MW01616598

GOOD BOYS

The Lost Tribe

WORKS BY JEREMY ROBINSON

The Didymus Contingency

Raising The Past

Beneath

Antarktos Rising

Kronos

Pulse

Instinct

Threshold

Callsign: King

Callsign: Queen

Callsign: Rook

Callsign: King 2 – Underworld

Callsign: Bishop

Callsign: Knight

Callsign: Deep Blue

Callsign: King 3 – Blackout

Torment

The Sentinel

The Last Hunter – Descent

The Last Hunter – Pursuit

The Last Hunter – Ascent

The Last Hunter – Lament

The Last Hunter – Onslaught

The Last Hunter – Collected Edition

Insomnia

SecondWorld

Project Nemesis

Ragnarok

Island 731

The Raven

Nazi Hunter: Atlantis

Prime

Omega

Project Maigo

Refuge

Guardian

Human After All

Savage

Flood Rising

Project 731

Cannibal

Endgame

MirrorWorld

Herculean

Project Hyperion

Patriot

Apocalypse Machine

Empire

Unity

Project Legion

The Distance

The Last Valkyrie

Centurion

Infinite

Helios

Viking Tomorrow

Forbidden Island

The Divide

The Others

Space Force

Alter

Flux

Tether

Tribe

NPC

Exo-Hunter

Infinite^2

The Dark

Mind Bullet

The Order

Khaos

Singularity

Hunger – The Complete Trilogy

Nemesis

Point Nemo

Good Boys – The Lost Tribe

GOOD BOYS

– THE LOST TRIBE –

JEREMY ROBINSON

BREAKNECK MEDIA

He might be a genius, like his father, but on a mission this important, he is our biggest liability.

"He smells like the discharge of a post-coital Garumpthian mole." Gruunlo-kar huffs at his own joke while Harth's booming laugh gets a smile out of me. Even Torel is covering her mouth.

"Oh, that's it!" Chirk shouts, putting the *Prowler* into a spin and angling us toward the moon's surface.

It does little to stifle the laughter. We have been through this before. It is a kind of pre-game warm up. A way to burn off tension and relax the nerves.

Chirk pulls up at the last moment. The moon's gravity, combined with the g-forces of the maneuver, presses me into my seat. A cloud of moon dust billows behind us as we circle the inside of a massive crater and slow to a gentle hover. He sets us down in the center, where we will have a clear view of our target planet.

The ceiling above becomes milky and then transparent. All eyes turn up.

"Looks like Kyno," Torel says, a wisp of longing in her voice. Been a long time since any of us have been home. The Kyno Corp's top exploratory fire team has been in high demand. If we get R&R, it is on a star base while the *Prowler* is restocked. Happily, most of our recent missions have not required violence.

And I hope our current mission will be the same. It is a rescue mission, after all, 37,000 years late.

"Baarfolir," I say.

He does not hear me. His gaze is locked on the planet above us. I do not blame him. Planets like this, with fertile land, oceans, and breathable air, are hard to come by. It is surprising that one of the factions has not claimed it yet. And if the Lost Tribe is here, I have no doubt that the Council of Kyno will have us stake a claim. A 37,000 year long habitation record all but guarantees acceptance without conflict.

"Baarfolir," I repeat, loud enough to sneak past his insistent thoughts.

"What? Yes? How can I help?"

Beside me, Chirk rolls his large eyes, but keeps his mouth shut.

"It has been a long time since the Lost Tribe has had contact with our people." I turn around to look him in the eyes. "What are the chances they will be un-receptive to our arrival?"

"Oh. Yes. Well, quite high, I'm afraid. There are too many possible scenar-ios to accurately project what we will encounter on the surface. For example, if the Lost Tribe crashed on this world, it's likely that knowledge of our people and technology would be lost over time. The civilization that developed in its place could be vastly different from our own. Our history and traditions would be foreign to them. It's also highly likely that they will look different from us and

1

PRAXION

"You smell something, Chirk?" I ask.

The little guy looks up at me, his nose twitching. "Meh," he says with a shrug. "I haven't smelled great since we landed on Pitchla-Nine. What a shithole."

"You haven't smelled great since—"

"Gruunlokar!" Chirk snaps. "I swear to God, if you make a comment about the way I *smell,* when I'm talking about the way I smell—the way my *nose* works when it draws air into it, thereby sending a signal to my brain, telling me how pleasant, aromatic, or God-damned awful a scent is—I will castrate you the same way your mother did your father."

Everyone has a good chuckle. Despite Gruunlokar being the scariest son-uvabitch operator I have ever encountered, Chirk is not afraid to snap back, whether it be with strong language or a hand-to-hand throw down. Despite his size, I have never seen him back down from a fight. Then again, he is a pilot, so he usually has a cargo bay full of munitions backing him up.

Harth's laugh bellows through the *Prowler*'s cabin. He is a good-natured gentle giant unless you piss him off. Luckily, that is hard to do. As our chief engineer, he would rather be fixing things than breaking them. It is not always wise to laugh so loudly at Chirk's expense, but since Harth is twice the size of Gruunlokar, our pilot's response is tame.

He jerks the controls back and forth, shaking us about as we clear the target planet's moon.

"You smell wonderful," Torel says, her practiced calm enough to soothe even the most panicked patient. She gives Baarfolir a nudge.

He looks up from his tablet, startled out of whatever tome he was mentally devouring. "What? Huh? What's happening? Where are we? Are we there yet?"

"Always with the questions, this guy," Chirk says. "The lady wants you to tell me I smell good, so I don't pancake us into this ugly-ass moon. Seriously, I could do it. No one would even notice another crater."

"I never observed whether you smell particularly good or bad," Baarfolir says, and he is not pretending to be neutral. Despite his race being known for their keen sense of smell and hearing, he rarely utilizes any sense beyond his eyes, peering into one book or another.

To those that came before,
and left me with a piece of their hearts:
Buddy
Sarah
Thor
Kenobi

that the hardships of living without technology for a long period of time would lead to adaptations and social irregularities. At least to us.

"Now, if they were able to land on the planet, retaining the technology contained in their ship, it is highly likely that our culture will have been preserved just as it has been on Kyno. They will understand what happened. Will know who we are when they see us. And will welcome us as brothers and sisters, lost so long ago."

I nod, feeling encouraged. It is the outcome I have dreamed of since hearing Baarfolir's father speak on the topic.

"Praxion," he says, "try not to get your hopes up. It has been…a long time. We need to be prepared for anything, including the possibility that our ancestors did not survive their arrival on this world."

I raise my hand toward the planet above, cast half in light and half in dark. The darkness is pocked by splotches of artificial light. "Evidence of habitation can be seen, even from space."

"Life is abundant throughout the universe," Torel says.

Baarfolir nods. "It's possible that this planet was already controlled by a dominant species when they arrived. Who's to say they survived that first encounter, though."

I sigh, feeling my hopes deflate to a more realistic level. "Okay, let us get into it, then. Harth, what are we receiving?"

He works the controls at his station, which are far too small for his meaty hands. Yet, he somehow manages to tap his way through the ship's systems with ease. "A lot, sir. Wow. That's…it's kind of a mess."

"Can you be a little more descriptive? And if you call me 'sir' again, I will have you on latrine duty."

"The ship cleans itself," Harth points out, and then he expands on his assessment of the signals we are receiving from the planet. "They appear to be using multiple wavelengths to transmit a vast amount of information, both from the light side and the dark. Data is flowing around the entire planet, which is a positive sign for civilization, but it's haphazard and chaotic. I can't make sense of it."

"Perhaps they are communicating with off-world species?" Gruunlokar suggests.

"The data appears to be broadcast from the surface and then redirected back to it. That we are receiving signals here is simply a testament to their sloppy data containment. It's like…" Harth frowns.

"What?" I ask.

"It's like they don't know that others might be listening. They're like a child splashing through the waters of a Thurocan breeding pool."

"Then they do not remember," I surmise. "Who they are. Where they come from."

"It would appear so," Baarfolir says, equally disappointed by the discovery, despite his insistence that we not get our hopes up.

"What is the content?" I ask.

Harth shakes his big head. "Can't make sense of it. There appears to be upwards of seven thousand languages spoken on this world."

"Seven *thousand*," Chirk says. "Hold on. Hold right fucking on. Are you telling me the fabulous fabled Lost Tribe is a decentralized civilization?"

"*Chirk*," I say.

"What? It's embarrassing! They come to this planet, and then what? Just forget who they are? Where they came from? Why we had to tuck tail and relocate to the far side of the universe? I don't care if they crashed here. When something is important, you don't just forget it. And now...now they don't even know how to communicate with each other?"

I decide to ignore the tirade because getting into it will reveal just how close our feelings on the matter are, and I do not want the others knowing how emotionally invested I am in this mission's outcome. "MIMIR," I say, speaking to the *Prowler*'s on-board artificial intelligence. "ETA on active translation services and image decoding?"

"One hour," MIMIR replies, voice calm and in control.

"Too long," I decide. "Can you isolate and translate a single term for me?"

"Of course," MIMIR responds.

"I would like to know the name of this world...or at least the most commonly used name in the most prolific language."

"Naturally," MIMIR says. "This will take a few moments."

"These languages are completely foreign to me," Harth says, listening to transmissions via his headset. "No trace of Kynolari. Honestly..." He looks up to make sure he has my attention. "There is a chance that the Lost Tribe never reached this planet at all."

"What about video?" Baarfolir asks. "That would be extremely helpful to—"

"Encoded," Harth says. "It's there, but we won't have access until MIMIR completes the translation process."

"I can think of one way to get a look," Gruunlokar says, raising a single challenging eyebrow toward me.

He is right, of course.

There is generally no better way to get the sense of a new world other than setting foot on it, breathing it in, and seeing things for yourself. We are all trained to pick up even the smallest of details in a short amount of time.

Even a brief visit could tell us a lot—and answer the question on everyone's mind.

I nod. "Everyone gear up. I want you prepped for a recon insertion in five beats."

"Still going with 'insertion,' huh?" Chirk says. "I'm telling you, it makes everyone uncomfortable. Gives me flashbacks to when I was young, and my mother had to check my—"

"Later," I say, cutting short his comment, not because I lack appreciation for his humor—we all appreciate it—but I need them to focus up and be clearheaded for what comes next. "Ten minutes on ground. Stay out of sight. Observe and extract. Then we will discuss how to handle things and revisit with translation services fully functional."

"Now we're fucking talking," Gruunlokar says, sliding out of his chair and heading to the armory. Harth and Torel follow him.

"Baarfolir, you will remain on the *Prowler* for now. If MIMIR finishes translation protocols before we return, find out what you can."

"Of course, Captain," he says with a bow and happily goes back to his reading.

"Where do you want me, boss?" Chirk asks.

"You might complain about your nose, but I know that no one can sniff out a problem quicker than you. You are boots on the ground."

"Any chance I can bring *Ridgeback*?"

"Any other mission, I would say yes. You know that." *Ridgeback* is a mechanized unit designed and built by Harth. It provides a more…robust body for Chirk, but that is not why he likes it. *Ridgeback* is outfitted with enough weaponry to level a city, which fills him with the confidence required to maintain his bravado when not sitting in the pilot's seat of an interstellar Kyno Corps gravity skipper.

"Right," he says. "Sneaky. Well, I'm good at that, too." He slides out of his chair and drops to the floor. Not many of his stature bother applying to the Kyno Corps. That he is here with us at all says all you need to know about him.

"Captain Praxion," MIMIR says.

"Yes?"

"I have the planet's name for you, sir."

"Let us hear it," I say, looking up at the mostly blue planet about to be named.

"Earth."

"Earth," I repeat. "Strange name."

2

MICAH

"Grover. *Dude.* Seriously, not right now." My leg continues to shake like I've got one of those old-timey, fat-reducing machines. The ones that shake the shit out of you with a vibrating belt. That's what having your leg humped by an eighty-pound Golden Retriever feels like. While it's funny as hell, it's also more than a little inconvenient when you're standing across from the first woman you've managed to bring home in more than a year. Longer if we're counting the years I spent on active duty with the Army Rangers.

To make matters worse, she's good looking, smart, funny, and *not* drunk. It's like the perfect quadfecta. Is that a thing? Quadfecta? Doesn't matter. I just made it a thing.

All that's left is to land the plane, so to speak, which includes her not think-ing that I just sit at home having a happy hump fest with Grover. Because I think this could go somewhere. With her. Like long term and not just a quick lay, though I wouldn't complain about a brief romp, because I haven't been with anyone since leaving the service. And before that, my sexual encounters were mostly listening to StewBeef jerk off out in the latrine. The man used entirely too much lube. I'm not even sure where he got the stuff. Doesn't matter if we were on base or lying low in some Afghan cave, he'd find a way to get his willy wet. Dick's probably soft as a baby chinchilla. Our fire team confronted him about it once, after a particularly long session that kept us awake. He claimed it was to prevent testicular cancer, and he insisted we all join in the fun, to save ourselves from a one-testicled future.

And now, here I am, getting dry humped by my only friend in the world while thinking about StewBeef's nuts.

I clear my throat, shake Grover off, and grab a dog treat from the counter. "Sit."

He drops into a sitting position, smiling like a happy dummy.

I crouch down and extend a hand. "Give me some skin."

He slides his paw over my hand.

"Good boy," I say, shaking my hands under both of his floppy ears. For a moment, we're just smiling at each other. Then I remember it's not just the two of us again, and I give him the treat. "Now go lie down."

I stand back up and give Jess what I think is a subtle up and down glance as I go. Her raised eyebrow and lopsided smile says I wasn't nearly as clandestine as I intended. She's not dressed in a way that encourages ogling—jeans and plaid flannel—but a woman endowed like she is sometimes has trouble hiding her curves, and my imagination is more than up to the task.

"You know, as a black woman in New Hampshire, I'm used to being looked at like a rarely seen and majestic peacock, but it's usually not as intense." She looks down at herself. "I have ketchup on me somewhere?"

I smile. "Pretty much everywhere, yeah."

She laughs. It's a lot cuter than it was back in the day. We went to middle school together. We called her 'Bender' back then. Her last name. Because it was fun to say. But now she goes by Jess, which suits her. She was a smart kid. I was a jock. We didn't spend a lot of time together, but I remember her laugh grating on me back then—like a congested woodchipper. It's much nicer now, but that might just have something to do with the effect her eyes are having on me.

"Well," she says. "Maybe you can help clean me up."

I'm startled by her sudden advance. "Uh..."

She steps toward me, hand reaching for the top button of my shirt.

Holy shit, this is happening.

I turn toward her, keeping it cool despite my heart now playing the drum solo opening for Van Halen's "Hot for Teacher." I reach for her hip, time slowing to a crawl. Every detail of her body, cloaked in New Hampshirite garb, ricochets from my mind to my crotch.

My hand slips around the top of her ass to the small of her back, pulling her close, as she expertly undoes my top two buttons.

I lean in to kiss her, lips parted just enough to—

A furry wrecking ball slams into my hip, driving me into the kitchen counter. Two paws vice grip my leg while a set of jaws clamp down on my belt.

"Grover!" I shout, and can't help but laugh at the interruption, in part because I always laugh when the Grovertrain goes on a hump fest. It often leads to a wrestling match that leaves me all scratched up. But that's when we're alone and not in the process of getting seduced by freakin' Jess Bender.

Happily, Jess is laughing, too.

She hasn't said so, but I knew she was a dog person as soon as she stepped in the house. And not just because Grover immediately fell in love with her. He's a Golden Retriever. He'd fall in love with Hitler if he walked in the front door and shouted, 'I demand to know vere you ah hiding all zee Snauzagez!' It was her response to his overwhelming affection that let me know she might be a keeper—for both of us. As he bounded up, she dropped to her knees. The result was an actual hug, during which he snuffled her hair, rubbed his head against hers, and smeared drool on the side of her face. What followed was a lot of licking. She didn't flinch once.

And she doesn't react with annoyance now. She just rolls with the furry frottage sneak attack, laughing and clapping.

Despite her positive reaction, I can't help but feel bad. Mostly for myself and the blue balls that might now be awaiting me. "Sorry. He's not always like this."

"Bullshit," she says.

"Okay, yeah, it's kind of a daily thing." I try to shove him off, but his little hooked talons are snagged on my jeans and the manic look in his eyes says he's not about to relent any time soon.

"You know he's not really trying to have sex with you, right?"

"Yeah," I say, leaning down to pry his forelimbs away from my thigh. He holds on to my belt a little tighter with his teeth and keeps the Elvis pelvis gyrating. "It's a dominance thing. He wants to be the boss."

"Or he's just really excited and doesn't know how else to show it," she says, giving Grover an out that isn't really negative at all.

With his legs detached, all of Grover's weight is now being held up by his jaws. He gives a playful growl and then shakes my belt back and forth before letting go and dropping to the ground. He's no longer latched on to anything, but his hips just keep thrusting as he walks around for a moment. Then he flops down, lifts a leg, and goes to town grooming his nuts.

Jess puts her hands on her hips. "Well, there's your problem, he's not fixed."

"My dad couldn't do it to him," I say. "Neither can I."

"Well, he's going to be a dry humping machine until you get him snipped or buy him a washable stuffed animal large enough to satiate his canine needs."

"Washable," I say. "Gross."

"In the meantime," she says. "I think he's got some energy to burn off."

And just like that, my hopes for an evening of hedonistic copulation bursts into nuclear flames, dousing the rural New Hampshire landscape in a radioactive dust of disappointment that—

"You have a tennis ball?" she asks.

"Huh?"

"You know, yellowish greenish bouncing thing that dogs sometimes chase?"

"Uh..." I point to a basket by the door.

It holds roughly 30 tennis balls in various stages of dismemberment, decay, and evisceration on a scale not seen since the horrors of Unit 731 during World War II. "A few."

"Good." She digs into the basket, which quickly usurps Grover's attention from autofellatio. She smiles at me. "Don't look so disappointed. It's not like we don't have all night." She opens the kitchen door and steps out into the early evening light, looking amazing.

Grover and I look at each other.

"Did you hear that?" I ask. "All. Night."

He cocks his head to the side and then turns toward the door.

"I know, right? She's totally into us."

He looks back to me, eyes wide, tongue dangling from the side of his mouth.

"Just no more humping, okay?"

Before he can reply, or I can imagine one, Jess calls from the yard. "Grover!"

His feet scrabble over the kitchen's old hardwood floor, then he tears out of the door and bounds off the back porch into the grass, where Jess awaits. She throws the ball in a way that reminds me she played softball a lot. For a moment, I just stand there, watching her clap and cheer as Grover does the one and only thing his breed was bred to do—retrieve. He leaps around her, taking part in the joyous ceremony befitting the return of a ball.

We're in the danger zone now.

And I honestly wasn't expecting it.

Jess was a match on a dating app. I didn't remember who she was until we met at the bar. But now, I'm looking out this door at a beautiful woman playing with my dog like she raised him, bathed in the summer evening sun. God damn, if there *is* such a thing as love at first sight, I might've just experienced it. I could do this until the day I die and be happy.

Maybe I will.

"Micah, get your ass out here," she calls to me.

I smile and head outside, thinking: *Don't fuck this up, don't fuck this up, don't fuck this up.*

3

"Do not engage unless fired upon," I tell the team. They know the drill. This is not our first insertion into an unknown world, but there is no room for error this time. "And if they are our people, relinquish your weapons and surrender immediately."

Gruunlokar grumbles.

He is not the type to relent, no matter the circumstances.

"We are not here to become the Lost Tribe's enemy," I say. "Am I clear?"

He nods. "Clear."

"Hit the ground moving. Tight, staggered column. We are recon only. Avoid contact at all costs. Evac to the *Prowler* on my command. Baarfolir will eval what we discover, and we will establish contact based on his suggestions when translation services are available. Do you copy?"

One by one, the team says, "Copy," confirming my orders.

The last is Chirk, who hitches his thumb toward me. "Didn't you say most of that a few minutes ago? Back in the cockpit?"

I wait.

He smiles. "Copy."

I turn to Baarfolir. He is standing in the Node Chamber's doorway, wringing his hands together. I do not blame him for being nervous. This is his first time on a mission. While he might not be heading to the surface, we are leaving him alone, on a moon, with only MIMIR for company. The A.I. is capable of getting him home, but I cannot imagine what that would feel like—returning to Kyno with no news about the Lost Tribe. While most in our culture have moved on from any kind of hope of finding the Lost Tribe, Baarfolir's father managed to rekindle enough interest to launch this costly and clandestine mission. There are some in the universe who would see our actions as expansionist, and that is strictly forbidden. "From now until we return, communications will be over encrypted comms. You are Prowler-One. I am Talon-Actual."

I motion around the circle of nodes, starting with 'Talon-One' at Harth and ending at 'Talon-Four' for Chirk.

He rolls his eyes. "Always last."

"It's in descending order by size," Harth says.

Chirk's already large eyes bulge a little as he looks from Harth to Gruun-lokar, then to Torel. She smiles and shrugs.

"What—the fuck?" Chirk says. "Are you serious?" He turns to me. "Are they serious? Because that's sizeist or something. I feel prejudiced against."

Somehow, I manage to just wait it out without smiling.

He sees me waiting, but gets in the last word, waving a dismissive hand toward Harth. "You're all just jealous because my body-to-dick size ratio is premium."

Torel clears her throat.

"Right, right. Sorry," Chirk says. "Your dick is huge."

And just like that, the tension breaks. I crack and laugh. "Asshole."

"Hey, somebody's got to lighten the mood around here. You're all so serious. Ooh. The Lost Tribe. Ahh. History. Blah, blah, blah. It's a mission. It's what we do. Let's launch these space teats, see what's what, rediscover our ancient ancestors, and go home, so I can strut my stuff in a parade with a bitch on either arm."

"Life goals," Torel says.

"Damn straight."

"Okay," I say. "Okay. Time to get serious."

He nods. "Copy that, Talon-Actual."

I toggle my comms and activate the nodes. "Prowler-One, Talon-Actual. We are 'go' for node insertion. Time for you to leave the chamber."

"Uhh," Baarfolir says, stepping back into the hallway beyond the Node Chamber. The doorway whooshes shut and seals with a flash of orange light. "Do I need to do anything else?"

"Negative," Harth says. "Prowler-One, you are clear to proceed to ops."

"Okay. Copy."

"That guy's adorable," Chirk says. "Like something you'd see on a kid's kibble box."

"Chirk," Gruunlokar grumbles. "Stow it."

"Talon-One, lock us down," I order.

Harth nods and gets to work. All around the cylindrical chamber, the nodes close around us. There is one for each operator. They are shaped like white tops, pointed on the bottom where they will impact with, and burrow into, the terrain. From there, they will provide each of us with a personal gravity bridge to the *Prowler*. This first ride to the surface will be a little bumpy, but every transport that follows will be smooth and will take just seconds.

The node's clear dome closes around me and seals. I check my buckles and the team does the same. There are no controls. No consoles. No way for the passenger to screw things up. A single indicator light is the only aberration in the otherwise stark white node. Orange is good. Purple is bad. Not sure why the designers included the purple light. Better to not know you are going to pancake into the ground. Die peacefully rather than in terror.

"I am orange," I say.

"Orange," Gruunlokar says.

Torel gives a two fingered salute. "Orange."

"Orange," Chirk says.

"That's five orange," Harth says. "MIMIR, we are clear for insertion at the predetermined coordinates."

"Understood," MIMIR says. "Node launch in ten, nine, eight..."

Our predetermined coordinates were chosen using several criteria, the first of which is low population density, away from cities, and in the kind of rough terrain we are all most accustomed to operating in. Temperature, oxygen levels, elevation. All of this was taken into consideration when choosing the IZ. There were several options, but the most ideal was found in a mountainous region not far from a continental coastline.

"Three, two—"

Chirk lets out a laugh. "Clench those sphincters and lick your fingers, things are about to get—"

"One."

I am slammed back into my chair as the node is launched from the *Prowler* via a magnetic rail that accelerates you fast enough to compress the air from your lungs. Some pass out immediately. Nearly everyone sees stars. But my team is so accustomed to the rush that it almost feels relaxing. That does not stop the g-forces from compressing my body, pulling my skin back, and flattening my ears against my head.

Before I am able to take my first breath, we are miles above the moon's surface and approaching the gravity bridge connecting this 'Earth' to its lone satellite.

I take the moment of calm to look out into the stars. I have seen this galaxy from dozens of perspectives, but never quite this far out. The view is stunning. The vastness of space has a way of making you feel small. If we do find the Lost Tribe on this planet, it will be a miracle. Harth would say that is the curse of advanced science—appearing as a miracle—but the odds of us finding our brethren amidst all...*this*...are infinitesimal.

One by one, the nodes slip into Earth's gravity bridge, accelerating again, this time more smoothly. I know all about the days of space travel before the discovery of the gravity web. The slow lumbering through space, sleeping in stasis for thousands of years, or generations of a people coming and going mid-flight. Had we known about the gravity web during the migration, the Lost Tribe would have never been lost.

The primitive satellites encircling Earth, slowly giving way to gravity's tug, reveal that its denizens have yet to discover the web as well. They might well look up into the night sky and wonder what holds everything together, where all the material binding things in place might reside. Gravity streams, webs, bridges, whatever you want to call them, might be akin to magic down below. But it is *not* magic. It is just science beyond the understanding of decentralized civilizations. And if I am honest, beyond my understanding as well.

What I *do* know is that all things in the universe, from black holes to molecules, have a gravitational force. It used to be viewed as an intangible force. Like wind. Unseeable, but its effects observable. Now we know better. Gravity is more like a viscous blob in which all matter is contained. It can be stretched so thin that it appears to not exist, but it is immutable, connecting all things. All peoples. All planets. And with the right technology, you can access it. Move along it, freed from the confines of physics. The greater the distance, the thinner the bridge, the faster the speed. Those are the basics.

That is also why the transition from normal space to gravity bridge is so smooth—and why the planet ahead is growing rapidly larger.

"Talon-Actual," Harth says via the comms. "Talon-One. Gravity bridge accessed. Insertion in fifteen ticks."

"Copy, Talon-One. Prowler-One, how copy?"

"Uh, yes," Baarfolir says. "Copy. Prowler-One. Ugh, that was all out of order."

"Do not worry about it, Prowler-One," I say. "Just keep the den warm and we will be back before you know it."

"Right," he says.

There is a gentle thump as we punch through the atmosphere. This would normally be a very loud, hot, and bumpy ride, but inside the gravity bridge, our travel is frictionless.

MIMIR's voice calls to us from the *Prowler*. "Touch down in ten, nine, eight..."

"Form on me," I say. "Maximum stealth. And stay—"

"Talon-Actual, Talon-Two!" The sudden boom of Gruunlokar's voice makes me jump. "I am purple! Repeat: I am purple!"

I glance down at my indicator light. Still orange. "MIMIR, what—"

"I am detecting a concentrated energy beam emanating from the planet's surface."

"Lasers?!" Chirk shouts. "They're using God-damn lase—" He grunts. "Talon-Actual, I am fucking purple as well. I am officially EMOS. Trajectory is fucked."

I glance to my left. Gruunlokar's node has a trail of smoke behind it and is drifting out of the bridge. Chirk is close behind. When they slip from the bridge, the pair are left behind. Their node emergency systems should prevent them from a fatal landing, but the fact that they were shot down, from *inside* a gravity bridge, means that we have underestimated the denizens of this world.

MIMIR's voice cuts into the conversation with, "Two...one..."

Gravity reverses course, and I am compressed downward, decelerating at a rate fast enough to compress and shatter a spine. Luckily, our armor more than compensates for the pressure.

Everything goes still.

Fog swirls around the node's exterior.

"Talon-Two, Talon-Actual, how copy?"

No response.

"Talon-Four, Talon-Actual, how copy?"

I give them a few seconds. Only reason they would not reply is if they cannot. Or they are dead. In either case, our job remains unchanged.

"Talon-One, Talon-Three, status."

"Orange," Harth replies.

"Orange," Torel says.

"All right then. We attempt to salvage this mission." The node's clear dome peels back, melting into the frame. I hop out and watch as the device that carried me to Earth drills its way into the rough ground. Moments later, all that remains is a metallic disc. I kick leaf litter over it until it is invisible and turn to find Harth and Torel standing ready behind me, both of them looking very concerned, but keeping it to themselves. I give them each a nod and then head out into the strange looking forest.

4

CHIRK

"Talon-Actual, Talon-Four, do you copy? Talon-Actual..." I sigh. "If you assholes can hear me, you better respond now or I'll—"

The atmosphere slams into me like a runaway gravity skipper. Leap Nodes were designed to take a lot of abuse, but I don't think the designers ever considered the possibility that one would malfunction and tumble out of a gravity bridge during the few seconds it takes to travel from a planet's Exosphere to its Troposphere.

And yeah, big words like that *do* get me laid. That and my God-damned primal good looks.

When the pod's rate of descent slows to its final terminal velocity, around two hundred miles per hour, I'm able to lift my head and look out the glass dome. Sky in every direction. Blue, like Kyno. Lots of clouds. Probably a pleasant place. Too bad it's populated by shoot-first, ask-questions-later, lipstick dicks.

A trail of smoke pulls my attention down. Gruunlokar's node. It's about a mile away and thirty seconds below me. By the time we reach the ground, we'll be miles apart. Rest of the team will already have boots on the ground, following through on the mission. They'll be torn up about losing us, but Praxion will keep things moving in a straight line. Always does, even if the shit gets covered in flies.

And he'll expect me and Gruunlokar to do the same, even if we crash land. Assuming my node works, I'll follow through. Recon, observe, and return to the *Prowler*, where I will send a very terse 'fuck you' message to the production team that made these Leap Nodes.

Then again, I'm not dead.

So, that's something.

That might change in the next, ohh, twenty seconds.

I look down at the terrain. A lot of trees and other green things. It's a fertile world. There's an ocean to one side. Mountains on the other. From an angle, everything looks green, but looking straight down reveals a line of cities, especially along the coast. I make mental notes about the locations of major landmarks. The biggest city is to the south, mountains northwest, ocean directly east. Based on that little information, I work out that we're coming down at least thirty miles to the south of the IZ, and in a much more populated area.

Gruunlokar's node deploys its emergency parachute and slows to a steady, swaying descent. Still plummeting, I reach nearly the same altitude and am once again shoved into my seat. Feels like I'm the new guy in a Golorian prison and everyone is taking their turn. My ass is going to be sore for days.

The good news is that my parachute has also deployed. So, I won't be turned into slurry upon impact. The bad news is that Gruunlokar and I are now easy targets for whoever disabled our nodes.

Going to have to hit the ground running.

But Gruunlokar might be out of luck in that regard. Looks like his node is coming down over the water.

I make one last attempt at contact, but I think my comms were fried by whatever energy beam knocked us out of the stream. "Talon-Two, Talon-Four, do you copy? If you can hear me, man, give me a sign."

I look to Gruunlokar's node, hoping to see a flash of light or some other indication that I've been heard. But the only thing I see is him splashing down in the distant water...and a large boat carving a path through the waves, heading straight for him.

They're coming for us.

I brace for impact just in time. I've hit the ground in a node more times than I can count, but not like this. The jolt forces a cough of pain from my lungs, the kind that if anyone were around to hear and comment on, I'd threaten their life out of shame. Despite being alone, I still feel the sting of humiliation, and that really just pisses me off.

I don't care if they're the Lost Tribe, I think, *I'm going to teach these pricks a lesson they won't soon forget.*

The clear dome melts away, exactly as it's meant to, and I leap out, my akimbo mini-railguns in each hand. I bounce back and forth, spinning, aiming, ready to fire.

At nothing.

I'm alone.

The node completes its own mission by drilling down into the soft soil, becoming a smooth silver disc in an otherwise pristinely maintained lawn of grass. I follow protocol, doing my best to cover it, and then take in my surroundings.

I'm just fifteen feet from the water, perched atop a retaining wall with a metal fence. I can't see the rocks below, but I can hear the waves crashing into them. It's an impressive view, but even the endless horizon doesn't hold my attention nearly as much as the massive stone structure with towers behind me. I squint up at it.

It's a castle. With turrets.

Crude stone masonry and misshapen rocks. Our ancient history books include images of places like this, but I've never seen anything like it up close. I get the appeal, I suppose, but I'm guessing that whoever lives here has to shit in a hole in the floor.

The idea of the Lost Tribe not advancing past some kind of iron age is disappointing, but it will make dealing with them a lot easier. At least, if they're violent for some reason.

Which they already were...

With lasers...

Making this castle...what? The preferred way of living, despite technological advances? I suppose it's possible. I've seen a lot of species throughout the universe living in ways I would never consider. Might have been a good idea to bring Baarfolir along for the ride after all. He might be able to make sense of the dichotomy.

See? Big words. My vocabulary is a panty dropping machine.

Weapons drawn, I lean my back against the castle wall and slide my way toward a stone archway that leads to a flowering garden. Seems pleasant enough. Can hear some flying things squawking nearby. I get a whiff of other lifeforms. Little ones. The kind that don't mind smelling like their own shit. Not what I'm here for.

A sound catches my attention. A hundred feet off and quiet. But it's unlike the animal calls, the shush of crashing waves, or the wind swirling around the stone walls. It sounds more like a language.

Someone is speaking.

I creep closer, ducking low behind some well-manicured hedges. The loose stone walkway beneath my feet isn't exactly conducive to stealth, but my light weight helps me keep the sound to a minimum.

There are two of them. They're dressed funny, in very bright colors. No way these two belong to some kind of military unit. Their clothing is tight and appears to be too small, revealing their skin.

Their bare skin.

"Fuck's sake," I say. I've seen things like this on Kyno. Fads where young people grow out hair in one area and shave it in another. But these two appear to have shaven their entire bodies except for the tops of their heads, which are both topped with dyed long yellow hair.

I'm going to have a really hard time taking the Lost Tribe seriously if they're all a bunch of freakin' whimsical eccentrics skipping through fields of flowers in their bright colors. I want to walk over there and give them a piece of my mind, shame them for debasing their species this way. But since their language sounds nothing like Kynolari, they wouldn't understand. Not until translation services are available, and I'm not sure when, or if, that will happen now. Data transfers between the *Prowler* and the team use different frequencies and transmission methods, though, so it's possible services will go live—hopefully in the next nine minutes.

Because I'm sticking to the mission parameters. Ten minutes of observation and then I return to the *Prowler*. We'll have to figure out what to do about Gruunlokar from there.

I roll between hedges, unseen in my approach.

Then a small gray creature catches me off guard. It's not threatening at all, just hopping along, content and foraging. There are animals like this on many worlds. All part of the complex network of life throughout the cosmos. But there is something about this...thing that makes me want to pounce on it. Tear it limb from limb.

And I nearly do it.

Takes all my restraint to not go off-mission, something that's only happened once before, on Tandor 5, with a sleek little curly haired—

A shriek spins me around, weapons raised. I nearly shred the creature standing before me. It's a primitive thing, dressed in a bright pink tube of fabric. Its hair, like the other two, is a faux yellow, and only present atop its head. The smell emanating from it, like a mix of flowers and the musk of several species, is pungent and repulsive.

How the hell did it sneak up on me?

Doesn't matter, I decide, because it's crouching down and reaching out for me, teeth bared.

But does it mean me harm? It's hard to say. While it's horrible to look at, the sound now coming out of all three of them is a kind of cooing. The way one might speak to a newborn.

"Back the fuck off!" I shout.

The big one laughs. At least I know what that means.

That's something, I think. But now I'm also pissed right the fuck off. Because they think I'm cute. They think *I'm* fucking cute!

I'm about to show them how cute a rail-shard hole in the foot looks when I'm startled by the appearance of a Kynolari. She's a beauty, too, but...she's also a prisoner, controlled by the largest of these horrible things.

It's worse than we imagined. The Lost Tribe isn't just alive, they've been enslaved.

5

MICAH

My wang-jangled nerves calm down after a good half hour of throwing the ball for Grover, during which Jess and I are able to catch up and talk like friends who are comfortable with each other, joking, ribbing, telling stories about mutual acquaintances. It's not a romp in the sheets, but it's a good...wholesome time. And probably the right order of things, if there's any chance of this becoming something more.

And at this point, I'm down for that.

Grover walks back to me, ball in mouth, tendrils of drool dangling from either side. The ball looks and feels like it's been dipped in enough ectoplasm to make Egon Spengler spontaneously orgasm at the sight of it. I'm afraid the G-man will want me to throw it again, but he's spent. He drops the ball at my feet, sits down, and then lies on his side, panting, tongue hanging out, a broad smile on his face.

"Gonna sleep well tonight, bud," I say, crouching beside him.

He rolls onto his back for a belly rub and closes his eyes when I oblige.

"You good with all dogs, or just this one?" Jess asks. She's smiling down at us.

"All dogs," I say. "Grew up with them. Buddy Boy, Sarah Elizabeth, Thor the dog of Thunder, Kenobi (aka Mr. Miggins), and now this ridiculous man." I rub his belly with both hands, prodding him to roll fully onto his back, spread his legs, and show his business to the world. "But Grover is the first of them that I technically own, because I inherited him when my parents— Well, you know that part of the story already."

"Well, I think this big man was destined to be yours. You suit each other." She crouches down beside me, rubbing Grover's head. He closes his eyes and leans his head into her massaging fingers. "You're both handsome, fun, and kind of dumb."

I stop petting.

Grover opens his eyes.

We both give her a sidelong stink-eye.

She raises her hands, laughing. "Okay, okay, not kind of dumb. Just a little dumb."

"Better," I say and resume petting. Grover closes his eyes again.

A cool breeze flows over the field between the house and the forest. There's a chill in the air tonight, which isn't uncommon in Sugar Hill, New Hampshire, atop an actual hill, just a few minutes' drive from the glacier-carved Franconia Notch and the White Mountains.

Jess shivers. Goosebumps rise on her arms. Without even thinking about it, I move behind her and rub her bare arms with my hands. It's not until she turns her head, and I see her raised eyebrows and smile, that I realize I might have overstepped.

Before I can ask, she turns to face me, plants her hand on my chest, and shoves. I topple backward into the grass. Before I can recover from the impact, she pounces on me, straddling my hips.

I want to say something cool, witty, or romantic, but I'm kind of just stupefied by how beautiful she is, and the subtle shift of her hips on my crotch. Pretty sure I manage to whisper an, "Oh my god," but I honestly don't know if I speak the words out loud.

She smiles down at me. "You ever been laid in the grass?"

I shake my head.

"Shouldn't…" I say, already kicking myself for being logical at a time like this, but the memory of Grover's slime covered ball is still fresh and my fingers are a little moist. "Shouldn't we wash our hands?"

She leans down over me, hands against my shoulders. "I don't want you to use your hands."

"What about ticks?" I ask. "This *is* New Hampshire."

"You can pick them off me later."

"Condom?" I ask.

She pauses to ponder that one. Shakes her head. "Period ended two days ago. Let's roll the dice like a couple of good Catholics."

"Haven't been to church since I was a kid," I say.

"Good," she says, leaning close to kiss me. "I guess no one will be watching, then."

When she presses her lips against mine, all my fears and anxiety melt away. I am at her mercy. Time loses meaning for a few minutes, and then her shadow moves off me as she leans up and pulls off her plaid shirt to reveal a well-toned body and a…Star Wars bra?

She sees my amusement and looks down at her chest. "I honestly wasn't expecting tonight to go anywhere…let alone here. Wait until you see the My Little Pony underwear. Going to drive you nuts."

I laugh and glance toward the sky above her.

Something looks off. Like the dimming blue is…distorted somehow.

"My C-3PO tits not doing it for you?" she asks.

The aberration grows stronger. Three streaks of light pulse down out of the sky.

She sees the look on my face and turns around at the same time Grover lifts his head to watch.

"The fuck?" I say, as all three of us bear witness to three, very not man-made-looking...things crashing into the woods downhill from the farm.

"We all just saw that?" Jess asks. "Right?"

I push myself up into a sitting position, Jess still straddling my waist. "Yeah..."

Grover gets to his feet and lets out a single bark toward the forest. His body is rigid, his tail extended out straight.

"Should we check it out?" Jess asks.

I'm at eyeball level with her glorious cleavage. The next word out of my mouth is spoken with more regret than I've ever felt in my life. "Probably."

"Don't worry," she says, placing her hands on my cheeks and lifting my face away from the award-winning macro view of her chest. "Like I said, we have all night. Think of it as adventurous foreplay."

"I might walk funny for a little bit," I say, "but yeah. We should probably check it out. Looked like they came down on my land, so I guess that makes it my problem."

"Or the CIA's. Men in Black. You know, guys like that."

She's joking, but she's not far from the mark. Whatever came down over my land...it wasn't a meteorite or anything else natural. That leaves just a few options. The U.S. military was testing something, and it failed. A private tech firm was testing something, and it failed. Or...well. UAPs. Not sure I buy into any of that yet, but I have plenty of friends in the military that do. No matter what it was, odds are it was detected. Eventually, Uncle Sam is going to come looking for it. If I can gift wrap it for them, that will keep my land—which my parents entrusted to me—from being torn up during the search and extraction.

That is, if there's anything left to find. They came in hot. Looked to be burning up. And I didn't hear any impacts. Might be nothing at all out there, and if I'm honest, that's probably the best case scenario. No fuss, no muss.

Jess rolls off me and gets to her feet. Looks down at my pants and raises her eyebrows. "Definitely going to be walking funny for a few minutes."

I tug my pants, trying to adjust, but it does little good. So, I roll to my feet and pretend it doesn't look like I'm hiding a corncob in my pants. Okay, corncob might be a generous comparison. Maybe a hot dog, but not one of those little ones. More like a Nathan's Colossal quarter-pound beef frank. That's fair.

Focus on the job, I tell myself, getting in the mindset of a Ranger.

Walking into the unknown is what we do. First on the battlefield, often months before other elements. I'm not expecting trouble, but again, this is New Hampshire. Lots of things with teeth, and more than a few good ol' boys who might not take kindly to us mistaking their land for ours.

"Be right back," I say and head for the house. I snap my fingers and point at Grover. "Stay here."

His only response is to look back at the forest, but I know he's not going anywhere without me.

I've got several guns in the house. Some are mine; some are Dad's. His are mostly hunting rifles. Mine are more for keeping my skills honed while at home. There's a SIG M400 TREAD kitted out with all the attachments I like: M600 Scout weapon light, Trijicon ACOG 4x32 Scope. Things like that. Also have an M4A1 and a Mk17 FN SCAR-H. But I'm not going for the heavy hitters. My everyday carry will work just fine.

I hide it in the living room, in the end table where my mother used to keep her sewing supplies. I don't have kids, and don't know any that might visit, so I don't worry about locking it up along with everything else. I open the drawer, pull out the unloaded Glock 19, slap one of three fully loaded mags in, and don't bother chambering a round. No point unless there's trouble, and if I'm honest, the odds of that, in this part of the world, are just about nil. But, I feel a little naked without it when venturing out into the wild. I don't bother arming myself when going into town, because every time I see someone open-carrying I automatically assume that they're the bad guy and watch them like a hawk. Don't want to scare people like that, because if the world is someday full of scared people carrying guns, a lot of people are going to get shot.

A lot *more* people are going to get shot. Already too many.

I exit the house, tucking the Glock into the appendix holster I keep with the weapon.

"You sure you'll need that?" Jess asks.

"Better to not need and have, than need and not," I say, furrowing my brow. "Or something like that."

"You got it right," she says. "Just...do me a favor. Don't take it out unless you really need to. Guns make me nervous."

"Yes, ma'am," I say. "Anything that can take a life in the blink of an eye should make you nervous."

"Oh," she says, pretending to swoon. "My woke hero."

I smile. "You'll change your mind if you see me use it." I make two clicks with my mouth and pat my hip once. A moment later, Grover is by my side, matching my pace.

"Why's that?" she asks, on my other side.

"I don't draw my weapon unless I feel force is necessary," I say. "Don't put my finger on the trigger unless I intend to pull it. And if I pull it, someone's going to have a very bad day."

"You've done that before?" she asks.

"Will it change your opinion of me? Still looking forward to the rest of the night?" I try to sound casual, but I'm genuinely concerned.

She smiles. "You're good. I just know I couldn't do it myself."

I give a nod. "Then yeah. More than a few times, mostly in places I can't mention."

"Is it...horrible?" she asks.

Strange turn the evening is taking, but I roll with it. Why not get the hard conversations out of the way during a stroll in the woods? Then we can go home, maybe take a shower, light some candles, and I can wage a jihad on her holy land. "Every time," I say. "Unless you're psychotic."

"Huh. Maybe I'd like it after all." She gives me a crafty smile and raises her eyebrows twice.

"Meh. I'll take the risk," I say, pausing by the entrance to a path. It winds through the forest, stretching down the hill that's closer to a mountain. I look to Grover and tilt my head toward the path. "You're on point, Gro Gro. Lead the way."

Head low to the ground, sniffing with each step, he quicksteps into the forest without leaving us in the dust.

"Guy with the gun and the tight buns goes next," Jess says. When I step onto the path, she swats my backside. "I'll let you know if I see any aliens back here."

6

PRAXION

"Keep alert," I say, "no surprises."

"Copy that," Harth says. "Not hearing anything unusual."

"That you *know* of," Torel says. "Alien world, remember. The way these trees are groaning in the breeze could be a warning signal for all we know."

"They're just trees," Harth says.

"Uh-huh." Torel eyes the swaying branches overhead.

She is not wrong to be suspicious of our surroundings. We have encountered a lot of strange things over the years, but...never sentient trees. What might *live* in the trees? That concerns me. There is movement everywhere, in the shadows and in the leaf litter coating the forest floor. Flying creatures darting through the air. My primitive instincts are shouting so loudly it is almost overwhelming.

This world is teeming with life.

Distractingly so.

"Catching a scent," Harth says.

The team stops in place. I take several quick sniffs through my nose. Nearly miss the new scent amidst the fresh vegetation, earthy decay, and the myriad of creatures. It is something new. A mix of smells. Living things. A synthetic aromatic smell. And...

I sniff the air again.

"Do you smell it?" Torel asks, also sniffing the air.

I nod. "Kynolari."

"But strange." Harth's deep voice is foreboding. "Changed."

"As we suspected," I say. "I am more concerned about the other scent profiles."

"How should we handle it?" Harth asks.

"Directly," I say, considering the time constraint I set on this initial recon mission. "But no contact. Observation only. We need to assess this whole world, and we cannot do that based on a single encounter. It is imperative we are undetected."

"Not to undermine you, boss," Harth says, "But we were already detected, and two of us shot down."

I close my eyes, restraining my emotions.

"That does not change the mission."

"Maybe it should?" he asks.

The silence that follows is brief but weighs heavily.

"The scent is coming from uphill. I do not hear them yet, so we have time. Flank and watch from the shadows." I meet Harth's gaze. "And if an opportunity arises in which we can gain more information about this world, and who might have acted against us, we will make use of it. Until that time comes, hand signals only."

I motion for Torel to take the lead. Her senses are heightened, and her feet are light. Without Chirk, she is our stealthiest asset.

She gives a nod and starts uphill, leaping between the large, exposed rocks that litter the forest floor. The firm footing makes her movement nearly impossible to hear, even up close. I go second, and Harth, whose heavy frame makes him the loudest of us, brings up the rear. I follow Torel's path, trusting her to choose the optimal route, each footfall carefully chosen.

We make good time, covering a half mile in just two minutes.

I glance at my watch. Only three minutes remain before we are due back on the *Prowler*. We are going to miss that mark, but potential contact with a Kynolari justifies the delay.

I toggle my comms. "Prowler-One, Talon-Actual, do you copy?"

"Talon-Actual, Prowler-One," Baarfolir says, his voice barely audible. "I copy. But why are we whispering?"

"I am being stealthy. You do not need to."

"Ohh!" he says, nearly shouting. "Right. Because you're down there and I'm on the, ahh, I'm up here. Goodness. Is there something wrong?"

"Just running behind schedule," I say. "If Talon-Two or Four return, please let them know we might have confirmation of the Lost Tribe's presence on Earth."

"Wait, what? You found the Lo—"

Ahead of me, Torel pauses and raises an open palm.

"Talon-Actual, out." I disconnect the comms and wait for Torel. Her head is cocked to the side, listening.

She motions for us to join her. Takes just a few seconds for the pair of us to reach her. Ducking low, she says, "Three scents. Two voices. Language unknown. They're being careful, but nothing close to quiet."

"Looking for us," I surmise.

"Saw us come down," Harth guesses.

"Odds of them being the ones who fired the laser?" I ask.

"Unlikely," Harth says. "If our trajectory was taking us to them, why would they have fired at all?"

"Then we are dealing with locals," I say.

"Would be my guess," Harth says.

"Agreed. We need to take a gentle approach." Torel glances down at the weapon gauntlet on my arm, activated and ready to fire.

It makes me uncomfortable, being on an alien world not fully armed and ready, but sometimes a lack of visible concern projects more power than a gun.

"Weapon systems cold. But be ready for anything. How far out?" I ask.

"Two hundred feet," Torel says. "Uphill but coming toward us along that game path." She points out a slender weaving path, the kind found on every world where there are jungles and a variety of large land creatures.

"Observe from above," I say, "then follow."

Harth grumbles but says nothing. His size makes grappling uncomfortable.

I draw the multitool from its holster on my belt, point it upward, and pull the trigger. The onboard guidance system targets a branch robust enough to hold my weight and launches the grapple toward it. Four ultragrade web tendrils wrap around the branch and constrict. I clip the bottom of the multitool to my belt buckle and, with the press of a single button, am whisked into the darkness of the forest canopy.

Torel arrives a moment later.

But Harth is nowhere to be seen. I toggle my comms, whispering. "Talon-One, Talon-Actual, situation report."

"Talon-Actual, Talon-One. Cannot locate a branch of sufficient…girth."

"Shelter in place, Talon-One. Stay out of sight."

"Copy that," he says. "Talon-One out."

There is a slight rustling below, but I see nothing. Harth's dark coloration and black body armor make him nearly invisible in the dark. But that does not mean they cannot sniff him out.

Hanging high above the forest floor, I watch the strangers approach. Satisfied they cannot see us and have not noticed our presence, I activate a spectral scan. The implant in my eye comes to life, seeing the world in a variety of spectrums that reveal a few important details, the first of which is that none of them are inorganic. That is the good news. The bad news is that the infrared spectrum reveals that the largest of the three is armed.

Across the variety of views, there is still too much foliage in the way to fully make out any of their features. Despite that, none of them look Kynolari to me. The upright pair lack the appropriate facial features, and the beast running around on all fours, snuffling along the ground…is, well, running on all fours, making it a simple being.

Some kind of livestock.

Or a pet.

This is not who we are looking for, but we should follow them anyway. I do not want to return to the *Prowler* empty-handed.

The three pass by, oblivious to us above and Harth below. Their senses are dull, illuminating their path with artificial light. They do not appear to be warriors. Their body language is casual.

"We should interrogate them," Torel whispers.

I was thinking the same thing, but there is a problem with that idea. "Language services."

"Shit," she says. "Right. Follow then?"

I nod and we both descend. Harth steps out of the shadows to greet us.

"See where they are going, and—"

"Praxion," Harth says. "The beast accompanying the two upright creatures. I believe it detected me. But it seemed to feel no fear and elected to stay with the others. Perhaps out of respect. Perhaps out of obedience."

"It does not matter which," I say. "I believe it to be a lesser creature, incapable of speech or understanding. It is of no danger to us. Stay tight, move fast, remain silent."

I step onto the path and find the hardened, leafless mud easy to walk on without making any sound. I double the strangers' pace and start downhill, curious about what we will discover. If there *is* a Kynolari in these woods, perhaps these creatures know where.

Or perhaps they are hunting it, I think.

Stay focused, I tell myself, raising my nose for a sniff.

I can no longer smell the trio, their scents whisked away by the air's downhill flow.

Cannot hear them, either. Strange.

I am about to hold up a fist and call a stop to our approach when a branch swings out from a tree and collides with my forehead, sprawling me back. My first thought is that we were wrong about sentient trees, but then I hear the threatening click of a weapon being readied.

The trio steps out from behind the tree. The largest of them speaks toward us, his voice confident and commanding. A man who has seen action and knows how to fight. Knows how to detect a threat without reacting. A dangerous adversary.

Without knowing what he is saying, I am not sure how to react. Best thing I can do is make no sudden movements and hope this culture values life enough that he will not open fire.

"Hold your fire," I say to Harth and Torel. "Stay calm. We are not here to start a war or make enemies."

Then a voice chimes in my ear. It is MIMIR. "Translation Services are ready, sir. Would you like them installed?"

"Yes!" I say. "Do it, now!"

The man barks at me again, slowly lifting his weapon and his illumination stick toward my face.

"Translation Services installed and activated, sir. You may now communicate."

The being's light shines on my face. It is bright enough to make me squint, and it turns him invisible behind its glare.

I hear a gasp from within the light. From the second, smaller, upright being.

Then the taller steps closer. "Holy shit… Holy shit." The light lowers, along with the weapon. His face is revealed, and though it is hairless and strange, I have no trouble understanding his arched brows and smiling mouth. He is shocked. Amazed. Bewildered, perhaps. But mostly…thrilled.

"You're…" He steps closer again, leaning in, crouching down, and reaching his hand out. "You're *dogs?*"

7

"I'm going to count to three, and then I'm going to put a dozen holes in your mammary laden chest!"

My threat is ignored. All three females close in around me, laughing, reaching, patting their knees. They don't understand what I am, that I'm not from this world. That the guns in my hands aren't...what? Props? A costume? Despite my bared teeth, they feel no fear of me.

I look back at the Kynolari held in the bag. She looks clean. There's no trace of abuse or malnourishment. All of that is good, but there is something missing: intelligence. She just stares at me through her large, beautiful brown eyes, her triangle ears twitching, her little body quivering with...what? Excitement? Fear? All the inner fortitude of our race is missing. Subdued.

She's been made docile.

She's...tame.

Controlled.

Contained.

But carried, fed, cleaned, and—

"Fucking hell," I say. "They're pets."

My arms lower to the ground, nearly dropping my weapons. Of all the outcomes our best minds envisioned for the Lost Tribe, this is the worst. So bad, in fact, that it was never even considered. I stagger back a step and sit on a stone.

How did this happen?

Why would the Lost Tribe allow it?

The trio crouches around me.

"I think he's lost," one says. "We should try to find his owners."

"If we don't find them, can we take him home?"

"Look at what he's wearing," the first says. "No way his person isn't here somewhere. It must have cost a small fortune to teach him how to walk upright like that. I mean, look, he's even sitting like a person, all manspreading. If he wasn't dressed, he'd be flashing his little ding dong."

Ding dong? Is she talking about my dick? "I'll have you know I've never left a bitch unsatisfied, so comment all you want, you hairless behemoth of a female. You couldn't handle what I have between my legs."

All three take a step back. They're looking at each other, and then back to me.

"What?!" I shout.

They flinch.

"Mom..." one says, the giddy grin melting toward something like horror. "Can...can Chihuahuas talk?"

The stunned matriarch in pink looks down at the Kynolari held in her bag. "No-no. I don't think. H-how..."

"Wait, wait, wait," I say, standing back up, which makes all three jump back. "You tall-ass bitches can understand me?"

"Uh, yeah?" one of the younger two says.

"Wwwwhoops," I say, forcing a smile.

Translation services updated, but MIMIR wasn't able to notify me.

"Well, in that case, maybe you three...lovely ladies—you *are* ladies, right? Maybe you can answer a few questions for me, starting with why the hell you're keeping *her*—" I point to their captive Kynolari. "—in a bag?"

The woman in pink is bugging out. Her lower lip trembles. The other two seem a little calmer, like they're maybe young enough to still have adaptable minds. But they also don't strike me as the types with answers to hard questions. So, I focus on the big pink one, stepping toward her as she starts backing away.

"Look, we can do this the easy way, with you all oohing and ahhing about the fact that I can talk, but the reality is, I have guns and I will shoot you if—"

"Aiiieee!" The big woman screams so shrilly that my ears fold back.

All three females sprint away. Opposite directions.

"Lick my taint," I say, lifting one of my mini-railguns. "Wound."

The weapon changes configuration based on my verbal command, reducing the projectile size and shape to ensure the exit wound is not a cavernous hole.

"Stop or I'll shoot," I whisper, technically following protocol. Then I pull the trigger. The single rail-shard leaves my weapon with the faintest of whisps. An instant later it slides through the woman's calf and exits out the front of her leg, flying off to land in the ocean.

With a pitiful "Ouiee!" the woman collapses into the loose stone path. Her handbag slides away from her. The female Kynolari slips out of its confines and shakes her little body.

I freeze.

"Holy..." She's amazing. Gorgeous. And...primal. Walking on all fours like our ancient—like *really ancient*—ancestors once did. That might be offensive to some, but honestly, that's kind of how I like to play in the bedroom.

"What did you do to me?" The big woman says, writhing around, holding her leg.

"Don't be so dramatic," I say to her, walking around her body so I can look her in the eyes.

The Kynolari sees me approaching and starts to shake again. Her thin tail wags back and forth, signaling she's happy to see me. My tail does the same. Not very professional of me but *look* at her. The sheen on her coat is mesmerizing. "Hey, baby," I say, working my swagger. "I'll take care of this. You just stay right here, okay?"

She licks her lips, but still looks like she might bolt.

"Just...sit, okay?"

She obeys, sitting on the ground, waiting, but still quivering.

"And you," I say, pointing my weapon at the woman's head. "You don't fucking move."

The woman sees my gun for what it is now and raises her hands. "W-what are you?"

I look back at the Kynolari bitch and try to think of something impressive to say. I decide the truth is good enough. "Special Operator Chirk of the Kyno Corps, pilot of the interstellar starship, *Prowler*, and I am here to...liberate the Lost Tribe."

"The Lost Tribe?" she asks, glancing from me to the female Kynolari. "You-you mean our dogs?"

"Is that what you call them? Dogs?"

"Y-yeah. They're dogs. *You're* a dog."

"*I* am a Kynolari," I say. "From the planet Kyno. *You* have enslaved my people."

She starts to speak, but I silence her by raising my second pistol. "Uh, uh, uh. I ask questions, you answer. Understand?"

She nods, which, along with raising hands in surrender, is pretty much a universal gesture understood by most species along with head shaking, laughing, pointing, and snarling. Life is diverse. Physical communication overlaps... except for this one species we encountered that made a jerking off gesture to say 'hello.' Most fun I've had on a mission. Spent half my time introducing myself and making Harth laugh.

"What are you?" I ask.

"What am I?"

"Your species. What are you called?"

"Human," she says. "People, I guess. I'm a woman."

"I noticed," I say, glancing at her oversized teats. "Okay, human. What's your name?"

"S-Sara Nobles."

"Is it S-Sara or are you stuttering because you're freaking out?"

"Stuttering," she says.

"Great. Now, Sara, what...is a dog?"

"Uh...she is." She points to the female. "Y-you are. D-dogs have four legs, waggy tails, uh, they...they're canines. Descended from w-wolves, I think. Evolved maybe. I don't really know. I'm a manager at Staples."

"Don't know what that is. Don't care. And in case you didn't notice, I have two arms and two legs." I point to the female Kynolari. "So does she... She's just walking on her hands...with stubby little fingers... Weird.

"Okay, Sara," I say, "What is *her* name?"

"Bacon."

"Bacon? What kind of name is Bacon?"

"Cute?" she says, cringing like there's more she doesn't want me to know.

"What is bacon?"

"It's from a pig."

"Sara," I say, losing my patience. "I am not from Earth. I understand what you're saying now, but if you're referencing something specific to this planet, like bacon and pigs, I have no idea what you're talking about. So, please explain to me, what is bacon? What are pigs?"

"Pigs are big animals. They live on farms. They're livestock. That...we eat." She looks at me, wondering if I'm following. I give her a nod. "Bacon is a cut of meat...from the pig...f-from its belly."

"You named her after a cut of meat?" I ask.

"Dogs love bacon," she says. "And...it's—"

"Cute," I say. "I heard. That's just fuckin'..." I shake my head. "Where are the mountains from here? Which direction?"

"Mountains?"

"Yeah, big pointy things coming out of the ground, usually made of rocks, sometimes glass."

"This is Hammond Castle. In Gloucester. In Massachusetts."

"Hearing a bunch of funny sounding words that mean nothing to me," I say.

She closes her eyes, thinking hard. "The nearest mountains are up north. And to the west a bit. In New Hampshire. The White Mountains. Maybe a three hour drive."

"And what about out there?" I point to the water.

"That...is the *Atlantic Ocean*." She says it like I'm stupid.

Like everyone should know that.

"Don't suppose you have geospatial coordinates for the water just south of here?"

She shakes her head.

I'm about to ask another question when I feel a bump against my tail. I twist around to find Bacon, nose lowered to my ass, sniffing. "What the—" Before I can react, she slips her tongue between my toned hind quarters and gives me a little lick. Had I not been wearing my combat armor, she'd have gone full asshole. "Whoa, whoa, whoa, baby. I am into some stuff, okay? Don't get me wrong, but I don't know you. I don't know where your tongue has been, and I'm kind of on official business here, okay?"

She says nothing, but steps closer, tail wagging fast enough to kick up a breeze.

"That's just how dogs greet each other," Sara says.

I pinch the fur atop my nose. "Are you trying to piss me off, Sara?"

"N-no. It's just...that's what dogs do."

"Fuck's sake," I say.

Before I can continue my interrogation, a loud screech perks my ears up. I stand tall, looking over the top of the hedge hiding us from the world and see two large, black vehicles. Eight men climb out, their faces concealed by dark eyewear. One of their coats is blown open by the breeze. He's carrying a weapon.

"Well, Sara, it's been real. Thank you for the information. Sorry about the leg. You'll be fine."

"It's okay," she says, catching me off guard. "You have a filthy mouth, but you seem like a good boy." She gives me an earnest smile.

The hell?

I holster my weapons and turn to Bacon. "Baby, I wish I had more time. Maybe we can—"

She licks my face. Really goes for it, too, slipping some tongue under my jowl. I am instantly aroused. "God damn... Maybe another time." I take off running, adjusting my pants crotch as I go. I need to reach the Leap Node and get back to the *Prowler* before these goons catch up to me. But I need to draw things out long enough that my boner isn't about to punch through my pants, or I will never hear the end of it.

I duck into an open door and find myself in a dark hallway beneath the castle. "Go away," I whisper to my pecker. "Go away. Go away. Go—"

My tail twitches and I spin around, ready to fire, but it's Bacon, sniffing my ass again. I'm about to chew her out when she does a little prance, turns around, and presents.

"You've *got* to be kidding me..."

8

MICAH

"They're *not* dogs," Jess says. "They're freaks dressed up like dogs. Like space marine dogs. Honestly, I didn't think there were many furries in New Hampshire, but hey, no judgement."

"Look at his face," I say. "The expressions. The way his eyes are moving. His eyebrows."

"Animatronics," she says.

"Who would spend that much money to be a furry?" I ask.

"People do weird things," she says. "Remember Janis Levonitis, from junior high? She became a freakshow frog woman with a traveling circus."

"She was born with webbed feet," I say.

"She tattooed her whole body green."

"Excuse me," the big one says. His voice rumbles through the nighttime forest. He's as tall as me, built like a weightlifter, and has the head and face of a Great Dane. His jowls jiggle a bit when he talks. "What is a...furry?"

"Okay," Jess says, a little panic creeping into her voice. "Maybe not animatronics. I mean, that would have been weird right? Not like talking dogs...from... from where?"

"We are from the planet Kyno," says the lead...dog. Looks like a Golden Retriever, but instead of a permanent smile and ever-loving energy, he's serious. Almost grim. "My name is Praxion." He motions to the big guy. "This is Harth."

I pull my hand away from Praxion. He wasn't going to smell it anyway.

The third upright alien dog steps closer, saying, "I'm Torel. Sorry if we frightened you."

Torel looks like a Bernese Mountain Dog, and the pitch of her voice suggests she's a female.

"He is *not* frightened," Harth says, motioning to me. "He looks...happy."

Forgot I was smiling. In fact, all my body language has changed to what I adopt when meeting a new dog, which is infinitely more friendly than when I meet a person. I take a step back and stand a little taller. Then I realize what I've done and move forward again.

I hold my hand out to Praxion, this time in a gesture of help.

After a moment's hesitation, he reaches up and takes my hand.

His fingers and palm are covered in thick, black pads. There are claws at the ends of his fur-covered fingers, but they've been trimmed down. No longer sharp. I pull him up to his feet, gauging his weight. Maybe a hundred and fifty pounds. Larger than Grover—who has disappeared into the woods—but smaller than most adult men I know.

Harth steps closer, squinting at me. "Why are you not afraid?"

"Should I be afraid?" I ask.

"No," Torel says, shooting a disapproving glance at the big guy. "Stop trying to intimidate them."

"*I'm* intimidated," Jess says. "In fact, I'm pretty close to freaking out."

"It's okay," I tell her. "They're...they're good."

"How could you possibly know that?" she asks.

I look each of the three alien-dog-things in the eyes. I see only kindness and concern. They might have a savage side. A lot of well-trained good dogs do. But you can always tell which dog has a real mean streak by looking in their eyes, by watching their subtle body language. These three have kind eyes and their ears are all perked. More than that, while Harth and Praxion have maintained a rigid, unmoving posture, Torel's tail has been slowly wagging. She is happy to meet us.

"Well," Jess says. "What now? Should we pet them?"

Harth's head snaps back. "Pet us?"

"Why would you do that?" Torel asks.

"It was a joke," Jess says, holding up her hands. Her fingers are shaking. She really is close to freaking out. Can't blame her. They're aliens. But...they're also dogs, which put me instantly at ease. "Sorry."

"Finally," Harth says. "They're intimidated."

"*They* are not." Praxion squints at me. "Why are you not afraid?"

"You're...my friends."

"Explain."

"All dogs are my friends."

"We...are dogs?"

"Right, that's probably a new word for you," I say. "You're, ahh, you're like Grover. He's a dog. An Earth dog, I guess. They're different from you. In some ways you're more like us. Like people. But you're also...dogs."

"Grover," Praxion says. "Your beast...is a dog?"

"Want to meet him?" I ask.

"Very much so," Praxion says, but he sounds more terrified than excited.

"Fair warning, he can be a little much when he meets new people...and dogs... I expect he will be the same with...people-dogs."

Praxion just grunts.

Oookay. Feels like there's a lot on the line here. I don't know what the fuck is going on, but it's weirder than that time Phil Ward and I decided to make a pizza with a half-pound of pepperoni and far too many Psilocybin mushrooms. I'm doing my best to just roll with all this, but my ability to cope with impossible situations is being stretched to the limits. I think the only thing allowing me to stay calm right now is that they're dogs, or at least they look like dogs. The part of me that is freaking out is balanced by the side of me that is ecstatic about the idea of dogs I can talk to.

I whistle. "Grover! C'mere boy!"

Leaf litter rustles.

Branches break.

He's like a freight train crashing through low hanging limbs, brush, ferns, and anything else between the two of us. I turn my flashlight to the sound, illuminating the forest. He's low to the ground, so all we can see is an approaching path of destruction…that's far too wide for one dog.

"Grover," I say. "Drop it." I turn to Praxion. "Sorry, he likes big branches."

Another grunt of disapproval.

Then Grover bounds back onto the path, wrestling an eight-foot-long branch. His limbs are covered in mud. Drool hangs from his jowls. Basically, he's having the time of his life. He runs toward me, excited to show me his prize, but it's far too long to fit down the path. He doesn't notice until he clotheslines himself. While Grover's head and jaws turn up, his legs keep pumping away until he flips over onto his back.

I would normally laugh at his antics, but this time I cringe. Feels like having a kid that can't swim being evaluated by an Olympic water ballet judge.

Grover flops around until he's back on his feet, covered in leaves and yanking at the long branch until it breaks. Then he's back to running up the path.

I pat my knees and hold out my arms. I realize a moment too late that I probably should have skipped this routine. But Grover is committed now and the only thing I can do is brace myself. He drops the branch and leaps over it. His double-sized tongue waggling from the side of his mouth, he jumps into the air and into my arms. Tail wagging furiously, he licks my face as if to say, 'Look! See! What I did! The branch! I did that! Yeah!'

Then all at once, he goes still. Slow turns toward Praxion. Sees him. I watch my dog's gaze dart from one of the alien dogs to the next, his eyes slowly growing wider. Then, he looks back at me and I can see the wild in him bubbling over into spastic excitement.

"*Grover...*" I say, despite knowing any effort to stop what comes next will be futile, like trying to contain a nuclear explosion beneath a ceramic casserole dish.

All at once, his body starts writhing. His limbs slap against me like he learned how to fight from some jackrabbit sensei. There is no winning this battle, so I let him loose, damn the consequences, whatever they might be.

Grover becomes a blur of motion that catches our visitors off guard. Praxion nearly falls over when Grover jumps up at him, not once, but about ten times in as many seconds, sniffing and licking the entire time. When it's Harth's turn, the big guy just crosses his arms and looks down at Grover with something close to disdain.

Jess leans close and whispers. "I'm not sure the dog-people are dog people."

"I know, right?"

When Grover makes his way to Torel, she crouches down to greet him, placing her hands on both sides of his face. He's thrilled that one of the three of them has returned even a fraction of his affection. His energy reaches an all time high, and I suspect he's about to tackle Torel to the ground.

"Grover," I say and snap my fingers. "Sit."

Grover is a bundle of excitable joy, but he's also well-trained. He sits down, contains himself, and leans into Torel's hands. She rubs him beneath the ears but looks at me with hostility. "You command him like a slave."

"A slave?" I say, holding up my hands. "What? No. Grover is my best friend."

My hand lowers toward my holster. It's not an aggressive move. More like instinctually defensive. But Praxion sees it and gets the drop on me, aiming his arm toward my head, some kind of weapon system glowing and humming to life.

"Take the dog," he says to Torel. "I want a full genetic work up. Find out if it has any relation to the Lost Tribe."

"You're *not* taking my dog," I say.

"The Kynolari are no one's property," he says. "Now, let us leave in peace. I do not want to hurt you, but I will."

"As will I," Harth adds, cracking his knuckles.

"You are literally the worst Golden Retriever I have ever met," I tell him.

Jess is about to fire back with some kind of comment. I appreciate it, but now is not the time for brash words or action. We are outgunned, out muscled, and outnumbered. We need to think. Strategize.

"C'mere!" Torel mimics me by patting her knees and opening her arms. And since Grover is a great Golden Retriever, he leaps into her arms, licking her cheek as she carries him away. Harth and Praxion backtrack up the path, weapons aimed toward us. Then they slip into the shadows, heading back to some kind of spaceship—with my dog.

I don't fucking think so.

9

PRAXION

"Prowler-One, Talon-Actual, we are en route to the IZ. Give me a sitrep on Two and Four." I glance over my shoulder and see nothing aside from Harth's broad back as he brings up the rear, keeping watch to make sure the Earth people do not follow us.

"Talon-Actual, Prowler-One," Baarfolir says. "I, uh, I haven't heard from either of them. Comms appear to be disrupted. But MIMIR tells me their language services updates were received and installed, suggesting that—"

"They are alive," I say, trying to hide my relief and stay professional. The longer you are in this job, with the same team, the harder it becomes to pretend the mission is more important than your teammates. Because, with enough time, you become a pack.

"Yes," he says. "And what about you? Have you made contact?"

"Direct," I say. "We are en route, plus one."

"Plus one? You're bringing someone with you?"

"Yes… I am…I am not sure, but he might be a descendant of the Lost Tribe."

"The Lost Tribe! You found them? Already? Wait… '*Might* be?'"

"You will see when we get there, Prowler-One. ETA, two beats."

"Understood, Talon-Actual," he says. "Ready to receive."

"Talon-Actual out," I say and look ahead to Torel. "How is he doing?"

She jogs ahead without missing a step, despite the heavy weight in her arms. The…dog, Grover, lies in her arms like a child. His tail is back, his legs loose and open, his head lolled back, and tongue hanging out. He is a strange creature, and yet he appears to be one of us.

"Honestly," she says, "I think he's enjoying the ride. Didn't know a Kynolari could relax like this. Though I could do without the closeup view of his dick and floppy testes."

"We don't know he's Kynolari," Harth says, sweeping his weapon back and forth, searching for targets. We have no desire to kill Grover's companions, but we cannot let anyone interfere with the mission.

"C'mon," Torel replies. "Look at his face. He could be Praxion's cousin. He's just…different. Evolved."

"*Devolved*," Harth says.

"That may be the case," Torel admits. "But neither option changes what he is, nor our commitment to him."

I find it hard to say, but add, "She is right. If this is what the Lost Tribe has become, we must liberate them, all the same."

"And do what?" Harth asks. "Set them loose to run wild on Kyno? Set up a social program where their needs are cared for by Kynolari who should be looking after our pups, elders, and sick? Or perhaps we will offer one to each pack? For companionship. As pets."

"It is not our task to come up with solutions," I say, leaping a rock and twisting around for a view of the forest. I take a quick spectral scan as I rotate. The infrared lights up our lone pursuer like a torch. It is the man. Grover's...owner. He is fast and closing. Has a disciplined stride. He must know that he cannot win this fight, and yet he comes regardless.

Strange. They are not the same species.

In all the cosmos I have not witnessed such a thing. Species might inhabit the same territory, but they do not...commingle. Do not form bonds. The concept of 'pets' is not foreign to me, but they are generally regarded as something pleasant to look at. Like indoor plants.

But this man is chasing us through the night, toward certain ambush and potential death. Why?

He called Grover his best friend. While I understand the implications of the term and find them laughable, it would be foolish of me to assume I understand the meaning from an Earthling's perspective. Perhaps someone incapable of caring for a best friend is ostracized from society? We visited one planet where the males of an avian species had their feathers plucked if they failed to conceive a hatchling by the age of five. One in five of those creatures spent the remainder of their days shunned, lonely, and featherless.

Without a knowledge of Earth customs, I cannot guess as to why the man persists. Only prepare for it. "Harth, the man approaches from behind. Hold here. Stop him...but do not kill him."

"Gladly," Harth says, slipping behind a tree.

"IZ in sight," Torel says. "Do we wait for Harth?"

"He will join us when he can," I say. "Returning Grover to the *Prowler* is priority one. Once that is complete, we will focus on getting our people back. All of them."

By the time we reach the clearing, I am beside Torel. While she holds the still relaxed Grover, I clear off the Leap Node pads. All that remains to do is stand on the exposed silver discs and verbally request transport. A moment later, we will be back on the moon.

Torel takes her place and starts to speak, "Talon-Three requesting—"

"—my ass," the human woman says.

She stands before us holding a round, yellow object and a branch. While the man approached from behind, loud and obvious, she flanked around. Clever. But futile.

"In her hand," Torel says.

"I see it." The object in her hand is strangely fascinating, but also reminiscent of a Bigapian thermal grenade. While I have seen no evidence of Bigapian influence on this world, I cannot discount the possibility of a secret alliance. The Bigapians are known for deception.

"Let him go," the woman says.

"Woman," I say.

"My *name* is Jess," she says, and I am curious as to why she would insist on my knowing, and using, her name rather than simply calling her 'woman.'

I wave her off. "I do not care to know or understand your customs...Jess. We will leave you in peace, but Grover must come with us."

"And I don't give two micro-shits about who or what you are, or whatever fucked up custom brought you to our planet. You are not kidnapping my friend."

"Your...friend," I say. "How long have you known...this Grover?"

"Uhh," she says. "About...two hours."

That catches me off guard. "Two...hours."

"He's a good boy," she says, as though that should make sense to me.

"You would give your life to rescue him?" I ask.

"Risk my life," she says. "I'm not giving you shit. Grover!"

The limp noodle posture of the dog's body shifts in an instant. His head perks up and turns toward the woman.

"Fetch," she shouts, and tosses the round object into the air.

Grover tracks its progress through the air, up and then down, but he does not move until the woman strikes it with the branch in her hands. The sound it makes and the way it springs away from the impact remove my fears about it being any kind of grenade, but the impact it has on the mission is equally grave.

Grover explodes with energy, bucking and thrashing in Torel's arms until she can no longer hold on. Then he is off, bounding into the dark woods far faster than any Kynolari can run. The Lost Tribe on this planet may be deformed, but they are not physically invalid.

What must life have been like for them to become like this?

I charge my gauntlet and point it at the woman. "You should not have done that."

She is defiant. Stabs a finger at me. "And *you* are a bad boy."

"Your words mean nothing to me," I say.

"How about a bullet, then?"

It is the man. Approaching from behind, weapon pointed at my back. "I have bested your giant, which means I am quite strong. And I've also bested—"

"Are you doing Princess Bride?" Jess asks.

"Yeah, so?"

"You're doing it all wrong," she says. "That's not *Wesley's* line. It's Vizzini's. When they're having the match of wits. 'You've beaten my Giant, which means you're exceptionally strong...'" She steps closer to me, looking me right in the eyes as she speaks. "'But, you've also bested my Spaniard, which means you've studied... You fell victim to one of the classic blunders'—never go in against a New Hampshire woman when a dog is on the line!"

She swings the branch at my head and nearly makes contact.

I lean back from the swing, and into a trap. The man wraps his arm around my neck and places his weapon against my head.

Torel aims her gauntlet toward the woman but holds her fire.

"Impressive," I say to the man.

"Just getting started," he says. "Now, you and your pals can either chill the fuck out and talk like the civilized people you appear to be, or you can zip on back to your spaceship and leave us the hell alone. I don't care which, but you are *not* taking Grover. I will kill all three of you before I let that happen."

"Why...do you care for him as you do?" Torel asks.

"Do space dogs *not* have best friends?" the man asks. "You guys have a lot to learn about being dogs, or Kynolari, or whatever you call yourselves."

Before I can think about how to respond to the situation, a roar precedes Harth's emergence from the darkness. He charges, incensed and apparently unconcerned about the man following through on his threats—because he leaps into the air and tackles us both.

10

CHIRK

"Clear," the man says, looking down at me with something between disgust and indifference. "Just a couple of regular Chihuahuas fucking."

Yeah, I did it.

Sue me.

How often do you have the chance to bone a bitch in the middle of a mission? Never. That's how often. And I know it's stupid. I know that if anyone finds out, I'm going to be in trouble. But the raw, primal beauty of her is impossible to resist. It's like she went into my chest, reached up, and took my brain, and then transplanted it directly to my pecker. Before I understood what I was doing, my clothing was shed, and I was going to town.

Then, just thirty seconds into the deed, the door opens to reveal one of the guys in black. The ones hunting me down. The ones that I assume caught Gruun-lokar out in the water. Much as I'd like to put a rail-shard through this guy's balls, my best chance of escape is to hide in plain sight. To become like this primitive Kynolari. The Lost Tribe that apparently lost their minds.

So, I focus on my dance partner and keep my hips gyrating, putting a little extra spice into it. Got to keep the ladies happy.

"You sure?" a voice over the radio asks. "Command says the one in custody looks like a dog."

The words 'in custody' give me hope. Gruun has been captured, but he's alive.

"Look more like rats than dogs, but yeah," the man says, exasperated. "I'll check..."

When he steps closer to inspect us, I enlarge my eyes and bare my teeth as a warning to not get closer. To my surprise and delight, the bitch does the same. The man stops. "Definitely Chihuahuas. Little psychos look like they might take my leg off."

"Just kick 'em," the man on the radio says.

I snarl and bark at that.

The man jumps and backs away. "Fucking Chihuahuas." Then he leaves and closes the door behind him, giving me the privacy I need to finish. Ten seconds later I dismount, stumble back a few steps, and say, "Minute thirty-two. New record!

I suppose the interruption helped, but still. I might be small, but I can go the distance, baby!"

I pick up my gear and start to dress, "Hey, sorry about that bark. Not really sure what came over me. Haven't done that since I was a kid."

Pants on, I say, "Not much for pillow talk, I guess. Hell, you can't talk at all, right? Can't say that's a problem. I'm not the best listener and tend to do enough talking for—" The silence gets to me. Something is amiss.

"Baby?" I say, turning around, expecting the man in black to be holding her at gunpoint.

Instead, I find her squatting, depositing a swirling dollop of shit onto the floor.

My jaw hangs open. "What..." She has no shame. No sense that she's being watched or doing anything out of the norm. She felt the urge for a post-coital shit and just... Right there... In front of me.

Her little legs start quivering as she forces the last of the poop from her ass. It falls...and then dangles, held aloft by a few—my stomach roils, *oh God*—by a few hairs. She looks back at her ass, panic in her eyes, then she takes off in a sprint spinning in tight little circles until centripetal force extends the length of the shit-mace's hair.

I dive for cover just before the turd becomes a projectile, flying past where I'd been standing.

"The fuck?" I say, getting back to my feet. "The fuck! Look, I know customs might have changed over the last thirty-seven thousand years, but holy hell, woman! Where I'm from we don't thrrreeee—" My voice transmogrifies into a high-pitched shriek of pure horror that I would die before admitting to.

I've never seen anything like it.

My world view—hell, my view of the universe—just... Implodes.

I take a step back, whispering. "*No*, nonono..."

I place my hand against my mouth, remembering the way she seduced me, her tongue under my jowl. "Oh, God..." I turn my head to the side and retch on the spot.

The bitch turns her head at the sound, pausing the feast on her own shit. Then she pads her way over to me, leans down to my vomit...and starts licking.

"Ahhh!" I shout. "Ahhhh!" I run to the door and crash through it with all the stealth of Harth passing gas. Back outside, the fresh air calms me, but only for a moment. The memory of her body beneath me, of her tongue's caress, of her own shit smeared on her teeth—

"Blarg!" I puke in the grass and then run away from the castle, heading for the Leap Node.

I need to get out of this horrible place.

Need to reach the *Prowler*, shower, rinse out my mouth, and then go through a full med-screening to make sure I haven't picked up any exotic STDs.

What the hell was I thinking? I was on this world for just a few minutes, and I've already broken a handful of protocols.

Finish the mission, I tell myself, dashing along a wall that will lead me to the Leap Node concealed in the grass, still clipping my armor back together. *Finish the mission.* I repeat it like a mantra, mostly so I don't throw up again. *Finish the mission.*

I slide to a stop at the sound of deep voices.

"You know what it is?" one asks.

"Not a clue," says another. "But I heard they found something like it in the water, along with the dog."

I peek around the wall. The node is uncovered. They've already started digging it up.

I nearly draw my weapon and gun them both down, but I've already dug myself a deep enough hole. Starting an interspecies war would not look good on my resume. I'm already up to my knees in the shit.

"God-damnit," I mutter, and duck back when one of them turns my way.

"You hear that?" he says. "I think someone whispered."

"Better check it out."

At the sound of footsteps, I make like a Flongorian Mangeloid and run, tail between my legs like a pup. I'm going to have to invent a whole backstory to cover for the monumental mistakes I've made.

For now, I need to escape, regroup, and come up with a plan to rendezvous at the original IZ...which is someplace up north, maybe near the White Mountains, if the beastly pink lady was telling the truth.

I follow my original path from behind the castle, into the garden of hedges intercut by stone pathways. I slip in and out of tall shrubs, ducking into the shadows when people approach. Some are the men wearing black. Others appear to be average citizens, departing for the day as night falls. I find my way to a paved clearing, full of what I assume must be vehicles of some type, on account of the wheels.

"Wheels," I say with a snicker, shaking my head. How did a civilization so primitive take us out mid-insertion?

I move among the vehicles, crawling under them when needed to avoid detection. At the back of the lot, I pause beside a small transport, low enough to the ground that I can reach the door handle. It's unlocked and swings open. I leap inside onto the seat and close the door behind me. My senses are quickly overwhelmed by horrible and somehow familiar scents, not to mention hundred-degree heat.

"Vehicle start," I say, unsurprised when nothing happens. I look for a start button, but there is only a small metal slot on the side of the steering mechanism. "Quaint. Still using keys."

I flip down the visor above my head.

No keys, but there is a photo revealing why the car smells familiar. The woman in pink is on display in front of a brightly decorated tree. She holds Bacon up. They're face to face—Bacon's tongue fully in the woman's mouth.

I reel back from the image, the heated smells really getting to me now. The animal musks. The synthetic flowery scent. All of it masks an underlayer of regurgitated shit. I run for the door, trip, and smack my face against the glass.

A muffled shout makes me flinch back.

Outside, a gruff looking man holds a hammer in his hand. He shouts something at me and then hauls the tool back. Before I can draw on him, he strikes the glass, shattering it.

"Don't worry, little dude," the man shouts. He's tall and wearing loose hanging clothing. Pants. An open plaid shirt. A second shirt with some kind of green leaf on it. He's wearing thick glasses and his hair billows around his head. I don't think it's a style. More of an unfortunate genetic circumstance. "I got you!"

He reaches inside, grabs hold of the armor behind my neck, and yanks me from the vehicle.

"I can't believe your owner left you in there. Assholes like that don't deserve to have a dog like you, man." He carries me to another vehicle. Looks faster than the last. It's black, low to the ground, boxy, and lit underneath. For a moment, I wonder if it might hover, but no, it has wheels.

Still, it's an improvement, and this...person, might reveal the location of his key.

He opens the door, places me on the opposite front seat, and slides into the vehicle beside me. "Welcome to my car, little dude. I call her *Peregrine*."

"Kind of a shitty name," I say.

"Well yeah, it's a mouthful, but peregrine falcons are the fastest—" His eyes open wide. He slow-turns toward me while smacking a small box in one hand against the other. "You just talk?"

"I did," I say.

He pulls a paper stick out of the box, places it in his mouth, and lights the end with a small flame. He sucks on it, filling his lungs with smoke and then blowing it out slowly. Then he laughs, a slow, high-pitched staccato, "Ahuh ahuh

ahuh. Ahh, man, that shit Casey gave me must have been laced. Thought it tasted funny. Anyway, my dude. You got nothing to worry about. You're with me now."

"And who," I say, "are you?"

"Ahuh, ahuh, ahuh. I, my good little sir, am Lord Sean Huempfner. The 'lord' is on account of me owning land in Scotland. Just a little bit." He pats the steering mechanism. "And this is my chariot, *Peregrine.*"

"Already covered that," I say.

"Right. Right." He takes another drag and starts the car with the push of a button. Definitely a better ride. I watch how he operates the vehicle and realize there is no way I'll be able to use it on my own.

We steer toward the paved lot's exit, where one of the large black vehicles is parked. Two men in black suits finish questioning the occupants of another car and wave them through.

"So, Sean, I'm with you now, right?"

He flashes me a big grin and nods. "That's what I said, little dude. You my dog."

"And what's that mean, exactly, to be someone's dog?" I ask.

"Means we're bros. Means we're...like, bonded."

"Like you'd save my life if you had to?"

"Dude," he says. "I *already* saved your life once in the last five minutes. Could totally go to jail for thrashing that window and taking you. So, yeah dude. A man and his dog. The bond is instant. Knew we were destined for each other the moment I saw you smash your little head against that glass."

"Huh," I say. "So, Hump...humpner?"

"Just use my first name, man. No one can pronounce my last name."

"Right. Sean. Seeing as how we're bro-dogs now..." I point through the windshield toward the two men in suits, waiting as we approach. "These goons in black. They're looking for me."

"Whoa-ho. What did you do?"

"Long story," I say. "But right now, I need you to help me get away. Can you do that, Sean?"

He looks at me with a smile, tapping out his burning paper stick. "Hell yes, but we're going to need a different kind of smoke. He tugs a rolled-up paper from behind his ear and lights it the same way he did the first. But the way he holds it and inhales the smoke is different. He holds his breath for a moment and then, while exhaling asks, "You want a hit?"

"Pass," I say.

"Your loss," he says, and then he pushes three buttons on the dash. The first turns on an interior light show. Bright colors shimmer all around us and pulse from front to back. The second recreates the light effect on the vehicle's exterior. And the third plays the loudest, most thumping music I've ever heard. "Tuck your tail and hold on to your pail. This is gonna be sick!"

He pushes his foot pedal to the floor, and I'm pinned to the chair.

The two men flash past, drawing weapons far too late. Then we're onto a road, accelerating as Sean cackles hysterically, shouting along with the song, "One, two, three, and to the fo'!"

11

MICAH

The gun falls from my hand when I hit the ground and the two large alien-dogs land atop me. The three of us spill apart on impact, which allows me to catch a breath and get back to my feet just in time to face the big guy, Harth, as he charges again.

While he's the biggest of the Kyno-guys, he's about the same size as me. A little bulkier maybe, and a hell of a lot faster, but pound for pound we're an even match. In that situation, discipline often decides the fight. And right now, I've got that in spades, while Harth... He's incensed, in part because I was threatening their leader, but also because I kicked him in the nuts on my way here.

"Rawr!" He opens his arms to grab hold of me again. He's a grappler. Would probably twist me into a pretzel if he got me on the ground.

I lean to the side, swat his arm away and allow his momentum to carry him past—straight into a sapling, which bends under his weight and then springs back up when he rolls away to the side.

"Just let us go," Torel says, as Grover thwarts our plan, returning with the tennis ball and dropping it at Torel's feet. She leans down and picks him up. "It doesn't have to be like this."

"Not without him." I point to my dog and say, "Grover, come!"

He starts writhing in Torel's grasp, trying to break free. He's not being violent, just struggling and flailing his paws against her face.

"He is not one of you," Praxion says, squaring off with me. "He does not belong to you."

"You want to see who he chooses, let him go."

He shakes his head. Raises his fists.

This one has a good head on his shoulders. He's also a Golden Retriever, at least in looks. He's got some mud marring his coat, but he's got the noble look of a strong Golden that's spent its years hunting ducks...or traveling the galaxy, I suppose. He might also have a fun side, but it's been buried by a lifetime of what? War? Conflict? Violence? Goldens will fight when they need to, but it's not exactly in their blood.

He closes the distance, poised in some kind of martial arts stance that I don't recognize. When he strikes, it catches me off guard. Everything about his movement says he's going to kick, but then he swings a fist and connects with the side of my head.

I manage to roll with the blow at the last moment, turning my fall into a tumble before getting back to my feet.

It's hard to defend against a fighting style I've never seen, but that goes both ways. A little Krav Maga, taught to me by a friend in the IDF, should be new to him. The combination of aikido, judo, karate, boxing, and wrestling makes it a hard fighting style for anyone to predict. Combine that with my willingness to fight dirty and it provides an advantage in most any close-up violent encounter.

I fight back with a combination of punches. The first two are feints, the third will put him on his ass.

Only it doesn't.

Not because I miss or he's really good at taking a punch, but because my fist stops just an inch from his furry face.

He squints at me, slaps my hand away, and sweeps my legs out from under me.

I cough when I hit the ground, gasping for air.

"You insult me," he says.

I try to explain that it's just not in me to strike a dog—if you ignore the nut-shot to the big boy. But a Golden? Can't do it. The bond between man and dog extends beyond whatever we might own. It's universal. Like a fundamental law of nature, forged in a time when one couldn't survive without the other. I want to tell him that, but I'm still catching my breath.

He raises a foot to stomp on my chest, probably aiming to break a few ribs and take the fight out of me. But he never gets the chance.

Jess tackles him from the side and hauls him to the ground. I can tell by her willingness to fight that she's a scrapper. Wouldn't have pegged her as one before, but she is fearless and knows how to take someone to the floor. Once there, she freezes, like me, unable to strike.

It's not a fair fight.

I get back to my feet and am hit from behind by a freight train that must have snuck out into the woods. I'm sent sailing. Beneath me, Jess is flipped off Praxion. For a moment, we lock eyes, bodies sprawling, each of us silently communicating something like, 'What the fuck do we do? I don't know! Ahh!'

Then I collide with a tree, hit hard, and slump on the ground.

"Shit," I grumble, trying to push myself back up as the big guy closes in on me.

"I lost him!" Torel shouts, as Grover drops from her grasp again. He lands on his feet and races toward the big guy.

I raise my hand toward him, trying to warn him away, but Grover isn't looking at me. His eyes are locked on Harth. His hackles are up. Ears back. Teeth exposed in a snarl.

Grover leaps and clamps down on Harth's forearm just as he's about to throw a punch. Harth reels back, shouting in pain. He shakes his arm back and forth and then throws a punch.

That connects with Grover.

My dog yelps.

Drops away.

Hits the ground.

I think Torel shouts, "Harth!" in anger, but I'm seeing—and hearing—red at this point.

Then I'm up and on my feet in an instant. All the pain and lack of oxygen in the world couldn't stop me.

I no longer care that they look like dogs. Right now, they are a pack that is threatening mine.

Grover has been injured, and that will not stand.

Not for one fucking second.

I leap and drive a knee under Harth's chin. His teeth snap together, and he grunts in pain. Probably made him bite his own tongue. He's dazed from the strike, but not out, so I follow with two strikes to his ribs, which lowers his guard. I follow them up with an uppercut.

The second strike to his chin staggers him back, but still fails to drop him.

So, I fight dirty a second time, reintroducing my foot to his nuts.

That does the trick. He folds in on himself, clutching his crotch.

I notice my gun near my foot, bend down, and pick it up. Then I turn around, point it in the air and fire off a round so everyone here knows I plan to use it if I must. I level the weapon at Praxion, prepared to offer them one last chance at leaving before I pull the trigger.

But he's not looking at me.

He's crouching—over Grover.

"If he's dead," I say, aiming the weapon at the back of Praxion's head.

"No." The lead dog's voice is quiet and full of regret. "He is breathing, but he is injured."

Torel and Jess arrive together, their concern over Grover overpowering their distrust of each other.

"We should get him to the *Prowler*," Torel says.

I point my Glock toward her foot and pull the trigger, putting a hole in the ground to make my point. "He is not going anywhere with you assholes." I pull out my cellphone and check the reception. As expected, we're in a dead zone. I take my keys from my pocket and toss them to Jess. "Pull the truck up as close to the trail head as you can. I'll be right behind you."

I shove Praxion out of the way and start to scoop my unconscious pup from the ground.

"Please," Torel says. Of the three, she seems to be the least aggressive and most reasonable. "I'm a medic. We have technology on the *Prowler* that can—"

"Not a God-damned chance," I say.

She raises her hands and takes a step back. "At least let me treat him here. I have equipment far beyond the capabilities of your people, designed for Kynolari physiology."

"In case you haven't noticed..." I haul Grover up. His dead weight is tricky to hold. "He's not a fucking Kynolari."

When I walk past them, Praxion does nothing to stop me. I glare at Harth as I pass, but he doesn't meet my eyes. He's ashamed about what he's done. But Torel walks beside me.

"Please," she says. "We are in a rural location, yes? How long will it take your primitive vehicle to reach help? Surely, he won't be treated at a facility meant for you."

She's not wrong. The nearest hospital is twenty minutes. The nearest veterinarian hospital—that's open all night—is an hour away. Without knowing how injured Grover is, taking him that far is a risk.

I pause to think it over.

Fuck.

"Jess," I say, stopping her in her tracks. She runs back and I hand her my gun. "New plan. Keep an eye on these two." I look at Praxion. "Torel will take me and Grover to the *Prowler*. You two assholes can stay here." I look back to Jess. "If they try anything, and I mean anything, shoot them."

She doesn't look super confident, but she tries to hide it and nods.

"Torel," Praxion says, "do not—"

She shoots him a look that silences him. He might be their leader, but Torel has no problem disregarding an order when it's dumb.

They're not just some kind of military fire squad, I think.

They're friends.

Maybe family.

"Here," Torel says, using her foot to brush away leaf litter, revealing a silver disk embedded in the ground. "This is a Leap Node. It will take us to the ship."

"And where is the ship?" I ask.

"On Earth's moon."

"Right. The moon. Cool. Sure." I step onto the disc beside her. "Always wanted to go to the moon."

She puts one arm around me and pulls me and Grover close. "Don't fight it. Just stand still. Only takes a moment."

"Prowler-One, Talon-Three, I have three incoming, one injured, one non-Kynolari. How copy?"

She listens to a response and then says, "Confirmed. One injured. One non-Kynolari. Node activation in three, two…"

12

GRUUNLOKAR

"We know you understand us," the man says, leaning down close to my muzzled face. "And we know you can speak."

His breath smells of recently consumed meat, much of which is stuck between the gaps in his teeth. I can smell his family. His children. Three of them. His wife. A mistress, perhaps, but more likely just leering too close to the women who work in this facility.

In addition to the muzzle, I am also cuffed and chained to a table. My feet are bound to the floor. They've stripped me of my armor, my weapons, and all my gear, leaving me in the fur, exposed to all who look my way. I would be humiliated if my captors didn't seem indifferent to my naked body.

The room I'm in is small, containing a simple table and two chairs. A one-way mirror hides observers, whose muffled voices I have no trouble hearing. The walls are painted bright yellow. A bit cheery for an interrogation space. But perhaps the people who work in this place, five levels below ground, get depressed without a little color in their lives.

They are attempting to question *me* but, in my silence, I have learned scores about these...humans.

Two main attributes seem to frame all that they do. Ambition and hubris. Their endless desire to be more—powerful, influential, rich, expansive—has brought this species far. The edge of space. To the boundary of understanding the cosmos. But their consummate belief in their own knowledge, choices, and understanding will be their downfall. Humanity is an infant on the cosmic stage, yet they believe themselves kings of all they survey, merely by planting a flag.

"Answer our questions and we can avoid any uncomfortable circumstances." His skin is dark compared to some other humans I've seen, and his hair is unusual, and not just because it's missing from his face. Plenty of non-Kynolari species lack hair. But very few have it in patches. From what I can see, the only hair to grace this man's body is around the fringe of his skull, where it bulges out several inches. And yet, the top of his dome-shaped head is completely hairless and glows in the bright light shining down from the ceiling of this barren room.

While he appears to be in charge at the moment, I get the sense that he also answers to someone very powerful. He's attempting to project a sinister aura, but the strongest odor in this place isn't the aged blood residing in the floor's cracks, or the chemicals used in an attempt to remove it. It's his fear. Of me. And of someone else.

"My name is Alton Applewhite," he says. "My wife calls me Apple. Most people call me 'Sir.' But since we're going to be friends, you can call me Alton. Now, what's your name?"

He waits a full minute, tapping his fingers on the table between us.

"Don't feel like talking, hmm?" he says. "I understand. You are, after all, a captive. Why should you trust me? But you need to see things from my perspective. Why—should I—trust you? Hmm? Why should I allow you, a stranger from another planet, to casually invade not only my world, but my country? You arrived unannounced, using technology far beyond our own, and invaded our sovereign land armed with enough weaponry to take on a battalion."

He's got a point, but there is something inherently untrustworthy about him. To divulge *anything* to this man would be a mistake.

"How about I tell you what *I* know, first? A little tit for tat. Oh, and if you don't understand that turn of phrase, it means I give you something, you give me something. And if you don't feel like giving something after my generous divulgence of information, then, we will simply take what we need. And that, my fine furry friend, will be torture for you."

He giggles at his own joke, covering his mouth with both hands.

He's excited about this.

Getting off on it.

"Okay," he says, rubbing his hands together. "Where to start, where to start? Oh! Yes. The thirtieth of June, 1908. The Yeniseysk Governorate in Russia, near the Podkamennaya Tunguska River. Not that any of that information means anything to you. Just setting the stage. It's a frigid place where no one in their right mind would want to live. So very few do. Which is fortunate, because on the date I've already provided, a twelve-megaton explosion tore through the area, leveling 80 million trees. Just flattened them out in a big circle. For a long time, no one understood what caused the event. There was no impact crater, after all. But then, the scientific community provided the answer: a two-hundred-foot-wide stone asteroid had entered Earth's atmosphere, and a few miles above the ground, it exploded with enough force to level Manhattan. Good thing it seemed to choose someplace less populated."

He leans back, twisting his lips. "Good thing."

I say nothing.

Don't need to.

The glare in my eyes says everything I want to express.

The man clears his throat. "For the record, 1908 was a hundred and six-teen years ago." He grins. "Your pupils dilated, just the smallest bit. Funny what the body reveals even when the mind is closed off.

"In 1947," he says, "and if math is not your strong suit, that's seventy-seven years ago, just thirty-nine years after the Tunguska event, a second phenom-enon took place in Roswell, New Mexico. Now, on the surface, these two events didn't have much in common. And as far as the world is concerned, one was a rocky meteor that exploded and the other, well, the other was a weather ball-oon. Not that anyone believes that, mind you, but the story is part of pop culture now. And no one knows the truth about what they found out there. Except me. And I'm guessing, you.

"Near as I or anyone can tell, the first of your two probes malfunctioned when it entered the atmosphere. It then directed itself toward an unpopulated area and detonated, erasing all traces of advanced technology. That was Tung-uska. The second probe was also adversely affected by our atmosphere, but the pilots crashed before they could self-destruct, which is fortunate because they would have killed twenty-five thousand American citizens.

"Now, here is where it gets interesting. The pilots. Funny looking guys with big eyes. They sure did cause a stir back in the day, but we both know they weren't ever alive, because they were robots. Drones. A mesh of living cells and advanced processing units. Living, but never alive. Biological machines. Why send a good dog to do a job when a flesh-robot can do it just the same without the risk.

"We've been using the same doctrine for years now. Drones. Thinking machines. And wouldn't you know it, I hear we recently cracked the nut on the whole brain-cell computer-chip combination. Going to revolutionize, well, everything. So, on behalf of the subsection of humanity I currently reside in and represent, I thank you."

He stands and paces.

"We learned all kinds of things about your technology. Reverse engineered cutting edge machinery that's now ubiquitous throughout households around the world. A few people thought to question how quickly things have advanced post-World War II. Most people credit the Nazis, but the Russians got nearly twice the amount of those super-minds and look at them now. What they were missing, and we had, was you. Well, not you. Not until now."

He stops pacing and looks me in the eyes.

"But...we did have help. Because you are not the only ones...out there." He points to the pocked white ceiling. "Earth has been a popular place of late, and some of you—aliens, I mean—share our values and ambitions. And boy, they do *not* like you. Took some convincing to hold off on the eradication of Earth's dogs. Something like that would have garnered far too much attention.

"Now that I see you, in the flesh, I'm surprised she listened at all. Because the resemblance is striking. Aside from the hands, feet, and other physiological changes, you are the spitting image of a German Shepherd."

He plants his hands on the table, leans closer to me, and starts barking. "Rouf! Rouf! Rouf!" Spittle flies from his mouth and he takes it up a notch, barking savagely and growling. "GrrrRouf! Wowowowow! Arghf! Arghf! Arrrrarghf!"

He leans back. "Huh. Nothing to say? Don't want to know who we're working with? How about that tit for tat we talked about? I just gave you a dog bowl full of intel. Now, why don't you be a good widdle guy and tell me what I want to know. Why are you here? Are there more of you coming? What is your purpose on Earth?"

He gives me a moment, but I say nothing.

"Let me break this down for you in a way I hope you can understand." He paces again. "If you don't talk, I'm going to extract information from you in a very uncomfortable way. Wait. I said I would make it easy to understand, didn't I? We're going to torture you. Violently. Then, when your mind is close to being gobbledygook, we're going to let our one and only MK Ultra graduate have a sit-down chat with you, let her dig around in your memories. And then, *then*, I'm going to tell our friend—the one working with us—about you. And when I do, I get the impression that you won't be long for this world, which is an Earth expression for 'she's going to kill you.' You seem like a tough guy. I'm sure none of this frightens you. But I also know you didn't come here alone. So, we can cooperate, or you can—one way or another—tell us everything we need to capture your friends and put them through the same shit strainer you're sitting in right now."

He watches me for a moment. "Heh. Going to be a real tough sombitch? Let me add this cherry to the top of your bad news sundae. Our mutual acquaintance... She really likes the color white. Dresses in white rubber suits outfits and gowns, like she's going to the MET Gala." He waves a hand. "You don't know what that is. But she speaks..." He taps the side of his head. "...directly into your damn mind. Strangest thing you'll ever feel, and if she doesn't like you, it's the last thing you'll *ever* feel before the inside of your cranium is liquified. Despite that, I get the impression that she is on the down and out. That for some reason, she needs *our* help. Against you."

He leans in close. "Her people...they call themselves The Draun. Kind of weird to include the 'The', but that's what they like. The. Draun. On the surface, they look and act like a bunch of interstellar druids, but also like space-nuns. It's their lack of a visage that really gets to me...just that chrome mask that distorts and reflects your own face. I don't understand how she can see much through that thin slit over her eyes, but she sure knows her way around technology. And is happy to share. Unlike *someone else*." He looks me in the eyes. Then he stands back and crosses his arms, all smug and sure of himself. "Now, do you have anything to say to that?"

I smile. "You're all going to die."

13

"...One." Torel stands still, waiting for the jump to begin. But beyond the creaking of trees in the windswept forest, everything remains still.

Something is wrong.

"Do we need to, like, make a sound effect or something, for your 'advanced technology' to work?" The human male's sense of humor is grating but reminds me of a less offensive Chirk.

"Prowler-One, Talon-Actual," I say. "Do you read?"

"Talon-Actual, Prowler-One," Baarfolir responds. "I hear you."

"Run a diagnostic on the Leap Nodes," I say.

"Right. Of course. How?"

I sigh. Someone should have stayed behind. It was foolish to believe our mission would be completed without complications requiring an experienced overwatch.

"Prowler-One, Talon-One," Harth says. "There is an orange button beside the main display. Press it three times."

"I did not know about that," I say to him.

Harth shrugs. "I reconfigured the *Prowler*'s systems. Built in shortcuts."

"Okay, excellent," Baarfolir says. "It's working. Let's see... The nodes still on board are showing all orange. But it looks like they're having trouble connecting to the others... Yeah, no connection."

"Does it show the cause?" Harth asks.

"Frequency interference," Baarfolir says. "Is that possible?"

"Not naturally," Harth says, "and we've only encountered one species with the technology capable of blocking—"

"Fuck this," the human male says, stepping away from Torel with Grover in his arms. The woman joins him, hurrying uphill. She glances back at Torel. "You, come with us."

Torel glances at me for permission, and I nod.

When they are out of earshot, Harth stands beside me. "Praxion, if The Draun are here, it changes everything. This is no longer a rescue mission."

"I am aware."

"What's our first step?" he asks.

"We will see this through." I motion my head toward the fading group. "The humans might have helpful information and, despite his diminished condition, if Grover is part of the Lost Tribe, I will not be responsible for his death. When he is healed, we will find out what we can and then decide on a course of action."

"We should summon the fleet," Harth says.

"I am tempted, but such a move would be noticed and could cause more problems than it solves. The Draun were routed ten years ago. Their numbers would not yet be sufficient to cause harm beyond this world."

"Hrm."

"I do not like it, either," I tell him. "But we must tread lightly, or this planet—populated by the Lost Tribe's descendants—might find itself at the center of a rekindled intergalactic war that left several charred worlds in its wake."

He gives a slow tilt of his head. "Understood."

I slap his shoulder and follow after the others. "Come."

The uphill journey does not take long. We emerge from the forest into a short cut field. The smell of it is intoxicating. This world's ecosystem is lush and primitive. Something about the cool air rushing down from the nearby mountains invigorates me.

We walk by a small round object lying in the grass. Looks like another yellow Bigapian thermal grenade. My gaze lingers on it as I remember how Grover chased it, finding joy in the activity. I want to pick it up. Inspect it. But I resist the urge.

The home's first floor glows with warm light. It is a simple structure built from wood, stone, and a synthetic shell. A crude dwelling. Horribly inefficient. And in a state of disrepair.

The woman opens the home's two doors and allows the man to enter with Grover, followed by Torel.

"If the one known as Grover perishes," Harth says, "you must be prepared to deal with the man's wrath. If need be, I will offer myself as a blood reparation. A life for a life. It is the right course of action...given my lack of control."

I pat his shoulder. It is a noble offer that I will not accept. Not with evidence of The Draun's occupation. But we will need to deal with the man's rage one way or another. "Let us hope it does not come to that."

Inside the home, Grover has been laid out on a table in a room that appears to be meant for food preparation and consumption. We have spaces like this in our dens, but they are much more technologically advanced and less...hands on.

"Micah," Torel says. "Scissors. Jess, hold this." She hands the woman a cranial scanner. Not only has Torel learned their names, but she is also putting them to work.

I turn to Harth.

"Watch the perimeter. No way to know if we were tracked."

He nods and exits. As much as we need to maintain vigilance, I also want him out of the house if things do not work out in Grover's favor.

"What can I do?" I ask.

"Stand there and wait," Torel says, holding a lifesign monitor to Grover's chest. Eight little arms jut out and pierce his skin, latching the device in place. Torel checks the display on her arm. The device pairs and then starts relaying vital signs. She gives no indication whether the results are good or bad.

"Here," she says, reaching out for the scissors when Micah returns.

She takes the sharp tool, leans in close, and carefully trims away two small patches of fur behind Grover's ears.

"What are you doing?" Micah asks, more nervous than angry.

"Saving him," Torel says. "His vitals are irregular. There might be damage to his mind, but there is still time to save him."

She takes out a small circular device that I recognize because we all have them. Cranial regulators. They help us compensate for things like G-forces or psychological attacks. They help us interface with translation services and also heal brain damage from combat or spacetime anomalies. They allow us to excel beyond our biology, and she is correct. It *should* repair any damage done. But is Grover still Kynolari? There is no telling what effect it might have on him.

With a twist, the regulator splits into two thinner discs, the bottom of each covered in thousands of wriggling, nano-scaled wires that appear to be alive, but are simply seeking out neurons to which they will connect.

"The hell is that?" Jess asks, eyeing the regulator.

"No way you're putting that on his head," Micah says.

"They go behind the ears," Torel says. "He won't feel them. You won't see them." She turns her head and pulls back her ear. "See? We all have them."

When Micah turns my way, I show him mine.

"What does it do?" he asks.

"Saves Kynolari," she says, keeping it vague. "Please. I don't know how much time we have."

I have heard her lie before and she is really bad at it. Torel is not lying now and is not using the injury as an excuse to get a regulator on Grover.

Micah looks up to Jess, their eyes meeting, conferring without saying a word.

"Not sure what other choice we have," she says. "But...he's your dog. Do what you think is right. Personally, I'd go for it."

Micah leans his forehead against Grover's, his eyes closed. Whispers, "Stay strong, buddy. The line of Taylor dogs won't end with you."

When he steps back, I am surprised to see tears in his eyes. While the Lost Tribe appears to have devolved, they also seem to have an almost symbiotic relationship with the dominant species on Earth.

I approach Micah while Torel places the regulator discs against the freshly trimmed areas behind Grover's ears.

"What is the line of Taylor dogs?'"

He wipes his eyes. "Taylor is my last name. Micah Taylor. The line of dogs... is like a lineage, but not blood relatives or even the same breed. There is a connection between dogs. Lessons learned. Personality passed on. Loyalty extended to each other and the family. My parents had Buddy when I was born, and there are traits from him that have been passed through overlapping generations of dogs since, all the way down to Grover. And when I get a puppy, he will pass that forward. The chain of dogs has been unbroken since my birth."

"How many...dogs...has your family possessed?" I ask.

"Including Grover, five."

"And how old are you?"

"Twenty-six," Micah says.

The number staggers me. "How long do they live?"

"Ten years if they're big. Fifteen if you're lucky. Buddy made it to eighteen. Kenobi didn't make it past nine. But there is a lot of overlap between them. Buddy never knew Grover, but he knew the others. And some of them knew Grover."

"Such a short life," I say.

He nods. "Too short. How long do Kynolari live?"

"Average?" I say. "Seventy years."

He smiles. "Seventy years... What I wouldn't give to have Grover around that long."

"Here we go," Torel says, activating the regulators. They pull tight against Grover's head as the filaments work their way through skin and bone, finding the mind beneath and connecting directly to it.

Grover's leg twitches when the connection is made.

"How long will it take?" Micah asks.

"The procedure is usually carried out on conscious Kynolari." Torel's ears lower. "Grover is neither of those things. There's no way to know how long it will take to repair any damage, or what the device's exact effect will be."

Grover whimpers. Then convulses twice before running in place, sideways on the tabletop.

"What is happening?" I ask.

"I-I don't know," Torel says, looking surprised.

"He's dreaming," Micah says, leaning down to gently pet Grover's side. "Easy, boy. I'm here. I got you." He leans his head against Grover's with more affection than I ever received as a pup. "You're okay, bud. You're okay…"

That is when Grover opens his eyes, rolls onto his back, and stretches his body to its full length, arms and legs reaching out. When he relaxes again, Micah leans over him. "You good, Gro-Gro?"

The dog smiles and licks Micah's face.

A moment later, Harth slides into the kitchen. He sees Grover, sighs in relief, and then turns to me. "Sir. We have incoming."

14

Tires shriek as we tear around a paved corner. I'm thrown out of the seat's inadequate restraints, constructed for a species far larger than me.

"Oof!" I shout when I hit the door.

"Oh-ho!" Sean says with a laugh. "Shit, man! You better hold on to something!"

"Oh, you think?!" I shout back, grasping the door's handle. "You always drive like this?"

"Only when I'm being chased by Men in Black, dude," he says, eyes wide, hands gripping the steering wheel, that funky smelling smoke pinched between his lips.

"They following us?" I ask.

He glances in the rearview and shakes his head. "I don't see anything."

"Not seeing anything isn't the same as it not being there." I climb the seatback and look out the rear window. "I count three vehicles. Large and black. Hiding in the dark. Looks like the drivers are using some kind of night vision devices."

"You can see them in the dark?" he asks, and then looks at me. "Ohh, right. Dog. *Talking* dog." He takes the rolled paper from his mouth and looks at it. "Psilocybin for the win. This is a crazy trip."

"How much are you going to freak out when you realize all this is real?" I ask.

He chuckles. "Man, talking dogs, man. That would be awesome."

He looks down at me and raises his eyebrows twice. Not sure what that's supposed to mean, but—

"Whoa!" I shout as we make a sharp right.

The back end of the vehicle swings out, clipping two others parked on the roadside. My face smacks into the gap between the chairs, leaving me looking down into the back seat, which is covered in wrapping papers. For a moment, I'm disgusted by the view. Then I catch a whiff of meat, fat, sugar, and salt. It's a mishmash of scents—a few of them vile—but my stomach roils with near insatiable hunger. Takes all my discipline to not jump into the mess and start tearing through it in search of morsels...

Like I'm some sort of animal.

When the car straightens out, I'm thrown the other way and pulled out of my strange food-lust. The impact was jarring but didn't slow us down. Which is good because, "They're gaining on us. Need to lose them."

"No worries, my man, we have the home court advantage. I grew up in Magnolia. Know these streets like the back of my scrote."

"That's not very comforting," I say.

"I mean, it's just a saying, but if I'm honest...I have one of those make-up mirrors. You know, the ones that magnify what you're looking at? Anyway, I got curious, right? So, I kind of squatted down in front of it and then bent way over for an upside-down view. Don't recommend it if you're not flexible, but wow, talk about expanding your mind. Twenty-five years without seeing a part of my body and then, wow, all at once, there it is. Upside-down. Darrel recorded the whole thing."

"That's...I just..." A chuckle escapes my lips. Finding it hard to focus. "Keep driving."

"That's the plan, my man! Whoo!" He makes another right-hand turn, heading uphill into a wooded area.

Behind us, screeching tires give away the position of the men pursuing us. A moment later, they give up on stealth and activate their bright headlights, illuminating us and the road ahead.

"Oh shit!" Sean says. "These guys are trying to give us an anal probe."

"Nah. Only Bigapians do that," I say with another chuckle, but he doesn't get the reference. I draw one of my mini-railguns. "Can you open the windows on this thing?"

"Yeah, but there's no need," he says.

"You want me to shoot out the back?"

"Nah, man. Just hang on to your fuzzy little nutsack, bro!" He opens a console between the seats, revealing a few switches and a button. He flips all three switches and hovers his thumb over the button long enough to give me a smile.

"Shit!" I dive down to the door handle and hold on tight.

He presses the button.

The engine roars.

G-forces tear me away from the door and pin me up against the seat.

Beside me, Sean howls with laughter, eyes wide. The dark forest passes in a blur.

"Bye, bye, Men in Ass! Fear the *Peregrine*! Fear—the *Peregrine*!"

Ahead, the road hooks lazily to the left. We're moving far too fast.

"Sean..."

"I got this!"

He pushes a button above his head. Doesn't seem to have any effect on our speed. Then he pushes the red button again and flips the three switches back. Our speed plummets. And I'm able to move again. I scramble up and look back. The three vehicles pursuing us are just small dots of light now.

"Hang on," he says, and this time I obey without question. He shifts gears, cranks the wheel, and we take the turn sideways, drifting around the bend, until he hits the brakes, puts us into a rapid spin, and drives off the side of the road backwards. I nearly scream but manage to hold it in when the sound of rough gravel grinds beneath the tires and we slide to a stop.

Sean reaches up and presses the button above him once more. In front of us, a pair of metal gates swing closed. He turns off the car, extinguishes the lights, and snuffs out his smoke stick after sucking in one last lungful and holding it.

A moment later, the three black vehicles roar past, pursuing a car that is now a ghost. After they pass, he turns Peregrine back on, but not the lights. Then he slowly reverses into a garage and turns the car off.

"Oh, ye of little faith," he says. "You know, I wanted to be a NASCAR driver, once upon a time. Or a getaway driver. For like, bank robberies."

"Well, it's good to have dreams," I say, not really interested.

"Meh," he says. "I found Mary Jane and never looked back. Or forward, I guess."

"That your girlfriend or something?" I ask. "Bitches can have that effect on a man."

"What?" He laughs. "Mary Jane? Marijuana? Weed. Pot. Dope. Grass. Ganja. Hash." He lights his smoke stick again. "This...is a joint. Or doobie. There are other names, too, but when it's small, it's a roach."

"A mind-altering substance," I guess.

He opens his mouth, turns his head to the roof, raises an index finger, and then just kind of freezes for a moment, before pointing at me and saying, "Yes. But this shit..." He takes a drag and coughs it out. "This shit is laced with something else. Something that's making me see and hear a talking fucking dog, man."

"You ain't seeing things," I say, fumbling my hands against the door, looking for the handle. The smoke filling the cabin is irritating my lungs. "And you sure as shit ain't hearing things."

I find the handle, pull it, and fall out when it swings open.

A cough bursts from my lungs when I land on the garage's hard floor. Sean leans over the seat, wide-eyed, looking down at me. We just stare at each other for a moment and then both burst out laughing.

"W-what is happening?" I ask. "W-why am I l-laughing?"

"Dat's da ganja, mon," he says in some kind of weird accent.

"You mean, the mind-altering substance you were smoking?"

"Yeah, man. Pot. This is what it does to people...and hallucinated dogs, I guess. We weren't hotboxing for that long, but you're a little guy. It must really be fucking you up."

Another pause and another fit of laughter.

This isn't funny, some small voice in my mind says from a swirling abyss. Need to make contact. Need to find the others. Need...to... "I'm not a hallucination!" I say and start laughing even harder.

Sean joins me for a moment, but then he seems to sober. "Wait. Huh? You're not? Hold on...isn't that what a hallucination would say? Naw, man, why would a hallucination say it wasn't a hallucination? And why a dog? I totally broke that window in the parking lot. That was real." He looks at me. "You were real."

"Still am," I say between chortles.

"So, you're a real dog...and I'm just hearing things?"

I raise a hand from the ground and point at the garage ceiling. "Negatory! I...am from up there!"

He leans out of the car and looks up. "You live in the ceiling of Mr. Jenkin's garage?"

"What? Who?"

"Mr. Andre Jenkin. This is *his* house. I do the landscaping at his mansion. He's on vacation for, like, the summer, I think. His daughter is primo, man. Like you wouldn't believe. I'm too old for her, I know, but a guy can dream, right? Then again, his wife isn't too shabby, either. I ain't picky."

"No one would think you were," I say, the silliness controlling me starting to fade as I catch my breath outside the car, which is still venting smoke.

Sean lies over the front seats, looking down at me with wide eyes. His halo of big hair surrounding his bald head strikes me as so ridiculous, I nearly start laughing again. Then he asks, "So when you said, 'up there,' you meant space, right? Like another planet? Or galaxy? Or dimension?"

"First three," I say. "Not the last. Only interdimensional species I've met look like little bioluminescent purple phalluses. They used to be blue and red, but something changed along the way. Anywho, they're not important. But yeah, I'm not a hallucination. I'm from another planet, separated from my fire squad, and I need to find them. *And* I'm here to rescue the Lost Tribe."

"Lost Tribe," he whispers, face going through a slow transformation from abject confusion, to understanding, and finally landing at abject gobsmackery. "Dogs. You're here to rescue dogs...from Earth...because...because dogs are aliens, too?! Holy shit! Holy actual shit! Dogs are aliens?! Deadass?"

I nod. "Yeah...but they've been here for thirty-seven thousand years."

"Mind...blown," he says, making a hand gesture that suggests his brains have been blown out.

I chuckle and mimic the gesture. "Probably a lot to take in."

"Like, yeah," he says. "I just...I mean...dogs. Wow." He blinks a few times and then seems to forget everything he just learned. "Hey, you hungry?"

"Like never before," I admit.

"Sweet," he says. "Let's go inside. I've got some Bugles and Dews. We can chill until the heat is off and, in the morning, we can see about finding your peeps. Dope?"

"What? No? I don't want to get any more of that stuff in my lungs."

"What?" he says. "Dope..." His eyes light up and he laughs, "Ahuh, ahuh, ahuh. Man, you chill as fuck. Dope instead of dope. Because they're the same words with different meaning. Psssh. I feel you, man. I feel you." He slides out of the car and motions for me to follow. "Let's go get some vittles."

15

MICAH

"Who is it?" I ask, and then quickly realize that the anthropomorphic Great Dane standing in the kitchen door won't have any idea who's approaching the house. "What kind of vehicle is it?"

"It's strange," Harth says. "It has wheels."

"All Earth vehicles have wheels," I say.

Harth shakes his head. "Such a backward world."

"Ignore the wheels. What did it look like?" I ask.

"Brown and green. Lights on top but extinguished. A star-shaped emblem on the side."

"Sounds like a state trooper," Jess says.

I nod and add, "Sounds like Steven Newell."

"Seriously?" Jess says. "Big Stevey Newell?"

He went to school with us. A few years ahead, so the overlap was mercifully brief, but he left an impression.

"He's a state trooper?" she asks.

"And my neighbor." I look out the kitchen window. See the patrol car rolling down the long driveway. While my property doesn't fall under the jurisdiction of State authorities, Steve is a bit nosy and likes to flash his badge. He's not a bad guy, but he might lack the mental elasticity to fully comprehend this ridiculous situation without calling in the cavalry. "I'll take care of it, but everyone stay inside and out of sight."

I point to our three non-human guests. "That means the three of you. We need to contain this."

Praxion nods and then turns to the other two, nodding twice more. They nod back, already going silent. They step toward the back of the house, turning off lights and disappearing into the shadows. While they seem intent on avoiding more conflict, I note that all three activate the weapons mounted to their arms before sliding into the dark.

Please don't be a dick, Steve. Please don't be a dick.

I help Grover down from the table and say, "On me." He stands beside my leg, waiting.

"Sure you want to take him out with you?" Jess asks.

"Would be stranger if I didn't," I say. "This isn't Steve's first visit, and he's never seen me without my wingman."

"Wingman, huh? That what he was doing when he dry-humped your leg into oblivion?"

I smile. "Worked, didn't it?"

"Almost," she says. "But I don't think we'll be recreating any Cardi B songs tonight."

"Cardi B songs—" The one and only Cardi B song I know piledrives into my thoughts, the lyrics flickering through my mind. I choke on the air I'm breathing, which gets a laugh out of Jess.

She smacks my back a few times, "Easy there, big guy."

I'm still coughing when I head for the door. This woman... Wish I'd connected with her sooner.

Hand on the door handle, I catch my breath and look down at Grover. Can't see the regulators, and he's acting like his normal self, though he seems to be mostly ignoring the fact that our home is full of people...and dog aliens, which would usually be enough to give him the zoomies. Nothing like an eighty-pound Golden sprinting circles through the house, off the couches, and drifting around the kitchen table before performing a tight spin worthy of an Olympic figure skater, culminating with a flourish as Grover catches his own tail and collapses to the floor.

"On me," I repeat, letting him know I'm not in the mood for shenanigans. He just looks up at me, calm and panting. "Good."

I open the door and step out into the night. The air has cooled enough that I can see my own breath. It was a warm summer day, but we're in the mountains. Things get cold and windy when the sun sets.

I tilt my head to the lawn. "Go pee."

Even if Grover doesn't actively need to pee, he can always squeeze something out. We got into the practice before going to bed and on long trips. He trots over to the grass and leans in close the way most Goldens do. Steve's high beams illuminate the scene, which presents exactly the way I want it to—we're just out for a piss.

I squint my eyes and raise a hand in greeting.

The car turns in the driveway, lighting up the forest from which we recently emerged with bipedal dogs from another world. He doesn't dim the lights. Doesn't shut off the engine. He just steps out of the car, places his brown hat upon his head—signifying that he is here on official business despite that being illegal—and moseys on over, boots grinding against the gravel driveway.

He's chewing gum.

He's always chewing gum. Blows the occasional bubble, and I wonder how he never gets any stuck in his mustache. He stands at six seven and weighs in at over three hundred pounds easy. Maybe four hundred. He could be an Adonis of a man if he put his mind to it, but he more closely resembles Stay Puft.

"Hey there, Micah," he says. "Busy night?"

"Not at all," I say. "Just chilling with the pup."

He grunts and gets down on one knee. Claps his hands toward Grover. "How is the dog faring? On account of losing your parents." To Grover, he says, "Here, boy."

"We have each other," I say.

"That's sweet," he says, forcing a smile and clapping for Grover again.

I make two clicks from the side of my mouth and motion my head toward Steve. Grover gives up on what he was sniffing and heads for the man, head low, unhappy about his ambassadorial role.

Takes a lot for a Golden Retriever to not like someone, but they say dogs can smell a person's guilt, and even intentions. If that's true, Trooper Steve might have some skeletons in his closet.

Steve gives Grover a rub on his head and then both ears.

Shit.

He pauses. The regulators aren't easy to see, but they aren't exactly soft and furry. "What're these, now?"

"Blood-sugar monitors," I say. "Poor guy has diabetes."

Steve clucks his tongue. "Shame. What with all he's been through." He pushes on his knee and grunts to stand. Tugs up his pants. "Well, reason for the visit is I heard a call out on the radio. Seems there were some strange lights in the sky earlier. Bunch of folks saw them. Called 'em in. From what I could tell, most of them claimed to have seen something out here over your folks' land. Well, *your* land now. Don't suppose you and some military buddies been having some fun out here? Maybe shooting off some ordnance?"

"Ordnance?" I ask.

"You know, flares and the like. I didn't mean— It's not like you're hiding a howitzer out here." He chuckles. "Just wondering if you might know something about it, is all."

I shake my head, pretending to think it over. "Nope... No. I've been busy the last few hours. Wasn't really paying attention to the sky."

"That so?" he says. The tone of his voice means he saw me out and about somewhere. Probably on my way to or from my date with Jess.

"Well, look what the dog dragged in," Jess says from the kitchen door. She steps out into the night. She's undone the top few buttons of her shirt, offering

just a hint of cleavage and an unmistakable suggestion about what Steve is inter-
rupting. "Stevey Newell."

"I'll be damned," he says. "Bender?"

"In the flesh," she says, wrapping her arms around me.

His eyes go wide. "I didn't know you two—"

"It's kind of a new thing," she says, squeezing me.

"Well, shit. Ain't that something." He backhands my shoulder like we're
friends. "Guess coming back home had at least one perk, eh? Went and bagged
yourself the only ethnic in—"

"How about those lights, Steve?" I ask, while Jess vents her anger by crushing
my hand. New Hampshire isn't known as an outwardly racist state, but we've got
plenty of backwoods types stuck living in a mental era that allows them to say
pretty much anything that pops into their heads without ever once considering
there might now be a better way to phrase something. "Anything we should be
worried about?"

"Not as of yet," he says, "but if my investigation turns anything up, I'll be
sure to let you know."

The presence of Grover puts Steve at ease, but the one-two punch of Grover and Jess has taken away all his bravado. Probably rehearsed what he was
going to say, and now he's forgotten all his lines. He's about to wave and leave
when he glances down at my waist and lingers for a moment.

"You carrying?" he asks.

"Huh?" I look down to find the shape of my holstered pistol visible beneath
my shirt. "Oh, yeah. Been a skunk around. Last thing I need is to give this big
man a tomato soup bath." I pull my shirt up so he can see the weapon. New
Hampshire is an open carry state, and even though I had it concealed under my
shirt, you can pretty much do what you want so long as you're on your own
land.

"Glock 19," he says. "Nice piece. Maybe we can fire some rounds at the range
some time."

"Maybe," I say.

"Hmm," he says. "Skunks. Never liked 'em much. Can't say I like most critters,
though. Coons. Opossums. Groundhogs. Weasels. Did you know we have weasels
in New Hampshire? Like a lot of them." He ticks off a finger with each named species. "Pine Martens. Minks. Fishercats. God-damn river otters. Otters. In New Hampshire. Who knew?"

I'm about to tell him I had no idea, just to make him feel like he's taught me
something so I can send him on his way. But I'm interrupted by the sound of
more tires grinding over my driveway.

I step to the side and look down the drive.

Three large black SUVs roll toward my home.

"Now, who's this?" Steve asks.

"No idea," I tell him, hand lowering toward my weapon.

He notices. Tenses. "You expecting trouble?"

"I'm an Army Ranger, Steve," I say, forcing a grin. "I'm always expecting trouble."

"Maybe so, but if they're looking to start something, best let me handle it."

I motion to the oncoming vehicles. "Be my guest."

Steve gives a nod, hikes up his pants and walks out to greet the SUVs as they roll to a stop, side by side, leaving just enough space to open all the doors between them and form a handy barricade. These guys aren't law enforcement. They're military.

"Steve," I say. "Might not be a good idea."

He waves me off and pushes forward, hand raised in authoritative greeting.

I glance to Jess. "Inside." She nods and I turn to Grover. "In!"

As they hurry for the kitchen door, I back away slowly, eyes on the tinted windshields. No way to know who's inside, or how many. The driver's side window of the SUV nearest Steve rolls down. Steve says something in greeting and then flinches. Staggers back a step. Goes for his gun.

Doesn't even reach the holster.

A gloved hand extends a Robocop-looking Maxim 9 pistol with an integrated sound suppresser and pulls the trigger three times, twice toward his chest, once to his forehead. Each round fired is quiet but sends a shock through my system.

Before Steve's body hits the ground, the rest of the SUV doors spring open, and I bolt for the house.

16

Micah is the last to enter the house, but his arrival is by far the most dramatic, diving through the door and sliding across the floor. Projectiles chase him, chewing up the dwelling's primitive wooden structure.

Before getting to his feet, he kicks the heavy wooden door closed and then starts barking orders.

"Big guy," he says to Harth. "Cover the front door."

He rolls to his feet, points to me and Torel. "Watch this door. I'll be right back."

"Must we take orders from this creature?" Harth asks.

"This *creature*," Micah says, "kicked your ass a few minutes ago. Only reason you're still breathing is because I like dogs."

"I am *not* a dog," Harth growls.

"*Harth*," I say. "This is his home, and we seem to have brought an enemy to his doorstep. He is a competent soldier."

"You have no idea," Micah says, a familiar glare in his eyes. I used to see it in the mirror when I was younger and full of confidence. I suppose it is still there, just tempered by experience and war.

Harth grunts, activates the Incinerator V17 gauntlet attached to his arm, and thumps over to the front door. Peeks out a window. "Counting twelve. Holding their ground."

Micah tells Grover to "Stay" and the dog obeys, sitting down, tongue hanging out, tail wagging. Despite what might be dire circumstances, he just looks happy to be alive. I cannot determine if it is endearing or the most pitiful thing I have ever seen.

"So," Torel says to Jess. "How long have you been his bitch?"

"*Excuse* me?" Jess responds, full of outrage, which is strange, because I did not hear anything out of the ordinary in Torel's question.

"His *bitch?*" Jess says, identifying the term that has offended her.

"Apologies," I say, "Translation services do not always work as intended. Is the word 'bitch' derogatory?"

"You think?" she says, and I am not sure what she means.

"What I meant," Torel says, "is, how long has he been your mate?"

"No one has copulated in this house for some time," Harth says from the front door, still peeking through the window, keeping watch.

"Well, that's good to know," Jess says, and then she adds, "Wait, how do you know that?"

Harth taps the side of his nose without breaking concentration.

"Gross," Jess says.

"Interesting," Torel says. "You seem...bonded."

"I was beginning to think so, too," Jess says, "before you assholes showed up." She gives me a smile, revealing her statement is in jest, but I detect true annoyance layered beneath the humor.

Micah returns from the second floor. He is wearing body armor over his chest and carries a second armored vest, which he hands to Jess. "Put this on." After she finishes slipping the vest on, he hands her a weapon with a long barrel and a broad opening. "Know how to use it?"

"I've fired a shotgun before," she says, taking the weapon and chambering a round. The sound the weapon makes is satisfying, despite its ancient looking design. "Gutted a deer more than once, too."

Micah nods and readies a much more futuristic looking weapon. He notes my attention and says, "SIG M400 TREAD with all the cool gadgets."

"Should that mean something to me?" I ask.

"Only that I mean business," he says.

"This is hardly the time for business dealings," Harth grumbles and shakes his head. "Capitalists..."

I activate my Sonizer M24 gauntlet. It wraps around my right arm, becoming an extension of my limb. It is capable of firing sonic blasts that will drop a Kynolari to the ground. The effect on other species varies to a degree but is never pleasant. If I need a more lethal option, I can crank up the power...which basically liquifies flesh and bone. I prefer to avoid the messy option, especially on an unclaimed world that is home to an unregistered species and the Lost Tribe.

"You were holding back," Micah says, eyeing my weapon. "In the forest."

I smile at him. "Very much so."

He grunts in displeasure.

Harth has a good chuckle at the human's expense.

"Got the impression your nuts weren't holding back," Micah says, sliding up next to Harth and peeking out the window. "Any movement?"

"None," Harth says. "And if I am unable to sire a pack someday, I will come for you."

Micah grins. This is good. There is no faster way for soldiers to bond than in the heat of battle...or even from the threat of it. Micah, Jess, and even Grover seem like they would be worthwhile allies to have on this world. That is, if Micah will forgive our transgressions. There are not many in the universe who would, but our appearance and relation to Grover and the dogs of this world seem to put him at ease.

A loud song emanates from his pants.

He flinches and pulls a device from his pocket. It is the most modern looking thing I have seen on this world thus far. In fact, something about the technology is familiar.

"Is that 'Gangnam Style?'" Jess asks. "You have Psy for a ringtone?"

Micah seems embarrassed, like he has been caught committing a petty crime of some sort, but he says nothing. He looks at the illuminated screen, taps it, and speaks into the device.

"Who are you?" he asks and taps a button on the device that allows us to hear the reply.

A monotone voice says, "Specialist Micah Taylor, you are harboring enemies of the United States of America. If you do not wish to be tried for treason, you will escort them outside immediately."

"To whom am I speaking?" Micah asks.

For a moment, silence, then a series of clicks.

Micah whispers. "We're being patched through to someone else."

A new voice comes on over the line. "Well now, Mr. Taylor, aren't you in an interesting pickle. On the one hand, you have the country you've served so faithfully since your eighteenth birthday. Enlisted before the party was even done it looks like. Bully for you. On the other hand, alien invaders that look like cute, fuzzy wuzzy dogs, man's best friend given a voice and wielding deadly technology that you would have a difficult time fathoming. The men outside your domicile are there to collect the invaders, unharmed if possible, as has been our mandate since 1947, when the Twilight Directorate was formed."

"Twilight Directorate?" Jess says, nearly laughing.

"Twilight," the man says, "is often associated with ambiguity. The in-between state of light and darkness. A time when things are neither completely visible, nor hidden. The unknown. Oooh. Aaah. That is where we operate. Directorate...well, that's exactly what it sounds like, an organized governmental structure. Kind of boring, but it was the forties. 'Twilight' was a good choice and, like a rising tide, it lifts all boats, which in this case is the word 'directorate.'"

Jess mouths the words, "What the hell?" toward Micah and he shrugs, mouthing back, "I have no idea."

"And you are?" Micah asks.

"Director Alton Applewhite," the man on the device says.

"You direct a Directorate?" Jess asks.

"Mmm," Alton says. "It is rather clunky, Ms. Bender."

"He knows who we are," Jess whispers.

Micah holds a finger to his lips, the universal gesture for 'silence' among species with fingers and mouths.

"You know," Alton says, "we are in an unusual predicament. Neither of you have family to threaten, so I'm just going to ask nicely—once—and then we'll shift gears. Please send the Kynolari outside, and you will be left in peace, along with an NDA."

"Give us a second," Micah says and then mutes the communication device. He looks to Jess. "Thoughts?"

"He knows who we are," Jess says.

"He knows who *we* are," Torel adds. "He called us Kynolari. He is the one who disabled the Leap Nodes. Who is jamming our comms and preventing us from leaving."

A ticking sound comes from the device, Alton clucking his tongue to accentuate the passage of time, and that we're nearly out of it.

"We cannot ask you to risk your lives," I say. "We will leave out the back. Make a show of it. Face them in the forest."

"Not that easy," Micah says. "He told us his name. Who he works for." He turns to Jess. "I'm sorry, but we've got targets on us. Even if they leave here alive—" He motions to me and then Torel. "We're both toast."

"Well, in that case," she says, "I guess we don't have much of a choice."

Micah turns to me. "You're good boys, right?"

Torel clears her throat.

"Good dogs," Micah says.

Harth groans. "I preferred good boys."

I hold my hand up, silencing the conversation. "Yes," I tell Micah. "We are. And we will not let you die today."

He nods and unmutes the device. "Alton?"

"Here."

"Go fuck yourself." He disconnects and looks up at me. "Hope you're ready for a fight."

"I have been ready for a fight since I suckled on the first of my mother's eight teats," Harth says, repeating the words of one of Kyno's most renowned and decorated generals. Then he yanks the front door open, aims his weapon, and pulls the trigger.

17

CHIRK

"What are these called again? Vittles?" I'm lying on my back, atop a plush couch, legs up on a pillow. My mind and body are in some kind of strange, relaxed state. I know it's from the smoke that filled the vehicle—a 'car'—aka *Peregrine,* which is a 'suped-up badass mother-fucking Mitsubishi Lancer,' according to Sean.

He's just about the strangest creature I've met in the entire galaxy, but he's warming on me. Could be the drugs in my system, but he seems kind and honest. Very much *not* like me, but they're attributes I appreciate in other people.

"Naw, man. Vittles is, like, a generic word for food. What you are partaking in are called 'Bugles,' on account of that they look like bugles, which are horned instruments used in the military to, like, I don't know, wake people up or something."

I look up at the yellow cones I have decorating the tips of my five fingers. "Well, they're now in my top five foods." I pluck one of the Bugles from my fingertip and munch it down.

Sean is seated in what he called a lounge chair, facing a display screen known as a TV. He's kicked back with a bowl of snacks, happily munching like an Archionic Field Slaugh with a feed bag.

A small human on the screen furrows his brow, pushes out his lips and says, "Watchu talkin' 'bout, Willis?" which is followed by laughter, both from the TV and from Sean.

He slaps his leg and laughs. "Ahuh, ahuh, ahuh. Classic. Gets me every time. You ever seen *Diff'rent Strokes?*"

"I can't even conceive of why someone would watch this," I say. "What is the point?"

"It's fun," he says. "Entertainment."

"I've seen entertainment, and this ain't it." I'm about to lie back and keep eating my Bugles when the screen shifts to something else. It's a Kynolari with a head like Praxion's, lying on the floor. Looks like it's dreaming of some kind of meat...

"What is this?" I ask.

"Oh, it's an old commercial. Advertising. This station plays old shows and old commercials. It's like traveling through time to the 80s."

I watch the Kynolari, or 'dog' as they call them here, wake up from its dream shouting of bacon. It runs around the dwelling, frantically sniffing out this bacon. Absolutely desperate. And then, it finds the source of the scent...and can't read the bag. But I can. "Beggin' Strips?" The scene plays out with a human female handing a strip of faux meat to the dog, who eagerly devours it. Then, a condescending voice declares that it's not actually bacon and it ends with the line, "Dogs don't know it's not bacon."

When the commercial ends and changes to something else, I turn to Sean. "That was the most offensive pile of shit I've ever seen. Are dogs jokes to you? You led me to believe that there was a bond between mankind and dogs. This... this is propaganda portraying the noble Kynolari race as stupid, gullible, and desperately ravenous for whatever processed garbage that was supposed to be. So much so that they would *beg* for it. *Beg?!*"

"It was the 1980s," he says, waving away my concern. "Everything was accidentally offensive back then. Also, have you ever had bacon? I mean, c'mon. Pretty sure *I* have begged for bacon. Oh! Maybe we have some!"

He lowers his footrest and springs from his chair, holding a remote control. He tosses it onto the couch beside me. "Here, watch whatever you want. But if you see any 'Yo Quiero Taco Bell' commercials from the 90s, I suggest changing the channel, el quicko."

"I want some Taco Bell," I say, translating his words into his common language.

"Habla Espanol?" he asks, sounding surprised.

"Thanks to translation services, yeah. Now, what is Taco Bell?"

"Not important," he says.

"More processed fake food shit, right?"

He thinks it over for a moment, "Uhh, yeah. That's basically right. But it's for people."

I shake my head and lean back. "This planet is fucked."

"Ahh, yup," Sean says. "And there are two things that make it better: Pot. And Bacon."

I look down at the remote, make quick sense of its labeled controls, and then change the frequency to receive a different video feed. Talking people. Click. Laughing people. A dog. In black and white. It's barking at people, telling them to follow. Seems smarter than the dogs I've witnessed thus far. They follow the dog, who appears well groomed, to a water well. And inside, a child who needs help.

"What is this documentary called?" I ask. "This dog is at least slightly competent."

He leans over, sees the screen, and says, "That's *Lassie*. And it's not a documentary. It's a show. Like *Diff'rent Strokes*. Fiction."

"Fiction..." I say. "Ugh."

He tears open a package of meat, presumably bacon, and peels strips away, laying them in a heated pan. The moment the smell of the meat reaches the air, I pick up on the scent. Though placated by the Bugles, my hunger surges, and for a moment I feel like the dog in the commercial. Like I would do *anything* to get that bacon. It's a kind of primal instinct, like what happened with...holy shit. Bacon. In my drug-addled state, I forgot all about Bacon.

I giggle.

"What?" Sean asks.

"Just remembered," I say. "I *have* had Bacon!" I crack up laughing, far more than is appropriate. This drug is strange, forcing my psyche to vacillate between states of relaxation, paranoia, and giddiness.

"Like the meat?" he asks.

"Oh, I gave her the meat," I say, giggling some more, and then quickly sobering when I change the TV frequency again and see a talking female human head. It's not the woman that holds my attention, though. It's the smaller video beside her head, displaying three streaks of light in a blue sky. A text label beneath the woman says, 'UFOs in New Hampshire?'

"Hey," I say, "what's this?"

He leans to look at the TV. "News. About stuff that's happening. Why?" He steps back into the living room, carrying a smell that can best be described as that moment right before an orgasm. "Whoa, is this about you? Let me see that." He takes the remote and increases the TV's volume.

"This was the scene earlier today over the mountains of New Hampshire, just north of the Franconia Notch, in an area known as Sugar Hill. Three streaks of light can be seen dropping through the clear blue sky, descending toward the mountains."

A video accompanies the woman's description, filling the screen. It was taken after me and Gruunlokar were separated, in the moments before the others would have landed. It's good to see that they made it to the ground, but this is going to draw a lot of attention and make it difficult for them to get around unnoticed. Then again, maybe they just exfilled and are waiting on the *Prowler*.

"Authorities say they received dozens of calls about the streaks, including one from a man kayaking at Echo Lake Beach, who toppled into the frigid waters and was taken away in an ambulance."

A man appears on screen wearing a cheap suit and a phony smile. "Well Janet, I know of at least one man who found it a chilling experience."

"Ha, ha, Chet. Right you are," the woman says, seated beside him. "No word on the man's condition, but we wish him a speedy recovery. And now..." She looks straight ahead like she can see us sitting here, "we want to hear from *you*. With all the recent UFO—or is it UAP, Chet?"

"I think you can pick and choose, but the government seems to prefer 'UAPs' these days. That's Unidentified Aerial Phenomenon, Janet."

"Thanks, Chet. Now then, we want to hear from you." The video of the Leap Nodes' descent plays again. "What do you make of this? Are we being visited by little green men? Are these travelers from another planet? Another time? Or even another dimension?"

"Our man on the streets, Steve Casey, is on location in Lincoln, New Hampshire, to ask just that," Chet says, and the video cuts to a man trying too hard to look casual in front of a sign for Hobo Hills Adventure Golf, speaking to random groups of people.

"What do you all think of today's UFO sighting?" Steve asks.

"UFO?" A young human female asks and flicks her hair. "All I saw was a bunch of creepy ass mannequin hobos and Andy Blankenship checking me out." She winks at the camera, gives a wave, and says, "Hi, Andy!"

"And what about you?" Steve asks an older couple. "Do you have any thoughts about today's UFO sighting?"

"What'd he say?" The man asks the woman.

"I think he asked if the mosquitos were biting," the woman replies.

The scene cuts again.

Steve looks a little exasperated.

He approaches a man and what must be his son.

"Hey there, folks. WMUR News. Steve Casey, man on the streets. Just wondering if you heard about today's UFO sighting, and if you had any thoughts about it?"

"UFO?" The older man says, his voice heavily accented. "Oh, ja! Wir haben das video gesehen. Ganz außergewöhnlich!"

Steve sighs. Looks at the camera. I think I hear a whispered curse before the dejected man says, "Janet, Chet, back to you."

"Holy shit, dude," Sean says, muting the TV. "Was that you?"

"My team," I say, no longer feeling the drug's effect. I point to the screen. "You know where that was?"

"Couple hours north," he says.

"Can you take me?" I ask.

"Yeah, dude. Of course. Your peeps are my peeps. But...can we eat the bacon first?"

I breathe in the scent Bacon was named for and only now realize how complimentary the moniker was. It's...divine. I nod. "Bacon first. Then we haul ass north."

18

I flinch away from the intense heat and brightness of Harth's weapon. It spews out twelve rounds of what can best be described as little pieces of the sun. Several of them burst against the ground, each of them like a flash bang. Several strike one of the vehicles and stick, melting through the metal like thermite. In the bright light, I lose sight of the men taking cover behind that vehicle's door. They might still be there. They might have fallen back.

"The hell is that thing?" Jess asks, leaning against the home's front wall, shotgun in hand.

Harth looks down as an orange line glows farther along the weapon's side. The light reduced with each fired projectile. *It's recharging*, I realize. No magazine to replace. Just time to wait. "Incinerator V17. Fires hot plasma."

"Kind of a shock and awe weapon, huh?" she says.

Harth grins. "Shock and awe. I like that."

He's about to lean back out and unleash another volley when 'Gangnam Style' bursts from my phone again.

I look at the screen. Unknown caller. I answer, suspecting who it might be. "You give up?"

As much as I want to go full-Rambo on these goons, I'd rather not have a dozen government corpses littering my family's farm...along with a state trooper's. That's already going to be hard to explain. Ballistics will clear me and place blame on the G-men...or whatever they are, but how do I explain why they were all here? And how many clandestine strings can Alton pull?

"You hung up on me," he says, sounding genuinely wounded.

"It happens," I say, and am about to repeat the act.

"But you didn't get to hear my final ultimatum. My *coup de grâce.*"

When no return fire drills the house from the outside, I know he's serious. Alton is strange and, when it comes to black ops, that makes him dangerous. Military personnel are predictable once you get to know them. But Alton seems somewhat unhinged. If he's telling the truth about the Twilight Directorate, that's not really surprising. But it means there's no way to predict what he's up to, if he's serious, buying time, or about to drop a MOAB on the house.

My phone chimes again, this time with an incoming Facetime call.

"*Bring bring*," he says, mimicking a ringing phone.

"What is that?" Praxion asks.

"Video call," I say, turning the phone away from him. "He knows who I am. Bad idea to let him see your faces."

Praxion nods.

With my back to the wall, I answer the video call.

On screen is the face of a dog. A German Shepherd. He's beaten and bloody, but alive. His eyes flare a little wider when he sees me. I'm not who he was expecting.

The camera moves back and a black man with a Saturn-like ring of hair slides into view beside the Shepherd like they're just two guys on vacation, taking a selfie. He's relaxed, calm, and smiling.

"You introduce me to your new friends, and I'll introduce you to mine," he says. "Not that he's told me his name, or anything at all beyond a veiled threat. But his mind is an open book to my soon-to-arrive friend. I'm afraid this poor fellow's brain won't be much good when she's done with him, but he's had his chance to talk. Of course, all this can be avoided if you just surrender the space-pooches. Not sure why you'd defend them. You owe them nothing. They offer you nothing aside from eventual capture, torture, and death. My bubbly exterior belies a dark, vengeful core that will take great pleasure in your discomfort.

"I'll tell you what. I've seen your service record. I could find a place for you here. You'd be in on secrets the rest of the world won't be privy to for decades. You'd have access to alien technology, including weaponry. And you'd serve a greater purpose, ensuring that humanity's entrance onto the intergalactic stage is such a grand spectacle that no one on this world or any other will think to claim Earth as their own."

"Is that possible?" I ask Praxion.

"Many things are possible," he says.

A deep voice speaks from the phone. "The Draun are here. He is in league with—argh!" An electric current stops the Shepherd from speaking.

"Gruunlokar," Praxion shouts, trying to look at the phone's screen.

I turn it away from him. "Stay focused. Think it through. He's goading us. There is nothing we can do for your friend."

"Not yet," Harth growls, and I give him a nod.

"Well, sounds like they're *all* noble and stubborn," Alton says, his face filling the screen now. "But what about you, Ranger Rick? You going to die for them? You going to let me torture your dog in front of you...for weeks? Months? I'd be interested in discovering what that kind of stress could do to a man. My good friends would be, as well."

"The Draun," I say, repeating the name for my own benefit.

"They are so much fun. You'll love them."

"Cool," I say. "Can't wait. Hey, why don't you tell me where you are, and we'll come to you?"

He flashes a big, toothy grin, revealing a mouth full of large, flat teeth. "You're fun. Alas, this is as close as you'll ever get to me without cuffs..." He leans back so Gruunlokar is in the image again. "...or a muzzle. Now, last chance."

Gruunlokar looks me in the eyes. Shakes his head. It's just about imperceptible, but it confirms he is a soldier of the hardest type. He knows the score. Knows he's in enemy hands. That anything other than fighting our way out of here and disappearing would be a trap. Mission comes first.

"Two things," I say. "First, your hair is horrid. Seriously. It's embarrassing. Go see a barber. Second, remember that time I hung up on you?"

He sneers, well and truly pissed off. "I did not enjoy—"

I hang up the phone, yank it open, and pull the sim card. "Do the same to yours," I say to Jess, and then I turn to Praxion. "These are your people, so I'll follow your lead and keep my people safe." I motion to Jess and Grover.

"Your people..." He says, pondering my comment. Then nods. "I suggest the direct approach. Our armor should protect us from projectile weapons—"

"Unless you get shot in the head," Torel says, shaking her head in exasperation. "I'm always telling them."

"You don't wear helmets?" I ask.

"They do not look cool," Harth grumbles.

"Can't argue with that," I say.

"Harth," Praxion says. "Full spread. Torel and I will sweep and clear. The rest of you follow behind." He turns to me. "Will Grover stay by your side?"

I nod. "But the noise is going to hurt his ears."

"The regulators will dampen sounds to a level that will not harm him."

"Huh," I say. "Going to have to get me a set."

Praxion taps a control panel on his forearm. "Talon-Actual, Prowler-One, do you copy?"

"Prowler-One, Talon-Actual, I hear you. Any luck?" I hear the response. Praxion has done me the same courtesy I did him by making the communication audible. A gesture of trust.

"We have found allies, but this world's government, or a faction of it, has tracked us down, and captured Gruunlokar. We are about to engage twelve hostiles who have come to collect us. Should the worst happen... If we fail... I need you to have MIMIR activate the automated return trip and deliver a message to the high council."

"O-okay. That sounds ominous."

"It is," Praxion says. "Tell them that The Draun have taken Earth."

"The Draun. Oh no…"

"*Taken* Earth?" I ask.

"Who is that?" Prowler-One asks.

"A friend." Praxion turns to me. "And yes, your government may not know it yet, but Earth no longer belongs to humanity."

"Well," I say, "I guess, *viva la revolución*, then."

"Are you sure?" Prowler-One says. "I could attempt an extract—"

"Negative, Prowler-One," Praxion says. "Keep your distance. Do not engage. If you even suspect we are compromised, return to Kyno."

"Copy, Talon-Actual," he says, trying to sound professional, but unable to hide his emotions.

"Hey, I don't know how things are on puppy-planet," Jess says, "but here on Earth, all this chit-chat is liable to get someone killed."

"Talon-Actual, out," Praxion says, and he turns to Harth and Torel. "As discussed in three, two, one."

The three alien dogs slide out the door, each of them unleashing a volley of fire from their otherworldly weapons. The already singed SUV explodes, bounding up into the air, propelled by a fireball. The heat and shockwave slap me in the face as I follow them out the door, swinging my weapon back and forth, searching for targets—

—that are no longer there.

Behind me, Jess says what we're all thinking. "What the hell?"

We pause in a circle, weapons aimed in every direction. The Directorate goons have disappeared, maybe into the darkness, maybe toward the back of the house, or perhaps—

Three pulses of light drop from the night sky to the hillside north of my home. They look similar to the Kynolaris' arrival, but larger, more energetic, and packing a kinetic punch that shakes the ground beneath my feet and levels trees.

All three Kynolari back step.

"Helions," Harth whispers and turns to me. "We need to leave."

"Now," Praxion says.

I point to my pickup truck. "The red truck!"

As we sprint for the vehicle, I shout, "Kynolari in the back, people in the front!"

"Is your vehicle fast?" Harth asks.

"Wouldn't say it's known for its speed, but the terrain here isn't exactly smooth—whoa!" Gravel grinds beneath my feet as I slide to a stop. I raise my weapon toward three Directorate men standing up from the far side of my truck and take aim.

19

Three shots ring out just as I notice the armed men standing behind what Micah called his truck. Each of the men snap back in time with the reports, headshots all. Sparks burst from the backs of their heads, and they drop out of sight.

I leap into the back of the vehicle with Harth and Torel as Micah, Jess, and Grover dive inside the cab and close the doors. The engine starts with an impressive roar.

A window at the back of the cab slides open and Jess says, "Hold on!"

A moment after I grip the side of the truck, we accelerate. Gravel spews out behind us as the wheels spin, and then grip the loose terrain, propelling us—straight toward the Helions.

"Why are we going *toward* certain death?" Torel shouts.

"It's a long driveway!" Micah replies, "and trucks can't drive through trees."

"I would demand a truck that drives through trees," Harth grumbles.

We speed closer than anyone should get to a Helion. The only thing that saves us is that they have just landed and are still changing form. A loud grinding fills the air as the predatory machines unfold their segmented, dark gray bodies and thick, stubby limbs tipped with long slashing claws. Electric blue shines from between their segmented oxium carapaces and joints. They are not stealthy, but they do not need to be. They raise their smooth, black heads and glowing eyes to the night sky. One by one, they open their mouths, full of razor-sharp incisors that cut through flesh with such microscopic precision that victims do not realize their thigh is missing until the open air touches the wound. These machines are capable of devastating enemy ranks. Once they entered the war, the Kynolari were forced to adopt new strategies, which never included being on the ground, or running away.

After we finish a long arc around the gravel driveway, the truck bumps its way over a dirt road.

"I am...beginning to hate...this primitive...planet!" Harth says, his voice interrupted as the truck's tires bounce over rocks and rumble over divots.

Behind us, three pulses of blue light signify the Helions' transformation is complete. I lean down to the open window and say, "They are coming."

"Any recommendations?" Micah asks.

"Do not slow down," I say. "And do not drive in a straight line."

"Shouldn't be a problem," he says, turning the steering wheel to the left, while braking hard. The back end of the truck swings to the right while he accelerates again, this time on a solid, smooth, paved road. To our left, a mountain. To our right, a valley. There appears to be only one direction in which we can flee.

"Praxion," Torel says. "Did you notice?"

"How screwed we are?" Harth says.

"His speed," she says. "He killed all three of those men—"

"They weren't men," Harth says. "They were drones."

"The point is," she says, losing her patience, "he killed all three of them before any of us had a chance to react."

"Meaning what?" I ask.

"Meaning his species is either highly skilled in the ways of war...despite their limited technology, or something is affecting our reflexes. Perhaps both." She looks me in the eyes. "When was the last time someone outdrew *you?*"

She is not wrong. I did notice, and tried to ignore the feeling of incompetence that came along with it. Micah all but bested us in the forest, and now he is saving us from enemies we brought to his home. He is a noble man, and perhaps a better soldier.

"Incoming," Harth says, and his regulator, locally connected to ours, gives us a sense of where he is looking without him having to say a word.

We turn uphill to the top of the mountain. A streak of blue light barrels down the steep grade, preceded by the thunderous cracking of the trees it is plowing through.

"You see?" Harth says. "Much more efficient to go *through* the trees." He begins charging the Incinerator to full power. "I'll take the first one."

The first Helion is always the easiest to dispatch. But they learn from each attack. They figure out your strategies, your arsenal. And they adjust until something works. And when that happens, there is no escape.

Harth raises his weapon as it begins to glow orange, tracking the Helion as it rampages down the hillside, undulating a dozen segments as its short limbs fling out to the side with each stride, pushing it down the hill like a runaway boulder. He thumps the truck's cab with his fist. "Faster!"

Inside, Micah grumbles, "Fuck's sake," but accelerates just a little bit faster. "You have ten seconds to do whatever you're doing and then we're either going to take a hard right or crash over the side of a cliff and die in an explosive inferno."

"Copy," Harth says, still tracking his target, totally unaware of three more enemies now behind us.

The two black vehicles sent by the Twilight Directorate have just entered the road behind us. And just behind them, the second Helion, fully unraveled, its six hydraulic limbs having no trouble keeping up. But it is not attacking. Not yet. And it will not do so until the first has completed its run, either in failure or success.

Harth's direct assault will not give it too much information to go on, aside from the fact that we have an Incinerator on board...which it will definitely know takes two minutes to recharge after a full power burst.

"Eyes!" Harth says, and we divert our gaze.

A loud *choom* bursts into the air, along with a momentary scorching heat. I cannot look at the fired round but know it will set alight everything it passes until it connects with its target.

"Hit," Harth says, almost casually.

I look back to the Helion. It is now sliding down the mountainside, the back of its neck a bright orange flare of hot, metal-melting sunlight that illuminates the terrain—including the road ahead.

"Hold on!" Micah shouts.

The truck brakes hard and then turns to the right. While we are still moving toward a steep drop off, the truck accelerates again in the opposite direction. It is impressive driving, but not nearly enough. The back end of the truck swings out over the cliff, but we are stopped when the rear wheels strike a metal rail. Tires screech as we tear forward again...straight toward the second Helion, which has cut through the forest and down the incline to attack us face-on before the Incinerator can recharge.

"Any ideas?" Micah calls from inside.

"Evasive maneuvers!" I shout.

"Evasive maneuvers!?" he responds. "We're on a twenty-foot-wide road surrounded by trees and death a la gravity!"

"Hit it with everything we have!" I shout.

I lean up over the cab and take aim with my Sonizer's secondary weapon system, a simple rail gun. Its rounds make short work of any metal or alloy but lacks the punch to take down a Helion.

"One minute," Harth says, counting down the time until he is ready to fire again.

Beside me, Torel activates her weapon system for the first time since landing on this world. While she is a deadly operator, she would much prefer to save a life than to end one. Good news for us, Helions are not alive. Nor are the Directorate's henchmen. Drone warfare is a clear sign that The Draun have influenced this world.

Like with my Sonizer, Torel's Lancer weapon system is integrated into her arm. Unlike my weapon, hers was designed to affect non-organics as well as organics, delivering a powerful electric charge. At a reduced level, it can also bring back fallen soldiers, as it once did me—the last time we faced Helions.

In that final day.

The Last Battle.

That is what our people called it. After decades of fending off The Draun, pushing them back to their home world and wiping the planet clean, there was speculation that some of The Draun had survived. But without their technology, without the resources of a home world, they would either die out, or live in squalor for millennia. But it seems they found everything they needed on the planet Earth, in the human race, hidden gems amidst a crowded universe.

And now war seems to be upon us once more. The Last Battle was simply the beginning of a reprieve.

I fire a series of rail-shards into the Helion, aiming for its left side shoulder joint. The best I can hope to do is weaken it. Sparks fly from the limb, but it carries onward, plowing a path straight toward us.

"Left forelimb!" I shout to Torel.

She takes aim and unloads on the same joint, sending a bolt of electricity that flows through the small holes I have punched in the outer shell. The limb goes stiff, and when the Helion attempts to put weight on the leg, it missteps and topples forward. Its massive weight plows a divot into the paved roadway... which it uses to its advantage. Pushing hard with its fully functional rear limbs, it launches its backside up and over, intending to crush the truck and everyone in it.

"Praxion," Torel says.

"I see it!" I say, quickly switching my weapon system back to its primary configuration and cranking the power to full.

I fire the weapon, unleashing a sonic pulse that slaps into the Helion's armored backside and heaves it upward. By a foot. It is not much but gives us an extra second to get clear.

The Helion crashes to the pavement behind us, its back punching deep into the ground, wedging it in place.

"Stop the truck!" Harth shouts, pounding the cab's ceiling, this time hard enough to dent the ceiling. When he slips his goggles in place, I know exactly what he is intending to do.

The truck screeches to a halt and Harth leaps out the back, his powerful limbs carrying him half the distance in one jump and then the rest in the next. As he arcs through the air, he deactivates the Incinerator, transferring all that power to the weapon system he prefers the most. Twin three foot long, glowing orange blades extend from his forearms. Neither of them are particularly sharp, but they do not need to be. The heat that radiates from the blades at the moment of contact is powerful enough to melt anything they touch.

Harth lands on the Helion's belly and slides over it, toward the head, while five of the six arms snap down, trying to crush him. He makes it through the gauntlet, dives over the Helion's head and spins, blades extended.

There is a luminous explosion of light from each impact, and then darkness. The Helion's glowing blue machine innards stop moving and go dark.

Lit in the truck's rear red lights, Harth jogs out from behind the Helion, a grin on his face. "Always wanted to try that."

I smile and take his hand, hauling him back into the truck. "Hope you got it out of your system. You will not be able to do it again."

"Let's go!" Harth says, smacking the cab's roof one more time.

From inside, Micah shouts, "Would you stop beating the shit out of my truck!" Then he steps on the accelerator, and we tear off down the road. There is a moment of stillness. Then the two black vehicles pursuing us round each side of the fallen Helion, racing toward us, a drone-man hanging from six of the eight windows, aiming their weapons, which they fire all at once.

20

CHIRK

"This is nice," I say, leaning back in the front seat of *Peregrine*, belly full of bacon, looking up through a 'sunroof' at the moonlit night sky. The car's interior is lit by a series of tiny lights oscillating between shades of cool blue. Feels like being underwater. "Relaxing."

I hope the others are having a similar experience.

Who am I kidding? After all the publicity they got on TV, they're definitely back on the *Prowler*, biding their time and looking for Gruunlokar and me. Can't wait for them to find me, though. I need to find their Leap Nodes, get back to the ship on my own, and let the others know Gruunlokar was captured. That's when things will get messy because we don't leave Kynolari behind. Ever. Even if they're already a corpse.

"Spent three years pimping out this bad boy." Sean rubs the steering wheel, like he's caressing a woman.

"You...rented your car out for sex?" I ask. "Can vehicles mate on this planet?"

"What? Ahuh, ahuh. It's an expression, dude." He laughs so hard that only squeaks come out. "Oh-ho, man, that's good. Pimping out means...it's like making it look good. I don't know where the expression came from. Maybe because pimps make their sex workers look good? Or because pimps are known for having nice cars, fuzzy hats, and furry coats."

I smile.

"Sex workers, huh? That's polite."

"What, you don't have sex workers on your fancy planet?"

"I'll have you know that the subjugation of any person for any reason is forbidden in much of the universe, including my fancy planet. That's what drones are for."

"So, robot sex is cool, but not paid sex," he says.

"Exactly," I say. "It's like...how do I say this to a lesser being?"

He scoffs and laughs. Knows I'm ribbing him.

"If your society survives the great filter and advances to the point of full automation and a global government—a requirement to take part in any intergalactic councils, by the way—do you think anyone would still choose to sell their bodies, or would they pursue something more fulfilling?"

"Couldn't tell you," he says.

"But what about, like, gnarly people? Like people *no one* wants to have sex with. How will they—"

"Asking for a friend, I bet." I smile at him. "*Full* automation. Like can't tell the difference, automation. Advanced societies across the universe agree that simulation, virtual experience, and drone technology designed to satiate our baser needs, or desires, is preferable to a labor force dedicated to pleasure, which often leads to abuse, trafficking, and more psychological problems than you can shake a Taboolian Sothcreant at."

Sean's eyes slowly widen along with a grin. "Whoaaa. Dude. We're, like, having a deep conversation, right? Like, I don't talk about this kind of thing with my friends. We mostly talk about weed and the *Project Nemesis* TV series. But like, social justice? Nah, man."

"Does that...mean something on Earth?"

"I think it means you my dog," he says.

"We've already established that I am *not* a dog, and I belong to no one."

"No, man. Not my dog, my *dog.*"

"What's the difference?" I ask.

"When someone is your dog...and you gotta say it like that, right? 'You my dog,' maybe with a 'bro' at the end. 'You my dog, bro.' It means we're tight. Means you're a good friend. Like elevated over other people or friends. Like top tier."

"Hold on, hold on. Let me get this straight. On this planet, when you want to express that another individual is in a peak friendship position, you would call them your dog? Like, as a compliment?"

"Hell yeah, man. Because dogs are man's best friend. Loyal. Unconditionally loving. Fun as shit. Telling someone they're your dog elevates them to a position of dog-hood. It's like saying that we are now all those things, in both directions, except you are actually a—well, a genetic relative of Earth dogs."

"Huh," I say.

"But it's not a saying everywhere," Sean says. "Like if you went to Russia and said whatever Russian is for 'You my dog,' they'd probably look at you funny, throw you in a gulag or something. I honestly don't know much about Russia beyond *Spies Like Us.*"

"And this is the problem with decentralized civilizations. Getting through the great filter and achieving genuine space travel takes a planetwide effort. Civilizations that don't come together for the betterment of the entire planet are doomed to destroy themselves. And only about ten percent of us make it. From what I can tell, this planet is on the wrong path."

"Well, shit, I guess. So, what's this great filter thing?"

"It's a concept, really. It's a point every civilization reaches where they have the power to either self-destruct, or rise above their petty grievances, base desires, and tribalism, for the betterment of the entire species. One side is primitive, mutually assured suicide. It's a kind of insanity. If I can't win, I'll burn it all down. The other option focuses on improving life for all."

"And only ten percent of people choose the betterment of life for all?"

"Well, more like nine percent," I say. "There is a smaller subset of survivors that choose the betterment of all...of their own kind. They retain their tribal, colonial instincts and apply it to the universe, rather than just their own planet. They survive the filter to become a pariah on other species, and as a result, people like me—soldiers—still exist. I'm a necessary evil, my friend."

"You ain't evil," he says.

"I do evil things," I tell him. "I take lives, and sometimes I enjoy doing it... Okay, what the fuck is in that drug? I don't tell anyone any of this shit."

"Been long enough that it's worn off," he says. "I'm telling you, man, you're my dog. And I'm yours." He holds his fist out to me.

"The hell am I supposed to do with this?" I ask.

"Bump it, man. With your fist."

I do as requested, and when our fists 'bump,' he opens his hand and draws it back, making the sound of an explosion. It gets a chuckle out of me. I'm pretty sure humanity is doomed, but I like Sean.

"You know," I say, "If all humans were like you—"

The car's interior flashes red in time with a sudden burst of haunting music that makes me jump and draw my mini-railguns.

"Whoa, whoa," Sean says. "Easy, man. Chill. It's just a phone call. Keep forgetting to change the ringtone. It's the theme song for *Stranger Things*, that's a TV show about these kids in the 80s... Anywho, one time at like four in the morning, that ringtone once literally scared the crap out of me. Thank God I was sitting on the toilet." He looks at a display, which reads Unknown Caller. "Must be a telemarketer. This will be fun."

He reaches out and presses a green digital button labeled 'Accept.'

"Allo," he says in a thick accent of who knows what. "Ow may I 'elp you today?"

"Who is this?" a man on the other end asks.

"You have reached the phone of Deepak Sharma. Perhaps there is something wrong with my Windows installation? Eh? Or perhaps I have won a lottery? Allo? Allo, are you there?"

The signal disconnects.

"Ahah, ahah, ahah. Works every ti—"

The music blares again, red lights flashing. Despite knowing what it is, I jump again. Same caller. Unknown.

Sean answers again, changing the accent once more. "Haro!"

The voice on the other end sighs. "Again?"

"Haro? Ah you they-ah? Haroooo? Youuuu have reached the phone of Moo-shoo Gaiking."

"Mooshoo Gaiking," the man says.

"That isa right! How may a herp today?"

"Your accents are incredibly racist, you know," the man says.

"Nah," Sean says. "They're established stereotypes. Hell, I'm an established stereotype. It's only offensive if you're a stick in the mud. Are you a stick in the mud?"

"Oh, I'm a lot worse than that," the man says, his voice oozing menace.

Sean glances over at me, suddenly not so sure about the conversation. Then he smiles. "Hold up, brah, are you doing, like, a stereotype of an evil megalomaniac? Because bravo, spot on."

"You're doing you," the man says. "I'm doing me. But I have no interest in speaking to a drug-addled high-school dropout whose highest prospect in life is mowing lawns but is much more likely to die beneath an overpass, forgotten by everyone he's encountered, like some nameless NPC. No, I'd rather speak to the pint-sized dog accompanying you."

The look on Sean's face in response to the man's brutal verbal attack enrages me. "Who the fuck are you?"

"Ahh, the little one speaks, too," the man says. "Adorable. My name is Alton Applewhite, and I am my government's response to you—a creature from the outers of space. We already have your friend, but he's not nearly as talkative as you've already been."

This is the asshole who caught Gruunlokar. "Fuck you."

"Though perhaps a smaller vocabulary, mmm?"

Sean holds a finger to his lips, shushing me. Then says, "Look, dude, if you want to talk to someone, you can talk to me. My number. My phone. My car."

"Ahhhh," he says, sounding like he's just finished a desperate piss. "You *are* driving. Thank you for confirming that detail for me. I do hate ordering strikes on the wrong target."

"What do you mean, 'ordering strikes?'"

"What do you *think* he means?" I shout and tap the button to break the connection. "How is he tracking us?"

When Sean's eyes go wide. He holds up the device called a phone. Then he rolls down the window and tosses it out. "Okay, we're clear. He can't track us now."

"Doesn't need to," I say, looking up through the sunroof, where a single bright blue orb of light descends toward us. "Turn out the lights."

A moment later, the vehicle's interior lights go dark, but the winding road ahead is still lit, revealing pristine homes with loose stone walls on either side. "*All* the lights."

"I won't be able to see," he says.

"But I will," I say and step onto his lap, taking the wheel. "Gas when I say. Brake when I say."

"Aww shit, dude. This is going to be sick." He turns out the headlights, plunging us into darkness—until the blue light above illuminates everything just before striking the ground.

21

"This is nuts," I say, gripping the steering wheel so hard that my fingers have begun to tingle. "This is so fucking nuts."

I glance in the rear view and see the two SUVs pursuing us. Directorate agents are leaning out of the windows, firing their sound suppressed Maxim 9s into the night. The rearview mirror disintegrates as it's struck by a round, spewing plastic and glass around the cab. Jess flinches away from it and shouts.

I look down at Grover, lying down between me and Jess. His head is low. Ears are back. He knows we're in trouble, even if he can't fully comprehend the situation. Dogs are masters of understanding the emotional state of humans. They can literally smell the minute chemical changes in our blood when we're happy, sad, enraged—or terrified.

I try to act calm for his benefit, taking a moment to put my hand on his head, but I'm not fooling anyone.

I've seen action. Been in warzones. But that was nothing like this. War is often slow moving. You fight for ground. You take the ground. But there aren't a lot of high-speed chases with giant robot monsters and gangs of stoic agents in the dead of night.

All around us, the road sparks with bullet impacts. Ahead, branches fall from the overhanging trees, mowed down by stray bullets. The agents don't seem to have a lot of experience shooting from moving vehicles, which is good, but there are enough of them that they occasionally get off a lucky shot. Eventually, they're going to hit somebody.

"Feel free to return fire," I shout out through the window. "Any day now!"

Tires shriek as I take a hard left turn, following the switchback road down the mountainside.

"If you hold the truck still," Harth says, leaning down to the window, "maybe we would be able to aim!"

"Have you never heard of spray and pray?!" I shout back.

He leans in closer and says, "I have not. Is it a tactic?"

"You point your weapon in the general direction of the enemy and hold down the damn trigger, creating a *spray* of rounds that you *pray* will hit something. It's basically what the assholes behind us are doing!"

"Kynolari are known for their conservation of ammunition. We aim and we hit our targets. One shot, one kill."

"And how's that working out for you right now?" Jess says. The difference between human and Kynolari combat techniques is apparent to both of us. These guys are accustomed to dominating the battlefield. I respect it. But we're neck deep in the shit and the only way out might be getting a little nuts.

Harth grunts and turns back to the other two alien dogs crouching in the back of my pickup truck. I think back on the night, trying to figure out how I went from being humped by my dog, nearly humped by a beautiful woman, and now about to get forcefully humped by a bunch of psychotic government agents. Even if I survive this, I'm screwed. Going to have to move to Guatemala or something. Fighting against the U.S. government, especially black ops who essentially answer to no one, is never a great idea.

"Spray and pray?" I hear Praxion ask from the back. They're discussing my tactic and taking way too long doing so. They look like dogs but are far more logical. Where's the instinct? The savage protectiveness?

Jess loses her patience before I do. She pounds on the back window and shouts, "Just shoot the shit out of them!"

"On my mark," Praxion says, and takes aim. "Fire!"

All three Kynolari pull their triggers, unleashing a chaotic spray of projectiles, most of which I can't see, aside from the small suns being launched by Harth's Incinerator.

The roadway behind us lights up orange, first from the Incinerator rounds, then from one of the two SUVs, which explodes, launching agents into the air.

"You see!" I say. "Spray and pray!"

Praxion leans down to the windows. "Who are we praying to?"

"I don't give a shit," I say. "It's an expression. You don't actually have to pray."

"Humans are strange creatures," he says.

"But you can't deny the results," I reply, as the second SUV drives through the fiery remains of the first and continues the pursuit.

A loud thud on the truck's hood makes me shout in surprise. It's a limb. An arm, dressed in a suit. And there is something off about it.

"I don't think that's human," Jess says, leaning forward to look at the arm, oozing black fluid.

"They're drones," Torel says, in the window. "Any injuries up here?"

"None," I say and glance down at Grover. He's shaking a little bit, but he's uninjured.

"I'm good," Jess says, clutching her shotgun.

"How do you know they're drones?" I ask.

"They are stolen Kynolari technology reshaped to look human. But they are not. They were designed to be explorers, to go places living beings cannot, but The Draun have used them as fearless, lifeless warriors. The drones couldn't save The Draun from justice then, and they will not now."

Her eyes flick to the road ahead and widen, her face cast in blue light.

The road ahead is occupied by the third Helion, its tardigrade-like body and limbs open wide to receive us, its flat-toothed jaws ready to engulf and sever.

Luckily for us, I grew up here. Played here. Hunted here. I know these woods and every way through them. "Hold on!" I shout, braking hard and turning a hairpin right onto a logging road that hasn't been used by a four-wheeled vehicle in forty years. My father and I used to take snowmobiles through the old trails crisscrossing the mountains, but the last time we had a chance to go out was when I was seventeen. Nine years ago. The paths were fairly overgrown then. Now?

"This is going to be rough!" I shout, and plow through a dead sapling.

Behind us, the forest flares blue as the Helion pursues, cracking through hundred-foot-tall trees like a razor through stubble.

The inside of the truck becomes a rock tumbler, tossing us around, wearing us down.

"Would this be...a bad time...to ask...for a second date?" I say between bounces, trying to lighten the 'oh my God, we're about to die' mood.

Jess laughs. "Yes!"

"Yes, it's a bad time?" I shout.

"Yes, to a second date," she says, and I'm honestly surprised because it requires a positive assessment of our survival chances.

"Well, all right then," I think and shout, "Whoa!" as a branch slaps across the windshield, shattering the glass.

"Though I might...need to drive."

"Turning right and uphill," I shout out the back, giving them a moment to hold on tight before cranking the wheel and thundering upward, toward a towering machine that has marred this hilltop for far too long.

"Harth!" I call through the window. "How's your charge?"

He leans down to the window. "Nearly full, but it will see that attack coming and have no trouble evading it."

"It won't see this coming," I say, pointing up and straight ahead through the windshield. He leans up and looks over the top of the truck, able to see what I know is there, but cannot see. "Shoot the base. Bring it down straight toward us."

He grins. "I'm beginning to like you, human." Then he stands back up, relaying the plan to the others.

It's going to be a close call.

While the truck is forced to stay on the old roads—basically two lines of dirt and rocks with a patch of four-foot-tall grass running down the middle—the Helion is cutting corners through the forest, creating its own path, oblivious to the tall pines.

"Wait a second," Jess says, leaning closer to the windshield, looking up. "I know where we are." She looks at me with wide eyes. "You're not?"

"Still sure about that second date?" I ask.

She responds by tightening her seatbelt, wrapping an arm around Grover, and pulling him tight against her. He wags his tail twice, licks her hands, and glances over at me for reassurance.

"We got this buddy," I tell him. "Today isn't our day."

I catch sight of Praxion watching me through the window. His face is so much like Grover's, it's uncanny, but his eyes are different. More intelligent, and more...damaged. Like mine. He's seen life and death for what it is and knows how quickly the first can become the second. He gives me a nod, and I gun the engine, fighting the wheel for control with every bounce.

"Almost in range," Harth says, leaning up over the hood, "but you're gonna have to stop if you want me to hit it."

"Just give me the word," I say.

"Which word?" he responds.

"Just tell him when to stop!" Jess shouts.

Harth goes silent, focusing on the job. Five seconds later, he shouts, "Now!" and I slam on the brakes. A brilliant orb of light, too bright to look at, launches uphill, not only illuminating the path ahead as it passes, but setting it on fire, transforming the forest into a pathway leading up and out of hell. Then it connects with the target, explodes its liquid hot material inside, and leaves a giant melted hole in its wake, more than half the diameter of the base.

The effect is immediate...and impossible to escape in the truck.

I kick open my door and shout, "Everyone into the forest!"

Grover and Harth follow me while Jess, Torel, and Praxion head to the road's far side. We run deep into the dark woods while the Helion charges the truck, nearly upon it, oblivious to the colossal threat descending toward it through the dark night sky. Then...it lands.

Two hundred and eighty feet tall. Two *hundred* tons of steel. The eyesore of a wind turbine slams down upon the forgotten road, crushing the truck I'm still making payments on, and then mashes the last Helion. Erases the thing like it never was.

The impact has enough kinetic energy to launch me forward. As I sail through the air, I see Grover beneath me, tossed—into the arms of Harth, who wraps my dog in a large embrace, protecting him as they collide with the ground... while I slam into another damn tree and lose consciousness.

22

"Are you okay?" I ask, leaning over Jess. Her forehead is bleeding, but the wound appears superficial. Then again, I am not a medical expert.

"Fine," she says, pushing herself up to lean against the fallen tree she was thrown into.

Torel crouches beside us. "Let me have a look."

"Said I'm fine." Jess tries to brush us away, but Torel does not put up with bad patients very well.

She shoves Jess's hand down and holds her med-glove over the wound. After a few moments, the med-glove sends the collected data to Torel's regulator. "Slight concussion."

"Not my first," Jess says. "Couple stitches and I'll be good."

"Stitches?" Torel says.

"You know." Jess begins mimicking some kind of procedure. "Needle and thread. Sew the wound together."

Torel's eyes widen.

"Is that what you do?"

She turns to me.

"Perhaps more primitive than we thought."

"Then what do *you* do?" Jess asks.

Torel furrows her brow. "It's already done."

"What?" Jess puts her fingers to her head, probing the wounded area, which has been regenerated by the med-glove. It does not work on every species, but humans appear to be biologically compatible.

"The damage to your mind will heal more slowly, but I don't see why it should stop you from active duty... Sorry. You're not Kyno Corps. Force of habit." Torel stands and offers her hand. Jess takes it and is lifted to her feet.

I have not known her, or Micah, for very long, but I find myself concerned about their well-being. I feel this way for my team, for the men and women I have served with for half my life. But these humans...I barely know them. I have known others longer and not mourned their loss in battle. But if these two humans, who initially fought against us, were to perish, I believe I would feel regret. Even the thought of it is too much to bear.

I turn and look back at the wind turbine that now separates us from the others. It is an insurmountable obstacle we will need to travel around, but first we need to coordinate with the others, assuming they are alive and unharmed.

I toggle my comms. "Talon-One, Talon-Actual, how copy?"

Harth's voice responds. "Talon-Actual, Talon-One, we are dusted, but mobile. How do you want to proceed?"

"What does Micah think?" I ask.

"You want me to ask the..." he sighs.

"This is his planet," I say. "His home. He knows this terrain. We do not."

"Very well." There's a moment of silence, then Harth returns. "He believes we should backtrack downhill 'double-time,' engage the Directorate agents, and commandeer their vehicle."

"It is what I was going to suggest," I say.

Harth grunts. "Me as well."

"Proceed as planned, Talon-One. Ears up. We are not out of this yet. Not even close."

"Copy that, Talon-Actual. Talon-One out."

"They're okay?" Jess asks.

I nod. "We will meet them below...along with the enemy. I will take alpha position." I turn to Torel. "Omega." And then I turn to Jess. "Your weapon?"

"Lost," she says.

"Stay between us. Ears up."

She smiles. "Cute expression. Ears up."

"It is not cute, it is—"

She holds up her hands. "I get it, I get it. But people rely more on their eyesight than they do hearing. We would say, 'keep your eyes peeled.'"

"You have keen eyesight then?" Torel asks.

"What? No. Horrible compared to most animals. Sense of smell, too. Hearing isn't super great."

I am confused. "What biological advantage led to you being the dominant lifeform on this planet?"

She taps her head. "Brain to body mass ratio."

She extends her thumbs, making a clicking sound for each.

"These bad boys."

"Opposable thumbs..." Torel says. "That...is it?"

Jess just smiles.

"Very well," I say. "We are traveling in darkness, so stay close."

"Just tell me if I'm going to run into a tree," Jess says, getting a laugh out of Torel.

We move through the night in silence, headed downhill, but not nearly fast enough. Jess struggles with her footing, whispering curses under her breath. After a few minutes, she says, "You should just leave me. I can find my way out in the morning."

"They know who you are," I point out. "Where you live. You will not be safe until they are defeated."

"Not sure the U.S. government *can* be defeated," she says.

"Regardless, there are other solutions."

"Such as?"

"I can carry you," I say.

Jess is silent for a moment, her fully dilated, but still unseeing, eyes roll toward the night sky.

"This is humiliating."

"No one will see you," Torel says, not disagreeing with Jess's assessment. There was a time in Kynolari history where the females of our species were not respected. They lacked the same rights as males. It has been many thousands of years since that time, but echoes of that ancient struggle still reverberate through time. I suspect the same may be true for Jess.

"Do not think of me as a man," I say. "Think of me...as a dog."

She smiles. "Can I pet your head?"

"If you want to lose yours," I say.

She sighs. "Fine. Shoulders or damsel in distress?"

"The first is inefficient," I say, "and the second leaves us vulnerable to attack." I do not offer a third option, because she might complain, and time is short. She yelps when I lift her up, arm wrapped around her knees and then grunts as the weight of her body falls over my shoulder.

"Okay," she says. "Let's go with the sack of potatoes method. Sure. Why not? I didn't need to breathe or be upright."

Her discomfort is noted, but our pace quickly increases.

After a hundred-foot downhill jog, I pause and whisper. "Smell them?"

Over my shoulder, Jess sniffs, but says nothing.

"Drones," Torel says.

"Were *any* of those agents human?" Jess asks.

"One," I say.

"How can you tell?"

"I heard his heart beating." I tilt my head to the side and lift my ears. "Still hear his heart beating. They are close, as is the turbine's top, which ends in a swath of destruction. Rubble. Fallen trees. Rough terrain."

"I get it," Jess says. "I'll keep my complaints to myself."

"Good," I say, and start the journey, leaping up and over fallen trees, climbing onto the turbine's massive blade, and sliding down the far side to the ten-foot drop. Jess coughs as the air is knocked from her lungs, but she manages to remain mostly silent.

I crouch behind a fallen tree and place Jess on her feet. A moment later, Torel lands beside me.

"Just ahead," I say, pointing. "Four agents. Each of them armed. Three are biologics."

"Bio-whatnow?" Jess says.

"Biologics. Another word for drones. Made of flesh and mechanical blood but operated by strategic artificial intelligence. Non-living entities."

"I guess we don't need to feel bad for killing them," she says.

"I would not feel bad either way," I confess.

"But, like, if they had kids, or a wife, or a do—a cat maybe. People who care about them, who are innocent."

"That's a lot of mental work to feel bad about something," Torel says. "Are humans generally depressed?"

"Well, yeah, but...never mind."

I toggle my comms. "Talon-One, Talon-Actual, come in."

"Talon-Actual, Talon-One. We are in position."

"Copy that," I say.

"The human man—"

I hear Micah whisper his name in the background.

"The human, Micah, says, and I quote, 'I can take them.'"

"Can he tell the difference between which is human, and which are biologic?" I ask.

"I believe the answer is 'No' given that he is looking at me like a pup seeing the Enchanorian Nebula for the first time."

"Then I will handle the situation," I say. "No debate. Talon-Actual, out." I toggle off the comms and turn to Torel. "Stay down. Stay quiet. This will not take long."

She nods, and I assume Jess understands the message was for both of them. Then I leap out from behind cover and maneuver my way through the trees, toward the four men sweeping the area with artificial lights. Staying in the shadows, I close to within range and activate my Sonizer. The weapon extends from my armor and wraps around my forearm and hand. When its slight hum does not give me away, I adjust the power setting to a frequency known to liquify the insides of biologics. No idea what it will do to a human being. Hopefully, it will not be too messy.

I wait for a moment when all four agents are turned away from my position. Then I step out from hiding, level the weapon at the quartet, and fire. An invisible wave of compressed sound flows out and away, striking the agents.

Three of the four drop straight down, their limbs no longer able to support their weight, their bodies liquified. Each of them lands with a splash of fluid.

But the fourth? He drops to his knees, shouting, "Oh, God! Oh, *God!* What the hell happened?"

I stand over the man and activate my neck lights, illuminating him as though in direct sunlight. His weapon lies on the ground a few feet away. He is twisted up in discomfort. He looks up at me with abject fear in his eyes, not because I am a Kynolari—he was expecting that—but because of the fate that has fallen upon him.

Harth and Micah arrive from one side of the ruined turbine. Jess and Torel from the other.

"Ugh," Micah says, placing a hand over his mouth. "You made him shit himself? You know what? I don't care." He levels his weapon at the agent's head. "Name."

The agent hesitates.

"Name or I'll have him do it again, but this time record it and put it on YouTube or whatever the kids use these days."

"TikTok," Jess says.

"That. Whatever that is. You'll be famous by tomorrow." He presses the barrel of his rifle against the man's temple, denting his skin, making an entirely different threat without saying a word. "What is your God-damn name?"

The man shakes, swallows, and then looks up with desperate tears in his eyes. "A-Alex…Alex Stuchbery."

23

CHIRK

"Okay," I say. "First question. Is there a road nearby that is less twisted than my small intestine?"

"Uh, yeah," he says. "That's where I was headed. 95 North. It's a highway. Like five lanes. But we have to go through a lot of roads like this to reach it."

"How much farther?" I ask.

"A few miles, maybe. Four, five minutes. Won't the winding roads help hide us?"

"All they'll do is slow us down." I point to the dense woods around us. "All this...won't matter to a Helion."

"Helion," he says. "That sounds like something bad."

"Very bad," I say. "With the others, we'd be okay. On our own... Well, the only thing we can do is run."

"Well, the good news is that I'm great at running."

"I hate running," I grumble. "But I know when to tuck tail. I ain't no fool with a death wish."

Brilliant blue light explodes off to our right, casting the nearby trees in silhouette. Won't be long now.

"Accelerate," I say.

We speed up, but not very quickly.

"What are you doing?"

"Accelerating," he says.

"Are you trying to make us easy to catch?"

"You said it so calmly that it didn't sound super urgent."

I rub my face. "Everything is super urgent right now. I'm just calm in the face of impending doom."

"Well, can you just add a little bit of emotion to your instructions, so I know how much pressure to apply when—"

"*Accelerate,*" I say, glancing in the rearview mirror. The Helion is there, closing in, its six stubby legs churning, and its razor mouth open wide. And all I can do to avoid it—without assistance—is swerve back and forth.

"That was better, but—"

The Helion disappears from the rear view.

It leaps toward us.

"*Accelerate!*" I say and shove my foot into Sean's knee. *Peregrine* surges forward, pressing me against his chest. I relax into him, letting his pectorals cushion me—a living race chair.

"Okay, that was great," he says, "but next time—"

I turn the wheel hard, narrowly making a bend in the road. Beside us, the Helion crashes down on some trees. Without the bend, it would have had us.

"Whoa!" Sean shouts, looking back at the explosion of blue energy pulsing from the now enraged Helion, and the devastation it has wrought on the forest. "*Dude.*"

"Gonna be us if we don't get the hell out of here," I say.

"Just keep on going, man!"

Swerving through the roadway, I get used to pushing down on his knees to affect our speed. We're making good time now. Driving the vehicle, even while using Sean as a long-legged proxy, is straightforward. Fast, slow, left, right. Inside thirty seconds, I'm cutting corners and accelerating faster. If Sean could see the roadsides, and how close we're coming toward them, he'd probably be screaming.

Me? I prefer a close shave, and I'm not just talking about driving.

When the ground begins to shake, I know it's not enough. Behind us, the Helion lumbers into view, closing, plowing through trees and homes, decimating the night, and leaving screams in its wake. This world would be helpless against an all-out invasion by The Draun.

"Holy shit," Sean says, glancing into the rearview. The Helion is right behind us now, its open jaws reaching down for us.

Sean guns the engine, propelling us forward to a speed far too fast for this road. It delays our becoming a snack for a ravenous machine but presents me with a new challenge—not pancaking into one of these trees, or into a house.

The road bends to the right, and I start making the turn. But we're not going to make it. So, I aim for what looks like a dirt roadway instead. We cruise past a home. I catch a glimpse of a man and woman sitting at a table, looking out the window, no doubt wondering what all the noise is. Then we're beyond them, bounding up and over a hill.

Behind us, the home is eradicated, exploding into a thousand tiny bits—its occupants along with it.

We cruise by a pair of trees and thump back out onto the road.

For the briefest of moments, it appears that we've lost the Helion. Then the forest behind us glows blue and bursts apart.

Won't be long before the Helion fully understands the terrain and the car's capabilities. They are learning machines. Every time I try something is the last time I can perform the maneuver without it predicting what I'm up to. And the moment that happens, we're a smear.

And while Helions are known for their savagery and adaptability, they are not known for their patience.

Bays on the robot's sides and back snap open.

"Shit," I grumble. "Shit, shit, shitty shit, shit."

"What?" Sean asks. "What is it?"

"How much farther?"

"I don't know, man! Maybe a minute. It's not like I'm a stopwatch or something."

"Too long," I say. "Suggest you hold on to something."

He grips the steering wheel.

"Something else," I say.

He takes hold of a handle above the door, and the armrest to our right, just in time. A dozen rockets launch up into the sky. If this were a Kynolari vehicle, alarms would be blaring, and I would be launching countermeasures.

I look up through the sunroof and watch the fiery tails jet up into the night sky, twist around, and plummet toward us.

The road ahead straightens.

I step on the gas via Sean's knee, pushing us faster.

Then I lock my eyes on the view above. Instincts will keep me on the road, but I really need to see when the rockets are about to hit.

The first comes in fast. Just before it collides, I swerve left, and the tracking mechanism isn't able to compensate in time. The explosion pelts the car with shattered pavement and nudges us farther to the left. What follows is a jarring series of last second swerves and explosions that destroy the road, batter the car, and draw a string of curses from my lips that shall not be repeated.

When the last rocket crashes down behind us, Sean breathes for the first time since the initial strike. "Ohhhh my God!"

"Hold on to your pecker," I say. "We're not out of the shit yet."

"Uhh," Sean says, trying to pull words out of his rocket-addled mind. "Sign! Green sign!"

"Gonna need more than that, buddy," I say.

He points ahead.

As the Helion closes in once more, the blue light emanating from its powerful innards illuminates a large green sign with an arrow pointing to the right. Attached to the large sign is a smaller one, this with the numbers 9 and 5.

"Right at the green sign!" he shouts.

I crank the wheel right and swerve onto a long, curved one lane road.

"Hate to break it to you, but we'd have done better staying in trees."

"N-No!" he shouts. "Fast! Speed! Go now!"

"Huh?" I say, glancing down at his right hand, working the device embedded between the seats...the one that propelled us away from the goon-squad and nearly pulled the skin off my face.

I grip the steering wheel. "Light the torch!"

With the flick of a switch and the push of a button, whatever illicit fuel he's got in this thing hits the engine and we're off, accelerating faster than a Helion could ever dream of.

At the bottom of what turns out to be a ramp, we blast out into a broad, straight road known as Ninety-Five.

"Whoooo!" Sean shouts. "One twenty! One twenty-five!"

"You counting something?" I ask.

"It's our speed, man! Honestly, I've never been brave enough to open her up for more than a few seconds. One-thirty-five!"

Behind us, the still-charging Helion begins to shrink in the rear-view. That's the good news.

The bad news is that we're not the only ones on this road and the other vehicles are traveling at half our speed.

Blue light flashes to my right. For a moment, I think it's another Helion, but then I spot a human vehicle beneath the lights.

"Aww, shit," Sean says. "It's the pigs."

"What?"

"Police," he says. "Law enforcement."

I swerve to the left and then the right, avoiding two cars. "You let the animals you eat—that my stomach is full of at the moment—work as law enforcement?!"

"Naw, man," he says. "It's an expression. Pigs are humans."

"I *ate* a *human?* You're *cannibals?!*' Few things worse in the universe than species that eat themselves. There is one particularly nasty species that eats its own body at the same rate it grows. From the day it's born until the day it dies, it's just coiled up, munching on itself in a perfect, lossless system. Some say that's a glorious representation of efficiency. I'd rather take a scorched earth approach. Wipe them all out. If only to let me sleep better at night knowing they don't exist.

"What?" he shouts. "No, man, just—just drive!"

We narrowly miss a large truck, swerving into a far-right lane that other drivers seem to be avoiding. A moment later, *Peregrine* begins to slow.

"What's happening?" I ask.

"Out of juice," he says, which again, makes no sense. "Gas... I normally fill up on the weekend."

I find the fuel gauge on the dash. Not only is the needle past the 'E,' which I assume stands for 'Empty,' but a glowing orange fuel indicator is lit.

The Helion is tiny in the rear view, but it is still coming. As is the pig, who has yet to notice the metal monster charging toward his rear end. "We need to take one of these other cars."

"How are we supposed to do that? No one is going to stop."

"Didn't say we were going to ask nicely," I say, and I crank the wheel to the left as traffic begins crossing a large metal bridge. *Peregrine* darts across lanes of traffic and clips three vehicles, including a large beast of a thing with eighteen wheels. What follows is chaos.

Glorious chaos.

24

"On your feet, Stuchbery." I motion with my rifle, but he doesn't budge.

"Don't make me get up," he says. "Please. It's...it's a lot. Everything, I think."

Based on the smell, I don't think he's lying. And if the man is going to be our captive...

"Oh my God," Jess says, hand to her nose, backtracking a step. "It's like all he eats is seafood."

I look at our three alien visitors and wonder what they'll think about me having compassion on this man. I wonder if they'll understand it's really not for him, but for us.

"I'm going to be ill," Harth says, stepping away.

Yeah, I don't think they'll mind.

"Do me a favor," I say to the man, "stay right there unless you want to find out if there is anything left in your fishy bowels."

The man just nods. Looks like he's near tears. His whole body is shaking like some little bird that's been abandoned by its mother. He's pitiful, which is perfect for our needs. But I wonder how he managed to become an agent at all. Who knows, maybe Praxion's weapon scrambled his head along with his intestines.

I squat by one of the dead agents, who was never really living to begin with. From a distance, they look human, but up close? Up close the illusion is broken. Their faces are masks of grim-faced men wearing sunglasses, like the agents from *The Matrix*. But they're not flesh and blood. The faces are magnetically attached to a blank shell. I peel one away to reveal a featureless silver head. No eyes.

Drones, though I think the actual term for these guys is 'biologics.'

Grover stands beside me, tongue hanging out, panting. He's jazzed from all the action but doing okay. Probably needs some water. Hell, I need a drink and probably something with a lot more kick. He gives the drone a sniff and then waddles away to inspect the other bodies.

I press my finger against the biologic's forehead. It's not solid metal. More like a pliable fabric alloy. There's about a quarter inch of gel, and then a solid skull. But none of it is alive. Now, or before. I sigh.

Biologics...

Killer robots.

Seems a natural evolution from today's weapon's systems, but about thirty years ahead of its time. Maybe fifty.

I undo the biologic's suit coat and shirt, checking everything for phones, IDs, anything that will help. But it's carrying nothing. Why would it? Someone dressed this thing like a giant Ken doll. It has no need for a wallet. No family to keep photos of.

The torso is surprisingly detailed, with human musculature that I'm sure has nothing to do with its actual strength. But someone gave it the body of an athlete.

Jess stands beside me as I work on the belt. "This is fucked up."

"I know."

She crouches. "On a scale of one to ten, how deep in the shit are we?"

"A lot higher than ten. This is beyond the President's paygrade."

"So, they'll want to kill us?" she asks. "Like forever?"

I don't see the point in sugarcoating the situation. "Until we're dead," I tell her.

She laughs at that. "Well, yeah, obviously. But is there a way out of it?"

I've been asking myself that same question. "Only two I can think of."

I start tugging down the biologic's pants and realize I've forgotten his shoes. I pull them free without undoing the laces. "Option one, we turn these guys in and join the Twilight Directorate."

"Which isn't really an option," she says.

"Not remotely," I say.

"Better not be," Harth grumbles. He's forty feet away, but his canine ears have no trouble picking up our hushed conversation.

"Option two..." I yank the biologic's pants down and his unnecessary boxers slip down, too. "We kill them all—Oh, *seriously?*"

"What?" Jess asks. She sees me staring down at the biologic's crotch and has a look for herself. "Whoa. Why...why would someone make a killer drone anatomically correct...down there?"

"I have seen it before," Praxion says. "It is a The Draun practice."

"'A 'The Draun?'" I ask.

"Since the first encounter with The Draun they have insisted on being called 'The Draun,' no matter the sentence structure."

Jess and I stare up at him for a moment.

Then she says, "Who gives a flying squirrel's fallopian tube what '*The Draun*' think? Just call them 'Draun' and use the 'The' when it makes sense. Fuck me. Talk about enabling. Back to the more important question..."

She thrusts her hands out toward the dangling twelve-inch Johnson. "Why?"

"The...Draun," he says. "Are all female. They reproduce asexually. However, they are still attracted to the males of a species. Of virtually any species. When drones are made to imitate those males, they are often made anatomically correct and fully functional."

"Cool," she says, oozing sarcasm, "A bunch of Lieutenant Commander Datas getting fully functional with the big bads. That's just...great. But *that*—" She motions to the big dick again. "—is *not* anatomically correct. That is too big. Way too big."

"Draun like pain," Torel says, looking down at the exposed robot cock. "They are sadomasochists. They desire pain. Crave it. And if it can be delivered by a facsimile of the male of a species, great. If it can be delivered by an actual male of a species, even better."

"That is what led to the Great War," Praxion says.

"What Great War?" I ask.

"Between Draun and...most other spacefaring civilizations. They were ruthless, treacherous, and caught the universe by surprise. Three civilizations met their doom before the rest could come together and mount a resistance, with Kyno leading the way."

"Hold on," I say. "You're telling us that an intergalactic battle was fought because an all-female species wanted to have sex with men, and no one was willing to give it up to prevent a war?"

"They were collecting the males of species and eradicating the females," Torel says. "When the males bored them, or failed to please them, they were slaughtered en masse. They used their moon as a dumping ground for the dead. It is roughly the size of your moon, but is now covered in a layer of corpses, ten feet deep."

"Okay, that's bad..." I say.

"The Draun were soundly defeated," Harth says. "We were there."

"Not quite soundly enough," I say. "Not if they're here on Earth, making big-dick biologics that no actual man without a megalopenis can compete with."

"I'm partial to 'macropenis,'" Jess says.

I furrow my brow at her.

"The term or the actual—"

"The term," she says, and smiles, "which I'm sure is a relief to you."

I stand with the dead robo-pornstar's clothing in my hands. "Very much so. Now let's—"

The sound of an openly weeping man cuts me short and turns me around.

It's Stuchbery, still seated in his own filth, smelling like a Fenway Park restroom immediately following a Yankees game. "It's true. It's all true." He looks up at me with pleading eyes. "You don't understand what it's like. They lure you in with promises. A big salary. Benefits. Paid vacation. Adventure and the excitement of knowing secrets. Then the next thing you know, a tall woman in white, with a chrome mask covering her face, she just takes you to town. And, you know, it's fun at first. The attention. For a few minutes. But then…oh God, then…you start to realize that you're just an object to them. A piece of meat. It's humiliating."

"Sounds like a typical college experience for women," Jess says.

"It's worse than that!" he shouts, shaking now. "Here! I'll show you!"

He stands up, cringing as what's in his pants slides down his leg. He strips off his jacket. Then his shirt. And finally his undershirt. Then he turns around to reveal a network of scars. There are healed cuts, whip marks, burns, and other injuries I don't recognize.

"Draun have a particularly painful copulation ritual," Torel says. "Not everyone survives their first encounter, let alone several."

He's a broken man, that much is clear. But that doesn't mean he's disloyal. Plenty of abused people would die in defense of their abusers. A moment ago, he was helping a task force of killer drones and giant robots attempt to kill us.

Won't be able to trust a word he says, but we can still ask. Before I question him, I need to show that he has options, that he can still choose a different path.

"There's a stream nearby." I point to the woods. "Just over there. Clean yourself up and change your clothes."

He looks surprised by the offer.

"We'll talk when you're done."

"R-really?" he asks. "You're not going to kill me?"

I smile at him. "I don't *want* to kill you. And no one here will harm you, but you need to help us. Can you do that, Stuchbery?"

He sniffs and wipes away tears with his arm. Then he heads toward the stream.

"I will watch him," Harth says, following the man.

"Hey, Stuch," I say.

He turns toward me. "Y-yeah?"

"How long until more of your friends arrive?"

"We were the closest unit," he says. "B-but they have other options that could be here soon. M-maybe twenty minutes."

"Be quick about it, then," I say.

"I will make him be quick," Harth says, giving Stuchbery a little shove toward the woods.

After they enter the dark tree line, Praxion says, "You are too kind," and he's not being complimentary.

"I guess Grover is wearing off on me," I say, looking toward the dog with pride only to find him nose deep in the ass crack of a dead drone. "Grover. Man. C'mon."

He looks up at me, tail wagging furiously. I expect that if the bodies were human and covered in blood, he'd be more concerned. To him, the dead biologics are more like giant chew toys.

Praxion huffs.

"Was that a laugh?" I ask. He's mostly been stoic so far.

"He reminds me of my son," he admits, "when he was a pup. Mischievous."

"Endlessly so," I say.

"And stupid," he adds.

Before I can argue the point, Torel says, "Praxion, stop. Do not cause friction with our allies. It is unbecoming of your pedigree."

He grunts and stands a little straighter. "Apologies," he says, blinking. "I am not sure what came over me."

"I, on the other hand," she says, "am known for my kindness and compassion." She kneels down and pats her knee. Grover responds instantly, rushing toward the person now at head level with him. When Grover starts sniffing her head, she doesn't back away. Instead, she laughs and then returns the gesture.

"What are you doing?" Praxion asks, sounding a little annoyed.

"Communicating," she says. "As our ancient ancestors once did. Before they had language, they had smell. Kynolari noses are some of the keenest in the universe. We can smell illness in a body before symptoms show, and the chemicals inside a body when it is happy or sad. We can also smell intention. Or could, at least. It is a skill that's been lost with time."

"Hasn't been lost," I say. "Grover can do everything you just said. All dogs can. And there is no better judge of character. Which is why I've decided to trust all of you. Because *he* does."

Torel places her hands on the sides of Grover's head and gives him a playful shake. He mouths her hand, eliciting a laugh. "Good boy," she says. "Good boy."

"We have returned triumphant," Harth says, deadpan.

"Keys," I say to Stuchbery.

"In my jacket," he says.

Happily, the jacket isn't covered in filth and I'm able to recover the key fob without needing to take a trip to the river myself. I open the driver's side door and climb in. Grover leaps into the seat beside me. Jess slides in behind him. Stuchbery and Praxion take up the second row, while Harth and Torel fill the rear.

I start the vehicle, which turns out to be electric and silent. Then I turn around and look Stuchbery in the eyes. "Where to?"

25

PRAXION

The drive has been silent since our prisoner gave Micah a destination. It is a city called Concord. The exact location means nothing to me, but Micah seemed bewildered by the possibility of it housing a secret government safe house. The man's intentions smelled honest. Also full of regret and fear, but not of us. So, Micah decided to trust him and started driving without needing directions.

It would appear that he has visited the McAuliffe-Shepard Discovery Center before.

After traveling through winding forest roads, we eventually make our way to what Jess called a 'highway,' which allows for faster travel. In the dead of night, we are the only vehicle on the road. According to Stuchbery, the government plates will keep us from getting stopped by authorities that monitor the speed of road vehicles.

Such a strange planet.

Being raised on a centralized world, it is always unnerving to visit a planet where trust between citizens and the government is not universal. Earth struggles with this more than most decentralized worlds I have seen. The distrust Micah has for a government he recently served is close to hostility. Then again, his home and land were just assaulted by our gravest enemy.

"Where are you going?" Stuchbery asks, leaning to look out the windshield as we exit the highway. "We're only halfway there."

Without responding, Micah turns into a brightly lit service station of some kind.

"I charged it up this morning," Stuchbery says.

Micah pulls behind the station, parking us in shadow. He looks back, eyes serious, voice grim. "Everyone out." He exits the vehicle, waits for Grover to follow, and then closes the door behind him.

Stuchbery looks around at the rest of us. "Well, that was abruptly stoic."

"I think you're rubbing off on him," Jess says to me and then exits the vehicle.

Torel pats my shoulder. "Always the butt of the joke."

"What?" I ask. "When have I ever been the subject of a joke?"

She slides past me and opens the side door.

Steps out into the night.

"Do you mock me behind my back?" I ask Harth. He just chuckles and slides out behind Torel.

I stew for a brief moment and then motion for Stuchbery to exit. Harth waits for him outside the vehicle.

"Wait here," Micah says when we have all left the vehicle. He jogs to the front of the building and around the corner.

"Is this behavior common for him?" Torel asks Jess.

"Couldn't tell you," she says. "It's been a long time since we've really known each other. He was in the military. A Ranger. Earlier tonight, he was a man protecting his family. His home. That I understood. This feels different."

"He recognizes what is happening," I say. "What is coming if we cannot stop it."

"What's that?" Jess asks.

Harth crosses his arms and leans back against the black vehicle. "War."

Jess turns to Stuchbery. "Is that true?"

"I-I don't know. I've seen a lot of strange things, but I don't...I'm not a decision maker." His eyes are wide, darting back and forth. "I just do what I'm told."

I step closer to the man. "Why do you look nervous?"

"W-what?" he says. "Why do you think? I mean, look at you guys. You're like people-dogs from another world."

"You knew that already," I point out. "You helped assault us. You have encountered the Draun. Why be afraid of us?" I lean in closer. "Man's best friends?"

A whistle from the front of the store interrupts the conversation and gets Grover's full attention. The dog runs to Micah, leaping up at him and licking like they have not seen each other in years. It is both disturbing and, if I am honest, endearing.

I give Stuchbery a shove toward Micah. "Move."

Micah leads us to the front of the service station where another, much older, vehicle waits. He opens the front side door for Grover and Jess, then says, "Everyone else in the back."

"Whose truck is this?" Jess asks.

"Remember Jason Infalt?" Micah says. "He works the night shift here. We've gone hunting a few times. Told him it was an emergency."

"Not sure he believes you now," she says, waving toward the station. A man's face is pressed up against the storefront's window, his eyes wide. "Hi, Jason. Good to see you. Just ignore the bipedal space dogs."

I wave at the man, too. "Hello, Jason."

His wide eyes roll back, and he plummets to the floor.

"What a frail creature," I say.

The back of this vehicle opens to a flat metal bed similar to that of Micah's vehicle. This one has a flimsy, latched-on roof. It is far less comfortable than our previous ride, but I have experienced much worse. Torel and Harth enter first, dragging Stuchbery in behind them. I roll into the back and close the hatch.

Harth pounds on the front cab, "Good to go."

Our new ride coughs, sputters, and rumbles as it starts. It smells of oil and rancid exhaust.

Stuchbery coughs, but Harth inhales it. "Reminds me of the atmosphere on Tanton Four. Few battles were more glorious."

"May the coming day end similarly," I say, smiling as I remember the scorched battlefield covered in slain Draun and their hordes of biologic warriors. And then, I feel something different and unexpected.

Remorse.

For the violence. For delighting in it.

There is no moral ambiguity when it comes to fighting the Draun. They must be destroyed to preserve life throughout the universe. They are a plague. Yet, I find myself feeling...sorry for them.

How did such creatures become so full of greed, ambition, and hate?

These are questions I have never considered.

The answers elude me.

"You okay?" Torel asks as the truck rumbles back on to the road.

She can smell my confusion. There is no point in concealing the source of my feelings. We are not in the habit of keeping secrets from each other. "I find myself conflicted."

"About?" she asks.

"The Draun," I say. "About...why they are...about how they came to be the vile creatures we have encountered on battlefields, in trenches, and in the void. I find myself wondering and feeling..."

"...despair," Harth says. "For who they might have been. Before. For who they might have become, had they not chosen a dark path."

"Yes," I say, turning to my battle-hardened friend.

He nods. "I feel it, too. Along with many other strange...emotions."

"I as well," Torel says. "Despite our situation, I feel lighter, yet, at the same time a greater weight about potential outcomes. We have learned to become detached in war, but I feel those boundaries collapsing within me."

Harth takes hold of Stuchbery's shirt. "What do you know of this, human?"

"N-nothing. I swear! I know the Draun c-can affect your mind...physically, but I've never heard anything about emotions."

Harth releases him.

"If—if you don't mind me making an observation..."

Harth growls at him.

"Easy," I say, placing a hand on his thick shoulder. Then to Stuchbery, I say, "Go on."

"I could be wrong. I haven't known you that long—"

"Nor will you," Harth says.

"—but it sounds...sounds like...you all are becoming more...compassionate? Or at least more in tune with emotions normally kept locked away." He motions to Torel. "Like she was saying. But, what I'm hearing you say is that you are able to feel what others do, by seeing things from their perspective. Through their eyes. That's empathy. Maybe it's why you spared me? Why I'm riding here with you, unbound and speaking plainly."

"I believe that is from a lack of bindings," Harth says.

"He's not wrong," Torel says. "Empathy. Compassion. Forgiveness. These are not things we are known for, and yet I find myself hoping this man—" She motions to Stuchbery. "—is able to redeem himself."

Harth grunts. He will not admit it, but he feels similarly.

We all do.

And it scares me. How can a compassionate soldier win a war against the Draun? This must be their doing. To weaken our resolve. To turn us into...

My eyes widen.

I glance toward the window separating the front cab from the truck bed. Grover is seated there, looking back at us, tongue lolling out, a smile on his face, eager to play.

"Dogs," I say. "We are becoming dogs."

A triple thump on the cab wall interrupts our mind-numbing realization. The window slides open. Micah leans over. "Six o'clock."

Harth cocks his head to the side. "What?"

"The time," Stuchbery says.

"Not the time," Micah says, getting frustrated. "I'm talking about a clock. Hands on a clock."

"He means look out the back window!" Jess says.

We all turn to look, peering out the dirty back window. For a moment, nothing. Then a light streaks through the night sky, arcing its way toward the ground, down toward the service station we recently left.

Stuchbery's jaw drops. "Holy..."

The light plummets below the tree line and is replaced by a large explosion. Billowing flames rise into the sky. A shockwave rattles our vehicle in time with a loud boom.

"How did you know?" Jess asks Micah.

"I guessed," he says. "I knew the SUV would have a tracker. That's standard operating procedure. I didn't know how long it would take them to respond, or that they would respond like that." He looks back through the window. "Bad news, looks like you're all expendable."

"We have been expendable our entire careers," Harth says.

Micah smiles. "Copy that."

"That includes you," Torel says to Stuchbery, making sure he is aware that his employer just attempted to kill him.

He gives a shaky nod and looks to the floor, most likely questioning every decision he made that brought him to this point. Then he settles back and closes his eyes.

I do the same, for what seems like just a moment. Then Torel's hand is on my shoulder, rousing me from sleep. "Praxion. We're there."

26

CHIRK

"Holy shit!" Sean shouts, as I swerve to the left. "Oh my god!" He yells, as we cut to the right. He finishes his string of expletives with, "We're going to fucking die!"

I press down on his left knee, and he mashes down on the brakes with proportional force. *Peregrine* screeches to a stop, just inches from the side of the large, eighteen wheeled vehicle carrying a large white tank on the back.

"We're alive," he says, patting his body, checking for injuries. "Holy shit. *Ho-lee shit.* That was some Fast and Furious, ball-sack shrinking madness, man. I-I feel great. I feel *alive.* What a high. But I also want to puke."

He opens the door, leans out, and does just that, spewing out a yellow mash of half-digested Bugles, which, for some reason beyond comprehension, I still find appetizing. Resisting the urge to lap up what Sean's just disgorged, I exit *Peregrine* on the passenger's side.

The highway behind us is full of screeching tires and crunching metal. The accident we—I—caused spans the width of the road and is a dozen vehicles thick.

I leap onto Peregrine's hood as Sean stumbles out of the car, gripping the door to stay upright. "You alright?" I ask him. That I'm worried about this human's well-being, after witnessing what they've done to the Lost Tribe firsthand, is out of character for me. I'm the ferocious, unforgiving, sarcastic member of the team.

He gives me a thumbs up and says, "Good to go, man. Just need to catch a breath."

"Better catch it fast," I say, jumping onto the roof and having a look back down the highway. The Helion is still lumbering toward us, and it will catch us if we're still here in two minutes.

I leap from the car and head for the side of the bridge upon which we've created a blockade. We're hundreds of feet in the air over what looks like a deep tributary leading out to the ocean. This will work.

I start back toward the large truck. The driver slides out, looking dazed. I point at him. "You!"

"Wha!" he shouts, caught off guard, all but throwing himself into the truck's side, raising his hands. What he doesn't do is look down. "Who was that talkin'? Where are you?"

I clear my throat. "Ahem."

He looks over me once more, but steps closer.

"Look. Down."

His bearded head turns downward. His eyes flare wide.

"There you go," I say.

He stumbles back into the door once more.

"Y-you're a dog," he says. "And you can talk..."

"*And* I'm from *space*," I say, mocking his amazement.

"Don't let it freak you, man," Sean says, joining us. "He's cool. My dog."

"He's yours?" the man asks. "How did you train him? Standing on two legs and all talkin' and shit?"

"Train me?" I say, starting to get offended.

He leans around and looks at the regulators behind my ears. "Are those speakers, like projecting a recording? But how do you get his mouth to move with the sounds?"

"You think this guy—" I motion to Sean with both hands. "—has the mental capacity, know-how, and gross motor skills to build advanced technical devices, embed them on my head, and train a living thing to do all that?"

He shrugs. "I dunno. Figured they were stapled or like hot-glued—wait a second. Are you telling me that you're real? That you are a talking dog—from space?"

He looks to Sean, who nods. "It's all true, my dude."

He gasps. "Why are you here?"

"In a general sense, I'm here to rescue my people from a bunch of primitives. In a specific sense, like, why am I here talking to you on this bridge? I need to blow up your truck and destroy this bridge before that—" I point toward the approaching Helion. "—arrives and either captures or kills us."

Just when I think his eyes can't get any wider, he sees the Helion. Then he turns back to me and says, "Okay."

"Okay?" I'm stymied. "Just like that?"

"Well, yeah, you're a dog. And a Chihuahua to boot!"

"And a stranger," I say. "From another planet."

"And a dog," he says, like that's the only important bit. "I just have one condition. Foxy!"

There's a skittering of nails on pavement and then the most petite little bitch I've ever seen comes strutting out from behind the truck, tail in the air, bulbous eyes already sizing me up.

"You've got to be kidding," I whisper to myself.

"I've been trying to find a suitable mate for Foxy for a long time. Want to start a breeding business on the side, you know. Right out of the truck. I'm guessing there ain't no better stock than that of a space traveling dog."

"You're not wrong about my stock," I say, "but this breaks so many regulations—"

"I'm giving up my truck, man," he says.

"God-damnit," I say, looking over the aptly named Foxy. She's even more alluring than Bacon, and she was nigh impossible to resist. "Fine," I say and am about to start barking orders when—

"Nobody move!"

A man aims a handheld weapon, first at Sean and then the driver, and then back again. He's dressed in a blue uniform. Has a badge on his chest. Law enforcement. I know the type.

"So, you're the pig, eh?" I ask.

His eyes dart to me in time with his weapon.

"Ahh!" he screams, voice suddenly high-pitched. "You're a dog!"

I look up at Sean. "This planet is just full of geniuses." Then I turn to the pig. "Yeah, okay, I'm a dog. That means you trust me, right? I'm a good boy. Never lie. Man's best friend."

He lowers his weapon. "Uh, yeah...yeah. All of that is true."

I lower my forehead into my hand, muttering, "They're all morons," then I look up again and put on a smile. "Listen, you need to get everyone off this bridge because in about sixty seconds, all of this is going kaboomee."

"It is?" the pig asks.

"Because I'm going to blow it up," I say.

"But...why?"

I lean to the side and point past him. "Because that."

He turns around and sees the Helion's massive form growing larger, stomping down the highway. It steps on a car that instantly explodes. He lets out another high-pitched, "Ahh!" and then says, "I'm on it!" before charging back into the wreck of cars that we caused, shouting for everyone to clear the bridge.

"You," I say, pointing to the driver.

"Jim Mock."

"Mock. Fine. Whatever." I point to the truck. "What are you hauling?"

"Gasoline."

"And that is?" I ask.

"Fuel. For vehicles."

"Same fuel that's in all these cars?" I ask.

He nods.

I survey the mass of cars stopped atop the bridge. This will be even better than I thought. Enough to make me change strategies. Slightly.

"Will it ignite with a spark?" I ask.

"Hell yes, it will," Sean says.

"Open it up," I tell Mock. "Let it spill. Join us on the far side." I look up at Sean. "Start running." I snap at Foxy. "And you, sugar teats, come!"

She yips out a bark and obeys, scurrying along behind me. I'd get slapped by Torel for saying it aloud, but if bitches back home were as attentive as Earth dogs, I might already be a married man.

By the time I'm halfway across the bridge, Sean is lagging behind me, and Foxy is far ahead. It's like she's hardly trying and can outpace me...on all fours. Behind us, Mock has just begun running. A clear liquid chugs from the side of his tanker, spilling onto the road, forming a puddle beneath the pile up of cars. I can't see the pig anymore, but I can't see anyone else, either. Hopefully, he managed to clear the bridge.

What I can see is the Helion, bearing down on us.

Despite not having a phone to track, it has a visual lock on me. Probably has since I stepped out of the car and looked back at it. Helions have superb detection systems, weaponry, and armor. What they don't have is the ability to swim. Because of their great weight.

When Foxy reaches the far side and turns around to bark some encouragement, I decide to experiment. No one's watching. Just Foxy, and she can't speak. So, I leap forward, extend my arms—and run.

It's awkward for the first three strides, and then it feels natural. My pace increases. Doubles! The road is rough on my hands—flying the *Prowler* doesn't build up many calluses—but the speed makes it worthwhile. At the end of my sprint, I dive forward, and tuck and roll back onto my feet.

"Pretty slick, right?" I say to Foxy.

She responds by licking me up and down.

"Holy hell, woman! Not yet." Earth dogs are the horniest creatures I've ever met.

I wave to Sean. "Hurry up!"

"I can't run on all fours!" he says, revealing that he must have seen me. I'm embarrassed for a moment, but it *was* pretty slick. He hacks and coughs as he approaches.

"I don't think it's the number of limbs you're running on that's the problem."

He waves me off and staggers to a stop, hands on his knees, trying to catch his breath. Mock, who is in much better shape, is nearly here. But we're also out of time. The Helion is seconds away from reaching the bridge.

"Keep running!" I shout while drawing both mini-railguns. I take aim and unleash a torrent of highspeed metal shards that ping and spark off the bridge frame, crashed vehicles, and the paved road. While the rounds strike at different times, they're traveling so fast that, to the naked eye, the resulting explosions seem to come from everywhere, all at once—which is the same moment the Helion leaps into and through the resulting fireball.

27

MICAH

"Okay," I say, looking up at the ninety-two-foot-tall replica of a Mercury Redstone rocket, "what now?"

"Stand back," Stuchbery says. "Outside the brick circle."

The red brick circle is divided into eight segments by lines of black brick, creating a dartboard pattern. The rocket is a bullseye. I look up at the lit rocket, wondering how many people knew that, while we were reaching for the stars, visitors from other worlds were already here.

I shake my head as I step back. Lies upon lies. People have a right to know. But for now, I'd just like to stay alive.

"Clear," Harth says when the last of us have stepped away from the bricks.

Stuchbery crouches down, hands hovering over the outer black ring. Then he taps them in some kind of sequence, thirteen times.

"Mary had a little lamb," Jess says.

"Huh?" Stuchbery says, looking up.

"If that were a piano, you'd have just played 'Mary Had a Little Lamb.'"

"Oh," he says, and then looks up at the rocket like he worships the thing, like he's waiting for the voice of God to descend from on high.

"Hedgehog," a robotic voice says. "Moist. Pedophile."

"What's happening?" Jess whispers to me.

I whisper back. "Challenge phrase, I think."

Stuchbery confirms it by standing up and saying. "Waxed. Gibbon. Conniption."

The brick segment in front of us lifts silently from the ground, rising up seven feet to reveal an elevator door.

"You've got to be kidding me," I say.

"This is an emergency entrance," Stuchbery says. "We only use it at night. The main entrance is inside the museum itself." He steps into the elevator and waits for the rest of us to join him.

It's cramped inside. Definitely not designed for three people, a dog, and three Kynolari spec ops soldiers. "Good thing I use Arid Extra Dry," I say, as I squeeze in.

"Not funny," Jess says.

"C'mon," I say, and sing the jingle. "Get a little closer…"

"Really not funny," she says.

"I think it's funny," Stuchbery says, grinning and then humming the full jingle as the doors close.

As the descent begins, Jess says, "Okay, can we address the elephant in the elevator?"

"What is an elephant?" Torel asks.

"Big animal. Long trunk. Not important." Jess turns her whole body around a little bit at a time until she is face-to-face with Stuchbery. "What kind of person chooses 'pedophile' for a challenge phrase?"

He suddenly looks like a teenager who's been caught stroking it to an A.I. generated nude photo of Julia Child rolling in melted butter. "Uhh..."

"It was *you?*" Jess says.

"I-I thought it was funny."

"Funny? Who would laugh at the word pedophile?"

"He is a sick man," Harth grumbles.

"Well, out of context..." he says, trying to defend himself. "Like if I suddenly said fellatio, or cunnilingus, or—"

"Stop," Jess says. "Just stop. Who would laugh at these things?"

I slowly turn my head away to hide my grin and notice that the otherwise silent Praxion does the same. He's been quiet for a while now, no doubt pondering next steps and what the presence of their enemy on Earth means for the future of humanity, the Kynolari, and intergalactic peace. But the barrage of questionable, multi-syllabic words is getting to him, too.

Being in the military, this isn't the first time I've heard any of these words used for humor's sake. And I've heard a hell of a lot worse.

Stuchbery stammers for a moment and then points to the doors. "They'll be opening in a few seconds."

Jess gives him a solid smack of stink eye and then spins around quick enough to catch me smiling. Her mouth drops, but I cut her outrage short when the elevator dings to a stop. "Here we go. Weapons hot."

We all attempt to aim toward the door, but the space is too cramped. If there is something with a gun on the other side of this door, we're screwed. The elevator opens to a long, white, well-lit hallway. Empty.

Grover is the first out of the door, his claws *click-clacking* on the linoleum floor as he prances his way down the hall, tail wagging like he owns the place.

"Any security measures we should know about?" I ask, stepping out behind Grover.

"Nothing else," Stuchbery says. "Don't need security for something that doesn't exist."

"And we'll be able to access the Twilight Directorate's systems from here?" I ask.

"Anything I have clearance for," he says.

"That does not sound encouraging," Harth says, behind me.

He's right. Stuchbery might be a long-term member of the Directorate, but he's far from intelligent. Nor is he loyal. I suspect his main purpose is to be subservient and obedient, but that's where his 'positive' qualities end. Hell, the poor man isn't even good looking. Looks like a mottled and abused goose that's had its beak filed away.

I feel bad for the man. Got in way over his head, was broken by sex-crazed aliens, and then was thrown to the wolves—almost literally.

"End of the hall," Stuchbery says. His directions are unnecessary, though, since there is only one door…at the end of the hallway.

I frame up beside the door, weapon ready. I look back at Harth. "Breach and clear?"

He smiles and nods.

Behind him, Praxion's and Torel's weapons extend out from their armor and cover their right arms.

"That's really not necessary," Stuchbery says.

"On three," I say. "One…"

"The door is unlocking," Stuchbery says.

"Two…"

Stuchbery sighs. "There's no one inside."

"Three!"

Harth steps forward and slams his foot into the door, just beside the handle. The frame buckles from the blow and the door breaks free, launching into the room beyond.

I slide into the room, sweeping back and forth looking for targets. Praxion and Torel are beside me, doing the same.

"Clear," I say.

Praxion confirms with, "Clear."

"I told you," Stuchbery says, stepping around the Kynolari. "I live here alone."

"But it was fun," Harth says, joining us with Jess and Grover.

Stuchbery crosses his arms. "And now I don't have a door."

"Don't think you'll be living here after today," I say, inspecting the large room. It's about the size of a classroom but feels more like a teenage boy's bedroom. Empty bottles of diet coke litter the floor and desk spaces. There's an un-made bed in the corner. Fast food wrappers spill out of an overfull trash bin. And in the midst of it all, a shining beacon of technology. A computer terminal with five large screens, each of them displaying a screensaver of an anime-style, Jabba's Palace, Princess Leia bouncing around the screen, letting out a little "Ooh" and "Ahh" with every impact.

"Cute," I say.

"I'll take care of this," Harth says, sitting at the computer.

"You'll need my passkey to—"

Harth's large fingers somehow fly over the touchscreens like he's Mozart ripping out a symphony. Then he says, "I'm in," and the screensaver disappears with an anime girl's "Teehee."

"What are these?" Jess asks, drawing my attention to the far wall lined with glass tubes, like human-sized transparent batteries.

"Charging stations for the biologics," Stuchbery says. "When they're not being used, they just kind of stand in there. They don't talk, or move, but I'm pretty sure they're watching me. Always watching me, which was embarrassing at first, because, you know, I'm a single guy...with urges, living alone."

"Gross," Jess says.

"Is that why you have images of naked human females on the back wall?" Torel asks, hands on her hips, head cocked to the side, looking at the most impressive collection of pinup posters I've ever seen. And they appear to be primarily from the 80s. There is more silicone displayed on the wall than can be found in all the world's gasket factories.

"Why do the females teats look so...rigid?" Praxion asks, stymied by the images. "They appear to be defying gravity. Is this normal for humans?"

He looks over at Jess, inspecting her chest. Despite wearing a plaid long sleeve shirt, it's still obvious that her rather ample bosom isn't defying gravity, despite her bra's best efforts.

Man, this night could have gone so much differently.

"No," Jess says, "it's not. And on this planet, it's considered rude to look at or talk about a woman's *teats.*"

"Humans are strange," Praxion says to Torel.

She nods. "It will take some time to unravel the complicated mysteries of this backward world."

Jess is about to protest when Torel smiles at her.

"Funny," Jess says, trying not to smile as well.

While everyone is busy, I place my hand on Grover's head. He looks up at me and mouths my hand. Means he's unsettled despite his perpetual gosh-golly happy face. I crouch down with him, and he steps in closer. "What's up, Grove?"

He licks my face, again expressing his nervousness.

"I know," I whisper. "It's been a crazy day. And we're not done yet. But I got you."

I kiss his forehead and muss his mane of fluffy fur. He relaxes and licks me again, this time more casually. "Okay, okay," I say. I know where this is headed and, for some reason, I feel a little awkward doing it in front of people, but even more so in front of intelligent dogs from outer space who might not approve or see the value in it.

I sit down on the tacky floor, straighten my legs, and open them in a V so Grover can approach. He pads as close as he can and then sits. I scoot the rest of the way in, and he lays his head on my shoulder as I do his. Then I wrap my arms around his back.

"You're okay," I tell him, almost cooing. "You're okay. I know, it's been a long day. And you're tired. We're all tired. But we can get through this, yeah?"

His tail wags.

"Yeah, you can," I say, petting his back a little.

His tail wags faster.

"Good boy," I tell him. "You're a good boy. Yeah, you are." I lean back out of the hug and kiss his forehead three times, after which he licks my chin…and then looks up, his eyebrows moving up and down as he looks from one person to the next.

When I look, too, I find that everyone in the now silent room is staring at the two of us.

Jess wipes a tear from her eye. "God-damn, that was about the sweetest thing I've ever seen."

"It really was," Torel says, smiling at us.

Even Praxion seems moved by it.

"I have a location," Harth says, turning back to the screen. Can't see his face, but I don't miss him rubbing a hand beneath his eye.

"How?" Stuchbery asks. "That fast?"

"Earth's digital security systems are…primitive. It was like wrestling an insect. What is an inconsequential battle to me would impress other insects."

"Oh," he says. "I think I get it."

"Not sure you do," I say, picking myself up off the floor. "What did you find?"

"He does not have access to many data sets, files, or systems. It's just a glorified, pitifully encrypted text network, but I was able to pinpoint the location of the server to which he's connected." He looks back at me. "Does 'Denver International Airport' mean anything to you?"

"Stuchbery is connected to Denver Airport?" I ask.

"Not to the airport itself," he says. "To something beneath it."

28

GRUUNLOKAR

"Can I tell you a story?" Alton asks, chin perched in his hands, elbows resting on the metal table to which I am now bound. "I want to tell you a story."

I don't dignify him with a response.

Because the few words I already gave him—*You're all going to die*—have been worming their way into the recesses of his mind, chewing away at, and shitting out, his confidence. In himself. In the Draun. In his chances of breaking me, of finding the others, of being victorious in any way.

Anyone could have spoken those words, but when I spoke them—*You're all going to die*—I was telling the truth.

And he saw it. He heard it.

And it unnerved him.

He's been making rash decisions since. Sending in hit squads. Unleashing Helions. I'm not thrilled that my words are having an impact on the rest of the team, but they can handle themselves. I have absolute faith in my people.

Alton does not.

So, while he gets more and more nervous, I remain calm, and will continue to do so, no matter what he throws at me, or what story he tells.

"I was standing on a precipice, looking out over a canyon, observing the layers of strata, wondering where it all came from and what had come before. Thermal winds, propelled upward along the cliff's edge, whipped through my hair and kept me from getting too close to the edge, as though God himself had his hand outstretched, holding me back. Because to trip? To fall? To step upon loose stone? Well, that would have meant certain death."

He leans in a little closer, so his breath is impossible to avoid, and says, "Can you see it? Are you there with me? Let your imagination carry you away, my hairy friend."

He taps his fingers along the sides of his cheeks, a little grin on his face, and then leans back. "So here I am, just admiring the world and wondering how it all came to be, when a lizard scurries up beside me. I don't know what it was, but even if I knew its name, it would mean nothing to you.

"I observe the small creature for a moment, and I swear to you, it's looking back at me, feeling the same connection—to me, to the canyon, to the world, and our place in history. Such a small creature, but its effect on my psyche in that moment was profound. I felt connected to everything. To the universe itself. And I knew, *I knew*, that I was destined to accomplish great things."

There aren't many creatures in existence that can feel connected to the universe and believe that they are the center of it. He's a narcissist of epic proportions, unable to comprehend that the things we do, the wars we fight, the people we love—it's all inconsequential to the universe. We are blips. Entire civilizations come and go, and the universe doesn't feel the change.

I am nothing.

He is nothing.

Kynolari fight and live for what *we* love, and what we feel is important, but we would never equate such things to the eternal.

"I can see you're drifting," he says. "Ruminating, perhaps. Hopefully, on my intriguing tale." He raises his eyebrows and continues. "I'm standing there with this lizard. Alone. Pondering. And that's when a raven flutters down and perches upon a twisted old tree leaning out over the cliff's edge, as though deciding whether to take its own life.

"I didn't know it in that moment, but it was the same question the lizard asked itself: 'How do I want to die?' It had two choices before it. Leap off the cliff and fall hundreds of feet to be dashed upon the rocks below. A moment of terror followed by instant, painless death. Or it could remain atop the cliff, risking a death by raven, picked apart while still living.

"The first option guaranteed death, but it would be painless. The second option left some room for survival—perhaps the lizard could outwit, outrun, or outmaneuver the raven? They are quite quick. It was a hard decision. I could feel the weight of it crushing down on its reptilian brain.

"So, I helped.

"I took the decision away from the creature, easing its mental anguish, and then took away its fear of pain—

"—by stepping on it."

He sits back. "It didn't have time to fear the end. Didn't feel any pain—at least not for more than an instant. All it really did was pop. After peeling its remains from the treads of my shoes, I laid it out for the raven and let it eat.

"Funny thing, that. The raven accompanied me for the rest of my time there, cawing at anyone who came too close, bringing me trinkets and coins—enough for soda and candy—and, in return, I killed for it. Again and again. It was a mutually beneficial relationship, forged in a day."

There's a knock at the door. A humanoid biologic leans in, its face flat and blank. "Sir. She is here."

"Send her in," Alton says, smiling down at me. "Your silence will soon come to an end, my friend. But first, my story's climax."

He leans back down, chin in his hands. "As the day wore on, each of us serving the other, I began to wonder. Does this raven think us equals? Or perhaps believe our relationship is that of a master and servant, with me as its hired hand? The possibility irked me. It was a ridiculous notion. A bird and myself, equals? On par? Proportionate? Peers?"

He laughs. "It was dusk when I killed the raven's next meal. A mouse. Its neck broken in a trap I'd set, but not yet dead, its small body twitching in my hand. I was God to it in that moment. I took it to the raven, waiting on the gnarled tree, and made my offering. But I did not place it on the ground. Nor did I bring it to the tree. I stood my ground, palm outstretched, my offering laid bare."

He smiles wider. "The raven came to me."

His smile melts away to reveal a sneer.

"And when its talons wrapped around my fingers, I took hold of its legs, wrapped tape around its beak and proceeded to pluck each of its feathers, one by one, until it, too, was laid bare. A featherless bird. A pitiful thing. There was no fight left in it after that, I'll tell you. I unwrapped its beak, gave it the mouse, and sent it on its way. Dominance established. As a Kynolari, a genetic ancestor of what we call dogs, I'm sure that's a familiar concept. Dominance. Humans understand it, too, perhaps me most of all."

The door opens. A woman steps inside the room and carefully closes the door behind her. Her hair is cut short and colored bright pink. Her eyes are round and unblinking. A pale, gaunt face completes the look of a living specter. She enters without a word and is not disturbed by my alien appearance. She doesn't look like much, but I already sense that, despite all his bravado, she is more of a threat than Alton.

"This," Alton says, "is Raven. Raven…please find out our guest's name?"

Alton rolls himself away from me until he thumps against the wall.

"Gruunlokar," I say, taking away the woman's first task, and reducing her power.

"Ahh, he speaks!" Alton smiles. "He *fears*. Find out everything else you can about—"

"My race is called the Kynolari. We are from the planet Kyno. We are on a peaceful mission of exploration."

Raven throws up her hands. "Why am I here?"

"You…" Alton says, waggling a finger at me. "Testing my patience. Making me look the fool. Delaying the inevitable. Your motivations for speaking now make no difference to me."

"Just trying to spare her," I say, looking at Raven. "Wouldn't want her to lose any feathers."

His grin is so broad, I see he's missing a tooth on one side of his mouth. He looks ridiculous. I can't stop myself from letting out a little chuckle at his expense.

"Carve your way into his mind," he shouts at Raven while thrusting his hands out toward me. "Extract all that you can, no matter what he says next! Do you understand?"

Raven sighs, rolls her eyes, and steps closer.

I don't bother speaking again.

She's committed to this course of action now.

Hear me.

She speaks directly into my mind. In some ways, it's reminiscent of the connection the Draun make before they explodes your head. A quick little hello, and then internal pressure beneath the skull rapidly builds before—

That's interesting, she says, her voice like a whisper. She saw my thoughts about the Draun. About what they can do.

How many are with you? She's digging deeper, looking for pertinent information first. She doesn't find it.

Who are your allies?

Allies? I think, and realize I've given up a piece of information I shouldn't. The others have formed an alliance with other humans. While that is good, it also reveals that they are in desperate circumstances.

You don't know them?

I focus on my youth, projecting images of open fields, my pack, my brothers and sisters. It was a joyful time, before the Draun. The memories are potent enough to cause me pain and are impossible for her to ignore. She must fight past them.

Dig deeper. Forge a profound connection, like the Draun.

And that is when the regulators attached to the sides of my head perform their primary function. A psionic feedback loop, replaying my vivid memories, again and again, unrestrained by the laws of physics, beyond the speed of light and the fabric of reality. For Raven, it becomes reality. One she cannot escape.

There have been plenty of tortures in my life, moments of great loss and sorrow. I could have trapped her in all of those. But...she is Alton's Raven. She wasn't born like this.

She was made.

So, I am merciful, trapping her mind in a moment of bliss.

When she goes rigid and falls flat on her back, there is a smile on her face.

Alton calmly stands up. Looks down at Raven. Turns to me. "You are to blame for what happens next. I want you to remember that."

"Careful," I say. "Wouldn't want *you* to lose any feathers."

"I do believe I hate you," he says, and exits the room, leaving Raven lying happily on the floor.

29

"How are we supposed to get to Denver?" Jess asks, throwing her hands up in the air. "I'm assuming that saving your friend from the Directorate is time sensitive."

"Not just for Gruunlokar," Torel says. "The Draun are on Earth. And they are aware of our presence. Whatever they're planning, the timetable will be moved up."

I find myself distracted from the conversation, thrown into my past. Witnessing the affection between Grover and Micah unlocked something in me. Suppressed memories, not because they are bad, but because they make me homesick. For family. For my parents. My siblings. Friends I have left behind in our fight to protect Kyno from threats like the Draun.

I suppose I did not realize how far out of my mind I put them.

But that hug between man and Lost Tribe, it brought me back to my mother, curled up with the litter, feeling nothing but safe. Warmth. Comfort.

It would seem that soldiers on this world do not give up such things entirely. Perhaps there is a lesson to be learned? Regardless, I find myself with an ache in my heart.

So, I bury it.

"How far is this Denver?" I ask.

"If we had a plane, we could get there in five hours," Micah says, "but there is no way the three of you are boarding a commercial flight, and I don't have the money to get us a private jet." He looks at Jess. "Do you?"

She shakes her head. "No one in the military owes you favors?"

"Not that kind of favor," he says.

"Then we call on Baarfolir," Harth suggests.

"Who is Baarfolir?" Micah asks, smiling.

"He's a historian." Torel squints at him. "Why are you amused?"

"The name. It's similar to Barfolomew, which can be shortened to Barf..."

"*Space Balls?*" Jess says, incredulous. "Seriously?"

"I mean, they're basically Mawgs, right?"

Jess attempts to hide her own smile but fails. I know not what they are referencing, but I get the feeling it is not complimentary.

Micah turns to me. "It's not important. Sorry."

"Humans," Harth mutters with a shake of his head. "A distractable lot." He sighs and continues. "The *Prowler* and MIMIR will do most of the work."

"The *Prowler* is our only way home," I say. "Our only way to warn Kyno of the Draun presence here. It is too great a risk. Baarfolir *is* our last hope, but not of rescue."

"I will infiltrate this world's banking system and transfer the necessary funds to Micah," Harth says. "Then we will procure a private plane, and—"

"Pretty sure that would be noticeable," Micah says, "especially since the Twilight Directorate knows who we are. They'd know we got a plane. Know our destination and arrival time."

"Then we steal a plane," Torel says.

"And get shot out of the sky," I say. "America doesn't really allow planes to just fly around without a flight path these days."

"How long will it take to travel by land?" I ask.

"If we don't sleep," Micah says. "A day, at least."

"Then that is our best option," Torel says. "I have stimulants to keep us awake."

"We'll be the ones driving," Micah says. "Any idea how your stimulants will work on a human being?"

Torel frowns. "Not a clue. But we can test it on one of you—"

"Test it on me," Jess says. "You'll need Micah later on."

"Not a chance," Micah says.

"I don't have a whole lot else to offer. I'm not a soldier. I don't know how to—"

"You're a dog person who knows how to shoot," Micah says. "And…you're…" He struggles to find the words. "…important. I don't want you to get hurt."

"Ugh," Harth says. "Humans are a pining species. Wonderful."

"Um," Stuchbery says, seated on his bed, petting Grover with one hand, and raising his other. "There might be another way."

All eyes turn in his direction.

"Speak," Harth says.

"I've only done it once, and I'm not really sure how it works, but seeing as how you all are from space—well, not all of you, just the dogs—well, not all the dogs, just the—"

"Stuchbery," Micah says. "Get to the damn point."

"Okay, okay." He holds up his hands. "It's just that this is kind of unbelievable, and I don't want you to think I'm lying." He takes a breath, seems to swallow it, and then continues. "Each state in the U.S., as well as other countries around the world… Well, they have teleporters inside major transportation hubs. Logan Airport in Boston. Denver International. LAX. Dubai International. Munich. You get the idea. And in New Hampshire…"

"Manchester Airport?" Micah guesses but doesn't sound convinced. "There are teleporters in Manchester Airport…"

"It's not impossible," Harth says. "With Draun help and technology recovered from a Kynolari intelligence drone, they could have recreated Leap Nodes." He turns to Micah. "That's how we transported from your moon to the surface of this world, and how we intend to return." He turns to me. "This also helps explain how they were able to detect our arrival and disrupt two of the nodes' trajectories."

Stuchbery gasps. "You've been to the *moon?*"

We ignore him.

"So, we go to Manchester-Boston Regional Airport, and if that's a bust, we find a van with tinted windows and go on a road trip," Micah says.

"How far is this airport from our current location?" I ask.

"Twenty minutes," he says. "We won't lose much time if he's lying."

"I'm not," Stuchbery says, "I swear."

"What about him?" Jess asks, motioning to the man. "We can't just leave him here. He could warn them."

"I don't want another human with us," Harth says. "Especially this human."

Torel nods. "He's a liability."

"I'll tie him up," Micah says. "If we succeed and survive, I'll come back to free him. Consider his debt to society paid. If we don't make it…he'll die here."

"Wellll," Stuchbery says. "There's a problem with all that, not that I mind being abandoned and left behind. My parents did the same thing." He shrugs. "I'm used to being unliked and ditched. That's why I like working with machines. They never complain about me."

"Save the guilt trip," Jess says. "It's not going to work."

"Oh, that's not why you'll bring me," he says. "It's the, what did you call it— Leap Node? You'll need my hand to make it function."

"I will cut off his hand," Harth says.

"Wait! Whoa!" Stuchbery pushes himself back on the bed until he hits the wall. "A dead hand won't work."

Harth grunts.

"He might be lying," Micah says. "But we shouldn't risk that he's not. He comes."

Stuchbery pumps his fist. "Yes." Then he sobers himself. "Sorry. It's just, I've been alone for a long time, and I honestly didn't know I was working for the bad guys. I mean, you're the aliens, right? I thought *you* were the bad guys. But you're dogs, and not at all like how they described you." He motions to Harth.

"Well, except for maybe him. But..." He pets Grover's head. "Who would want to kill a dog?" He lets out a long, satisfied sigh. "It's nice to have friends again."

"Not friends," all of us say in unison before heading to the door.

"It's okay," Stuchbery says to Grover. "I still have y—"

"Grover," Micah says, and the dog dutifully runs to his side as we file out of the strange, secret hideaway. I cannot help but wonder how many of these little bunkers are hidden around this planet. The number must be substantial if there are Leap Nodes connecting all the world's major transportation hubs.

I pause by the door and wait for our feebleminded guide. If the Twilight Directorate employs just men like him, our odds are much improved. I suspect the reason for his apparent incompetence is a matter of control. The Draun tend to eradicate species that pose an intellectual threat and subjugate those who do not. Some humans, like Micah and Jess, appear to have the cognitive wherewithal to join the interstellar community, but then there is Alex Stuchbery. Easily manipulated, desperate to please, and strange to look at. If there are many more people like him, it is no surprise the Draun chose this world as a starting point for the rebirth of their empire.

In truth, I suspect this world is at a turning point. The great filter has indeed arrived, but they might not get the chance to destroy themselves. The Draun might do it for them.

"It's okay," Stuchbery says, speaking to himself. He reaches beneath his pillow and pulls out some kind of paper booklet, the cover of which is adorned by a woman wearing a white lab coat. "I'll always have you, Ariel Ivanovici. You might have lost the Nobel prize for your work with ExoGen, but some day, I'm going to find you, and thank you personally. You'll see." He kisses the magazine. "I'll be back."

I clear my throat.

"Coming!" He returns the publication to the pillow and hustles toward the door. "I was just—"

"I do not care to know what you were doing." I place my hand on his chest, stopping him short of the long hallway leading back to the elevator. "But if you betray us, I will let Harth remove every extremity on your body, starting with your fingers."

"So, like fingers and hands? Or are we including feet? Arms and legs? Oh wait, you mean..." He looks down at his crotch, eyes wide. "Or maybe you meant my head? Because technically that's an extremity, too, if you count the torso as the core part of the—"

I grip his shirt.

"Do not make me change my mind about your hands."

He raises his hands, thinks better of it, and hides them behind his back. "Okay. Okay. I get it. No betraying. I promise."

I shove and follow him down the hallway. The path ahead is a ridiculous one. Following it leads to almost certain peril, but we have no other choice. To not walk the path before us means doom, not just for our team, but for this entire world.

30

CHIRK

"Ho-lee sputum crust!" Mock shouts, as the Helion is heaved into the air by a shockwave powerful enough to peel away its outer layers of armor.

None of us gets to see what happens next because that same shock wave slaps us silly. I hit the ground twenty feet from where I'd been standing, rolling back to my feet, ready for whatever comes next—which happens to be Foxy. She tumbles right into my arms. I ease her back, lessening the impact. She looks up at me, wide eyed and trembling. Then she licks my nose.

I place my hand against her mouth and say, "Soon, baby...soon."

She licks my hand, slipping her tongue between my fingers. I nearly lose control and mount her right then and there, but a resounding crash of metal on metal turns my attention back to the bridge.

The Helion has landed atop the column of fire rising from the spilled gasoline and burning vehicles. It's partially obscured by black smoke churning into the night sky, but I can clearly hear its pain-fueled cry.

It's unnerving. Not just because of its volume, but because this is the first time I've heard a Helion express pain. They are known for their relentless and brutal pursuit of enemies, no matter how excruciating, right up until the moment of their destruction.

But this one is different. This one...isn't just a machine. There's something *living* inside it. Something being tortured by what I've done.

I am not to blame, I tell myself, not for the first time. I did not lock the creature inside that metal shell. I did not send it on a mission of death and destruction. I simply defended myself, and others. I won't allow myself to feel guilt for this, but rage...white hot and pure.

A secondary explosion rocks the bridge. The Helion pitches itself upward with a shriek and comes down hard. The bridge buckles, groans, and then gives way. A fiery torrent of metal, machine, and beast plummets into the dark river below.

I glance over at Sean and Mock. The far less agile humans are sprawled on the side of the road, both of them unconscious. I take two steps toward them, intending to rouse them from the realm of unconsciousness, when I think better of it. Not because they're better off, but because I'm not really an exhibitionist.

There's a tree line at the side of the road. Plenty of nighttime privacy to be found in there. "You," I say to Foxy, who is immediately by my side. "Let's get this done."

I head into the woods, and she follows. The flickering orange light from the still burning cars remaining on the river's far side is almost romantic. "Okay," I say. "How do you like it?"

She just stares up at me, tongue sticking out from the side of her mouth, legs jittering.

"Right," I say, undoing my armor. "I'll lead."

Five minutes later, I strut back out of the woods feeling relaxed and a little more spent than I should. Foxy was just as eager as Bacon, but not as easy to please. She also had a strange habit of snarling and nipping at me. That was a first. Have to admit, I kind of liked it.

Made me howl. Haven't done that since I was a pup, and that was pretending.

When I arrive at the roadside, Sean is sitting up, watching the blaze on the bridge's far side. From behind, he appears to be spasming. Beside him is Mock, holding his head...also shaking a bit.

"What the hell is wrong with you two?" I ask.

Both men whirl around with God-damned tears in their eyes.

Mock reaches out, shouting, "Foxy!"

The dog springs to life, bounding into the truck driver's arms. He hugs her tightly while she licks his face.

I debate telling him where that tongue has recently been, but I don't think he'd care. Earth dogs seem to lick everything they encounter.

"What's all this about?" I ask Sean, waggling a finger at his tears.

He wipes his eyes with his shirt. "Nothing, man. We just thought. You know. Because of the explosion. And you weren't here—"

"We were in the woods," I say, with a smirk and a double tap of my eyebrows. "Mock came through, so I fulfilled my end of the bargain. Simple as that. And listen up, both of you." I wait for Mock to look at me. "This stays between us. I am *not* allowed to fraternize with alien species, and I am certainly not allowed to impregnate a member of the Lost Tribe."

I shake my head. I should never have done it.

Not with Bacon. Not with Foxy.

I just can't seem to control my urges.

Problem for another time. Right now, we need to find a new ride before whoever sent the agents and the Helion after us realize we didn't go down in a blaze of fiery glory.

"Hey," a woman shouts. "Are you guys okay?" She's running to us from the far side of the highway, where a large truck-like vehicle with flashing red lights has just stopped.

Not law enforcement, I think.

Medical services of some kind.

She lays her hard case on the ground between Mock and Sean. "You okay?" she asks Mock.

"Little shook up," he says, "but fine."

"Same," Sean says before she has a chance to ask him.

"Great. Hey, did you guys see what happened?" she asks.

"I'm fine, too," I say, waving up at her. "Thanks for asking."

She looks down at me. Her eyes go wide and then roll back. Her legs crumple beneath her and she falls to the roadside.

"Whoa!" Sean shouts, looking at me. "Was that like some mental telepathy or some shit?"

"What?" I say, scrunching up my face. "No. Some people just can't handle coming face to face with a superior being."

"Pff. Right on, man. Right on."

I point to the red truck with flashing lights. "We need that."

"What, the ambulance?" Sean asks while Mock checks on the medic. "There's still a driver."

"Not for long," I say, brushing myself off. I point to Mock. "You. The deed is done, but I make no fertility guarantee. Are we good?"

Mock gives a thumbs up. "Square. And hey, it was an honor to meet you."

"You're God-damn right it was," I say, and strut my way across the empty highway, toward the oncoming lanes, which are starting to congest with late night drivers no longer able to cross the bridge.

We stop at the divider and peek into the ambulance. The driver is a thick, bearded man lit by the flames on the bridge's far side. He looks bored, but also like trouble, like he'd rather be out somewhere brawling with other simpletons. Probably why he's driving the ambulance and not attempting to help anyone.

"I don't like him," Sean says.

"Same," I say.

"That means we can kick his ass, right?" Sean says. "You'll do the heavy lifting, obviously, but we get in there, you do some dog-fu and then we jack the ambulance and jet."

"Look," I say. "Sean. See these?" I motion to the regulators embedded on the sides of my head. "They have translation services, meaning I understand your language, and speak it. But, if you use your language in ways it was not intended to be used... Point is, I don't know what it means to jack or jet anything in the context we have going on here."

"Can't you, I don't know, extrapolate or something?" he asks. "Like from context?"

"Can," I say, "but don't like to."

"Well, why not?"

"I'm an operator in the Kyno Corps, the most elite unit this side of the universe. We do not conceive or execute plans that require colloquial interpretation."

"Yeah, you do," he says. "We've been doing it since we met, brah. Because we're simpatico. BFFs. You're my dog, remember?"

I stare at him for a moment. "Fine. Just...stay behind me."

He giggles, ducks low, and gives two thumbs up. "Awesome."

We approach the ambulance from the back and sneak up the side. I watch the driver in his side mirror, making sure he doesn't look back. When we reach the door, I hold a hand out to Sean, stopping him in place. "I got this."

I climb up to window height and knock on the window. A moment later, it rolls down. "Somebody out there?"

I lean out in front of the window, taking hold of his side mirror, feet planted against the door. "Hey, you ever seen a talking dog before?"

The man's eyes widen, brow turned up in a look of abject shock, but he doesn't lose consciousness. Seems like that only happens with some humans, but not all.

"I'll take that as a no," I say.

And then the man reacts very differently from other people I've encountered up until now. He screams, unlatches the door, and then kicks it outward in an attempt to dislodge me.

I hold on tight as the door slams open—and then bounces back. I pull myself in tight, using all that momentum to my advantage, shoving both feet out and kicking the man right in his shocked face, putting my superior Kynolari strength to work and achieving my initial goal of rendering him unconscious.

I climb inside the open window while Sean opens the door.

He's ecstatic. "I knew you knew dog-fu! That was some Hong Kong Phooey shit right there."

"Just...help this guy down to the ground."

Sean slides the driver down, laying him out beside the ambulance. Then he climbs in, and I take my position atop his lap, grasping the steering wheel. "All right. Back on the road..."

"...and allowed to speed," he says, reaching forward to flip a switch. A siren blares. "Law enforcement won't stop us like this."

"Nice," I say, and put the car in drive. Then I step on his knee to accelerate and turn the ambulance around, using the side of the road to go the wrong way down the highway.

Sean chortles. "This is just like Ratatouille, but with a space dog!" He gasps. "Can you teach me dog-fu?" He gasps again. "You could be my sensei! Like Master Splinter, but a dog. How cool would that be?"

"Remember what I said about using your language in a way that makes sense."

"Yeah…"

"Wasn't a question," I say. "I'm telling you to remember."

"Right. Got it. You don't know who Master Splinter is…"

"Correct."

"Do you know what a turtle is?"

"Not a clue."

"Okay," he says, "that's where we'll start." He then proceeds to regale me with the story of four ninja turtles that makes me wonder how many other alien species humanity has encountered before. I just let him talk, while listening to the human chatter on the communication device mounted to the console. The people speaking on it use code, but it's not complicated, and I soon have it figured out, which allows me to avoid some threats, while the lights and sirens keep others at bay. We're making good time, but I can't shake the feeling that we're going to be far too late to find the others.

31

MICAH

I've been to the Manchester airport dozens of times and the only thing out of the ordinary I've ever seen was the new offramp meant to make getting there easier. I just take the side streets like always and have no trouble finding it. The passenger terminal is open all day and night. Getting inside won't be a problem.

But the moment we walk through those doors, with three upright dogs dressed in futuristic black-ops gear, things are going to get tense. The biggest threats the airport has faced were probably a rogue raccoon or a confused deer, but it's still an American airport post 9-11. Security, while not over abundant, will be well-armed.

Which means my assault rifle is staying in the vehicle. The Kynolari won't give up their weapons, called 'gauntlets,' but they're futuristic enough that they might pass for props long enough for us to locate and use the teleportation system hidden inside the airport.

"Okay," I say, standing at the parking garage end of the sky bridge, which leads across the parking lot and road, directly into the terminal. "Everyone stay calm and relaxed. We're supposed to be here. We're having a good time. This is just silly fun."

"You don't sound like this is silly fun," Jess says.

"You sound like you're going to pass out," Harth adds, fiddling with a device he's been working on throughout the drive. None of the tech looks familiar, which means he's pillaged his own gear to create it. Not sure what it does, or will do, but he's just snapped it closed and appears to be done.

I take a deep breath and let it out slowly. "Everything we say and do from here is going to be recorded. What happens next could very well define how your species is regarded on Earth. If it ends in confrontation…"

"We will not raise arms against those guarding this facility." Praxion looks to Torel and Harth, who confirm with a nod. Then he turns back to me. "But you do look tense."

I put on a smile. "How's that?"

"Somehow worse," Jess says, patting my shoulder.

I sigh and look down.

Grover is there, his harness on. He's not an official emotional support dog, but the red harness might get the job done. Plus, he's a Golden Retriever. I could set him loose inside the airport and everyone he came across would be thrilled to see him.

He licks my face when I crouch down in front of him. "You ready for this?"

His tail wags faster, not because he understands, but because I'm speaking to him. I run my hands over his soft ears, and then again, running his ears between my fingers. When I was a kid, I used to sit at the top of the stairs with old Buddy. Would do the same to him, imagining that, if he went blind someday, he would know it was me because of the way I pet his ears.

I move my hands to Grover's fluffy mane, giving it a shake and leaning my forehead against his. It's like a two-man huddle, but we're not formulating a plan, we're emotionally regulating. With his coat good and tousled I take hold of his cheeks, give him a kiss on the forehead and stand back up.

"Okay," I say. "I'm ready."

"What was that?" Harth asks. "A pre-battle ritual?"

"I believe it was simple affection," Torel says.

"Between two species..." Harth says.

"Well, I think it's sweet," Stuchbery says.

Harth grumbles at the man. "No one cares what you think."

Praxion says nothing. Just looks down at us with a furrowed brow, either deep in thought or disapproving. I don't really give a fat deuce because, after that little love-fest with the pooch, I'm feeling a lot lighter. "Let's get this shit show on the road."

I lead the way down the long, empty hallway. The windows on either side reveal the terminal ahead, adorned with glowing signs for Delta, American Airlines, and Southwest. We've walked by a few cameras already, but no one has shouted at us to stop. Yet. We're not technically in the airport. Once we go down the flight of steps at the end of the hallway, things could change.

I almost skip down the stairs, hand on Grover's harness, casual as can be. And when I reach the bottom...nothing. The terminal is empty. No airline personnel. Not a single traveler. That might be business as usual for Manchester airport at four in the morning, but the lack of guards is disconcerting.

Puts me right back on edge. Hadn't considered this part of the journey might be a trap.

I snap at Stuchbery. "Where to?"

"Right there," he says, pointing to the iconic metal statue of a moose standing at the front of the terminal.

"The moose..."

"What is a moose?" Torel asks.

Jess points to the sculpture. "That's a moose. Native animal."

"It's quite large," Harth notes.

"They get a lot bigger than this." Jess approaches the statue, inspecting it. "Talk about hiding in plain sight. So, how's this supposed to work?"

"I will enter the destination code," Stuchbery says. "Then you just place your hand against—"

"That is not how a Leap Node works." Praxion's not buying it. "You must stand atop the node to—"

"Oh, we're standing on it now," Stuchbery says. "It's beneath the floor. Touching the moose just activates it. They made them large enough to transport large numbers of people—of biologics—from one place to another."

"What's the ratio of biologics to humans?" I ask.

"I couldn't tell you that," Stuchbery says. "But I've only ever met a few actual humans. I would guess actual humans are outnumbered by biologics...maybe fifty-to-one."

"That's horrifying," Jess says.

"Not until today," Stuchbery adds. "They were my quiet friends. Always listened. Never judged. I shared everything with them."

"Mm," I say, only half listening. "Sorry we killed them."

Torel shakes her head. "They were never alive."

"But they felt alive!" Stuchbery shouts, suddenly in tears. "They were alive to me!"

Grover being Grover, he walks to Stuchbery's side and leans into him. The groaning man falls to his knees and weeps into my dog's fur.

"This guy..." Harth says to Praxion, pointing at Stuchbery.

"Patience," Praxion says.

"Empathy," Jess says, scolding. "He thought he was protecting the world from aliens. He's been abused. Broken. Brainwashed. His only friends were automatons. We took all that from him. Violently. In the last two hours. He's..." She lowers her voice. "He's a freak of the first order. I get it. But give the guy a break. He's been through a lot and is helping us, despite the risk to his life."

Praxion nods. "She...is right." He looks down at Stuchbery. "We owe you a debt of gratitude. You have sacrificed much. Have entrusted us with much. I...am sorry for the...things you have lost today."

Stuchbery looks up, face wet with tears, snot in his nose. "Thank you, kind alien dog."

"Praxion."

"Praxion," Stuchbery says. "I hope that I—"

"How you folks doing tonight?" a man asks.

I spin around to find a somewhat portly airport security guard.

Doesn't look like he's up to chasing anyone down, but he's armed with a pistol. He flinches back when he sees the Kynolari. "Holy shit, what in the hell are you all?"

"Furries," Jess says. "We're on our way to a convention."

"Furries, huh?" He looks our alien friends up and down. "My wife was into that sort of thing. Dressing up. Acting a fool. Like an animal. Debasing herself if you ask me." He clucks his tongue. "Never was my thing. You ever been with a woman that howls in bed?"

"Just once," I say, giving Jess an obvious wink.

She makes a playful aghast face and swats me.

The guard chuckles. "Well, for what it's worth, I can tell you spent money on those things. Looks like you have some fancy animawhatzits in those faces. Suggest you take them off before boarding, and you're definitely going to have to take off those heads. Need to see your faces, and you're liable to scare some kid shitless."

"Yes, sir," Praxion says.

"I'll be damned," the guard says. "Even the mouth moves when you speak."

"They spent way too much money on them if you ask me," I say.

"Tell me about it," the guard says, and then he looks down at Stuchbery. "He okay?"

"Girlfriend broke up with him," Jess says.

The guard's eyebrows raise. It's the most suspicious thing he's heard all day. "Girlfriend... *Him?*"

"She was...*special*," Jess says, and I can tell she's cringing on the inside.

"Ah," the guard says with another cluck of his tongue. "Gotta love them special kids. Well, all right, you folks have a good flight. If you need anything, I'm around."

"Thank you, sir," I say.

He gives a wave as he struts away, high on his very limited power.

"What..." Harth says, glowering, "is a 'furry?'"

"Uhh," Jess says. "People who dress up like animals."

"And that is all?" Harth asks. "I detected an undertone."

"Definitely an undertone," Torel says. "And I believe it to be sexual in nature."

"Harth. Torel." Praxion sounds frustrated. "You are Kyno Corps. Keep your focus on the mission. What it means to be a...Furry...on this world is of no consequence."

"Apologies, sir." Harth nods. "I've been finding myself distracted by inconsequential things since our arrival on this world."

"I believe we all have," Praxion says, turning to Torel. "Perhaps a detailed analysis of the atmosphere is in order."

Torel nods, tapping the controls on her forearm touch screen. "Sample taken. Analysis in progress. Details when complete."

"Very good." He turns to Stuchbery. "Are you in control of yourself again?"

"Y-yes. Sir." Stuchbery stands and gives a salute, which means nothing to Praxion.

"Time to go," I say to him.

"But first," Harth says, placing his device in the fake foliage surrounding the moose. Before I can ask, he glances back at me. "A beacon, transmitting on all frequencies." He faces Praxion. "If Chirk hears it, he will be lead here."

"Can the Leap Node be left active?" Praxion asks Stuchbery.

"Yeah," he says. "Sure. So long as no one else touches the moose."

"What happens then?" Torel asks.

Stuchbery looks stunned, like he's confused anyone would ask a question with such an obvious answer. "Well, they'd be transported to Denver. Duh."

"Great," I say. "Let's...let's just do this."

Stuchbery nods and steps into the moose statue's display. He walks around to the back and lifts the creature's tail. From here, it looks like he places his palm against the moose's anus, but I'm guessing there's a hand scanner hidden beneath the tail. Makes sense, I guess. Who would think to look for a moose's asshole?

"It's active," he says. "Ready to go?"

I give Praxion a nod, and he says, "Do it."

"Heeya!" Stuchbery shouts and gives the moose a slap on its hindquarters. A moment later, the world disappears.

32

PRAXION

Our destination is pitch black. The kind of darkness that not even a Kynolari's eyes can pierce. Something is not right.

"Feels like limbo," Micah says.

"I am unfamiliar with this term," Harth responds.

"It's a religious concept," Jess whispers.

"Religion," Harth says, and then huffs.

"Red light?" Micah whispers in my direction, understanding what the rest of us are doing, and confirming that human eyes function similarly to Kynolari eyes, even if they are inferior. Red light will allow us to see without forcing our dilated pupils to contract.

"Affirmative," I say.

"I've got Grover," Micah says.

"I would like to hear more about limbo," Torel says. We are in the same positions we occupied when we left the terminal. And all but one of us is accounted for.

"It's a place with no direction," Jess says. "No up or down, left or right. It's a place of perpetual waiting."

"Waiting for what?" Torel asks.

"Judgment," Jess says. "The end of days. I'm not really sure."

"Is this something all humans believe?" Harth asks.

"Not remotely," Micah says.

"That is good," Harth says.

"Performing spectral scan," I say, my tone flowing with the conversation. No one responds, not even the humans. Their instincts are sharper than I would have guessed.

I spin around slowly, taking everything in as the implant in my eye shifts spectrums, revealing the things none of us can see without enhanced vision. And part of me wishes I had not. First, because I can now see Stuchbery, hands clasped over his mouth and nose to conceal his laugh, which Kynolari ears have no trouble hearing. It confirms what I feared would happen: we have been betrayed.

Tricked by a fool.

I knew it was bad the moment we arrived. I can smell the biologics. Can hear the faint echo of a massive chamber. I might be blind, but my other senses more than make up for it. That said, my enhanced vision has revealed a factory where all kinds of biologics, from the humanoid to the monstrous, are being constructed. Many are unfinished, in various stages of construction, laid out on belts, hung on hooks, mounted to walls. But just as many are active—and closing in on our position.

"Weapons hot," I whisper. "Limbo is not as empty as we were led to believe."

"Should have brought my rifle," Micah grumbles, and I agree. Another armed operator would be ideal. And while there is an option, it would be dangerous, if not catastrophic for a human being.

"Torel," I say. "Regulator count?"

"Two remaining," she says. "You're not thinking—"

"I am."

"Thinking what?" Micah asks, "because I'm kind of getting the idea we might be screwed."

"A regulator," I say. "The same as ours. Same as Grover's. It would allow for integration with a weapons system...which would make enhancements to your body as well."

"That doesn't sound horrible," Micah says.

"It could kill you," Torel says.

"They are *not* meant for use by non-Kynolari," Harth says, sounding a little angry, and not out of fear for Micah's well-being. He is a noble warrior. A non-Kynolari has never worn a regulator, nor been integrated with our weapons systems.

"I would normally agree with you, my friend," I say. "But we will not survive what comes next without help. And we are short on time."

"Just do it," Micah says.

"Again," Torel says, a fresh regulator in hand, its two parts held to the sides of Micah's head. "It could kill you. The system was designed for Kynolari physiology, but our psychology as well. It will integrate itself with your mind, and it may well root out the parts of you that it does not recognize as Kynolari. You may be a different person when you wake up."

"But if it takes?" Micah asks.

"You will be able to use our weapons systems," I say.

"Of which I carry spares," Harth says.

"Of course he does." Jess doesn't sound convinced. "Micah, I'm not sure this is a good idea."

Micah nods in the dark. He understands the risk. "But it might be our only chance." He looks toward me, though he cannot see me. "Right?"

I scan the space one more time. We are surrounded. These biologics are unarmed, but we will run out of sufficient charge long before they have all been destroyed. We are going to need to fight our way through them. "Affirmative. Torel, do it. Harth, we need his hand."

"Was hoping you'd say that," Harth says, extending his Incinerator weapons system's glowing hot blades. The orange light illuminates Stuchbery, whose eyes spring open in surprise.

"Wait, wait, wait," he says, extending his open palms toward Harth, hoping to beg for mercy.

He finds none.

Harth swings one blade.

Two hands tumble through the air, rolling to the ground.

Stuchbery looks at his stub wrists. "My hands... My hands! Oh my God, my hands!" Harth's blades are so hot that they cauterize as they cut. In theory, they are useful for dispatching enemies—even with the toughest armor. In reality, they cauterize wounds and prevent messes. In situations like this, they also leave the enemy alive—and capable of running.

Which Stuchbery does, making it all of two steps before his feet are removed by Harth's second blade. He sprawls to the floor, screaming and squirming.

"Traitors are worms," Harth says, looking down at him. "And now you are one of them. Crawl down into the pit from whence you came."

Harth's next swing cuts through the torso of the first biologic to arrive. Its clothing-free form looks like an unfinished human. No genitals. No eyes, nose, mouth, or ears. Just stretched artificial flesh over a synthetic body. "I'll take care of the first sacrifices to arrive. Make sure the human survives the bond—"

"I'm okay," Micah says, hands on the sides of his head.

Torel looks him over, confused. "I don't understand... Perhaps they're not fitted correctly?" She attempts to adjust the regulators attached behind Micah's ears, but they are bonded, the nano-thin sensors already through his skull and working their way into his brain. "How do you feel?"

"Kind of tickles," he says. "Where you put them. Other than that, I feel nothing."

"No headache?" she asks. "No discomfort in your limbs, or lack of control?"

Harth grunts as he swings upward, splitting another biologic from crotch to head. Its two halves fall to either side of him.

"How long does it normally take to kick in?" Micah asks.

Torel looks me in the eyes as she responds. "It...it should be done."

"I don't feel any different," Micah says.

"How is that possible?" I ask Torel. "His physiology. His brain."

She shakes her head. "It's as though he is Kynolari."

"Or," Harth says, spinning and hacking the head off a third drone. He looks back at us. "It didn't work at all. But there is one way to find out." He kicks a fourth biologic in the gut, sending it flying back into two more. He turns to Micah. "Projectiles and blades or lasers and claws?"

Micah doesn't hesitate. "Lasers and claws."

Harth gives an approving nod, reaches behind him, and pulls a cylindrical case from his pack. Hands it to me and then returns to the fight, but he is only guarding one side, and the enemy is closing in all around us.

"Put it on him," I say to Torel, and then I activate my own weapon system, which slides up over my arm. A sonic burst disables a dozen biologics, but then needs to recharge, so I switch to my railgun and start gunning them down. But not one by one. That is too slow for this lot. I line them up before firing, each rail-shard snapping through the heads of at least three biologics before crashing to a stop inside a wall or machinery.

"Put your arm in here," Torel says, opening the case, which appears hollow. He does so without hesitation. "Okay, now this is *definitely* going to hurt."

Before he can ask why or second guess his decision, she activates the gauntlet integration system. The first part is the most painful as the components drill through flesh and attach to bone. After that, the disparate pieces attach to one another, initialize, and finally connect to the regulated brain. I do not know what will happen if the system attempts to connect to an unregulated mind. I suspect it will just remain a dormant lump of alloys, quantum cores, and a fusion power cell.

Before my system is done recharging, Micah's is up and running, glowing with thin orange lines that are simultaneously pleasing to the eye and reveal his power levels. Full charge. Fully connected.

"Okay," he says, smiling at his arm. "How do I use it?"

"Think of it as an extension of yourself. Use your thoughts to control it, but do not rush it. These systems can take some time to get—"

"Not my first field test," Micah says, holding his hand up. "I think I get it." He extends and retracts five razor-sharp oxium claws, and smiles. "I'll call it...*Hell Hound.*"

Harth shakes his head, disapproving. "That is not what this model is called. It's—"

"It's Hell Hound now, big guy," Micah says.

His hand blooms with orange light as the illuminated lines running down his forearm drain to nothing. Torel and I see it in time to leap aside. Then he unleashes a beam of energy so powerful that it punches a three foot in diameter hole straight through countless layers of biologics—and the wall beyond them. At the same time, the energy pulse lifts Micah off his feet and turns him into a projectile headed in the opposite direction. Bound by the laws of physics, he does not make it nearly as far, but collides with dozens of biologics on the way, taking a beating for his efforts. And when he recovers, he will be surrounded by the enemy, power drained and helpless.

33

GRUUNLOKAR

"You've had me in three rooms now," I say, "and I've come to the conclusion that you need a decorator."

I'm speaking now. But only sarcasm because I know that it gets under my captor's skin. His irritation amuses me and throws him off balance. He's not sure what to do with me, so he's relinquished control. Called in the Draun.

Meeting one of their kind, face to face, has never been done before. At least not by anyone who has lived to tell the tale. And I do not intend to die today. Or tomorrow.

They have me in a padded cell. A fifty-foot square space that is cushioned on the floor, all four walls, and the ceiling, twenty feet above my head. I'm not sure if it's meant to make me nervous or comfortable, but I will not risk either. My first instinct was to harangue Alton, but it's not fun or distracting when he refuses to reply. For all I know, he's not even listening. So, I change tactics.

Sitting in the room's center, I close my eyes and focus on a mental exercise, imagining what fate has befallen the others, picturing what has happened and what might yet still.

Chirk's angle of descent was disrupted, same as mine.

But where I dropped into water, he touched down on land, in an area that appeared populated.

I clench my eyes tighter and picture his first moments.

His small stature allowed him to go unnoticed. He followed protocol, searching his immediate surroundings for danger while the node finished recalibrating. But...it didn't work. He couldn't leave. Our nodes were non-functional, as were our comms. Chirk is scrappy. He would find a path to safety, outwitting the agents sent by Alton. He's out there, free, but alone, fighting for survival and hunting for the others.

Who are where? On target? Or were their flight paths disrupted as well? Did they follow through on the plan and return to the *Prowler*? Are they searching for me, or are they stuck on this world, too? Will they mount a rescue or find their way to a different padded room?

There are too many unknowns to imagine their fates.

My concentration breaks.

I open my eyes. And I am not alone.

Standing silently at the far side of the room, is a tall feminine figure dressed in a white, hooded, flowing cloak. Her legs, hips, and hands are all covered in tight silver fabric that reflects the pattern of the room's padding. The rest of her clothing, interwoven with the silver, is white, matching the cloak. Her true face—whatever it might be—is hidden behind a polished chrome mask, featureless, aside from the horizontal slit that allows her to see, though I'm not sure how anyone could see through such a narrow opening.

This is the closest I've ever been to the Draun.

She doesn't move. Not even the slightest twitch. She exudes total calm and absolute menace simultaneously.

Searching for a way into my mind, no doubt.

She won't find one. The regulator will see to that. She might be powerful enough to resist the device's defenses, but she will not worm her way into my thoughts.

I sit patiently, resisting the urge to run across the room, bite down on her with my jaws, and tear her apart.

I blink out of the imagined attack.

Killing people is part of my job, but I have never imagined doing so in such a savage manner. It's more like some dormant instinct that's been awakened by her presence.

Or perhaps it is her, attempting to trigger my baser self, revealing a weakness.

Despite the proximity of my greatest enemy, I close my eyes, focus on my breathing, and wait.

It feels like an eternity.

The weight of her in the room compresses my chest, making breathing difficult.

I breathe in. Hold it.

Breathe out.

Over and over until the pressure on my body subsides.

Mind and body under control, I open my eyes again to a distorted view of my own face, bent in the mirrored visage of the Draun's facemask.

"Hello," I say.

She just stares. I can feel her eyes, hidden behind the small slit, scratching at my mind, but unable to find a chink in the armor.

"You are far from home," she says, standing up. She's at least six feet tall.

"And yet I am much closer to my people than you are to yours," I say.

She huffs a laugh, and then turns to a wall, like someone is standing there. "Does he truly believe The Draun now cease to exist?" She goes still for a moment and then looks down at me. "Do you *all?*"

She laughs louder this time. "How wonderful."

With just a few words, she was able to extrapolate far more information from me than Alton could during hours of interrogation.

I remain silent and intend on saying nothing more.

She senses as much and crouches down in front of me. "You know, I have never seen a Kynolari before. The duration of my life has been spent here, on this world."

How long have they been here? I wonder, realizing that this Draun might not be a refugee of the war.

"You are...uglier than I imagined," she says. "Nothing like your feeble cousins who occupy this world."

What is she talking about?

"The enslaved masses. The mind-addled mongrels. The weak comforting the weak. Would you like to meet one? Of your cousins? The fabled Lost Tribe? They've been here for some time, though not nearly as long as we. Still, their impact on this world is...humorous. Behold." She raises her hand and motions for someone to join us.

The door through which she entered slides open without a sound. A small Kynolari is revealed, standing on all four limbs, and completely naked.

"Come," the Draun says.

The Kynolari—a female—trots into the room, tail wagging, tongue hanging out. It appears to have been lobotomized. Her body is shaved down to her gray skin, aside from the end of her tail, her hands and feet, and her head. She looks ridiculous, like five fluffy gliffins have nested on the extremities of her body.

"What did you do to her?" I ask.

"The only thing that changed her into the obedient creature happily walking its way toward us is time and the air we breathe. The Lost Tribe is far more lost than any of you imagined."

The small female stops beside the Draun.

"Sit."

She sits.

"Lie down."

She obeys.

"Do not listen to her," I growl.

The small Kynolari leaps to its feet, unleashing a high-pitched bark and baring its teeth, *defending* the age-old enemy of our people.

"What do you want from me?" I ask, reeling from the Kynolari's physical state and behavior.

"To educate you," the Draun says. She motions to the Kynolari female. "This, is Ling. She is a dog. As are you. Her breed is called a 'Chinese Crested Dog.' And yours, a 'German Shepherd,' though your fur is darker than most. As a dog, you are born and bred to serve my kind."

"Your kind..." I say. "How many of you are there on this world?"

She grins. "The number increases faster than the steady beat of your heart."

My brow furrows. It's not possible. The Draun were defeated. Eradicated. I saw it with my own eyes. Took part in their undoing. Took pride in our accomplishments and received medals from worlds throughout the cosmos. If all of that was a farce...

I need to escape this place.

Need to get word out.

"There is no point in trying," she says.

She's not wrong. Taking on the Draun up close and personal is a death sentence. My head would burst before I could wrap my hands around her throat. She might not be able to read my thoughts, but she can still project her telekinetic will on those around her. And there is no way to tell how powerful she is. Not all the Draun are created equal, but some are strong enough to level buildings or tear ships from the sky.

When I relax, she says, "Very good. If I had a treat, I would reward you."

I grumble but say nothing.

"You're just how I imagined you," she says. "I know everything there is to know about your kind but seeing you here? It's different. I'm far less impressed than I had hoped. You are more like them—" She looks down at Ling. "—than you'd ever want to admit. So much pride in those eyes."

"Ask your questions so I can refuse to answer them," I say.

She waits a moment. "What is your name?"

There is no harm in a name, so I give it with the hopes that she will relax and reveal more than she means to, as I already have. "Gruunlokar."

"That was hardly a refusal," she notes.

"I want you to know my name when I kill you," I say.

"Gruunlokar. Sounds strong." She sits across from me, legs crossed. Ling leaps into her lap, tail twitching. She settles the moment the woman starts stroking her back. "Well, Gruunlokar, I would like to tell you a story. About how my people came to this world, and about how yours joined us."

"*Joined* you?" I ask.

She reaches up and pulls away the white hood, revealing a chrome head. She presses three tabs along an invisible seam, two on the sides, one on the top. They hiss when she presses them, releasing a seal. The front of the mask peels away and I become the first Kynolari to ever see the Draun and not have his head immediately explode.

She smiles at my surprise.

"You..." I say, mind reeling. "You're...*human.*"

34

"And then you find out that it's Michelangelo. I mean, whoa. The way he fought, I thought he must be Raphael for sure, but Michelangelo? Dude. Mind blown."

"Huh," I say. I did my best to tune out the long-winded story full of ridiculous names and battles, but found myself drawn to the characters. "So...this is a popular story on Earth?"

Sean nods. "I'd say so. Even if you haven't watched the movies or read the comics, you at least know who TMNT are. They're...what's the word? Ubiquitous. Like Superman. Or Nemesis."

"Earth has a lot of stories?"

"Tons."

"Are they all about anthropomorphized creatures?" I don't like thinking of myself that way, but given the story I've just heard, it might be a theme on this world.

"Not all of them," he says. "But there's a lot." He starts ticking off fingers. "Bugs Bunny, Winnie-the-Pooh, Redwall, The Jungle Book, Pinocchio, Stuart Little... Oh! Chip and Dale's Rescue Rangers, the Gummy Bears, really pretty much everything from Disney."

"Any of those about dogs?"

He shakes his head. "No, but there's Martha Speaks, Scooby Doo, Lady and the Tramp, Up—man, that movie made me cry. Uhh, Underdog, Space Buddies— that's dogs in space, you'd like it. Mr. Peabody and Sherman, Clifford the Big Red Dog, Ruff Ruffman, and—"

"Okay," I say. "I get it, I get it. There's a lot of them."

"Loads," Sean says.

"Has it always been that way?"

"Well, I'm kind of an expert in what's on TV, but yeah, dogs are pretty important to people. Always have been. Like, there was this one guy, Odysseus. He went on this epic journey around the world. Fought in the Trojan War, which is just a bananas story on its own, and a cool movie. Before leaving, he entrusted the protection of his family to Argos, his dog. When Odysseus returns home, twenty years later, he's older and bedraggled and in disguise. Nobody knows who he is...except for Argos, who greets his human, is thrilled at his return, and then relinquishes his protective duties by lying down, closing his eyes, and dying."

"That's..."

"Heartbreaking, right?"

"I was going to say it was a perfect example of the Kynolari code of honor, but sure, that too. This is the human experience of dogs?"

"For those of us lucky enough to find the right dog." Sean smiles down at me. "But yeah, people have depended on dogs for protection, survival, and friendship since...well, since there've been dogs. I suppose you could say that the relationship between people and dogs has been more of a partnership, historically anyway. Not as much now that we have modern technology, I guess, but you still bring out the best in us—what the hell is that sound?"

"Huh?" I turn my senses outward. I'd become so invested in the conversation that I stopped listening to the world, including the radio, which is now unleashing a series of high pitch chirps.

"Sounds like an emergency broadcast thingy, but there's no message."

"Is that common?" I ask.

"The emergency broadcast? Yeah. It's for like hurricanes and wars, and natural disasters and stuff. They run tests all the time, too, but they don't keep beeping forever."

He reaches for the radio's power button. I place my hand on his. "Wait."

"What?" he whispers. "Is it, like an alien thing?"

"I think you might have been right the first time," I say. "An emergency broadcast."

"But there's no message," he says. "Just beeping."

"The beeping is the message," I say. "Take the wheel."

We trade off driving responsibilities and I leap into the passenger's seat. The truck's dim interior glows when I activate the control panel on my forearm.

As I tap buttons, Sean glances at me several times. "What are you doing?"

"Translation services are designed to detect and translate languages. That's why we can understand each other. But it can also crack codes and ciphers, even the most complicated ones."

"This is a code?"

I nod. "Every beep contains hundreds of individual tones, spaced so closely together that it sounds like one long note. If you're a human. But to me... I can feel the vibration. The slight distortion. This is a message *from* a Kynolari, *for* a Kynolari." I shake my head with a grin. "Harth. Has to be."

"What's it say?" he asks.

"Almost there." I wait, tapping my finger.

Then a very basic message appears on the screen. I read it aloud. "Manchester Airport... Touch the moose."

"I know where that is," Sean says. "We were cutting through ManchVegas on our way up North via 93."

"Hold on," I say. "There's more."

As the text unfurls on my forearm, a sense of dread sweeps through my body.

"Beware. The Draun are on Earth."

"The Draun," Sean says. "Were they, like, drawn? Are they artists or are they—"

"Your worst nightmare made flesh," I say.

"Oh. That doesn't sound great."

"It's the opposite of great, and it means your whole planet is waist deep in a slurry of Gulvarian mucus plugs."

"That doesn't sound great either."

"It's basically the worst thing you can imagine. Being waist deep in it. You'll never be the same. Trust me."

"Been through some shit, little man, huh?"

"Through it, around it, beneath it, got some in my mouth."

"Dude..."

"Yeah..."

I snap out of that unpleasant memory and back to the current dilemma.

Harth managed to get us their location, but also warned of the Draun. That means we might be in for a fight.

"Can you shoot?" I ask.

"I mean, I've *seen* it done. Doesn't look too hard. Aim and pull the trigger. Not a lot to it."

"The aiming bit takes some practice, but yeah. Know a place we can get you a gun?"

"We're in the United States," he says, like that should mean something. "In New Hampshire."

"In the middle of the night," I add. We've driven by plenty of storefronts, and all have been dark.

The roads are also nearly empty.

This society shuts down at night.

"Just look for a bright blue sign that says Walmart," he says and extends his hand in the shape of a gun...sideways, pretending to pull a trigger. "Then we'll be all pew, pew, pew!"

"The hell is that?" I ask.

"A gun," he says. "I'm shooting it."

"Huh..." I say. "You know what, never mind. I think we—not to mention any innocent bystanders—will be safer if I'm the only one shooting. And if we're lucky, I won't need to fire my mini-railguns at all. Again."

"Wait, you shot someone?"

"In the leg," I say, waving away his concern. "A large, pink female. Bacon's... owner. It was a small wound."

He gives me a suspicious side-eye.

"What?"

"Did she have it coming?" Sean asks.

"Well..."

He gasps.

"Desperate times, Sean! Desperate times! Just...get us to the Manchester Airport and bring me to that...moose. Whatever it is."

"It's a moose, man."

"Not. From. Earth."

"Right. It's an animal. Like a really big deer."

I stare at him, damn near close to snarling.

"Uh, it's got four legs, and short hair. Long snout. The males have these massive antlers, like sideways horns that grow all weirdly shaped." He puts his thumbs against the sides of his head and splays his fingers out. "Like that."

"Wheel," I say, and he resumes steering.

"They weigh like a thousand pounds. Probably more if they're a big dude."

"Better," I say. "And there is one of these at the airport?"

"Right," he says. "But it's not real. It's a statue. You said we need to touch it? Like pet it, or like more of a—" He makes two clicking sounds, gives a wink, and caresses the air in front of him.

"First," I say, "never do that again. Second, just touch it. And before you ask, I don't know what will happen when we do. That he wasn't more specific means they were in a rush. And if he mentioned the Draun, that probably means they were being chased."

"So, we're walking into what...a trap?"

I smile. "Naw, Sean, it means we're the God-damned cavalry."

35

MICAH

Here's what I remember. One, an alien weapon system being attached to my arm. Two, me 'jumping the gun' and firing said weapon system before fully understanding it. Amateur move. Three...being tackled from behind by every single member of the Patriots' defensive line. That's what it felt like, at least.

Honestly, I don't remember much after the third impact. Just a vague sense that there were more.

And now I'm lying on a hard floor, curled up like a newborn foal, struggling to break free from the stupor of birth and into the blinding pain of full consciousness.

I flop over onto my back, looking up into darkness that dances with little dots of light. It's pretty, but I also understand what it means. I've been knocked silly.

Because I fired a laser cannon attached to my arm.

Because it launched me across the factory floor.

Which means I'm now alone, lying on my back, surrounded by killer biologics that I can't see.

A distant voice shouts to me. "Use your thoughts to control the gauntlet! It's paired with your regulator!" The voice belongs to Torel and sounds distant. Which isn't great.

Okay, class, I think to myself, *what did we learn?*

First, the alien weapon system is called a 'gauntlet.'

Second, I can interface with it via the regulators connected to my brain, which I also have no idea how to use beyond a *Reading Rainbow* style, 'Use Your *Imagination*,' kind of way.

Third, I'm on my own.

And fourth, I make numbered lists while in a semi-conscious state. Makes sense, I suppose. It's a quick way to find order in chaos.

I close my eyes and the view doesn't change. Darkness overlaid with happy swirling spots. *Imagine,* I will my mind, *imagine...* What will help me understand the gauntlet's limits and abilities?

Lines and words flicker in my vision.

The hell is that?

I haven't opened my eyes yet.

Information is displayed in my periphery. When I think about it, I can see it more clearly. Power levels. Weapon mode. Damage indicators. Language selection. Comms.

Holy shit, it's a heads-up display.

I focus on the power level. It's recharging, but pretty close to zero. Next is the weapon mode indicator. Right now, it's full-on laser beam—if the graphic is to be believed. But I can also see that my claws—so awesome—are still extended. So, what if I...

With a thought, I transfer the limited laser power to the tips of my claws. I lift my hands over my face and open my eyes. The claws glow orange, lighting my surroundings and revealing a mass of biologics, their blank faces turned down toward me, watching, waiting to see if I'll recover.

In the distance, I hear fighting. Praxion, Torel, and Harth. Grover is barking. Jess is shouting his name.

"Can I get a hand?" I ask one of the biologics, reaching my hand out to it. "No? I guess that's—whoa!"

I catch a glimpse of a biologic raising its foot to crush my head...but I don't see it with my own eyes. It's like a sudden, out-of-body experience, like I'm seeing myself from a distance. It's almost like a visual sixth sense. Is there a fisheye lens built into the gauntlet?

I roll to the side as the biologic's foot crashes down with enough force to crack the concrete floor. My head would be paste if I hadn't moved, and these guys are a lot stronger than I thought.

They're not people, I remind myself. They're drones. Robots.

Like less Schwarzeneggery Cyberdyne Systems Model T-800s.

Step one, don't get caught.

Step two, stop making damn lists. Seriously, what the fuck?

I duck as a pair of arms reach for me from behind. Again, I see the attack coming from outside of myself.

Then I go on the offensive. My fingertips glow orange, guiding my path as I rake the claws down the front end of a biologic, slicing deep into its body and severing something important enough that it collapses to its knees and faceplants on the floor behind me.

The drones standing around look down at their fallen comrade, expressionless, but somehow exuding some sort of surprise. Then they turn to me in unison.

"Shit," I say, and, rather than waiting to be put on the defensive, I charge the nearest biologic and drive my fingers, like the tip of a spear, into its head. The sharp blades, coupled with the white-hot laser light, let my hand slip straight into the skull. Once through, I grip the head, twist my body around, and flip the robot into a third biologic that falls back from the impact.

It's a good start, but it's hardly a dent.

More of a ding that will buff out.

And then the biologics surrounding me switch from *What the fuck?* mode to full-on battle mode.

I'm instantly on the defensive, ducking, weaving, and blocking. The only advantage I have now is that the gauntlet, even with its low power setting, allows me to slice through everything my hands come into contact with. So, as I'm blocking, I'm also severing limbs. A few punches find their way to my back, chest, and gut, but I'm able to roll with them, reducing the impact, again because of my strange new sixth sense.

During the action, I catch a glimpse of the others, faring much better than me, but facing the same never-ending army. We need to communicate. Find a way out of this mess.

Comms, I think, and the indicator in my vision blinks. Connection made. "Talon-One, Badass Human-One."

"Who is this?" Harth responds over the comms, sounding angry. "How did you break my encryption?"

"Didn't break shit, big man," I say. "It's me."

"Me who?"

I duck a punch and disembowel a biologic, which is a lot less disgusting than it sounds. When it doesn't drop, I move around behind it, dragging my claws along until its top falls away from its bottom.

"The only person you've given a gauntlet and regulator to!" I shout, turning toward the others, watching as Harth figures it out, turns toward me, and makes eye contact. He's genuinely shocked. "How?" he manages to ask before we're both struck in the back and sent to the floor.

I roll with the strike, severing the legs of two drones as I roll back to my feet. I'm holding my own, but I'm getting tired. "Talon-Actual, Badass-Human-One. We need to reconnect. Find a way out of here."

"Badass-One," Praxion says. "'Human' is redundant and long-winded. Also, I agree. Talon-One, Talon-Three, clear a path."

Harth takes action first, launching a dozen liquid hot spheres of orange light that pummel, melt, and dismantle every biologic they strike. Each molten blob bursts upon hitting the floor, splashing drone legs by the dozen. Half of the biologics between us fall to the floor. Most of them are destroyed, but those with functional top halves are still dragging themselves along, desperate robotic zombies.

My sixth sense spins me around. I dodge a punch aimed for the back of my head and then cleave the arm away at the bicep. With a backhand, I remove its face and then kick it away to stumble into the encroaching horde.

I see outside myself again. It's just a flash, zooming in on a hand reaching for the back of my neck.

I spin around to catch it—

—but Grover beats me to it. My dog leaps into the air, grasps hold of the arm, and yanks the biologic to the ground, shaking his head. I've never seen Grover like this. He's almost savage. Hackles raised. Teeth bared. Growling. And then, through all the bravado, he glances up at me, making eye contact just long enough for me to understand what he's thinking. *Look at me, Dad! I'm doing it, too!*

"Good boy," I tell him and his tail wags for a moment. Then he glances to the left and, for a flash, I see what he sees.

My sixth sense…is *Grover?*

I kick out toward the onrushing biologic and catch it in the gut. If it were a living, breathing human being, it would be crumpled over, gasping for air. Instead, it plows forward through the impact, lifting my leg and toppling me onto a pile of destroyed or malfunctioning drones. An arm wraps around me from below.

The advancing biologic stands above me. Cocks its fist back. Throws a punch that will indent my face.

I block the strike with the gauntlet. Mostly. The biologic's fist doesn't connect, but the gauntlet slaps against my forehead.

And now I'm seeing stars again. Dazed, I won't be able to block a second blow. My head lolls to one side, and I see Grover, surrounded and biting. I loll my head to the other side. Jess is struggling to get to me, but Harth is holding her back.

"Do it!" Praxion shouts, his voice like a distant echo.

Torel steps toward us, raising her gauntlet, which is primed with luminous blue energy.

I turn away, knowing what's coming. Face turned to the ceiling, looking up at the biologic about to turn my face into a bowl, I watch as the air fills with arcs of pure energy, branching off between the nearby drones, sending them into upright spasms, like it's a new dance craze for all the naked faceless people.

The lightning strike ends with a loud crack, and all the biologics in a thirty-foot radius drop to the floor. I lean my head to the side and strike the machine-man still holding me. With a hole in his forehead, he loses control and I roll away.

Grover nearly tackles me back to the ground, but I catch him in my arms and receive all the kisses. By the time he's done, I look and feel like I've just splashed my face with water.

"Revolting," Harth says, standing beside me, catching his breath.

We're all winded, beat up, and unsure about what comes next. Our reprieve will be brief. The remaining biologics, possibly thousands of them, are already trying to reach us, but they seem to be having trouble climbing over their pals' limp bodies—perhaps because they're not yet fully formed. Doesn't really matter why. We've still got just seconds to come up with a plan.

"We need to get the hell out of here before these faceless assholes figure out how to walk over their dead buddies."

"Assholes have faces on Earth?" Harth is revolted.

"What?" I ask. "Not literal assholes."

"Ahh, it is a slur, then."

I'm befuddled. "What? Just... Can we focus on not dying?"

"We do not know how to exit this place," Praxion says, "or where we will be when we do."

"But we know someone who does," Jess says, looking toward Stuchbery, who's still trying to worm his way across the floor, one of his hands clamped in his mouth.

I sag in frustration. "Fuck. *Stuchbery.*"

36

PRAXION

"How the hell do we get out of here?" Micah shoves Stuchbery with his foot, rolling him onto his back. "Tell me now or lose the last appendage you have. It might be tiny, but I'm willing to bet you care about it a hell of a lot more than you do your hands and feet."

As a show of force, he flashes his new claws, brilliant with laser energy.

"Whoa!" Stuchbery shouts. "Whoa! W-what do you want?"

Micah looks at me with a shake of his head. "This guy..." Then he punches Stuchbery square in the face. "How do we get out of here?"

"Th-they'll explode my head if I help you!" He tries to worm away. "They'll kill me."

"I'm going to explode your nuts and then let you live."

"*I* will kill him," Harth says.

"You see?" Micah says. "Exploded nuts followed by whatever kind of horrible death this guy can cook up."

"We will slow roast him," Harth says. "He would not be the first alien species I have consumed."

Micah flinches.

Looks back at Harth, no doubt wondering about the statement's veracity.

I am not sure he would like the answer.

"E-eat me?"

"Just your legs to start," Harth says, his blades glowing orange again. "You can watch. Then your arms. Then, maybe we will let you live, as a stump. I'm sure the Draun will find some use for you. A doorstop, perhaps."

Harth lowers an Incinerator blade close enough to Stuchbery's leg that he can feel the heat and remember the searing pain they cause.

"Okay!" Stuchbery shouts, his voice a few octaves higher than usual. "Okay! Okay! I'll show you the way!"

"Tell us," Micah says.

"It's a big place." Stuchbery leans over to look at the encroaching biologics, some of which are not based on human forms, but on alien species the Draun have eradicated. The hulking Gobi. The long-limbed Tyrne. And the many tentacled Plata-mots. Like the humanoid biologics, they are unfinished, lacking faces, hair, and other defining features. Despite that, they are a haunting reminder of what is at stake. "And there isn't time!"

Harth grunts. "Very well. You will show us the way." He hauls Stuchbery up, slings him over his back and straps him on, cinching him tightly in place. "Directions. Now."

Stuchbery points the way with his stump of an arm. "That way."

A quick glance reveals that Micah's weapon is near full charge.

"You take alpha position," I tell him. "Torel, back him up. Jess, you are behind her. Harth, you are next. Keep Stuchbery *alive.* I will take Omega."

Despite using Kyno Corps terminology, Micah seems to understand. He gives a nod and strikes out in the direction Stuchbery has sent us. Grover stays by his side. They do not move like servant and master. More like a team. Trusted comrades. Seeing them in battle together dredges up mixed feelings. Grover is Kynolari, despite his current condition. I believed him to be diminished and felt similar about humans. And yet, together, they were able to act as one unit, complementing each other and coordinating with an uncanny sense of the other's whereabouts and actions.

As we charge toward a fresh wave of biologics, Micah shows restraint, unleashing controlled bursts of laser light from his fingertips, focusing on targets directly in our path and leaving the rest to scrabble over the smoldering remains.

But the enemy is not attacking all of us. Their focus is on Harth, or rather, the man strapped to his back. If they can kill Stuchbery, they can keep us from escaping and eventually overwhelm us with numbers.

Torel and I keep that from happening. While she cuts down some with brief cracks of electricity, I put rail-shards through their heads, sometimes two or three at a time when they line up for me. It is not really a winning strategy but might buy us enough time to reach where we need to be.

Where that is, I wish I knew. But Stuchbery continues to point the way, this time to a set of double doors that had been nearly invisible. We might never have found them without guidance. "Through there," Stuchbery says. "There's a stairwell. Head down to the bottom. Might be a long way."

"And then?" I ask.

"Through the lobby and out the door. After that…just try to blend in, I guess."

"Blend in?" Micah asks. "Where the hell are we?"

The question is interrupted by the thunderous arrival of a Gobi biologic.

It is nine feet tall, leaning much of its girth on its thick forelimbs.

It pounds the floor twice, as though demanding we stop.

"It's like a giant, hairless gorilla," Jess says.

The Gobi were a large, but peaceful people. Non-expansionist. Gentle.

Like the Kynolari, they did not become warriors until there was no other choice. Fight or die. They died regardless. I take aim with my railgun. I fire a three-round burst, each one of the rail-shards punching through the thick skull in the shape of a triangle, increasing the odds that one of them will strike something vital.

The biologic stumbles to the side but is not disabled. Micah drops it by extending the lasers at the ends of his claws and using them to slice though the beast's thick leg. It topples to the side, spasming.

He is learning quickly. It takes time for Kyno Corps cadets to adjust to using a weapon system. Many, like Chirk, choose to use traditional weapons, especially if their primary function requires the full use of both hands at all times—like a pilot. But Micah is integrating faster than most, allowing his mind's eye to guide the weapon's power.

It could simply be that he is already a seasoned soldier with experience using a variety of Earth weaponry, but I suspect it is something else. Perhaps something unique to him.

Micah kicks through the doors, revealing a stairwell that only goes down. "Let's go!" Torel takes the lead as Micah holds the door open. Jess and Harth follow, heading down the stairs. Grover waits at the top step.

"Good boy," I tell him when I arrive.

Micah and I are both caught off guard by the comment. Then I grumble, "Later."

Micah closes the door and uses his gauntlet to weld the seam. "Won't hold them back forever," he says and then snaps his fingers at Grover and points to the stairs. "Down. Go!"

Grover leaps down the stairs, tail spinning in circles as he follows the others.

"I'll take Omega," Micah says, adopting our terminology, and I do not bother arguing the point.

Our footsteps echo up and down the concrete encased stairwell. Looking over the edge, there appears to be upward of fifty floors.

"We are either descending a very tall tower," Jess says from below, "or taking the express route to hell."

"What is hell?" Torel asks.

"A religious concept. Where bad people go when they die, to be eternally tortured."

"It will be full of the Draun," Harth says. "Perhaps we can go there and torture them ourselves?" He bursts into laughter, but it is cut short when the first impact shakes the door above.

The seal holds, but it will not last for long.

"Double time!" Micah says, taking the stairs two and three at a time, bouncing off the walls as he goes, setting a brutal pace. "Which floor?" he asks Stuchbery.

The stumpy man has a hard time responding as he bounces around on Harth's broad back. "W-w-what?"

"Which floor is the lobby at?" Micah says.

"S-s-second!"

"Keep going," Micah tells me. "And keep Grover safe. I should be right behind you."

"What are you doing?" I ask.

"Making it hard to follow us." His gauntlet flares to life as he holds it to the floors above us.

I am caught in a moment of rare indecision. I am not normally in the business of taking orders or blindly following another plan. Neither is Micah, and he has been—thus far—willing to share the burden. But this is something else. His plan is not without risk. He could very well sacrifice himself to save us.

"I'll be right behind you," he says. "Thanks for caring." He pats my cheek the same way he does Grover's, but with a gleam in his eye. Knows it will bother me. I give him a good-humored growl and then continue the journey downward.

Three flights below, I hear the blast of Micah's gauntlet, once again on full power. It is followed by a thump, a muffled, "Holy shit," and then a laugh, which is then promptly punctuated by a "Fuck me, it worked."

When his footsteps start down the steps above, I lean out over the railing and look up. The top five flights of stairs have been vaporized, as has the ceiling above, revealing a bright blue sky.

Not underground.

Not yet, at least.

The door is struck again, booming from above.

Micah catches up to me, waving for me to increase my pace. The others are four flights below now, making us the first line of defense should the doors be breached, and the fall survived.

Another boom, this time accompanied by the sound of wrenching metal.

I am not sure they are through until a humanoid biologic sails past us, striking a railing, and then a dozen more on its way down, torn farther apart with every impact.

Below, Harth bellows a laugh when it passes him in pieces.

Micah and I pause to look up. A torrent of biologics fills the air, spilling into the stairwell like water. Most slap into the stairs above and are destroyed. Some make it down the center but meet the same fate as the first. The narrow gap chews them up and swallows them down. Non-living meat in a grinder.

But the tunnel will soon fill with biologics and, like the creatures that burrow and dig on any world, they will eventually find a path through. Hopefully, we are at the bottom when that happens, but I have a feeling nothing will be that easy.

My concerns prove to be merited a moment later, when the top half of a biologic falls past me but manages to reach out and take hold of Micah's clothing, yanking him over the railing faster than I can react.

37

I used to be a night person. Back in my younger military days. Drank too much. Flirted too much. Was all kinds of full of myself. Thought I had a right to be, seeing as how I was risking my life more than the average grunt, making it back to base in one piece, and feeling God-damn high on life. So, when I found myself in a bar, surrounded by pale-skinned Korean women with fake tits, giggling at my every word, I didn't question it.

Thought I was in for the night of my life.

Even when they suggested we leave out the back.

Even when it took two of them to hold me upright.

And then, with one swift kick to the crotch, I was undone.

My bravado imploded.

Ego shattered.

The badass operator was brought down by a few princesses in high heels and short skirts. I was too ashamed to fight back. Too drunk, too. They could have robbed me and left, but I'd apparently been rude. Maybe a little handsy. So, they taught me a lesson. One I've never forgotten and would thank them for if I had the chance.

I learned humility that night.

Thought the lesson had stuck, too.

But the moment I was dragged over the railing, by the torso of an unfinished man-thing, the humiliation I feel lets me know that some pride—in my abilities, in the nobility of my part in this quest—has crept back in.

It's eradicated the moment I'm jarred to a stop, upside down, ankle grasped by Harth. I dangle there, looking down at the biologic still clinging to my clothing.

"You are heavier than you look," Harth says, struggling to hold on.

"It's not me," I say, reaching up for the hunting knife sheathed on my belt. "It's the heavy ass robot hanging on to me."

"The robot has no ass to be heavy," he says.

"Not a literal ass!" I shout, swinging the knife down, burying it in the biologic's composite skull. It twitches and goes still, its rigid fist still clinging to me. I peel three of its four fingers away, before the weight tugs it free. The biologic falls away, bouncing off rails and shattering on its way down. A fate I nearly shared.

Free of the extra weight, Harth hauls me up. Jess and Torel help me over the rail and back to my feet.

"Graceful," Jess says, trying to mask her genuine concern.

"Like a cat," I say, and then I hold my hands out toward our Kynolari friends. "Sorry."

"What is a cat?" Torel asks.

"An animal," I say. "Dogs tend to not like them."

"Why would dogs not like a specific animal?" Harth asks.

"Because," I say. "They're assholes." I point at Harth. "Not actual assholes. You'll...you'll know if you meet one."

Footsteps announce the arrival of Praxion and Grover. They look like siblings that have been separated by time and space. One adopting a simple life, the other becoming a galactic warrior. It's not too far from reality.

"Keep moving," Praxion orders as Grover leans himself against my legs.

"Don't need to ask me twice," Jess says, and takes the lead. With no enemies below us, no one complains. And she sets a blistering steady pace of someone who runs up and down mountains in the morning—she does—and knows her limits.

The sounds of our pursuers fade a little with each flight we descend. Body parts occasionally topple past, pulled faster by gravity than we could ever hope to run. But the stairwell above is still clogged by a broken mass of never-living, faceless corpses.

"There is a story on our world," Torel says, as we wind our way downward. "A Kynolari is stuck inside a downward spiraling tunnel that appears to have no end. Only able to see a few feet in front and behind, he is never quite sure if he's making progress or walking in place."

"Sounds horrible," Jess says.

"Kept me up at night," Torel says, "imagining what it would have been like."

"How did he get out?" I ask.

"Never does," Torel says.

"Okay," Jess says. "Now it's depressing. Is there a meaning, or do Kynolari parents like keeping their kids awake at night?"

"It's an illustration of always pressing forward in life," Harth says, "of not stopping to look anywhere but forward."

"I thought it was a lesson in patience," Praxion says. "Facing the Draun...it felt like this sometimes. Always pressing forward. Never making progress. Until one day, the tunnel opens, and you find a way out."

"Except," Torel says. "We're right back in the tunnel again. My point was that I finally know how the guy felt, all that time, round and round.

"What about you?" Torel asks me. "Are there any human stories that might provide distraction during this time of perpetual downward motion?"

She's trying to boost morale, keeping us from focusing too much on the fight to come, on the long road ahead, or the hopelessness of our situation. Her role as a medic must include psychological well-being, too, which is kind of impressive.

"A story," I say, leaping down four steps, pushing off the wall on the next landing and taking the next flight down in two steps. "I'll tell you about Grover's namesake."

I regale them with a retelling of my favorite childhood Grover story—the Sesame Street Muppet, not the dog. I imitate his voice and do my best to project his abject fear and discomfort.

When I'm done, Torel gasps. "*He* was the monster at the end of the book?"

"A strong moral," Harth says, nodding his head. "To not become that which you fear the most."

I'm not sure that's the story's meaning, but I don't argue the point. Fiction allows people to come to their own conclusions about morality lessons, character motivations, and whether the author has a bias he's trying to shove down people's throats. If someone takes away anything positive from a story, that's great. Grover would be happy.

"He was the monster the whole time," Torel says. "He didn't become it. He was it." She takes a flight of stairs with a single leap. "A profound revelation."

Praxion grunts in agreement. "We are all monsters. At one time or another. Denying it is ignorance."

"You said this book is for children?" Torel asks.

Jess laughs and says to me, "Wonder what they'll think of 'Lord of the Flies?'"

"We're going to have to ease them into that," I say. "Maybe 'The Giving Tree' first."

Jess's voice rumbles as she sprints down the next flight. "Oh God, no. They'll want to kill themselves."

"Is trauma a normal part of human childhood?" Torel asks.

"Pretty much," I say, leaping four steps. "But it never really stops. Case in point." I motion to the staircase we're charging down.

"Perhaps humanity is simply more aware of their hardships," Praxion guesses.

"Or," Harth says. "Perhaps they're simply whiny martyrs."

"I think Harth is right," Jess says, impacting a wall. "Oof!"

"Are you all serious right now?" Stuchbery shouts from Harth's back. "Is this a book group? Is Oprah hiding at the bottom of the stairs?! And boo-hoo, life is sooo rough!"

The pitch of his voice becomes shrill as he screams, "I don't have any hands or feet!"

"Do we still need him?" Harth asks, motioning to Stuchbery. "I would like to drop him now."

He's not deadpanning. If Praxion gives the word, Stuchbery is going to take the express route to the ground floor.

"No, no, no!" Stuchbery says, waving his pitiful stumps around. "I'll shut up!" He attempts to make a lips-zipped gesture, but without hands and fingers it looks more like a throat-slitting threat. Despite being from different worlds, the Kynolari have little trouble understanding gestures.

"Dump him," Praxion says.

Harth heaves Stuchbery off his back and over the rail. I catch him before he falls out of sight and drop him—not very gently—onto the stairwell behind us. Then I look up, into the eyes of each Kynolari. "I understand how things can get during war, but we do not kill unarmed men."

"Was that an attempt at humor?" Harth asks.

"Ha. Ha." Stuchbery says. "Unarmed. Very funny." He raises his stumped arms and waves them around. "Still got my arms, mutt!"

Harth steps toward him, fire in his eyes. "What did you call me?"

I step between them. "We do not have time for this!"

Grover backs me up with a loud bark. When I glance down at him, I realize that he's not actually taking my side. He's warning me, hackles raised, eyes up. I follow his gaze and find a large, many tentacled biologic squirming its way down the stairwell, the way a squid might fit itself through a tight hole...and it's doing so faster than we can.

"Go!" I shout. "Go, go, go!"

We break into a downward run, pursued by something out of the 'Inferno,' if it had been written by Lovecraft. I glance down. Thirty floors to go. I glance up. The biologic is not running so much as controlling its fall. If we reach the bottom, it's going to be with seconds to spare.

38

CHIRK

"Okay," I say, lying in a wooded area just outside the Manchester airport, "that's a problem."

"Yeah, dude. I've never seen so many cops in one place before." Sean lies beside me, following my every command. I'm starting to understand the appeal of having a human around.

"I thought they were pigs," I say.

"Well, yeah. Cops. Pigs. 5-O. The heat. The fuzz. And if you don't want a ticket, police officers."

"Do humans have that many words for everything?" I ask.

"Naw, just things that are important...or stand out for some reason. Like weed."

"That stuff we smoked."

He whisper-chuckles. "Yeah, man. Something like twelve hundred words. And that's not counting the twenty-three hundred strains. I mean, if you count all that, it might be the most important thing in the whole world." His eyes widen. "Whoooa. I never thought about this before. You're expanding my mind."

"If only it helped solve this problem."

There are dozens of flashing vehicles.

Cars, trucks, and some kind of armored hulking things that say 'SWAT' on the side. At least a hundred cops, fanning out through the airport. But they're not really doing anything. Just securing the area. Turning people away. Controlling the scene.

"Do cops perform other duties beyond site security?"

"Some of them, yeah. Detectives. They're the guys who figure shit out."

"See any of them?" I ask.

"They don't wear the blue uniforms or body armor," he says, "so they shouldn't be hard to find."

We spend a few silent seconds scouring the area. Sean is using his bare eyeballs, but my ocular implant allows me to zoom in a hundred times with a lossless resolution. Handy when flying in space, trying to avoid asteroids approaching at thirty thousand miles per hour.

I don't see anything like what he's talking about.

Which means they're not trying to figure out what happened, they're just providing security.

"Coming up dry," Sean says.

While his word choice makes no sense, I understand what he's trying to communicate. "Same. These guys are here to keep us out." I take a deep breath through my nose, sucking the air in with several quick sniffs, saturating my olfactory receptors with odor molecules flitting through the air. The scent is faint at this distance, but even a hint is enough to confirm what I already suspected. "They're not cops."

"Huh? How? They've got uniforms. And the cars. And—"

"They're not even human," I say.

He gasps. "Shapeshifters?"

"What? Shapeshifters? How..." I shake my head. "You know what? Never mind. They're biologics. Drones."

"Like robots?"

"Like robots. Yeah, but they can look and act like whatever species the Draun mold them to."

"Like that Helion thing?" he asks.

"Yeah, but not really the one we faced. Pretty sure there was something alive beneath that shell."

"So much to keep track of, dude."

I pet the top of his head. "Don't worry, big man, I'll do the thinking for both of us."

He smiles and nods.

"So," he says, immediately trying to do the thinking, "we sneak past them, find the moose, and lay hands on it like we're in church."

"Lost me at 'lay hands,'" I say.

"Touch it. Sorry. Grew up Pentecostal."

"Still not making sense, but yeah, that's the basic plan. We just need to map out the path of least resistance."

"Okay, but...if all those guys are here to stop us from getting there, that means they know, or at least think, that we'd come here, yeah? If you knew, or at least thought, that your enemy—who is, let's be honest, a normal dude and a badass Chihuahua—would be coming your way, would you just stand around waiting or would you—"

"Shit," I say, spinning around, scanning the woods behind us. Sean's right. They'll be looking for us. Monitoring the surrounding area.

I hear a crunch of leaves. Catch a whiff of something human. It's nearly upon us. I dive behind a tree, leaving Sean on his own.

"Don't move, asshat!"

Sean lets out a high-pitched shriek, springs into the air, spins around, and lands on his back. When he sees the cop standing over him, gun aimed, Sean raises his hands and says, "Don't shoot!"

A warrior, he is not. But the cop is both focused solely on Sean, and human. They've got the biologics in the airport and the humans—who don't know better—scouring the area.

"Whatchu doing out here?" the cop asks.

"J-just trying to see what's going on." Sean is nervous, but a decent liar. "It's crazy man. All those officers down there. Is it a terrorist attack or something?"

"Or something," the man says, frowning. "Truth is, I have no idea. But they don't want anyone watching, and that means you."

"Yes. Absolutely." Sean looks for me and is confused by my sudden disappearance. "I'll go. I just need to—"

I sigh and then do my part for the greater good. Gear and clothing removed, I strut out from behind the tree on all fours.

The cop doesn't even aim his gun at me. Just smiles and asks, "He yours?"

"Yeah."

The cop holsters his weapon. "What's his name?"

"Chirk."

"Weird name," the cop says, and I nearly blow my cover for a chance to bite his nuts, which is an urge so disgusting I won't be sharing it with anyone. I don't bite. It's not in my wheelhouse. But right now, in this moment, I would take joy in sinking my teeth into his flesh.

The fuck is wrong with me?

The cop pats his knees and crouches. "C'mere, Chirk. Here, boy."

As I walk closer, he double takes on my hands...which are definitely hands and not paws.

"He like a special needs dog?" the cop asks. "Bet you picked him up at a shelter, yeah? Good on you, I guess. Me, I like the pure breeds, and by pure breed I mean not inbred. Kill shelters don't really sit well with me. They're still dogs. But man, some of these guys... I'm sorry, but I couldn't look at his fucked-up legs all the time." He laughs at me.

I stop and look up at Sean.

We need to work on our man-Kyno synchronicity. Here I am, taking a full load of insults, right to the face, and Sean has yet to figure out that I'm providing him with the mother of all distractions.

"Not the nicest dog, is he?" the cop says, standing back up. "Can't expect much more from a Chihuahua, though. Rats of the dog world."

"He's not a rat, dude," Sean says, just starting to get offended.

The cop laughs. "Right. Look at him. Surprised he's not shaking." He scoffs. Waves his hand at me. "This might be the single most retarded dog I've seen in my life. No offense, but man..." He digs into his pocket and pulls out a phone. "...I just need to get a pic to show my wife, or she won't believe me."

"No pictures," I say, patience evaporated like the mist of a Bolvarian Swamp Beast's anal secretions in the hot Tomelari sun.

The cop's head snaps back. "Huh?"

Then a large branch shatters over the back of his head, toppling the man to the ground.

Sean stands above him, chest all puffed out and proud of himself. "No one calls my dog 'retarded.'"

"He said a lot of horrible stuff before that, you know," I complain, pulling my clothing back on.

"Yeah, but *retarded?*"

"He called me inbred. Inbred! Me!"

"Is it possible," Sean says, "that there are things that offend your people that would not offend my people, and vice versa?"

I stare at him for a moment. "I like you better stupid."

He rolls his eyes. "Now what?"

"I'm thinking subterfuge."

"I don't think there's any water around here."

"Okay, back to stupid." I sigh. "You know what. Just do what I say, okay? Step one, put on the cop's clothing."

"Ohh, I get it. It's kind of a trope, though."

"A what?"

"Trope. Like overdone. Cliché. In TV. Movies. Happens all the time."

"Well, good thing this isn't one of those things," I say. "Now, change your clothes before Captain Sphincter Hole wakes up. It's almost time to bring the thunder, and by that, I mean 'take a shit.' I'll be behind this tree."

39

PRAXION

Being Kynolari means that, in times of great intensity, I am capable of sensing and comprehending every detail around me while simultaneously planning for what is to come. A moment in real time crawls as the neurons in my mind fire. It feels like time has slowed. While everyone experiences time at a steady pace, for me it moves through sludge.

And in that frozen moment, I feel something strange.

Pride.

And not in my people. That is normal. They are the best of the best, and I am always proud to serve with them. What is new is that I feel proud of the humans among us...and the dog. Grover is...different. Not the ideal Kynolari strive toward, but he is far from a simple creature. Dogs on Earth are loyal, brave, and compassionate, unlike any lifeforms I have ever come across.

Left alone on this world for so long, the Lost Tribe adapted to life by becoming an indispensable part of the alpha species' lives. They work, play, and live side by side. And, in turn, that has changed humanity. They might be an unrefined culture with a tribal governmental system prone to infighting, but everything I have seen of Micah reflects the highest moral compass of any Kynolari. And his fighting prowess matches that of those in the Kyno Corps.

These things have felt like a mystery to me, until this moment, watching him catch Torel as she loses balance, making sure he is between Jess and the railing, putting himself in greater danger so that she is protected, and having absolute trust in Grover, who returns that trust without question.

It is a unique discovery—a species that is so different from the Kynolari at first glance, but so much like us upon closer inspection. They have learned a lot from each other, but how deep does it run?

Question for another time, I think, a half second into my slow-motion rumination. In the next fraction of a moment, I consider the writhing beast descending from above.

It is a biologic Platamot. Something I have never faced before. The Platamots, despite being a peaceful, advanced species, were large and powerful after millennia of fighting for survival in the vast oceans of their world. I fought alongside the last of their warriors before all were wiped out.

Seeing this unfinished version, plummeting toward us with vicious intent, is heartbreaking, but also nerve-wracking. It is capable of taking on large numbers of adversaries and, in this form, it will not react to pain.

Both Torel's and Harth's weapon systems are recharging. That leaves Micah and me...and if the biologic is built like a true Platamot, my Sonizer will have little effect.

But if we do not fight, none of us will survive.

The moment passes, and I shout. "Jess, guide Harth and Torel to a vehicle. Micah, you are with me. Aim for the limbs."

He gives me a glance and a nod. Understands the stakes. Fight and win or fight and die. It is the same in every battle.

"Grover," Micah says. "Go with Jess."

Grover barks. He doesn't like it.

Micah snaps his fingers and points to the door at the bottom of the stairwell that Jess has just yanked open. "Go!"

Grover whines, but obeys, running down the rest of the stairs and out the door.

"What's the plan?" Micah shouts. "Blast another hole straight up and through the roof?"

To be honest, it was the first thing I considered as well. But Platamots are agile and flexible. If he misses the drone's core, it would just keep coming and he'd have no power to sustain his weapon.

"I will hit it with a sonic blast," I say. "It will not do any damage, but it will repulse the creature's descent for a moment, allowing you to—"

"Make sushi out of its limbs."

"Does that involve cutting them off?" I ask.

He nods. "Into little pieces." He looks upward. "Incoming!"

The Platamot folds its many arms inward, dropping the last few flights. When it reaches the bottom, the creature's arms will unfurl and tear us apart.

"Now!" I shout, aiming the Sonizer up before unleashing a full power blast. Its intensity is increased thanks to the stairwell's concrete walls. The Platamot strikes the invisible force like it is hitting the floor. If the drone had bones, they would have broken. Instead, its limbs are forced out to the side. They writhe in the air and slap against the walls.

Lasers stretch out from Micah's fingertips.

He is unpracticed and has trouble aiming with much precision. But then he adjusts his lack of experience to a new tactic.

He says, "Coochie coochie coo," and just wiggles his fingers all over the place like he is tickling the beast. He cuts holes in the walls, through the steps, the railings, and the biologic, carving the faux creature into little bits, far smaller than was required.

"Edward Scissorhands, eat your heart out," he says with a grin.

Bits and pieces of synthetic flesh fall around us, slapping against the floor.

"You see?" he says. "Sushi! A little rice and soy sauce and we'd be—"

The defeated Platamot bursts apart, but it has nothing to do with Micah's laser tickling. A second creature has survived the descent and is removing the last obstacle in its way.

The long, rigid snout of a Tyrne slides through the fleshy remains now splattering down the stairwell, propelled only by gravity.

"Fall back," I say. "Through the door!"

The Tyrne lets out a shrill, warbling battle cry and tears the Platamot biologic's corpse in half, dropping down the stairs after us. Its long limbs stretch out, catching railings and propelling it faster than it could fall. They're normally majestic things, but this incomplete biologic is shrouded in loose black skin, flapping around in the breeze. The flesh of its unfinished face fills with air, inflating it and providing a clear view of the machine beneath.

Micah exits first but waits at the door. He slams it shut behind me and locks it before turning around to see what has stopped me in my tracks. We are in a four-story lobby for some kind of modern business. There are towering glass windows revealing a busy metropolis on the other side of the doors.

"Where are we?" I ask, noticing that none of the people in this place look at all like Micah or Jess. Humanity is a very diverse species.

He jogs toward the nearest person, waving his hand. "Hey! Can you tell me where we are?"

The man's response is unintelligible to both of us. Whatever part of the world we are in, it is not one translation services deemed necessary for our mission, meaning we are a long distance from where we began. Micah turns around, frowning. "Japan." He motions toward the windows and a vast, colorful, and busy city beyond. "Tokyo would be my guess."

"Is it far?"

"From New Hampshire?" he says. "Other side of the planet. From Denver… still pretty damn far. The good news is that this is Tokyo, you're not going to stand out as much as you think."

"Why is that?"

The suited man sees me for the first time and his eyes light up. He shouts in Japanese, summoning several more people who had been at the glass, looking down the street, probably at the others after they ran through.

"What do we do?" I ask.

Several of the men take out devices, turn around, smile, and capture images of themselves with me behind them.

The door behind us begins to shake. The Tyrne are not as powerful as the Platamots, but they have keen intellects. It will be through that door once it understands the obstacle. Likely a matter of seconds.

"Just smile and do this," Micah says. "Extend your index and middle fingers and keep speed walking like Tom Bosworth."

"Who?"

"Fast walker. Never mind." He waves his hand at me and then turns to the men capturing images. "Arigato." He bows his head a little, moving through the lobby. "Arigato."

The men respond with big smiles, bows of their own, and "Domo arigato."

Before we have reached the exit, still with a collection of onlookers, the stairwell door booms and shakes. The men with us gasp and turn around.

"You all need to run," Micah says to them. When they do not respond he tries to shoo them away with his hands. "Sumimasen! Sumimasen! Go, go, go!"

Before our admirers understand exactly what Micah is attempting to communicate, the stairwell door bursts open. It is not the Tyrne that emerges first. It is the gelatinous remains of the Platamot. Its long tentacles slide out over a puddle of slime.

The men let out a collective, "Ohhh!" and step back.

One of them shouts a question at us, but we do not understand.

"Sumimasen," Micah says one last time, then something about the tone of his voice gets the message across. What is to come will not be pleasant.

"Wish I could say more to them," he says, "but the only Japanese I know I learned from James May in Japan, and he didn't know much, either."

A wet gurgle rolls out of the stairwell.

The men skitter farther back, holding onto each other, terrified, but too interested to run.

"Here it comes," I say, readying my railgun.

"Anything I should know?"

"They are faster, more agile, and stronger than you. I have never known one to be beaten in hand-to-hand combat."

"Anything good?" he asks.

"No."

The Tyrne steps into the lobby, head low, teeth bared, the loose black skin on its face now hanging like jowls. It walks on two short hind limbs and on the elbows of its forelimbs, its long forearm lifted high, ready to strike out with its fearsome dagger-tipped long fingers. A true Tyrne is a majestic thing, covered in bioluminescent plates that rattle and change color based on their mood. They are very bad at keeping secrets, fearsome hunters, and, at one time, they were close Kynolari allies. Now, like the others, all that remains of them is this mockery.

"You shoot the shit out of it," Micah says. "I'll flank right. Hit it from the side."

I give a nod, take aim, and begin firing. I am careful with my aim, not because I have limited ammunition, but because this world's structures are not strong enough to stop a rail-shard in its tracks. The projectile will likely punch through several buildings before coming to a stop. They are not large enough to do any real damage to the structures, but this city seems congested. It is possible that the shards will strike innocents as they pass through. I will not be using Micah's 'spray and pray' tactic here.

The rail-shards punch through the drone's body, guaranteeing its attention is fully on me. But I am unable to strike the creature's head, which is in constant motion. All I have really accomplished is sealing my own fate if Micah fails.

He runs parallel to the Tyrne, extending his claws and filling them with laser energy.

Our audience sees this and lets out another collective, "Oooooh!"

Micah cuts in, approaching the Tyrne from the side, on a collision course.

But he is too late.

Not going to make it.

His eyes widen when he sees it, but the look is quickly replaced by determination. He turns his hand back, pointing it to the floor, and unleashes a powerful blast of laser light that burrows a hole in the floor and launches him forward. I have seen Kynolari use the technique on the battlefield, using an energy burst to quickly scale a wall, but none of them could match Micah's total lack of grace.

"Whoa!" he shouts, sprawling through air, but always on task, never losing his focus. As he passes over the Tyrne's back, just before it reaches me, he drags those laser claws over its spine, severing it in four places.

The biologic collapses and slides to a stop. It attempts to drag itself closer and gnaw on my feet, but I step back, aim my railgun and fire three shots into its head.

Lying upside down against the far wall, Micah raises a fist, gives a thumbs up and says, "Yes!"

I flinch when the men watching erupt into cheering, laughing, and clapping quickly. No idea what they are saying, but they appear to be fans. Micah picks himself up and hobbles over to me. "You okay?"

"Fine," I say. "You?"

"Peachy keen."

I sigh. "Your language is confusing."

"It's slang," I say. "Means I'm fine. But we can both tell Jess I'm pretty roughed up and maybe I'll get a sympathy bang when all this is over."

"A...what?"

He smiles. "A sympathy...mating."

"Ahh," I say. "Yes. That is pleasant."

Behind us, beyond the lobby, out in the road, a large black and white vehicle screeches to a stop. Torel leans out the window, waving and shouting something I cannot hear. I understand the message, nonetheless. "Time to go."

40

"Is…is that a panda bus?"

"I do not know what a panda is," Praxion says.

I feel like I'm hallucinating, which pretty much confirms we're in Tokyo. It's a half-sized bus with large windows. Some kind of tour bus. The side has a black and white pattern and a slab of advertising. But it's the front of the vehicle that steals the show. It's molded in the shape of a bear, with a mouth, black nose, and two bulbous eyes. And while I recognize that it's supposed to be a panda, it doesn't really look like one. It's more like a melted anime version of a panda.

We step outside and head toward our awaiting freakshow chariot. That's when it winks at me and sends a chill up my spine, unleashing all the tension I've been holding since encountering the horrors inside the biologic factory. My shoulders shimmy like my name is Bunnie and I'm shaking my tits on stage at the Rose Petal Pavilion.

I'm not sure what will happen now that we've escaped, but it's also not my problem. This is not where we need to be to stop the Draun or rescue Praxion's friends. Best guess is that they'll cover it up. Those guys in the lobby are in real danger because they were witnesses.

But witnesses of what? I'm pretty sure they thought it was a show of some kind. A marketing stunt. Talking space dogs and tentacle monsters are par for the course in this part of the world. Maybe they'll be okay.

The door closes behind me as I climb into the bus. I'm surprised to find a wide-eyed driver behind the wheel, dressed in a spiffy blue uniform. There's a stuffed panda seated beside him, panda paraphernalia all around, and the seats are topped with multi-colored panda ears.

"Strange," Praxion says.

"For both of us," I say.

"You sit down now!" the driver shouts in passable English.

Praxion takes a seat near the front of the bus. I sit opposite him, next to Jess, who seems to be the driver's point of contact.

"Go," she says. "Drive!"

The bus wheels screech as we pull away from the curb and into traffic, eliciting more than a few honking horns and shouted Japanese curses.

"Where you want to go?" the driver shouts.

I lean forward and place my hand on his shoulder. He flinches. Unlike the men in the lobby, he sees the talking Kynolari for what they are—a mind numbing impossibility, even in the land of Godzilla, Hentai, and the Kanamara Penis Festival. "Hey. Bud. You're okay. They're...they're good dogs."

He looks me in the eyes for a moment and then glances back into the bus where Praxion, Harth, and Torel sit, looking out through the windows, ready to shoot down anything that comes our way.

That's when I see the true object of his concern. Stuchbery. He's unconscious on the floor, still missing his hands and feet.

"What happened to him?" I ask Jess.

"Harth turned around too fast. Hit his head on one of the metal support beams." She smiles through her frayed nerves. "Claims it was an accident."

The driver looks at me again. Leans in real close. "They are talking dogs?"

I nod. "Yeah."

"Where ah they from?"

"Another planet," I say, seeing no reason to not be honest with the man. "Also, eyes on the road."

"Eh!" He looks forward and brakes before running into another, much larger, tour bus. He sighs and looks back one more time. "Shinjirarenai..." He remembers I can't understand him and whispers. "I can't believe it."

"I hear you, man. It's..." I gesture like my head is exploding.

He laughs nervously and nods. "Hai. Hai."

"Here's the thing..." I look at his name badge. "Roger? Really?"

"Haruto," he says.

"Haruto. This is the situation. These guys... The dog-people, they're here to help us. To help all of humanity from an evil alien species that wants..." *What?* I don't really know what they want, but I trust the Kynolari. "...to conquer the world."

"Masaka..." he says, sounding amazed.

"And we need to help them," I say. "We need *you* to help them."

This time, when his eyes widen, there's a little gleam. He takes a deep breath. Puffs out his chest a little. "What do you need?"

"What's the nearest airport?" I ask.

"Haneda," he says.

"Any animal sculptures there?"

He nods. "Hai. Hai. Mooon." He says it like he's a cow, drawing out the 'moo.'

"And that is?"

"Majestic blue bull. It is in the North Wing. Very beautiful."

Sounds about right, I think. "Take us there."

He gives a nod.

"Hey," I say, offering my hand. "I'm Micah."

He shakes my hand and gives a little bow. "Pleased to meet you."

I smile. "It's okay if you're not. We did hijack your bus."

He waves his hand at me. "No choice. Saving the world, right?"

"You're a good man, Haruto." I pat his shoulder and take a seat next to Jess. "Hell'uva first date, yeah?"

"If it turns out this is an elaborately staged ruse you do for all the ladies, I'm going to be pissed."

I smile. "Only for the ones with wife potential."

The fuck *did I just say?*

"Oh, wow. *Wife,* huh? In the sandwich making you a kitchen?"

"Huh?" I say, looking at her.

She's flustered. "You know what I meant."

We look into each other's eyes for a moment. There's a real connection there. Something I'm not sure I've felt before, which is ridiculous because this is our first date. I knew her before, but not like this. I've seen combat. Fought against alien-dogs, and giant robots, and unfinished fleshy drones. But none of that made me as nervous as I am right now.

Jess leans forward and kisses me. Gently. All my anxiety melts away. I feel serene. Known. Hopeful.

"Human mating rituals confound me," Harth says, shaking his head.

All three Kynolari are watching us. Our affection is peculiar to them. As is our adoration for Grover, who's sitting beside me, watching, tongue hanging out, panting. When we make eye contact, he wags his tail and places his head in my lap.

"I love you, too, buddy," I say, rubbing his head and realizing I've just unleashed another word bomb. *Love you, too.* There's two ways to hear that. I'm returning Grover's love. Or, I love Grover in addition to Jess.

Can you love someone that fast? Is love at first sight real?

"Very sweet!" Haruto gives a thumbs up, smiling and nodding. "Very nice! Love is what we fight for most, yes?"

I wish I was a hermit crab with a shell to crawl into. I'd dig myself back into that Fibonacci spiral and never come back out.

Grover breaks through my tension by climbing up on the bench seat between Jess and me. We both throw ourselves into petting him, ducking, and weaving away from the sudden blossoming of romantic energy.

Not the time, I tell myself. *Not the place. And slow your fucking roll, man.*

Grover licks my cheek and I lean into him.

"Micah." Praxion, elbows on knees, leans across the aisle between us. "What is happening? What is...this?" He motions to me, Grover, and Jess.

"People don't show affection on Kynolari?" I ask.

"Not like humans do," he says. "And not...like dogs."

"Maybe it's something Kynolari used to do, but forgot?" Jess asks.

Praxion furrows his brow and, I have to say, he's adorable, and it takes all my self-control not to scratch the top of his head.

"And now he looks at you with affection!" Harth says.

"Maybe mating rituals on this world are interspecies?" Torel says. "Like the Flargarian reproduction bacchanalia?"

"Do not speak of that unholy festival of debauchery," Harth says.

"That does not happen on Earth," I say.

"He lies," Harth says. "I heard his heartbeat increase."

"We all did," Praxion says.

"Okay," I say, raising my hands, "listen. I'm sure not all Kynolari are perfect, right? You have criminals? Aberrant behavior? There are bad dogs on Earth, too." They look at me like I'm wrong. "The point is, yes, there are some...disturbed people who might partake in...uh...interspecies activities, but we—the mentally stable—look at their behavior the same way you would."

Harth bursts out laughing. "He's so uncomfortable."

Praxion smiles. "Kynolari are a flawed species as well."

Torel slaps Harth's shoulder and then says to Praxion, "You two are horrible."

The Kynolari might not express affection like people do, but they clearly care for one another, and enjoy each other's presence. Perhaps there are some Kynolari that behave more human-like. Praxion, Torel, and Harth are the alien equivalent of the toughest Navy Seals, and those guys can be downright cold. I haven't sensed that kind of hardness from the Kynolari. They're warriors, but... deep down, they're still dogs. Like it or not, they have more in common with Grover than they'd want to admit. They're just burying it.

"Ahh, scuse me, Micah and puppy people," Haruto says, waving his hand. "I very much wish for you to continue your expressions of love and affection. Very adorable. Hai. But, ahh, I think a problem is emerging."

"I believe the human needs to defecate," Harth says. "Can you hold it until we reach our destination?"

"Harth," Torel says. "He doesn't need to defecate." She points out the back window. "Look."

We all look.

Far behind us, the façade of the building from which we escaped explodes into the road, raining debris on people and vehicles. And out of the billowing dust steps a familiar sight. "Helion," I say, but this one is different from the others. It's larger, and it has a long, whipping tail with a fleshy covering. It turns in our direction, unleashes a mechanical roar, and charges.

"Holy shit!" Haruto shouts, stepping on the gas, swerving around a car, and banging a right. "What I do? What I do?!"

I lean up close to Haruto. "Airport. We have to make it. Do not stop. Not for anything."

A moment later, he slams on the brakes, sending me crashing into the dash.

41

CHIRK

"We're gonna die. We're gonna die. Holy shit, we're gonna die."

"We are if you don't stop saying that," I grumble, standing on all fours, to-tally nude—*again*—waiting for the elevator doors to open.

"I'm wearing a police uniform, strolling into an airport *full* of police."

"They're not police," I remind him.

"Even worse," Sean says. "Alien drones."

"Biologics."

"Whatever. Same difference."

"That makes no sense."

"None of this makes any sense!" he says.

"Dude," I say, "you need to calm down. The moment these doors open, you are a police officer and I...what am I?"

"My canine unit...dog. Man, I don't know what you're called. I'm not a cop."

"You are a cop," I tell him. "For the next ten-ish minutes, you are a blue-light-flashing pig." I stand upright, grab the bottom of his new uniform's shirt, and tug his attention down to me.

"You hear me, Sean?"

I give him a little snarl for effect.

"Yeah, man. Yeah. I just...I was never good at trick-or-treating."

I release him. "What?"

"Trick-or-treating. It's part of Halloween, a holiday where people dress up in costumes and walk around to other people's houses saying, 'Trick or treat,' and get candy. If they don't have candy, you're supposed to pull a prank on them or something. I don't know. I've never done it."

I pinch the top of my nose. "This backward planet... And you were bad at this how?"

"I'm...not a great liar," he says. "First of all, you have to pretend to be some-thing you're not, which is kind of a lie, but then 'Trick or treat?' Woof. It's like a bluff, right? Like telling someone, 'I'm going to fuck you up,' when you know you can't. And trick or treating is like a promise to TP or egg someone's house—if they don't give you anything. I have a guilty conscience, man."

"I've seen you routinely break your society's laws," I say.

"Well, yeah, that's different. That's the government. The man. The law. I don't respect them."

"I got news for you buddy. If the Draun are on Earth, and have been here for a while, they *are* your government...or will be soon."

"Oh... Shit..."

The elevator dings and the doors slide open to reveal two straight-faced biologics in full human skins, pretending to be law enforcement.

Sean flinches and says, "Trick or treat!"

The biologics frown and glance at each other. While they're not fully conscious beings, they are capable of independent thought and do confer with each other. That moment of silent connection between the two of them gives me time to leap up behind Sean and pluck the mini-railguns from his pants pockets. I land on the floor sideways and put a round in each of their foreheads.

They crumple at Sean's feet.

"Real slick," I say, looking up.

"I almost threw up on them," he says, bending down and taking hold of one man's wrists. He drags him into the elevator without needing to be told. He's got promise, but it's going to be a very long uphill battle to turn him into anything resembling an operator.

Sean releases the drone's arms. "They feel so real."

"And these are the simpletons," I say. "The grunts. Others—the ones that infiltrate governments and militaries... They're smarter. Kynolari can sniff them out, but most species can't tell the difference."

We drag the second biologic into the elevator and let the doors close.

"Listen," I say. "Just glance and nod. No need to engage. Biologics don't make chit-chat."

He nods. "Got it. But...can't they tell I'm not a biologic?"

"Only if you give them a reason to attempt a direct connection," I tell him. "So. Don't."

"Okay," he says, rolling his shoulders. "I got this. I got this..." He takes several deep breaths and gives me a nod. "Let's go." He takes a step and stumbles. Steadies himself against a wall. "I'm okay. Just took too many deep breaths. Made me lightheaded." He stands up straight. "Okay. I'm good."

We're gonna die, I think, but I keep it to myself. Then I slip the mini-railguns into his pockets and strut my buck-ass naked stuff beside him like an obedient Earth-dog.

At the end of the long hallway, we descend a staircase toward the airport's main terminal. At the bottom of the steps are two dozen biologics, just mulling around, pretending to make conversation.

I glance up at Sean. He's wide-eyed but keeping his face even and unwrinkled. Passable for a short time. I walk next to him, doing my best impersonation of an obedient Earth dog.

Then, all at once, all the biologics turn and wave, flashing phony smiles. On its own, that's creepy enough, but they do it in unison.

Sean stops in his tracks.

I think he's blowing our cover already, but he's waving back in time with them, a big grin on his face.

After that momentary greeting, the biologics return to their fake conversations. Sean moves between them, and I skitter along beside him.

The moose is easy to spot, even though I've never seen one before. Sean's description was spot on. I go rigid and stare at the large metal animal, straightening my tail the way Sean said a dog might indicate a direction. When he starts to the moose, I follow him until we're standing in front of it.

"What now?" he whispers.

"Not sure," I say. "I need to sniff around." I hop up onto the sculpture's base, which is decorated with faux plants. I can smell Praxion, Torel, and Harth. They were all here. There're also distinct scents of humans. Three of them. And another that has traces of Kynolari. An Earth dog. They were all here, and—

"What are you doing?"

Sean and I spin around to find a biologic in full cop garb, hands on his hips, legs spread a little too wide to look natural.

"Inspecting the scene," Sean says.

"It has already been inspected."

"I have been instructed to test out this new canine unit," Sean says. "Ironic, isn't it? A Kynolari serving our needs."

The biologic nods. "Indeed." But he's not convinced. "I should have been informed. I will need to scan your—"

"You are not interested in what we uncovered?" Sean asks.

The pretend officer cocks his head to the side. "It is unlikely that you have discovered something we do not already know. The Kynolari and humans used this Leap Node, as we intended, and fell into our trap. Right now, they are most likely just pieces of human flesh on a cold and unforgiving floor."

"Oh," Sean says, a little shaken. "That *is* wonderful, but...come. See." He walks around the moose to the far side, where the other biologics can't see us.

He points at the moose's limb, and I back him up, striking the same pointer pose, straight at the leg.

"You have to look closely," Sean says. "I believe a message was left behind."

"A message?" The biologic asks, leaning in close.

As he bends down, Sean is revealed behind him, holding one of my mini-railguns, his pinky finger on the trigger. He aims at the back of the drone's head, closes his eyes, and turns away his face. For good measure, he puts his free hand over his eyes.

"I do not see a message," the bio-pig says, "prepare for—kck."

Sean catches the body before it hits the floor. He lowers it down, easy, just out of sight. Job done, Sean bends over. "I'm gonna hurl. What do we do?"

"We're the calvary, remember?" I say and place my hand on his head. "We're going to kick some ass." I place my free hand on the metal moose, activating the disguised Leap Node.

In a flash of black, we're transported to the same location as the others.

Sean announces our arrival with a loud retch and a spatter of vomit. I clamp my hand over his mouth and instantly regret it. Instead of launching forward, his puke deflects off my hand and sprays in every direction, a fountain of partially digested questionable food choices.

And for some God-forsaken reason I can't—from the bottom of my being—explain, the smell of it makes me hungry.

I shake off my hand, smearing what's left on Sean's pants. Then I pull the mini-railguns from his pockets and survey the area. We're alone. Smells like a biologic factory. I've been to one before. A short visit before blowing it sky-high. But it's not the kind of smell you forget.

I move onto other scents. Praxion. The others. Harth fired his Incinerator here. Torel, her Lancer. There are corpses in the dark, but I don't smell blood. They escaped.

"This way," I say, following the scent through the darkness.

"Can't see," Sean says.

I sigh and snap my finger. "My gear."

He hands me my body armor and I quickly dress. Then, I grimace and say, "Pick me up. I'll guide you."

"Seriously?" Sean says, excited.

"Don't get a boner or anything," I say as he lifts me up, cradling me gently in a way I will never, not on my life, admit is quite comfortable. I give him instructions and he dutifully follows them through the maze of bodies. We come to a stop at the top of a stairwell lit by emergency lights.

"This make sense to you?" Sean asks, pointing at the twisted tunnel of tangled and mangled unfinished biologics. Some of them are still functional, but they've been crushed into position, forming a spiraling tunnel leading downward. Something powerful shoved its way through them, chasing...

"Praxion," I say. "They made it out. Fled down. These things chased them."

"It looks like intestines," Sean says. "Like the inside of them. You know, like how I imagine it would look. I've never actually seen the inside of an intestine."

I grunt and say, "I have. It's more...pink." Then I shove him into the hole and jump down after him.

He screams around the first few spirals, and then starts groaning.

"Don't you do it!" I shout, sliding down behind him, around and around.

He starts dry heaving.

"Don't you fucking do it."

"Huuarrgg!"

I splash through chunky bile, waving my hands, coughing and sputtering.

"How much fucking food can one man hold in his stomach?!" I shout.

The next two minutes are a living hell.

Then we slide to a stop at the bottom, where a door is missing.

I get to my feet, shake off and turn to Sean, who's mostly puke free. "You will never speak of this. Not to your therapist, god, wife, or mistress. Comprende?"

Sean raises his hands. "Swear, man. I wouldn't diss you like that."

"Great," I say and turn toward the door just in time to witness the interior wall burst open and give birth to a freak-show of a Helion that doesn't even look in our direction. Instead, it charges across what I think is a lobby, and crashes through a forty-foot tall, segmented window, taking the front of the building with it.

Outside, people and vehicles are crushed, screaming for help that won't be coming unless we can stop the Draun ourselves.

"Move!" I say, chasing the Helion out into the street. Dust and screams fill the air, but I catch sight of both the Helion and, further down the road, what it's chasing—a long black and white vehicle that tears around a corner and disappears.

I look for Sean in the dust but can't find him. "Sean!" A flare of worry churns my insides. "Sean!"

A motor spins me around. Sean is sitting in a small red vehicle that is low to the ground and looks fast. Not surprising, I guess. Sean said that before me, his only real friends were 'pot and speed, but not the drug.'

He pats the passenger's seat. "Get in, my dude!"

I leap into the seat, face forward, and smile as Sean guns the engine and we tear off in pursuit of the rogue, flesh-covered Helion hunting my team.

42

PRAXION

"Take my hand," I say, reaching down to Micah, sprawled on his back at the front of the bus, his feet up and over the dash.

He looks up at Haruto. "What part of 'Do not stop for anything,' did you not understand?" He reaches up, takes my hand, and allows me to heft him back to his feet.

We both look out the windshield, curious about what could have possibly stopped us while fleeing from certain death. A line of children, dressed the same in white blouses and plaid skirts, cross the street in front of us. They all smile and wave at the panda bus. Some hold up two fingers. Others make a heart shape with their hands.

"Okay, Haruto," Micah says. "You're off the hook."

"They are...adorable," I say, feeling a strange kind of affection for the small humans I have never seen before.

Grover barks and leaps up on a bench, wagging his tail and scratching at the glass, desperate to say hello to the children. They see him and react with vocal joy. The connection between them is instant, requiring no introductions. No time spent together. Grover is beloved by these strangers, simply for existing.

Jess leans between us, sees the children and says, "At least they're not ducks."

I do not know what ducks are, and I do not really care. I give Micah's shoulder a pat.

"You are unharmed?"

"Wouldn't say that." He rolls his shoulder. "But I'll live, if that's what you mean."

As the line of children comes to an end, we return to our seats.

"Resume fleeing, Haruto," I say.

The driver gives a nod and steps on the gas, giving the horn a playful honk at the waving children now safe on the side of the road. I fear it is a wasted effort. With a Helion on our tail, screaming and death will follow in our wake.

"Harth," I say. "Helion status?"

"Still pursuing," he says, looking out the bus's back window. "It has halved the distance, but we still have time to formulate a plan of attack."

"Attack?" Jess says. "Here? In the city?"

49999

"Helions are engines of destruction," Torel says. "Its main goal might be to kill us, but it will destroy everything it comes across on the way. The longer we run, the more people will die. Our best chance to minimize the damage is to destroy it."

"Wait, wait, wait!" Haruto shouts. "What happen to airport?"

"Keep going," Micah says. "Just...be ready to stop in case we come up with a plan that—" He looks at me. "—will *not* get us killed. Can't save the world if we're dead."

He is right, and clearly understands the concept of collateral damage. Sometimes to save the most people, you must allow some to perish. It is a harsh truth of war that is hard for many to understand.

Including Jess. "We can't just leave that thing here. What happens if we escape? If we leap to another place on Earth and that thing is just loose in Japan? What will it do?"

"It will delight in a murderous rampage until there is no one left to kill, or its power cells run out...in roughly ten years." Harth shrugs. "Whatever comes first."

She glares at Micah. "We can't leave it here, Spock be damned."

"Who is Spock?" Torel asks.

"An Earth...philosopher," Micah says. "Taught that the needs of the many outweigh the needs of the few. Or the one."

"A wise man," Harth says.

"We are not abandoning Tokyo," Jess says. "Is that clear?"

She speaks with conviction and command, fueled by a passion to protect her fellow humans, demonstrating the same connection to strangers that Grover generates. Human compassion would be seen as a weakness by many of those who have faced the dangers of the wide universe, but I find it inspiring.

"Very well," I say. "We will face the beast. But not until we reach the airport."

"Hear that?" Micah asks Haruto.

"I hear! I hear! You all talk! Let me drive!" He swerves back and forth, narrowly avoiding several vehicles and fleeing pedestrians.

"Okay," I say, "Ideas?"

"Assuming it has learned from its fallen brethren, it will see a direct Incinerator blast coming. Perhaps I could incinerate the sides of one of these buildings, toppling it onto the—"

"That's a horrible idea," Jess says. "You'd kill thousands of people."

"Spock would approve," Harth grumbles.

"I could stun it with a shock," Torel says, and then looks at her Lancer. It is not yet fully charged. Nor is Harth's Incinerator. It will not be long but, for the moment, their plan is shelved. And not just because of power levels. There is very little we could do to stop a Helion that would not risk turning a portion of this city into a steaming pile of wreckage.

"I have idea!" Haruto shouts, twisting the wheel and taking us around a ninety-degree turn fast enough to tip the bus up onto two wheels for a moment.

"Does it involve getting us all killed?" Harth asks, deadpan.

"Ha! Ha!" Haruto says, mocking. "Big dog be quiet!" He turns to Micah. "We need open space, yes? To fight mecha-monster?"

"Preferably," Micah says.

"On the way to airport," Haruto says. "I know a place. No people. Lots of places to hide. Places to flank enemy. Attack from all sides. Never see coming."

It would appear humans are naturals when it comes to war. At the moment, it is an advantage. In the long term, warring species never last that long on a cosmic scale. War leads to rapid advances in technology, but society usually lags behind and self-destruction becomes inevitable.

"Proceed," I say.

Around us, the buildings start shrinking in size as we exit the city's vast core.

"Harth, ETA?"

Behind us, the façade of a building collapses. From the debris, the flesh covered Helion emerges, roaring and charging. "Thirty seconds."

We are not going to make it...

I look ahead and spot two bridges over water. "Upcoming bridges! Take them out!"

Harth shatters the rear window and leans out of the truck. We pass over the first bridge. It is not large, but Helions cannot swim. If it does not clear the gap in one jump, it will be slowed.

The Incinerator pops three times as Harth fires at the bridge's core. The rounds reduce metal, concrete, and pavement to slag. The bridge collapses in seconds.

The Helion reacts with uncommon speed, as though it—or one of its brethren—has faced the sudden destruction of a bridge before. It clears the distance with no trouble, digs its hooked claws into the roadway and doubles its speed.

The second bridge is larger, requiring five Incinerator rounds to destroy it. The Helion leaps again, lunging into the air so high and fast that it might not just land on the road, but on top of us.

"Hit the gas, Haruto!" Micah shouts.

The bus speeds up...slowly.

Our concern was unnecessary.

The gravity on this world is unforgiving, yanking the Helion down just short of the bridge. While its body plummets out of sight, the creature's claws dig into the road and keep it from falling into the water.

As the Helion pulls itself up, Stuchbery wakes. "Where am I?! What's happening?!" He lifts his stump arms and remembers everything, and lets out a high-pitched shriek—"Aieee-uv-uv-uv!"–that is cut short by an electric shock from Torel, rendering him unconscious once more.

The road bends to the right into a three-lane straightaway. To our left are several large buildings. To our right, a collection of large metal containers.

"Are those shipping containers?" Micah asks.

"Hai," Haruto says. "The port is to our left."

"Good thinking," Micah says.

"I know. I know. That's why I say, 'you talk, I drive.'" Haruto taps the side of his head. "I have only great ideas." Then he cranks the wheel hard to the left, tipping us onto two wheels again before straightening out and dropping back down.

Grover is bounced hard by the impact, yelping a bit. Micah has him in an instant, holding him tightly, whispering into his ear. "I got you, bud. We're going to be okay." He kisses Grover's head. "I got you."

"Why do you speak to him if he does not understand you?" I ask.

"He understands my tone," Micah says. "The words are for me. But...I think he understands more than he used to. Since..." He places a hand on the regulators behind Grover's ears. "I feel connected to him. More than ever. Is that possible?"

"Possible," Torel says. "Yes. Between Kynolari. But he is...not fully Kynolari, and you are human. What you are feeling is more likely—"

"Now you talk about emotions when you should be talking about fight!?" Haruto is outraged. "What is this, Star Trek: Discovery?! You going to scream out emotions now?!"

Jess sighs and shakes her head. "So many Star Trek references."

I do not understand exactly what Haruto is referencing again, but he is not wrong. Tires squeal as we take one last turn onto a road lined with brightly colored, large metal containers. Beyond them, the ocean.

Haruto crashes through a chain link barricade, turning into a path between crates just as a building behind us is peeled apart in the middle. The Helion appears to be in some kind of distress, thrashing as though injured or under attack from some unseen force, but it never wavers in its pursuit, closing the distance quickly.

"Everyone out!' I shout. "Into the maze. Attack from all sides. Force it toward the water. Do *not* hold back."

The door opens, and we charge out, leaving Haruto and Stuchbery inside. The driver steps on the gas, peeling away with his lone passenger. The rest of us spread out, Torel and Harth heading south. Micah leads Jess and Grover to an aisle framed by red metal. He makes eye-contact with me. Gives me a nod. Slips into the maze, heading north.

I hope I will see him again but know not to get my hopes up. I have been in similar situations before and rarely escape without casualties. When a blue container spirals past overhead, shedding its brown boxed innards, I disappear into the shadows and prepare for guerilla warfare.

43

"You saw what that thing did to the buildings, right?" Jess says. "I don't think metal shipping containers are going to deter it much."

"Can't attack what it can't see," I say, rounding a corner deeper into the maze. I'd like to say I'm leading the way, but Grover is on point. Seems to comprehend that we need to get lost, and fast. His body language has changed, too. Tail, head, and ears are down, walking low like he does when he's about to do something he's not supposed to, like eating deer shit, or munching on mushrooms, or chasing after a critter.

I've always taken the body language as rebellious. A kind of 'Don't bother telling me what to do right now because I'm not going to listen,' kind of posture. But in this circumstance, I see the truth. He's saying, 'I'm getting shit done.' Hell, maybe vacuuming up deer shit is important to Kynolari, too. Or maybe dogs are just sometimes gross.

Nothing worse than having to go to a vet and tell them your dog's stomach is full of poop pellets. Actually, that's not true. Worse than that is not knowing about it until you get a shitty lick on the lips and finding out the hard way.

"I'm telling you," Jess says. "This isn't the best idea."

"It's our best play that doesn't involve getting a lot of people killed," I say.

"I'm concerned about us getting killed," she says.

She's not wrong to be concerned about that. The Helion is a beast, but we've seen the Kynolari take them down before. Just need to attack it in a way it can't see coming, and—

A shipping crate flies through the air above us, casting a shadow over us for a moment, before sailing out of sight. A moment later, a crash of metal on metal and then, high above, a tower crane leans out over the maze of crates, slowly bending toward its breaking point. A crate still attached to its cable swings out like a wrecking ball, fifty feet overhead.

"Well," Jess says. "Shit. Being right sucks. We need to get out of here."

On our own, it might take a while to find our way out, especially when backtracking isn't an option. But we have Grover. I give a whistle. "Grover. Out!"

He barks, breaks left, and leads the way.

"Seriously?" Jess says.

"Trust him," I say, though I'm not entirely sure why I feel so confident—not just in his ability to navigate a maze, but in that he understands what I'm asking of him.

Since the biologic factory, when I got a glimpse of the world through his eyes, I've felt more connected to the dog than ever before. Understanding each other without words. Without body language. We're in sync.

A distant explosion shakes the ground. The boom and shockwave slides through the maze, kicking up dust and rattling the metal containers.

The hell is going on?

I'm about to snap at Grover and give him the command to stop, but he stops moving the moment I think it. Looks back, panting. Waiting.

Holy shit...

With a thought, I activate my comms. "Talon-Actual, Badass-One, you copy?"

"Badass-One," Praxion replies, sounding a little winded. "Talon-Actual, I copy."

"The hell is going on out there?" I ask.

"The Helion is unlike any we have encountered before," he says, and then he grunts like he's just jumped and landed hard.

"It's smart," Torel says without identifying herself.

"It is herding us," Harth said, offended by the idea. "Using the environment to force us into the open."

I glance up at the crane above us, still bending toward its breaking point. "I noticed."

"I think we should give it what it wants," Harth says. "Just all at once. Give it everything we've got."

"And if that doesn't work?" I ask.

"The water," Praxion says. "If it follows us there, it will sink."

"Copy that," I say. "ETA..." The time it will take us to reach the central clearing pops into my head. "Two minutes."

"Two minutes," Harth says. "Confirmed."

"Confirmed," Torel repeats.

"Confirmed," Praxion says. "Do not hold back. Out."

Grover barks the moment we finish and begins moving. I motion for Jess to follow him while I bring up the rear, keeping an eye on the crane, now bent over like a weeping willow.

Grover leads us through the winding red, blue, and yellow passages with confidence. Never wavering. Never pausing to sniff or listen. He's a trouble-seeking missile and never loses sight of his target.

The result is that we reach the clearing a full minute before we're supposed to. Which feels off. I was so confident about how long it would take to—

To what?

To say goodbye, I realize, turning to Jess and Grover. "This is where you two get the hell out of here."

"What?" Jess says. "We're in this."

"But you can't fight," I say. "Neither of you can. While you're here, I'm distracted. I'm worried about you. Both of you." I look down at Grover. "If anything were to happen to him." I look back up at Jess. "And for some reason, you—"

She smiles.

"I'm not sure how I'd handle it. I need you to head north, out of the crates. Don't stop until the fight is over. And if the Helion is still standing...keep going. Do not come back. For any reason. You hear me?" I look down at Grover. "You hear me. Don't you?"

His closed mouth opens in a puppy grin, and he starts panting. Not exactly confirmation of what feels true, but I'll take it. I crouch down, place my hands over his ears and kiss his forehead. "Be careful, buddy."

He licks my chin and I kiss him again.

When I stand, Jess has tears in her eyes. "This better not be goodbye forever."

"Won't be," I say, trying to sound confident. "We can take it."

"You better," she says, and then she kisses me. When we part, she keeps a hand on my cheek—and gives me a slap. "Kick its ass." Then she looks down at Grover. "You. Lead the way."

"Go," I tell him, snapping my fingers and pointing north. He spins around and leads the way.

When they're out of sight, I check my gauntlet power levels. Full charge.

Back to a container, I slide to the edge of the maze and lean my head out. The Helion is three hundred feet away, its back to me.

An easy target.

But no war has ever been won by jumping the gun.

"Talon-Actual, Badass-One, I am in position."

"Badass-One, Talon-Actual, copy that. Ten seconds out."

"In position," Harth says.

Torel chimes in next. "Almost there."

"Any specific order we want to hit this thing in?" I ask.

"I will stun it," Praxion says. "The three of you—"

The Helion swipes its massive arm to the side, colliding with a shipping container that slams into the next, closing the gap between them. The force of the impact creates a shock wave that shoves dozens of containers inward, compressing the space between them.

"Talon-Actual," Harth says. "Talon-Actual, do you copy? Are you okay?"

No response.

Fuck.

"Hit it!" Harth shouts, "Hit it now!"

Bright Incinerator rounds launch into the air in a high arc, drawing the Helion's attention skyward. While it's looking up, several more white-hot rounds launch out of the container maze to the north, striking the Helion's left flank, setting the creature's unfinished flesh ablaze.

Lightning tears through the air, splitting around and embracing the beast.

But it doesn't react... Not with pain or spasms of malfunction. Instead, it simply turns toward Torel—and returns the lightning from where it came. A burst of sparks is all I see before bracing myself and taking aim at the monster's back. I'm about to give a full charge blast but, at the last moment, I hold some power in reserve. Because I've got a bad feeling.

Something is off.

The beam of orange energy that tears from my arm, carves a clean line through the Helion's flesh, but doesn't punch through its body. Instead, the raw energy reflects off its back and heads skyward, punching a hole through the clouds and exiting the atmosphere.

It was ready for us. For every weapon we've got.

The Helion's flesh melts and tears away, revealing a shimmering metal body that can resist the heat of Harth's Incinerator, return the energy of Torel's Lancer, and reflect my Hell Hound's laser.

Helions learn, but this one seemed smart from the get-go, like it was designed to fight Praxion's team specifically.

We need to attack it in a way it won't expect.

That it will never see coming.

I extend my claws and charge toward its back. "Talon-One, Badass-One, collect your people. Get them to safety. I'm going to introduce myself to this asshole."

Harth grumbles in my ear. "I should help—"

"Your people need to survive," I say. "Get them out of here. Now. I'll keep it busy for as long as I can."

There's a moment of silence, followed by, "Copy that, Badass-One. Knew I liked you for a reason."

I smile, climb onto the roof of a forklift, and then leap onto the Helion's hind leg, digging my laser claws into its metal body. The lasers don't help much, but the blades dig in just fine. The Helion must not feel pain, because it doesn't react to my arrival. But it does turn toward Harth, now racing through the maze toward Torel's last known position.

I haul myself up onto its back, trying to come up with some attack plan that will put it down. But before I can think of anything, the rapid approach of a car engine draws my attention.

A red sports car cruises into view. Must be going eighty, ninety miles an hour. Crouched down on its trunk is a small dog. A Chihuahua?

No, I realize, *a Kynolari. This is one of their missing friends!*

The car crashes head-on into a concrete barrier. While the front-end folds inward, the backend is propelled upward, catapulting the Kynolari warrior into the air. As he sails overhead, he draws two small weapons and opens fire on the Helion's back. His rounds spark off its metal hide. Then he lands just a few feet in front of me and looks back.

He's small and very silly looking but manages to muster more machismo than Clint Eastwood when he looks back at me and notes the regulators on my head and the gauntlet on my arm. "Who the fuck are you?"

44

CHIRK

"You must be Chirk," the human says, clinging to the Helion's metal hide using a Kynolari weapon system. That alone confuses the hell out of me, but he's also wearing regulators. The newest and best. Same as the rest of the team. Which means he got them from Praxion.

"I know who the fuck I am," I shout, digging my claws into a seam in the giant drone's armor. "Who are *you?*"

"Micah," he says, sliding over the Helion's back as it begins to buck. "But I think names are a low priority at the moment. You have a plan?"

"Honestly," I say, "My plan was to launch myself onto the Helion's back and then improvise it to death."

Micah smiles at that. "We had the same plan!" He drags himself higher and then reaches his free hand back for me.

I gotta say, it's nice to meet a human that isn't either horrified or thrilled to see me, who doesn't talk to me in a cutesy voice or have expectations based on the dogs of this world. He treats me how I'm used to being treated—like a badass fucking operator who's seen more shit than a Dengalarian Festering Pit. I appreciate him for it and understand why he's here, even though I'm a little offended that he appears to have been adopted as a teammate, replacing me or Gruunlokar.

Then again, I've got Sean on Team Chirk. It was his idea to smash the car into the concrete barrier, launching me into the battle in style. We probably should have worked out the details of what came next, but there wasn't time. This Helion was ready for everything the team threw at it.

But not me.

And not this guy.

"Motor controls are buried between its shoulder blades!" I shout. "If you can carve a hole, I'll tear it apart."

"Look at that," he says. "A plan! Good boy!"

I level a bulgy-eyed snarl in his direction—and the sonuvabitch smirks.

He's screwing with me. In the middle of a life and death battle.

I think I like him. He reaches his hand out again and I take it.

The Helion really throws itself into bucking us off, thrashing up and down. We slap against its back twice, and then Micah slides me upward, hard as he can. I'm flung up, bouncing over the armor plates before coming to a stop between the shoulder blades.

He's not far behind me, dragging himself up with the claws between trouncings. When he reaches me, he scratches an X in the Helion's armor. "Here?"

"Looks about right," I say, and he wastes no time.

Micah's claws glow magma hot as he stabs the blades into the Helion's armor. He grinds his teeth from the effort, almost growling as he pulls the blades through metal strong enough to deflect railgun fire.

He fights like this is personal. Like he's trying to protect someone.

That's when I spot them, fleeing to the north. A human woman and an Earth dog who's also wearing a set of regulators. Glad I'm not the only one who threw regulations out the window, but I am surprised Praxion went so far. Then again, I will be leaving out the majority of what I've done since arriving on this world from any and all reports I'll need to write.

I have no way to explain the primitive urges I've been feeling, and I've given in to, on more than one occasion. I've bedded two bitches, with the very real possibility of impregnating one, if not both of them. I've partaken in illicit drugs, eaten unsanctioned foods, and befriended a denizen of a decentralized, backward culture.

Micah finishes hacking away a rough circle and digs his claws inside. Pulling together, we tear away the segment of armor. It slurps out of position, pulling strands of viscous brown sludge with it.

The Helion bounces up onto its hind legs, roaring in frustration. Then it slams back down, failing once more to dislodge us.

I've dismantled a number of Helions in my day, but they've never had liquid insides.

The plate falls away and I look inside.

I'm expecting a mishmash of moving metal parts. Instead, I find flesh. And muscle.

"Holy shit," I say.

"I thought Helions were biologics," Micah says, looking at the wound. "Or robots."

"God-damnit," I say, feeling an upwelling of rage that makes me snarl.

"What is it?"

"It's a source beast. An original from which biologics are designed."

"Is that bad?" he asks, grunting as we slide back and forth.

"It's tragic," I say. "Helions were modeled after an alien species—the Grokar— that we knew existed at one point, but never encountered. They were one of the first to fall to the Draun. This is one of them. A survivor. And that's bad…"

"Why?" he asks as I draw one of my mini railguns, setting the rounds to burst on impact for maximum internal damage.

"Because," I say. "I have to kill it."

I place the mini railgun into the wound Micah created, and pull the trigger, sending a fusillade of rail-shards into its flesh. Each shard breaks apart, in a spray of supersonic splinters that move through flesh like it's air. I can't see what's happening inside the massive beast's body, but it's not hard to visualize a thousand needles coursing through its meat and bones, ricocheting off the armor's insides. On its own, a needle won't do much damage, but together, bouncing around the armor's interior, the shards' kinetic energy will slowly turn the creature's insides to mush.

And it's not happy about it.

The Helion gives up on trying to dislodge us and switches tactics to crushing us beneath its girth.

"Jump!" I shout as the Helion careens to one side, intending to roll over and pop our insides out of our mouths. Instead of jumping, this asshole human takes my arm and flings me clear.

Flings me, like I'm a sack of shit to be discarded and—

"Oof!" I hit the ground much farther away than I would have if I'd actually jumped. He must have known I'd never get clear, so he threw me at great risk to himself. I roll to my feet and look back at the toppling Helion.

Claws dug into the armor, Micah bends his legs, and when he's 90 degrees to the ground, he releases and springs away.

He lands atop one of the shipping containers and is back on his feet in time to leap again before the Helion rolls into him. He lands on his back, leaning up and aiming his gauntlet back at the Helion. Unleashes a controlled, narrow laser blast that just misses the opening on the Helion's back.

Micah attempts to stand again but is knocked off the crate as the Helion completes a full revolution, smashing into it. He lands on his back, thirty feet from me, coughing and gasping for air. I aim both mini-railguns and open fire as the Helion gets back to its feet and turns its full attention on Micah.

"Get up, asshole!" I shout at him, but he has yet to catch a breath.

I fire at its face, aiming for the eyes, hoping to get its attention. "Over here, you Glafarian genital mite!"

No use. It's focused on Micah, and impervious to my attacks.

I look for help but find none.

And Micah...I think he's confused. Had the brains knocked out of him.

He swipes at the air as the Helion stands in front of him.

"No! Don't!"

The Helion draws its massive arm to the side, winding up for the mother of all backhands.

Micah staggers to his feet. "No! Please!"

The hell is happening? He looks blind. Like he knows what's coming but can't see.

My mind races, trying to think of a way to help him, but I'll never get there in time. Even on all fours, I wouldn't nearly be fast enough—

A golden blur nearly knocks me down as it barrels past.

The fuck was that? I think, and then I recognize the Earth dog I saw fleeing with the woman.

It came back.

For Micah.

The Helion's arm swings forward.

Even if Micah saw it coming, he couldn't avoid it.

But he doesn't have to.

The dog leaps up, tackling him to the side—

—and putting himself in the path of danger.

The backhand strike connects with the dog. Its yelp of pain is suddenly silenced.

The golden blur topples in my direction, hits the pavement, and rolls to a stop at my feet.

My heart skips a beat.

His face looks like Praxion's, but he's not Kynolari. Not fully. An Earth dog, but based on what I've just seen, he has the heart and bravery of the best Kynolari.

"Grover!" Micah shouts, voice cracking with emotion, looking over at me... looking down at the dog. When our eyes meet, I shake my head. No way a hit like that was survivable.

The man screams.

It's close to a howl, filled with more rage and sorrow than I've heard in all my life. And like a good soldier, he redirects all that turmoil toward the creature—willing or not—that caused his pain. With a burst of laser light, Micah uses the gauntlet to leap up over the Helion, coming down on its back once again.

Then something I've never seen before happens.

He takes aim, unleashes another agonized scream, and then his partially charged gauntlet fills with enough power that I need to look away from its brilliance.

"It can't be," I whisper. "No fucking way."

A moment later, all that power is unleashed as an intense and narrow beam of energy that tears through the Helion's body at the speed of light, bounces off the inner armor an untold number of times, vaporizing the insides, the pressure building until its head explodes and the laser beam launches skyward.

The Helion lurches and falls, bouncing Micah off its corpse.

He slides down its flank, lands on his feet and runs to Grover's side, tears in his eyes, sobbing like his entire world has just been destroyed. I've never seen anything like it. Like him. And it brings tears to my own eyes.

Then Micah gasps and leans up. "I think he's alive."

I'm about to argue when I see the dog's—Grover's—chest rise for a breath.

His eyes open and turn up to Micah.

"I got you, bud," he says. "You're okay. I got you."

The dog moves its mouth and then does something I believed impossible.

"Love...Micah," Grover says, voice coming from his regulators, and then he lets out a long sigh before falling still, his chest no longer rising or falling.

45

GRUUNLOKAR

I'm seated alone, in another large, white room. The floor is hard, almost like stone. Walls are bare and slightly rounded. The light in the room is dim, coming from a single illuminated beam running down the ceiling's center. In the middle of the space is a primitive viewing screen wrapped in a white case and standing on four legs. I am seated, and bound to, a white chair. There is a second beside me, empty for now.

And that is fine with me. I am content to sit here alone, contemplating recent revelations without distraction.

The Draun have been on this world for millennia. Were here long before the Lost Tribe's arrival thirty-seven thousand years ago. They commingled genetically with this world's primitive inhabitants, who gained physical advantages that allowed them to become this world's dominant species.

As the original human species went extinct, this new breed of Draun spread over the planet, building a fresh civilization and wonders of technology until something changed.

She wouldn't say it, but I'm guessing that change took place thirty-seven thousand years ago—when the Lost Tribe arrived. Progress slowed. The Draun left behind to rule this world went silent. When that happened, the planet would have been deemed a failed colony. Ever efficient, the Draun would not return en masse. An envoy or two, perhaps, but when they failed to return or report in, the planet would have been considered a loss. At that point, the surviving Draun and the Kynolari survivors from the Lost Tribe would have been left to coexist. To evolve...and devolve together.

I grind my teeth without showing any external emotions. But I am enraged and offended by the idea. Kynolari made lesser. Made slaves to a species as repugnant as the Draun.

Though they are not all the Draun. Not fully. Not anymore. Despite what my interrogator would have me believe that her story of awakening to her power and the knowledge of her people tells me that she alone is the only true Draun on this world. She claims to have been awakened by a signal from the depths of space, a beacon sent long ago, seeking to alert any of their kind on other worlds. She received that signal and, while she once considered herself a champion of the human race, she now understands her true place in the universe. And seeks to wake up the rest of this world.

Tomorrow.

If that happens, there will be eight billion new Draun in the universe.

Eight *billion.*

If they are able to get off world, the great war will begin anew.

I need to stop her, but I do not know how. I am bound and unable to escape. Security isn't just tight, it's invisible. I know I am watched, but I do not know where from, or by whom. The best I can do is wait for an opportunity to present itself and be ready to strike without mercy when it comes.

"Hello again."

I flinch out of my thoughts, caught off guard by the woman's silent approach. Her clothing also seems to hide her scent. She carries Ling in one arm and a bowl of some kind of puffy food in the other. She remains maskless.

"I realize this might seem a primitive display to you, but it is a human tradition: gathering in front of the television—the video display—to communally watch the dramas of life play out. Often, the stories are fiction, but this is closer to what people on Earth call, 'news.'"

"Where is your peon?" I ask.

"Alton?" she asks with a roll of her eyes. "Preparing for guests...if any survive."

I do my best to show no trace of concern, but it is a challenge.

She raises a hand toward the television.

"Wait," I say. "Before you begin..."

She turns toward me while Ling begins plucking the puffed food from the bowl, wagging her tail while she munches. "Delaying what is to come changes nothing. The events we will be watching are already in progress."

"I want to know about you," I say.

"I'm sure you do."

"You were raised human," I say. "Not the Draun."

"You can lose the 'the' before Draun," she says. "It sounds ridiculous in English."

"Are you afraid to answer the question?" I ask.

She grins. "I was raised human...but never felt at home."

"And you received a signal," I say. "From space?"

"Nearly died in the process," she says. "But yes. And it changed me. Woke latent abilities. Allowed me to become more. Not long after, I began to...remember who I am. Who we all are. A secret knowledge passed down in human genes that, once unlocked, reveals our true ancestry, power, and destiny."

"How long have you been like this? A Draun?"

"Nine years," she says. "I took control of the Twilight Directorate five years ago and we have been preparing ever since, locating ancient troves of technology, building factories and transit systems, and coordinating with those of my kind not of this world. The Kynolari genocide managed to miss a few outposts when you purged my kind from the universe."

"We *prevented* genocide," I blurt out. "Your people destroyed entire worlds. Civilizations."

She waves me away. "I have seen the truth with my own eyes. I know what you are. What you have done. And now, thanks to your arrival on my world, plans have accelerated. Tomorrow, the rest of my people will have their eyes opened. They will embrace their destiny as one unified species, resilient in the face of canine oppression. Now..." She raises her hand to the television and snaps her fingers.

An image winks onto the screen. It's distant at first, slowly moving closer to a scene of absolute chaos already unfolding.

At the center of the screen—a flesh-covered Helion.

The Draun takes a bite of the puffed food and then offers the bowl to me. "It's popcorn. A traditional Earth food during entertainment. You can eat straight from the bowl if you'd like. A little drool never bothered me."

I turn away from the bowl, though it takes an effort to fight the hunger pangs that kick in when I smell it. I have not had anything to eat or drink since my capture.

"Ooh!" The woman says as the Helion's flesh burns and falls away, revealing a hardened metal shell. We are still too far away to make out details, but I know the effects of Harth's Incinerator when I see it.

A blast of lightning strikes the beast but is deflected.

It's followed by a powerful laser blast, which ricochets into the air, narrowly missing whatever drone is watching the scene playing out.

"Closer," I grumble.

She smiles and snaps her fingers again.

Our view shifts to another hovering camera, closer, but off to the side.

She tilts her head like she's hearing something, despite the television feed being totally silent.

"I'm told your leader—Praxion, I believe, has already fallen. Crushed between shipping containers it would seem. A pitiful fate. And it appears your other comrades aren't faring much better. Would you like to know why?"

I snarl. Can't help myself.

I'd tear her throat out if I could.

"That's not a Helion. Not really. That...that is the real deal. A Grokar, armored, but in the flesh. Apparently, there is a farm on some distant moon where they are raised, lobotomized, and prepared to push back against your people's genocidal warmongering."

"Grokar..." I say, leaning forward, shaking my head. The poor creature, once peaceful, now a weapon of death.

"What's this?" she asks, snapping her fingers. Our view shifts high above once more. She points to a red vehicle racing into the scene. But it's not alone. There is a human there, too. A male. He leaps onto the Helion's back and clings to it.

"And there he is," she leans forward. "The man of the hour, Micah Taylor. He's proven himself to be a competent enemy. And he'll be the first to stand beside me. If he survives."

"Can we get closer?" I ask, no longer interested in what she's saying.

The drone's camera zooms in enough for me to make out a few details—including the gauntlet attached to the man's arm. *It's not possible,* I think, but I guard my surprise. Praxion would not grant another species access to a weapon system unless his trust had been fully gained. More than that, the technology shouldn't be compatible with a being that is not Kynolari and, even worse, a Draun.

The vehicle careens into the shipyard and immediately crashes. The wreck elicits a laugh from the Draun, but she's missed the small speck that's flung onto the Helion's back. *Chirk,* I think, trying not to grin. *They've found each other.*

The man and Chirk manage to tear a hole in the creature's back before being flung away. The human—this Micah—saves Chirk, puts himself in harm's way, and then, just as he is about to be struck down...*he* is saved.

By an Earth dog.

I find myself torn between confusion and anger. Despite our view being from high above, I can sense the human's pain. Can almost feel it when he screams.

And then...the impossible. His partially drained weapon system charges to full and tears into the Helion's back, destroying its insides and bursting out through its mouth.

The Draun's hand pauses, popcorn held in the air before her open mouth. She turns toward me. "Is that normal?"

I lean over to the bowl and bite down on a mouthful of popcorn, not just because I'm hungry, but because I want to hide my smile. If what I just saw is real, that man on the screen is *not* Draun.

He can't be. Because he was prophesied about...thirty-seven thousand years ago on the day the Lost Tribe went missing.

46

MICAH

I know this pain. Have felt it before.

But not like this. Not so sudden. And not with so much guilt attached.

When a dog passes...when *your* dog passes...guilt is always part of what comes next. Their lives are so short in comparison to ours that you can't help but wonder if you should have fed them something different, gone on more walks, shouldn't have sprayed for ticks, should have sprayed for ticks... There's no escaping the concern that you had something to do with their demise.

But this... Grover gave his life for mine.

He should have never been here.

I should have left him in New Hampshire, with Jess.

Should have done a thousand different things.

But I didn't. I kept him by my side. Because I'm selfish. Because I'm weaker without him. Less resilient. More afraid. And because of my shortcomings, he's dead.

And that...

That is God-damned fucking unacceptable.

I drop to my knees by Grover's side and scream, "Torel!"

No idea if she's still alive, if any of them are still alive, but I know she's Grover's only hope. "*Torel!*"

"Here," she says, limping out from behind a container with Harth's help. When she sees Grover on the ground, she releases the big Kynolari and hobble-runs toward us. "What happened?"

"He took a hit," I say.

"A big hit," Chirk says.

"Chirk!" Harth says, smiling despite the circumstances.

"Just in time for the shit show," the tough little dog says. Their conversation continues, but I hear none of it. My attention is on Grover and Torel. She kneels beside me, holding her hand out over his still body. Data scrolls onto the screen on her forearm.

"What is it?" I ask.

"A lot," she says.

"What are you waiting for?" I ask. "Use your gauntlet. Bring him back!"

"That's not how it works," she says, looking at me with the most empathetic eyes. I'm nearly undone right then and there. "You know that's not how it works."

"But you could save him, right? You travel through space. You're an advanced civilization. Your technology... It would be enough."

She nods. "Maybe. But not here. Not in the field." She places her warm hand on the side of my face. "I'm sorry."

"No!" I look up. It's Jess, hand to her mouth, tears in her eyes. "Oh God, no." She drops down beside Torel, placing a hand on Grover's side.

That's when I lose it, arching over to unleash a sob that wracks my body and nearly splits my ribs.

"He was a brave warrior," Harth says, placing his large hand on my back. "A true Kynolari."

"Oh shit," a man says. "Oh *shit.*"

I glance up to find the stereotype of a pothead kneeling next to me. I don't know him. Grover doesn't know him. But he's crying just the same.

"Was he yours?" he asks me.

I nod, whole face quivering, small squeaks coming from my throat.

He puts his arm around my back and side-hugs me. The affection of a random stranger provides a moment of comfort, but it's the voice of Praxion that re-ignites my sliver of hope.

"Torel." He stands above us, face grim and dripping with blood from a head wound. "Prognosis?"

"He's gone," she says. "There's nothing I can do for him here."

"And on the *Prowler*?" he asks.

"Perhaps," she says.

"That is enough." He toggles his comms, allowing all of us with regulators to listen in. "Prowler-One, Talon-Actual, do you copy?"

"Talon-Actual, Prowler-One," says the voice of a Kynolari I have yet to meet. He sounds older. Gentle. Not an operator, which is probably why he's still with the ship.

"Prepare for Earth-drop. We need immediate evac. Prep the med bay while en route," Praxion orders.

"Whoa, whoa, whoa, you're not going to let Baarfolir pilot my baby," Chirk says.

Praxion looks down at Chirk. "*You* are going to pilot. Remotely."

The fog clouding my thoughts starts to fade. There is a chance, however small, that Grover can be saved. If that's true, I need to snap out of my emotional malaise and get my fucking game face back on. I wipe my tears away with my sleeve.

"Micah," Praxion says, no trace of sympathy in his voice.

"Sir," I say, blinking the last of the wetness from my eyes.

"We are being watched." He looks up and I follow his gaze. A drone hovers overhead. I scan the area and find two more. "Take them out."

I nod and stand, extending three fingers. The first laser blasts from my ring finger and I put it down when the drone explodes. The second laser comes from my index finger and erases a second drone. With my middle finger extended, I raise it toward the last drone high above, now retreating. Then I point the finger at the device and slice it in two.

"Okay," Chirk says, cracking his knuckles. "No problem. Flying remotely. Through an atmosphere and hostile territory."

"You got this, bro," the strange pothead says, and the pair fist bump.

Chirk's hesitation is gone. He nods. "I got this." He pulls a visor down over his head. "Establishing uplink."

The man sees me watching. Extends a hand. "Sean."

"Micah," I say. "You know Chirk?"

Sean gives a casual smile. "He's my dog."

"He's *my* dog," Chirk says.

"We're each other's dogs," Sean says.

I glance at Harth. He shrugs.

"Ready to go," Torel says. She and Praxion have Grover on some kind of levitating stretcher. "ETA?"

"Five minutes," Chirk says.

"Five minutes," Jess repeats, not liking the sound of it.

"I'm flying from your moon, halfway around the planet, through your atmosphere, and straight down to us. Ain't no one in the universe who can do it any faster." He taps several buttons that we can't see but must be projected in his visor like virtual reality.

Jess is right. A five-minute wait while Grover lies still, his heart not beating, feels like an eternity. But people have been dead far longer and brought back. I won't give up hope.

A honking horn turns me around.

It's the Panda bus tearing toward us. The brakes lock. Smoke from the screeching tires billows past the vehicle when it comes to a stop. Haruto emerges from the gray smog, waving his arms. "We must go! Go now!" He spots Grover lying still. His concern melts to heartbreak. He turns to me. "Oh no...not the nice one."

"We can save him," I say.

"Hai!" he says, suddenly enthusiastic again. "But not here. Many, many creatures come this way. Following path through the city. Must leave now!"

From the Panda bus, I hear Stuchbery laughing. He falls out of the side door, dragging his stumpy body across the pavement. "They're coming for you now, suckas! You're all going to die, and I will delight in the—"

Harth lifts his Incinerator toward the man.

"Aieeeee!" Stuchbery screams, raising his stumps.

Harth fires a single Incinerator round. It strikes Stuchbery in the chest and transforms his whole body into a white-hot flame that flares with blinding intensity for a moment and then puffs out, leaving only a small pile of dust behind.

"You disapprove?" Harth asks me, noting my frown.

"I don't shoot unarmed men," I say.

He squints at me. "He wasn't unarmed. He was unhanded."

His gaze lingers until I crack a smile, which becomes a chuckle. "He was an asshole."

"Okay, okay!" Haruto shouts. "Stupid man dead! Now we go! On the bus. Hurry. Hurry."

While the others climb aboard the bus, I run out of the shipyard and into the street, looking back toward Tokyo. The distant city looks massive and imposing, but it's nothing compared to the wave of flesh-colored machines roiling down the road. The Twilight Syndicate has sent everything still functional after us. Some are nearly complete—human and alien biologics—while others have fleshy coverings, and still more are just metal skeletons. And there are hundreds of them, tripping and falling, each vying for a place at the front of the pack, eager to reach us first.

The bus skids to a stop beside me. Everyone is on board. Grover hovers in the center aisle, held still by the passengers, each one of them with a hand on his body, as though praying for his recovery.

"Hurry!" Haruto says. "You get on now!"

I climb in. The door closes behind me, but I don't take a seat. Instead, I smash the glass and lean outside as we speed away in a giant panda, aim my gauntlet back the way we came, and—nothing. My power is drained. It filled so quickly before, but I'm not sure how that happened.

I lean back inside and ask Praxion. "Hey, how do I get this thing to recharge faster?"

"It takes as long as it takes," he said. "Have patience."

I shake my head. "That's...not right. After Grover, it recharged in seconds."

His brow furrows.

"Saw it myself," Chirk says. "He's telling the truth. But it wasn't seconds. It was faster than that. A lot faster."

This must mean something to the Kynolari, because the four of them look between each other, a realization slowly spreading across their faces.

"What?" I ask.

"*Him?*" Harth says, near outrage, pointing at me. "*He* is the *Axiom?*"

I look to Praxion. "...the what-now?"

47

PRAXION

It is not possible, I think, but I keep it to myself. The idea of the Axiom being non-Kynolari is...offensive at best. That said, Micah has proven himself to be a true ally, naturally loyal to our ways, and beloved by a member of the Lost Tribe...who sacrificed himself to save Micah.

Perhaps the Earth dog knew more than we suspected.

Perhaps *all* Earth dogs know more than anyone—even the humans—realize.

"Questions for another time," I say.

"Only asked one question," Micah says.

"Later," I tell him.

The Axiom is not a subject to be hurried. While many in our culture have written the prophecy off as the last desperate broadcast of our lost people, just as many hoped—still hope—that those brave Kynolari had not lost their minds. That they understood something about our people the rest of us had not fully comprehended.

I turn to Harth and raise my eyebrows. "Later."

He gives a nod and heads for the back of the bus. Harth, like the rest of the team, always believed the Axiom was real, but he also had hopes it might be one of us, though he frequently took pleasure in ruling out Chirk. He shatters another window, checks his gauntlet power levels, and waits. The approaching horde is still out of range.

"How are you doing?" I ask Haruto.

"Be being better if people and dogs stop breaking bus windows!"

I grunt. "The panda bus is serving a noble purpose in an intergalactic war against tyranny, genocide, and—"

"Ooh, ok. I didn't realize fight was sooo noble. Why don't you break all windows while you're at it, huh?" Haruto is angry and sarcastic. I do not blame him. The bus is his livelihood. But all the large windows, and the glass that fills them, are a danger to us all. A single projectile could become a hundred.

"Not a bad idea." I place my hand against the window beside me and activate my gauntlet, acquiring the resonant frequency of the material. I then hold it up and unleash a blast of energy that irritates everyone in the vehicle and shatters every single window out and away from us.

Haruto is aghast. "Eh?! What!? Chikushou!" He swivels around and levels a waggling finger at me. "Bad dog! I tell you no and you do anyway? Kuso!"

"You're going to be a hero, Haruto," Micah tells the man. "Japan...hell, the whole world will know who you are. I doubt you'll ever have to drive a bus again."

This placates the man somewhat, but our other driver is losing his patience.

"Could you please tell the very angry man to focus more on driving and less on being a whiney little bitch?" Chirk bounces in his seat as we strike rough pavement. "Trying to punch a hole through the atmosphere here!"

"Hey," the human named Sean says to Haruto. "Chirk says you need to stop being a whiney little bitch and—"

"He call *me* whiney little bitch?" Haruto shouts. "I call *him* very *little* bitch. Look like little girl dog. Take you to China. Make you into soup."

All eyes turn to Haruto.

"What did he just say?" Harth asks.

"Something about soup," Torel says.

"Bro," Sean says. "Not cool!"

I know next to nothing about Sean, but he seems to have Chirk's complete trust and, somehow, friendship. Chirk can be...abrasive. He does not have a lot of friends outside the team, and his quick temper often keeps the bitches at a distance. Sean, it would seem, is immune to Chirk's personality quirks or, even less likely, is able to diffuse them somehow.

I am not sure what they have been through together, but they have somehow become comrades. Sean is ready to fight on Chirk's behalf, which is admirable, but this is not the time or place.

Micah places a hand on Haruto's arm. Speaks to him in a calm, deliberate, and slightly threatening tone. "Stop shouting. Stop threatening. We are trying to save Grover. Nothing else matters. Not your feelings. Not your God-damned bus. All that matters at this moment, is that you drive as fast and as well as you can so that the little man back there can remote pilot a spaceship to Earth from the God-damned moon. Get us to the airport. That's all you need to do, okay?"

Haruto glances at him. Sighs. "Okay. Save dogs. Save the Earth."

"Something like that," he says.

Haruto's driving improves. He utilizes the entire road to avoid bumps and moves smoothly between lanes.

"Better," Chirk says. "ETA, three minutes. I heard something about an airport?"

"Almost there now," Micah says, looking up at the road signs.

"You read Japanese?" Haruto asks.

"What? No, I—" Micah double-takes the sign as we pass beneath it. It is written in the Japanese language, but like me, he has no trouble reading it thanks to a recent update in translation services. His mind continues to access the regulator without error.

"MIMIR," Chirk says. "Need a little help with the stabilizers."

"Copy that," MIMIR says. "Compensating for user deficiencies."

"User deficiencies? Who taught the A.I. to be funny?" Chirk says, leaning back and forth as he pilots. "Coming in hot."

"Are you okay?" I ask Sean.

He raises his hands. "Sorry 'bout that. Just riled when people rib my peeps."

I pretend to understand him. "Ahh. Yes."

"Sit down, broski," Chirk says, using an Earth term that neither I nor our translation services recognize. "Let the bossman do his thing."

Sean sits, and I lean out the bus's shattered window, looking back. For a strange moment, I feel great. The wind in my hair, the smells whipping past, something about it relaxes me. I could stay here for hours. Instead, I look up toward the sky and find a bright orange spot. The *Prowler* is slipping through the atmosphere and, aside from the sun, it is the brightest object in the sky. She will be an easy target.

My fear is confirmed a moment later when Chirk says, "Taking fire. Same shit that disabled the Leap Nodes."

"Is it a danger?" I ask.

"The *Prowler* ain't no Leap Node," Chirk says. "She is a battle-ready, ass-kicking machine of doom that has survived more—gah!" He recovers from the surprise quickly, thanks to not being on board. "Took a hard hit. They've increased the power. MIMIR, set a chaotic course. Make it unpredictable."

"Affirmative," the A.I. says.

"Eyes on the airport," Chirk says. "Rendezvous at the southernmost airstrip. Looks like it's on an island of its own."

"Hai!" Haruto says. "Entering airport entrance tunnel now."

"Here they come!" Harth says.

Behind us, the biologic horde closes in, pushing to catch us inside the tunnel where there is nowhere to hide. But there is something odd about them. The way they are moving. At first, I thought it was a jumbling mess of eager drones.

But drones are not eager.

Biologics share a common goal. They do not vie for position.

With this perspective in mind, I see them for what they are.

An *it*.

A singular.

They are not fighting for position or grappling with each other. They are holding on to one another, conjoined into a single, massive creature. Every body making up the mass works together, undulating the massive whole as one inorg-anic organism composed of faux flesh, metal bones, and hundreds of independ-ent biologic minds united to complete a common task—

—our destruction.

"Micah," I say.

"I see it," he says, leaning out the side window as we plunge into the tunnel. "I might be able to slow it down, but I'm still not sure how to super charge this thing."

"Channel your emotions," I say. It is the best advice I can give in such a short time. There was a time when the gauntlets were more...intuitive. More in tune with the warrior using it. It has been said that those with the heart of a warrior, fighting for what they love, could recharge a weapon system using energy derived from their spiritual selves. Not their bodies. Nothing tangible. That has mostly been written off as superstition and lost technology, but the Axiom—representing an essential, and unknown, principle governing the entire universe—would no doubt have access to ancient truths, whether he knows it or not.

The tunnel is lit by long strings of circular lights on either side. Walls appear to be large rectangular blocks, but I suspect it is solid, reinforced concrete. It would have to be. The ceiling overhead holds back the ocean.

For now.

"Harth," I shout.

"Full charge!" he responds. "But I'm not sure it will do much good. It will just shed the affected components and keep coming."

In response, I point up.

His eyes widen. Then he nods and leans out the back window.

He takes aim, straight up.

"Umm," Jess says. "That might not be a good idea. There's a lot of water up there. And we—in case you didn't notice—are down here."

"Not liking the sound of this!" Chirk says, leaning back and forth, tapping buttons only he can see.

Sean turns around and sees Harth. "Oh, damn."

"I don't like, 'oh, damn,' either," Chirk says.

"Everyone hold on," I say. "Physics is on our side."

"Oookay," Chirk says, reaching out a hand in reality. Finds Sean's lap and crawls up onto his legs. "Seatbelt me."

Sean wraps his arms around our small pilot, holding him tight while he pi-lots the *Prowler*. "Something I should know about physics?"

"Aside from everything?" Chirk says, shaking his head. "It gets bumpy."

I give Harth a nod, and he fires.

His Incinerator round strikes the tunnel's ceiling, reducing it to dust and burning its way upward. A quarter of the biologic monster makes it past the round before the ceiling implodes, instantly filling the space and launching water, biologics, and a wave of pressure in our direction.

48

CHIRK

As a pup cadet in the Kyno Corps pilot training program, I spent a lot of time in sims, wearing a headset, controlling a variety of vehicles that didn't exist in the real world. After purposefully crashing every vehicle I could—for fun—I excelled and graduated to remote piloting military aircraft that *did* exist. Spent years training. To be the best of the best. And it wasn't until I achieved that goal that I was promoted to the role of actual pilot. There aren't that many of us. Kyno Corps crafts are controlled remotely by a combination of A.I. and Kynolari safely tucked away in a control center.

Point is, I have a lot of experience. I've been trained for every scenario.

That's what I was told.

Now I know exactly how big a pile of shit that was.

Big. Really big. Like the size of a Sklaug's pendulous testicular pouch.

To be fair, I studied thousands of possible strategies for just about any situation I could imagine. But not one of them included remotely piloting into an unknown planet's atmosphere, while under laser fire, while being thrashed in a moving panda bus being driven by a lunatic with a penchant for potholes, all while being chased by a creative horde of biologics that have merged to form a writhing attack phallus.

When we get back to Kyno and I suggest this scenario for future trainees, they'll see a rapid drop-off in graduates with perfect scores.

But not me.

I got this shit.

Sean does a good job keeping me steady. He moves with me, while buffering me from the worst of the bus's movement. It's awkward, not only from a piloting point of view, but also trusting a human being enough to let one hold me like this.

The hardest part is when I lean left with the *Prowler* and the bus goes the other way. Screws with my equilibrium. Nearly puke a few times, but there's no time for it.

MIMIR does her job, keeping the *Prowler* steady and compensating for my erratic maneuvers, adding a few of her own—as requested—to avoid laser fire. It was strange, at first, co-piloting with an A.I., but I'm used to it now. There are a series of symbols in my heads-up display, each of which lights up when MIMIR is a fraction of a second away from making a course change, allowing me to move with it rather than against it. To the outside observer, we move as one.

Not that there's anyone observing my epic entry into the atmosphere, careening through and around clouds, maneuvering like a madman to avoid laser fire. We take a few hits, but the *Prowler* is tough and has been hit by heavier weapons before. She'll survive.

No idea about the rest of us. I'm uncomfortable knowing we're directly under attack, but there's nothing I can do about it.

Focus, I tell myself as the *Prowler* punches through the lowermost cloud layer. A vast blue ocean comes into view. Far to the north: land. It's highlighted with a tall orange beam of light, pinpointing the team's location.

Thanks to the planet being round, the ground-based laser fire ceases as we descend.

The *Prowler* levels out just feet above the water's surface, kicking up a wake behind it.

"Damage report?" I ask.

"Huh? Well, the windows are broken," Sean says in the real world.

"Not you," I say. "MIMIR."

"Minimal damage to secondary systems that will be repaired within the hour. However, thermal shielding was damaged during entry. I do not recommend leaving the atmosphere until repairs can be completed."

"How long?" I ask.

"It gets the job done," Sean says, bouncing me around as he laughs.

I grin but ignore him.

"Two hours," MIMIR says.

"Understood. Passing full control to you. Keep us on course and perform rapid evac maneuver thirty-seven when you reach the coordinates."

"Copy that," MIMIR says. "Course plotted. Preparing for maneuver thirty-seven."

"While you're at it, prep weapon systems."

"Which systems would you like to activate?" MIMIR asks.

"Sean," I say, "how bad is it? The thing chasing us?"

"Uh," he says, twisting his body around. "On a scale of one to ten, it's kind of a 'Holy shit, we're about to die.' Honestly, I'm kind of freaking out. If my ass wasn't so clenched, I'd probably be shitting myself."

"MIMIR," I say.

"Here."

"All of them."

"Are you sure?" she asks. "Have you consulted Prax—"

"All. Of. Them." I'm not a fan of repeating myself, but I maintain my composure because MIMIR's concern isn't completely unfounded. I'm a pilot, not a gunner. That's more Gruunlokar's forte, but he's not here, and I'm not about to entrust Baarfolir with the ship's weapon systems.

Then again, some of the others might prefer the historian behind the trigger. Because I like to cut things close. I've never hurt anyone. Never officially been a purveyor of friendly fire. But there have been...incidents. Occasions when Kynolari had a tuft singed. Nothing serious, but I've altered a few hair styles.

"One minute until maneuver thirty-seven," MIMIR says. "Weapon systems active."

"Might want to tell Baarfolir to buckle up."

In the real world, Sean says, "Baarfolir... *Baar*folir."

"Prowler-One was buckled before entering the atmosphere," MIMIR says.

"Is he screaming?" I ask. "Please tell me he's screaming."

My heads-up display switches to an interior view of the cockpit, where Baarfolir sits in my God-damned chair, grasping the armrests, eyes wide, mouth open in a silent scream as he watches the ship career over the ocean, toward the land ahead.

I laugh. "Oh, that makes me happy." I switch my view back to the gunner's HUD. "Okay, let's get messy."

"What did he just say?" Harth asks. "You. Human."

"Who me?" Sean asks.

"Yes. What did Chirk just say?"

"Don't tell him," I whisper.

"I, uhh..." Sean is unsure what to do. Harth is intimidating, and if I heard the background noise correctly, he just shot out the inside of a tunnel.

"Shh!" I say, zooming in and watching the tunnel from the outside, a few miles out still.

"He said I'm his bestie," Sean says.

I'm thrust back into Sean's body as the bus is propelled forward from behind. It's a surreal experience, feeling the movement, but watching the ocean above the tunnel drop down, filling the concrete tube with water and pressure. The bus launches out of the tunnel, heaved by a horizontal fountain of water. A segment of the biologic worm makes it through behind the bus, but much of it is crushed beneath the massive water weight.

I'm thrashed around inside the bus while watching from a distance as it lands, bounces from side to side, and eventually settles onto all four wheels, tearing through the middle of the airport, weaving in and out of other vehicles.

I try to line up a clean shot at what now looks like a ball of biologic fury. It's thirty feet tall, and large enough to swallow up the bus.

"Keep going straight, Haruto!" I shout. "No matter what happens. Do not turn away from that final runway."

"I get you!" Haruto shouts back. "I get you! Geez. Little dog is backseat driver. Not enough he piloting fancy spaceship, but now he want to drive panda bus, too?"

"I ain't piloting," I mutter, still trying to lock onto the ball of biologic death closing in on them.

"I heard that!" Harth says. The big bastard moves closer to me, listening in amidst the chaos playing out around him, like me being behind the barrels of a dozen weapon systems scares him more than being dismantled by drones.

"You do your thing," I say, "I'll do mine!"

"You're doing Gruunlokar's thing," he says.

"Chirk," Praxion says. Sounds like he's crouched down beside me. "What are you doing?"

"Saving our asses," I say. "You do realize I'm in the God-damned bus, too?"

"There is gate ahead!" Haruto calls out.

"Through the gate, Haruto!" Micah shouts. "Through the gate!"

A moment later, I hear the metal gate crash against the front of the panda, feel the bounce of metal beneath the tires, and see the whole thing play out like I'm watching one of Sean's Earth movies.

"Thirty seconds, Praxion," I say. "Maneuver thirty-seven. Might want to get everyone situated."

"Everyone take a seat!" the bossman shouts. "Hold on tight. Harth, Torel, help me steady Grover."

I tune out everything that's said next. None of it matters. I'm in two places at once, feeling all kinds of fucking calm. The *Prowler* twists into a sudden ninety-degree spin, sliding up beside the end of the last runway. The cargo bay's side hatch opens, the ramp lowering to the runway.

As soon as we stop moving, my weapon systems lock on target.

"Get under your sheets and hold on to your teats," I say. "Time to feel the mother-fucking heat!"

I fire an array of weapons all at once, unleashing splintering rail-shards, particle beams, gravity torpedoes, and rockets. The *Prowler* shits out a wave of death that careens toward the dented-in panda face. I squint my eyes, hoping I haven't just killed us all.

In the real world, I hear the projectiles and energy pass in time with Harth's, "I don't want to die like this!"

From my gunner's seat point-of-view, I watch the array of death miss the bus and strike the biologics. The ball implodes and then bursts. Body parts are flung. Gore splatters the end of the runway.

Hell yes, I think. Only thing I can be accused of is maybe a little bit of overkill. But this is the Draun we're talking about here. Overkill usually isn't nearly enough.

I'm bounced out of my headset when the bus strikes the ramp and surges up into the *Prowler*. Everyone is alive and safe.

Except for Grover.

The moment the bus comes to a stop, Torel takes hold of the stretcher and shoves her way down the center aisle. "Everyone out of the way! Baarfolir, meet me in the med bay." She pauses by Micah. "You can come if you let me work and don't say a word unless I ask you something."

He gives a nod, and then they're off to save the first Kynolari casualty of a reignited war we'd thought was won years ago.

49

MICAH

I've never had a panic attack before. Usually feel like I'm in complete control—maybe not of my circumstances or surroundings or other people, but of myself. I can mold my emotions like a child with a case of Play-Doh. Can compartmentalize trauma and save it for later, when I'm sitting in front of a therapist. That's the way hard jobs get done.

But right now, I'm freaking out.

It's taking every trick in the book for me to not be a blubbering mess. I'm breathing intentionally, pacing out my inhalations, making a mental checklist of chores to do at home, and telling myself everything will be fine, that there's no way Grover can die. It's just impossible.

I've had dogs pass before. It is the brutal reality of befriending a creature that lives a decade on average. Fifteen years if they're lucky. Far fewer if they're not.

But Grover... He's not just young, not just my closest companion on this planet, but he's also the last living vestige of my parents. Losing him will feel like losing them again, or at least what's left of them.

I focus on the back of Torel's feet, following her through the ship. I barely notice my surroundings. White hallways. Arching support beams. Mesh walls. Some part of my mind registers all of it as strange and new, but I'm not impressed, moved, or distracted by it.

It's not until a hand takes mine from behind that I snap out of my battle between mental breakdown and my grip on reality.

I gasp at the touch.

"Hey, hey," Jess says, squeezing my hand. "I'm here with you. You don't need to do this alone."

I squeeze back, probably harder than I should. But I can't speak. If I attempt to make a sound, it will come out as a sob. People tend to think that being a special operator means you're a soulless killing machine whose emotions are so stunted that you can wade through a sea of bodies and come out the other side chuckling like a villain in a Japanese anime. Truth is, we whittle our lives down to a core group of people without whom we're lost. Often times, that's just a fire team and the family we grew up with. Then a wife and kids. Relationships are intense.

Losing someone from that tight knit family stings. I've seen battle-hardened war-riors openly weep—in a medic's tent, on an evac chopper, and again at too many funerals.

Losing someone that has saved your life—as Grover did mine in the wake of my parent's passing—feels like an amputation, but not of some limb. The hacked away part of you comes from inside, like the still-beating heart in the hands of Mola Ram in *Indiana Jones and the Temple of Doom.*

"There," Torel says, pointing to a curved bench mounted to the wall of a domed oval room. The entire ceiling glows with bright ambient light. Feels like we've just walked out into a sunny day. My spirits lift just a little and I see my surroundings for the first time since entering the ship.

We're in a futuristic med-bay. Lots of equipment and machines I don't recognize, including six robotic arms hanging from the ceiling. We're on an alien space craft... The *Prowler.* A ship that can traverse the stars, created by an advanced society of beings whose physiology is more similar to Grover's than to any human's.

If anyone can save Grover, it's them.

It's Torel.

I watch her work, lowering Gover onto an operating table beneath the six arms.

"I'm here, I'm here," says a new voice. Sounds a little older than the others. Scratchy and yeah, a little cute. A wizened looking Bearded Collie hurries into the room, dressed in pants and what looks like a black knit sweater. Black ops casual. "Just tell me what to—"

He sees us. Staggers back a few steps.

I haven't met him, but this must be Baarfolir, the attached historian left be-hind on the *Prowler.*

"Oh! My. Look at them..." He steps closer to me and Jess, looking both of us over. "Fascinating. Nearly hairless. Primitive, but there is intelligence in their eyes, isn't there? A hidden potential...but for what?"

"Little man," Jess says, and points to Torel and Grover.

He follows her finger and remembers why he's there. "Oh, yes! Of course, of course. Torel—"

"T-scan," she says, pointing to a large, arching device.

Baarfolir presses a touch screen, and the T-scan device hovers over the floor. He moves it with little effort, guiding the machine over Grover. It settles down around him, its interior glowing with pulsating lights.

"All crew prepare for rapid maneuvers." It's Chirk over comms, back in the pilot seat.

"We'll be fine," Torel tells me. "Might feel some bumps, but we could flip over, and you wouldn't really know it."

"Hey, Micah," Chirk says, "if you're up to it, I could use a destination. Someplace we'd be hard to find with Earth tech."

The direct strategic question helps me separate myself from the desperation of the moment. "How is the *Prowler* at handling pressure?"

"Can fly through the heart of a gas giant," he says. "Why—ohh. The ocean. Gotcha. Dumb question."

A moment later, I feel the ship shift, but it's subtle, and I can't tell if we've shot up into the sky, or down into the water.

"T-scan running," Baarfolir says, stepping back, looking at the large touchscreen with Torel. It's like an X-ray, Cat-Scan, and MRI all in one, quickly viewing Grover's insides in high resolution detail, highlighting all the damage done to his body.

"Oh my," Baarfolir says. "What happened?"

"Helion," Torel says, and then looks to me. "If it helps, I've seen worse, but...Grover is not Kynolari. Best we can do is try."

I nod my understanding.

"What can I do now?" Baarfolir asks.

"Distract them," Torel says, motioning to me, and adding, "This is going to take some time. Being in the room won't do you—or me—any good. I will contact you the moment anything changes, for better or worse."

Baarfolir turns to me. "I'm sure this is all very disconcerting for you both, but you must trust the process. No field medic in the universe has more experience than Torel. Grover is in the best hands possible."

He's kind and gentle. Instantly trustworthy. And his words help. A little.

"There is something I could use your input on," he says.

I look back to Torel and Grover. She's plugging lines of who knows what into his body, attaching electrodes to his head, and the robotic arms above him are coming to life, lowering down from the ceiling. They're right. I can't watch this.

"Okay," I say, fighting back emotions once more.

Before leaving, I head for the operating table and lean over Grover's body. I pet his ear and neck. Kiss his forehead. "See you soon, buddy."

I place my hand on Torel's shoulder. "Whatever happens, thank you."

She gives me a nod and goes back to work.

Then I follow a very sympathetic looking Baarfolir out of the med-bay and into a winding hallway. The ship's interior is surprisingly organic. The walls are solid but composed of a weblike structure. It appears random, but I'm sure it's not. A door whooshes open to what can best be described as a study. There are actual bookshelves on the walls, full of ancient tomes from another world. At the center of the room is a circular bench surrounding a glass table.

"I've been doing research," Baarfolir says, taking a seat at the table and motioning for us to join him. He waves a hand over the glass, and it glows a gentle blue. Above the glass, holograms—I think they're holograms—of books appear. Human books.

He sees our surprise and says, "Go ahead. You can touch them as long as they're within the table's circumference."

"What are they?" Jess asks.

"A small sampling of humanity's ancient texts. Many of them are similar to those of our people." He motions to the books surrounding us. "Poems. Epic tales. Religions. Philosophies. You can read any of them you like. I sampled a few on my own, but it is much simpler to let MIMIR download all of the data and then answer questions you might have."

"I'm familiar with the concept. People—*Earthlings*—have just begun playing around with A.I. ourselves."

"Indeed," he says. "Primitive, but similar enough. I'm curious about something though... Do your people have oral traditions? What I mean is, do you have knowledge about your people that might not be in books?"

"Only of a personal nature," Jess says. "Or maybe if you're an expert in a particular field."

"I don't suppose either of you are experts in Earth history? Anthropology, perhaps?"

"I'm a soldier," I say. "Like the rest of your crew."

"You're much more than that," he says, looking at the gauntlet attached to my arm. The regulators behind my ears hold his attention for a moment, as well. He turns to Jess.

"I'm an artist," she says. "Trying to be."

"The universe needs more artists," he says with a smile. "Regardless, perhaps you can help. I've come to a conclusion and was hoping to get confirmation from an outside source." He taps his hairy chin. "Perhaps there is another way." He looks back and forth between us. Lands on me. "Would you mind submitting to a genetic sequencing and brain scan? Neither will take long, but I believe both will be revelatory."

"How revelatory?" Jess asks, flipping through pages of holographic ancient papyrus.

"The kind that reshapes your entire view of history and your place in the universe, not to mention whether your species will be a friend or foe to the

Kynolari. If war returns to the universe, Earth might be the first battlefield. It would be beneficial to know what side your people—as a whole—would take.

I'm not sure I like the sound of anything he's just said, but it's keeping me distracted from the potential that I'll never see Grover again. "Let's do it."

50

"Are we being followed?" I ask.

Chirk shakes his head. "Nothing detectable."

"This planet is too backward to pursue us into the water's depths," Harth adds.

"They are not as backward as we would like to believe," I say, thinking about the things we have witnessed. The things we have seen Micah do. "I agree that appearances are not encouraging, but there is something about them—some of them—that gives me hope."

"Hope will not be enough to save them," Harth says.

"That's our job," Chirk adds.

"Hell yeah, it is," the man named Sean says, pumping a fist.

I had forgotten he was here, seated beside me in the *Prowler's* cockpit, listening to our conversation about humanity. He does not seem offended by our harsh critique of his people. In fact, he is conducting himself like...he is one of us. As if his newly forged friendship with Chirk—a miracle on its own—supersedes his previous experiences and allegiances.

Humanity might very well be the strangest creatures I have encountered in the universe, despite the fact that, visually, they are quite bland. They make up for it with a great capacity for compassion, love, and trust—things I know I struggle with after years of conflict. Yet, despite being a soldier, Micah excels where even I fall short.

And Grover.

He has single-handedly managed to change my assessment of the Lost Tribe's fate. They *have* changed, but it might not have been for the worse. They are fierce protectors, loyal companions and, in some ways, they seem to complete a human who treats them like family. Over the past millennia, Earth dogs have become an integral part of this planet's evolution.

But I am still uncertain about humanity as a whole.

They are wracked by division and infighting, guided in some way by the Draun, whose influence on this planet might have just begun...or might have been present for some time. They seem well established, but also, not yet organized or widespread.

There are few Draun worlds where we would have been able to hide simply by plummeting into the depths.

"Recommendations?" I ask.

"Our first priority should be getting word to Kyno," Harth says. "They need to know the Draun are still a threat."

"Not without Gruunlokar," Chirk says.

"Leave no man—or dog—behind," Sean says, backing up Chirk.

I share their sentiment, but can we justify risking the universe for the sake of one soldier, even Gruunlokar?

"Plus," Sean says, "their operation is small potatoes, right?"

"Small...potatoes?" I ask.

"New," he says. "At least on a Galactic scale. I mean, sure, they've got a lot of freaky robotic drone things, but most of them weren't even finished. They threw some Helions at us, but if they work the way I think they work—"

"Learning from each attack and adapting strategies with each new wave," Chirk gives a nod.

"—then they didn't really have many of them. What good is learning from mistakes if you've only got five tries? And the last of those five was an OG Helion, right? The original species, which you all thought was extinct...and might be now. Sounds like a desperation move. Have you considered that they've been tossing everything they've got at you to give you the impression that they are strong here? That they've got more than a bunch of airport Leap Nodes, and a bunch of people-shaped drones? Hell, these fuckers are gaslighting you."

"I am unfamiliar with the term," I say.

"Means they're presenting you with a version of reality that is bullshit, in the hopes that you will buy into it, that you'll believe it, and give them control. Bro, you guys need to watch some Dr. Phil. It's human psychology 101."

"We are *not* human," Harth says.

I scratch an itch behind my ear.

"Aww, let me get that for you, buddy." Sean leans over and scratches behind my ear, somehow knowing exactly where and how to drag his nails. When he does—before I can swat him away—my right leg begins to twitch, thumping the floor.

"Stop that, fool," Harth says, slapping Sean's hand away. He looks at me, and then down at my leg. "What was that?"

"I...do not know," I say, looking down at the limb I just lost control of.

"It's normal," Sean says. "Happens all the time. Look." He leans forward and scratches Chirk behind the ear. Chirk's leg twitches like mine, an involuntary response.

"Ahh," Chirk says, leg thumping. "That's the sweet spot." When Sean stops, Chirk looks back at Harth and me. Sees our skeptical eyebrows. "Don't judge. I'm telling you, it might look weird as a Merflog's prolapsed shit spout, but the Lost Tribe got a lot right on this world."

Before I can respond, Baarfolir's soft-spoken voice speaks to me via the comms. "Praxion?"

"Baarfolir. Status?" I ask.

"On Grover," he says, "I'm not sure. Torel is seeing to him. I'm with Micah and Jess in the study. We've made a discovery."

"Can it wait?" I ask. "We are...attempting to devise a strategy."

"I'm sorry, sir, it cannot wait. And I believe it might very well affect every decision you make from here on."

Baarfolir is not known for exaggerating. He prefers precision and facts.

"Very well."

I stand and address the three of them. "Come up with some actionable options. We will discuss when I return."

"We're on it, boss," Sean says, offering a strange kind of salute.

Harth harrumphs. "I do not like his casual disregard for—"

Chirk waves him off. "Ahh, you'll get used to it, big guy. Just be a good boy and go with the flow."

"Who *are* you?" Harth asks as I leave.

The study is not far, but I have time to consider Sean's point of view. He does not strike me as intelligent. Then again, he might simply be disguising a sharp mind. But the Draun cannot be underestimated. We have only faced their minions thus far. A Draun is a far different and more dangerous challenge.

I enter the study to find it looking more like a laboratory. Micah is seated, a neural scanner attached to his regulators, wrapped around in front of his eyes.

"On a scale of one to ten," he says, face turned to Jess, seated beside him. "How much do I look like Geordi La Forge?"

"A solid seven," she says. "Too much hair and a near complete lack of melanin are working against the illusion."

I clear my throat. "What have you found?"

Baarfolir sits up and looks over the top of a medical tablet. "Thank you for coming, sir. I wouldn't normally bother you with—"

"Get to the point," I say, not in the mood for long winded explanations.

"Yes. Of course. Right. Well...you see... I've tested Micah's DNA. And while much of it is biologically unique to this world, there is also enough foreign DNA that they are, in theory, a different species now, than they were one hundred thousand years ago."

I squint but stay silent.

"You see, there was a point in human evolution where Neanderthals—a more primitive branch of their evolutionary tree—co-existed with modern humans. What they call Homo sapiens. For a long time, humans believed that they received a biological advantage through crossbreeding with Neanderthals before their extinction forty-thousand years ago. But...there is evidence that their DNA was altered—radically—a hundred thousand years ago. It was at this time that humanity really started to migrate around the planet and could have led to the Neanderthal's extinction."

"The DNA," I say, suspecting that its source is the point of this conversation. Earth would not be the first planet where the development of an emerging species was altered by forces from outside the planetary system. On occasion, it happens accidentally. More often, it is done on purpose by those with a need for slave labor. "Where did it come from?"

He clears his throat. "T-the Draun."

"You said humanity could be a different species now," I point out. "Did you mean...?"

He nods. "Technically, more like cousins of the Draun. But they are enough Draun that..." He glances at Micah and Jess. "...Earth would be purged."

"Which is not cool," Jess says. "Just in case you are open to opinions."

My instinct is to power up my gauntlet and kill them both. Nothing good has ever come from the Draun. If these two really are what Baarfolir claims, they will betray us. They are our enemy. They...

I focus on Baarfolir. "Why are you smiling?"

"There's more," he says. "As you know, the Lost Tribe found themselves marooned on this world 37,000 years ago. They found a humanity that was just beginning to form civilizations, long since altered by the Draun, and long before they posed a universal threat. Over time, humanity came to depend on the Lost Tribe. For protection. For companionship. More than that, many of this world's early religions revered the Lost Tribe, even worshipped them as Kynolari technology was used to create some of man's oldest megalithic structures. Do you recognize him?"

He waves his hand and a blue image of a familiar Kynolari breed is displayed. But his head dress represents a specific historical—some say mythological—figure.

"Anubis," Micah says, catching me off guard. "God of the dead in ancient Egypt."

"Is he still?" I ask.

Micah shakes his head. "Not for a long time."

Baarfolir continues. "Over millennia, the Lost Tribe changed. Their minds shrank, they reverted back to a four-legged gait, they became hunters and lost the ability to speak. But they also seemed to gain empathic abilities our heroes of old once possessed. It wasn't long before human and Kynolari were perfectly integrated into each other's lives."

"But they are *not* human," I say, offended by the idea of Kynolari living in harmony with Draun.

He holds up a second neural scanner. "Put this on."

I do as I'm told and wait for the short process to complete. When I hear the chime, I remove the device and look at the medical tablet Baarfolir has turned around. It shows a colorful image of my brainwaves.

"Your mind," he says, "the way it works, is distinctly Kynolari. Every single one of our scans looks just like this, no matter the size, upbringing, health, or breed. It is one of the things that truly unites us."

"I know all of this," I say.

"Of course, of course." He waves his hands. "This is the important part." He works the medical tablet upside down, pairing it with the neural scanner still on Micah's head. He runs the scan, and the results are displayed.

Before I can ask, Baarfolir brings up my results and displays them side by side with Micah's. Then, just to make sure there is no doubt, he overlaps the results.

Identical.

"Is this real?" I ask, stunned.

"I've rerun the test a dozen times. It seems that humans—at least the ones who spend a lot of time among the Lost Tribe—are positively affected by the relationship, which literally changes their thoughts and their brainwaves, to those of a Kynolari. They might have Draun DNA, but some of them, maybe many of them, are as Kynolari as you. I suspect that this is why Micah integrated with the regulator so quickly, and the gauntlet had no adverse effects."

I take a seat.

Micah removes the headset. He looks all twisted up with emotion. And it's not just concern for Grover. This revelation has moved him. Humbled him. "My mother used to say that every time we lost a dog, it took a piece of our hearts, but at the same time left a piece of its own for us. And that, with enough time, enough dogs, we would be just as loving and compassionate as them. That we would be more dog—than human. I don't think she knew that for a fact, but I think all long-time dog owners know it. In their core. We feel the change, from human—to dog. To Kynolari."

It doesn't seem possible.

A Draun.

A human.

A Kynolari.

All in one.

"Do you know what this means?" Baarfolir asks.

I nod. There is no doubt now. "He *is* the Axiom."

51

CHIRK

"Okay, okay," Sean says. "Hear me out. We nuke the site from orbit."

Harth and I stare at him.

"It's the only way to be sure," he adds, smiling like an idiot.

"Wait a second," I say. "Are you quoting something we couldn't possibly have seen on account of coming from another world, light years away from Earth?"

His smile gets wider. "Well, in this other movie, Explorers, TV transmissions—"

"Don't care," I say. "Look, buddy...Sean, Praxion wants us to come up with serious, save-the-mother-fucking-day ideas. The kind that help win a battle against a superior force. Not the kind that's based on a movie."

"Wait," Harth said. "I liked the scenario in which we nuked the site from orbit. Was that not a genuine option?"

"We do not carry nuclear weaponry on the *Prowler*," I say, "or any other Kynolari ship. Mass innocent casualties ain't our style."

"This is true," Harth says. "But it sounded fun."

"But..." Sean says, thinking hard as he looks at the ceiling. "These Draun guys. Didn't you, like, wipe them out? Completely?"

Harth and I share a look.

"That's different," I say. "There are no innocent Draun. They're corrupt to the core. From birth. And there's nothing that can change that."

"Huh," he says.

"You sound judgmental," Harth says.

"All he said was 'huh,'" I point out.

Harth crosses his arms. "It was a judgmental 'huh.'"

"Look, Sean," I say. "War changes the rules, especially when you're dealing with a genocidal species like the Draun. They enslaved worlds. Committed genocide on a galactic scale. When flesh becomes diseased, you don't just take most of the rot away, right? You take it all or it will just spread again. The Draun are a disease. Only way to make sure it never returns is to cut it away with nothing left."

Sean gives a slow nod. "I get it."

Gets it but doesn't like it.

A low priority proximity alert chimes from the cockpit control panel.

"What's that?" Sean asks.

"Means we've got a visitor," I say.

"Anything we should be worried about?" he asks.

"It's large," I say, pulling up the object's data stream. "But fully organic. Not a threat."

Sean attempts to peer through the cockpit viewscreen. I chuckle. "That's not a window, asshole."

"Well, how the hell was I supposed to know?" He smiles. "Can we see what's out there?"

"Sure," I say, tapping my touchscreen panel. Lights on the outside of the *Prowler*'s hull snap on, illuminating the water around us. The cockpit viewscreen displays what's directly ahead. And it's nothing like what I expected.

Its eight arms and two tentacles flow through the water, casually probing the darkness for food. An eyeball that's larger than me rotates toward the *Prowler*, drawn by the bright light in the darkness.

"Holy Cthulhu," Sean says. "It's a giant squid."

"You seen one before?" I ask.

He shakes his head. "Only in videos. They live in the deep ocean. For a long time, we only knew they existed because of scars on whales—those are really big mammals. Mammals are—"

"I got it," I say. "Big animals eat other big animals. It's kind of a universal theme."

"Our biggest animal—a blue whale—eats the smallest," he says. "Filters them out of the water."

"Huh..." is all I can say.

He leans closer to the screen. "I watch a lot of Discovery Channel."

"Figured it was something like that," I say.

Praxion returns without a word. He just sits with the same brooding expression he had upon discovering the location of the Draun homeworld. The weight of the discovery, combined with the knowledge of what needed to be done weighed on his golden brow...just as it does now.

He just stares for a moment, and then lets out a long sigh. "Options."

His eyes drift to the view screen where the giant squid has closed in on the *Prowler* and is attempting to gnaw on the hull. It's a fascinating view, but Praxion isn't interested.

"Way I see it," Sean says. "We only have one solid play."

All eyes turn to him. Harth looks dubious. I'm suddenly wishing Sean knew when to keep his mouth shut. He doesn't understand what the look on Praxion's face means.

"Speak," Praxion says.

"Two-pronged strike. One with the *Prowler*. Big, violent, obvious. Make lots of noise, draw their attention. Meanwhile, a strike team, or whatever you call them, uses the blue bull thing. In the airport. Go to the other airport all stealthy. Infiltrate during the hubbub. Find your man. Exfil with him. And then bring the pain. Kaboomy. Job done. Bob's your uncle."

Not everything he said made sense. Some of it was just nonsense, but the core of his plan works. It's strategic. Solid. Doable.

Praxion grunts.

"Are all humans naturally strategic?" Harth asks.

"Some of us," Sean says. "I've just played a lot of Call of Duty. That's a video game."

"Wonderful," Harth says before turning to Praxion. "What is weighing on you?"

Praxion blinks and looks up. "Micah. His DNA."

"What of it?" Harth asks.

"A portion of it is Draun. And it is not just him. It is all of them."

"Draun?" I say, glancing at Sean, who looks just as contentedly dopey as always, immune to the ramifications of this revelation. "How *much* DNA?"

"Enough," Praxion says, and he quickly places a calming hand on Harth. The big guy's cue was subtle, but he was about to throttle Sean. "There is more. While their DNA was meddled with long ago, the arrival of the Lost Tribe appears to have also influenced the human race, or at least some of them. We don't know yet. And until we do, no larger action can be taken."

"I don't understand," Harth says. "If this world is genetically Draun, then it is only a matter of time before—"

"Micah's brainwaves are Kynolari," Praxion says.

I nearly fall from my seat. "What?"

"Impossible," Harth says, then his expression melts with realization. "Unless..."

"We have all seen it in him," Praxion says. "Sensed it. From the moment we met, I suspect, despite our reluctance to acknowledge the possibility. Micah is human. And Draun. But in his heart and mind, he is Kynolari, through and through. No corruption of genetics can overcome that."

Praxion looks us both in the eyes. "He is one of us, and more. He *is* the Axiom."

"*Awesome*," Sean says. "What's the Axiom?"

"A legend of our people," Harth says, "A being whose ideals represent a universal truth and knowledge, whose very existence is capable of generating power, recharging gauntlets in an instant. Perhaps more. It has only ever been a story...of how our people once were."

"Ha! You see?" Haruto says. He's been seated in the cockpit with us this whole time, head back, eyes closed. I'd assumed he was sleeping, but he was just listening. "Not only Earth dogs that have changed, eh? Not just people. Change part of universe. Ebb and flow like the ocean. You believe you better than people because our DNA is different, but in heart, in here..." He taps his chest. "...we just like you. In mind, we think alike. I listen to dog-people talking, all this time, and I wonder, *Why do they think they are better?* And I am right. Not better. We are the same."

Praxion nods. "Loud but correct. With one caveat. It appears your people have a choice. Most are oblivious to the option and remain human—neither Draun, nor Kynolari. Some, like Micah, have made the choice without ever knowing it."

"Dog people," Sean says.

"Kynolari," Harth corrects.

"Naw man, not you guys. Dog people. People who like dogs. Like, really like dogs. Like Micah. Me and Jess, too, even if we didn't have our own. We're just drawn to dogs. Feel the kinship. Get down on the floor, in the slobber, soak up the love, you know?"

"Perhaps," Praxion says. "But there is at least one human on this world who chose to embrace the Draun. We must find them. We must kill them, before this world can be fully corrupted."

"How we do that?" Haruto asks. "Only hippie-boy has plan."

"Am I hippie-boy?" Sean asks, smiling.

"'Am I hippie-boy?'" Haruto says, rolling his eyes and shaking his head.

"Yes," Praxion says. "Sean's plan sounds simple and effective. We will rescue Gruunlokar and, if we encounter the Draun, destroy them."

"For Kyno," Harth says, thumping a fist against his chest.

"For Grover," Micah says, standing at the back of the bridge with Jess and Baarfolir.

Harth stands and approaches Micah. He is one of the largest Kynolari I've ever seen, but he stands eye-to-eye with Micah. He offers his hand. "For Grover."

Micah nods and takes Harth's hand. "Let's fuck some shit up."

Harth grins. "Indeed."

52

We've split into two teams. The first, led by Chirk, is staying aboard the *Prowler* to cause a ruckus and draw attention. Staying with him are Harth, Baarfolir, Jess, Sean...and Grover, whose status is still unknown and won't be known until the array of procedures being carried out are complete. That they are being attempted at all gives me hope, but Torel is impossible to read when she talks about it.

Team two is led by me—a surprising honor, but also logical. Earth is my home turf, and I've been to Denver's airport a few times, not that my knowledge of what's above ground will be much use. Joining Praxion and me is Torel. Haruto will be joining us as well, but just for the first part of the mission. I wasn't keen on Torel leaving Grover's side, but her job is done, she says, and it's standard operating procedure for any fire team to include a medic.

Jess insisted she come with us, but I put the kibosh on that, but not because I'm sexist or overprotective. When Grover wakes up, I want him to have a familiar face looking down at him. Plus, she's not a soldier, even though she looks the part now, kitted out in Kynolari body armor. Her brain wave results were similar to mine.

Apparently, she grew up with dogs, like me, and lost her last just a few years ago. A Dalmatian. She was too heartbroken to get another, but it explains why she took to Grover so quickly. And it explains why her brain waves are also Kynolari.

Sean's results were close, but not quite there. Baarfolir believes that will change in time, that the more time humans spend with dogs, the more in sync their brainwaves become. He also revealed that Earth's atmosphere is similar to their original homeworld's early stages. The longer they spend on Earth, the more they feel those ancient stirrings, driving them toward instinct, empathic connection, and a primitive lifestyle. They have no fear of becoming like Earth dogs. That would take generations. Thousands of years. But they all agreed they were feeling the effects, especially Chirk.

Right now, we're fifty feet deep, just off the coast of Tokyo, ready to deploy our four-man rescue team. There's just one thing left to do.

"Are you sure about this?" Torel asks.

"I've got the brain waves," Jess says. "Should work."

Torel nods. "In theory. But Micah is…different."

"The Axiom," Jess says. "I know. I heard. The more you all mention it, the bigger his head is going to get."

"Is that something that happens to humans?" Harth asks.

"It's an expression," I say. "Means my ego will get big."

"He is the Axiom," Harth says. "His ego *should* be big."

Jess laughs. "Just…let's get this over with. These things already worked, right?" She pats the regulators attached to her head just behind her ears. Like mine, they connected with her mind and body like they were designed for us. Jess doesn't really need a gauntlet. She'll be safe inside the *Prowler*. But no one could argue when she pointed out how every moment since their arrival had been FUBAR. So, she's getting a gauntlet, too. Just in case.

"This is a gauntlet integration system," Torel explains, holding the same non-descript metallic tube that upgraded my arm to a weapon system. "Just slide your arm inside and hold still. It will hurt, but it won't take long."

Jess slides her arm inside. A moment later, she grunts. I remember the pain, the feeling of something punching through my arm, tapping into my bone, but it's so quick that bearing it isn't difficult.

When Torel says, "Done," Jess is surprised.

"That's it?"

"Advanced alien civilization," Torel says with a smile. "Remember?" She turns to me. "And now you… Are you sure? No one has ever worn two gauntlets simultaneously before."

"Why?" Jess asks.

"One has always been enough," Praxion says, watching from the doorway, dressed for battle and ready to go. The team is waiting on us.

"Well, you've never prepared for battle with an American before," I say, and slide my left arm into the integration system. Torel activates it and I feel the familiar sting of connectivity. Then it's complete. I withdraw my arm, flex my fingers, and then extend the claws—now on both hands. "Sick."

I charge both with laser energy and view the readouts in my heads-up display. Everything looks normal as far as I can tell. I extinguish the gauntlets and smile at Praxion. "Good to go."

He nods and activates his comms. "Prowler-One, Talon-Actual, we are 'go' for insertion. How copy?"

"Talon-Actual, Prowler-One," Chirk responds. "Strapped, wrapped, and ready to clap. Wait. No. That's what I say to the ladies. We're orange."

Praxion smiles. Seems that, like human operators, Kynolari de-stress with humor before a mission. "Copy that. We are orange. Take us up."

Jess and I face each other as the *Prowler* ascends.

"Well," I say. "Want to go out again?"

"Only if you survive," she says, "I'm not big on dating corpses."

"I'll do my best," I say and kiss her.

"Do all humans rely on romance to form bonds?" Torel asks.

"Only one bond," I say. "At a time. Usually. It can get complicated, but sometimes we're lucky and find someone special."

"Sounds like a lot of work," Praxion says, motioning us to follow him.

"Nothing worth doing is easy," I say.

Praxion grunts and smiles. Then he glances over at Torel, his gaze lingering for a moment. She doesn't notice, but I do. "Inside," he says, motioning to a small oval room.

Jess hugs me. "Be careful."

"Always am," I say.

"She is Kynolari," Torel says, "and we are exceptional at smelling lies."

I smile, squeeze Jess's hand, and then we're separated.

By the time the *Prowler* reaches the surface, the rescue team is gathered inside a small, oval space. There's a hiss around us. The walls grow glossy and slick for a moment before going opaque, like a thin filament has just formed a dome around us.

"Talon-Actual, Prowler-One," Chirk says. "Ready for deployment on your go, no go."

"Prowler-One, Talon-Actual," Praxion says, "we are go."

"Copy that," Chirk says. "Happy hunting, and do me a favor when you see the Draun, call them a—*what did you say?*"

In the background, I hear Sean whisper, "Dick-whore."

"Call them a dick-whore for Sean," Chirk says.

"No promises," Praxion says.

A hatch opens above us, revealing a ten-foot-tall tube. Water pours in from above. When the tube is full, we're launched upward toward the sunny surface. As the paper-thin bubble surrounding us breaks the water's surface, it dissolves away, leaving us standing on a disc, from which we can easily step onto the seawall bordering the Haneda airport.

"Come! Come!" Haruto says, waving us along like we're a lost tour group. "Just walk straight to terminal. No one pay attention."

He's not wrong about that. There are no planes leaving and none coming in. The chaos we brought through the airport not long ago has shut everything down. Sirens wail in the distance. Lights flash over the runway to our south, where the Draun remains lie scattered. Helicopters spin circles around the airport. I'm sure we'll be caught on camera, but as long as no one zooms in on Praxion or Torel, we should be okay.

Haruto sets a blistering pace across the tarmac. There's three hundred feet of open pavement to cross before we reach the maze of parked planes and the airport terminal beyond. All in search of a blue bull. Sounds like Indiana Jones on LSD to me, but hell, we got here thanks to a control panel on the ass end of a moose statue. Say what you will about the Draun, but they either really like animals, or they have a sense of humor. Perhaps that's a side effect of being partially genetically human.

When Haruto starts waggling his hips to either side, Praxion asks, "Do all humans walk with a strange gait?"

"Only speed walkers," I say, trying to keep up without looking silly.

"Is good exercise!" Haruto shouts back. He's ten feet ahead of us now. "Easy on the knees!"

I scan the tarmac, looking for anything out of the ordinary, but aside from the emergency vehicles, it's just another day in Japan, post destruction by monsters. When we reach the shadows of plane wings, I relax a little. We're no longer visible to the helicopters, or whatever small drones might be watching. The Twilight Directorate was playing fly on the wall during our shipping container battle. Last thing we need is for them to spot our rescue team before we reach Denver—or the blue bull.

Haruto reaches a service entrance. Tries the handle. Locked. He bangs on the door until it opens. Then he speaks loudly in Japanese. I understand bits and pieces thanks to the regulators, but he's talking so loud and fast that it's difficult as a non-native speaker to make it all out. And he keeps on going until the person holding the door relents and allows us to enter, giving each of us a quick nod as we pass.

"I told her you were famous TikToker kemoners. That is Furry in America. Very popular here. Said you had been stuck on plane and needed to find hotel, or airport get sued. She says airport evacuated, but we can walk through terminal to front door."

"Excellent work, Haruto," Praxion says.

Haruto opens a door at the end of the hall. He turns around, smiling. Gives a deep bow. "It has been an honor Praxion-san." He sweeps his hand to the side and steps back, revealing the airport terminal, and the blue bull, exactly where he said it would be. "May I present, Mooon."

The bull lounges on a stand surrounded by a short rope meant to keep curious children at bay. It's blue, as advertised, and covered in white speckled stars.

Its back end is painted with pine trees. I'm not sure what it represents to the Japanese, but it looks like it would be more at home in the state it leads to.

"Okay, we found the bull," I say, "but how are we going to activate it?"

This is a part of the plan I hadn't thought of until this very moment. Torel, on the other hand, has been ready for it since we left the factory. She pulls out one of Stuchbery's severed hands. She waves it like he's saying hello from beyond the grave.

Stuchbery. What an asshole.

Praxion steps over the barricade, inspecting the bull. He squints at the statue's backside. "The panel is hidden in plain sight, painted to match the pattern of the bull, but visible in the infrared spectrum."

"You see in infrared?" I ask.

"Only when I want to," he says. "Along with many other spectrums, thanks to an implant."

I lean over to Haruto. "Predator vision!"

"Ahh, yes. 'Get to da choppa.' Arnold-san." He's tense, but working hard at hiding it, just like the rest of us.

"Hand," Praxion says. She tosses it to him. He looks it over in disgust and then places it against the bull's side. A gentle hum fills the air. "It is activated."

I shake Haruto's hand. "This is when you get to go home, collect insurance on the bus, and tell a story no one will believe."

Haruto grins. Then he offers me his business card, which features a large happy panda bear. "In case you need me again. Or want to send post card."

I pocket the card, give him a smile, climb over the rope, and place my hand atop the bull. A moment later, the Leap Node hidden within the metal sculpture sends us across the Pacific Ocean, California, Nevada, Utah, and smack dab into the center of the United States—Denver, Colorado.

I breathe in the crisp, but thin, nighttime air and look up—directly into an oversized set of veiny blue testicles.

53

GRUUNLOKAR

"This is a little melodramatic, don't you think?" I ask, as I'm wheeled down a long, white hallway. The Draun pushes me along telekinetically, too proud to do the physical labor on her own. Ling's paws skitter over the hard floor, moving fast to keep pace.

I'm not even bound to the chair. The weight of her mind keeps me planted, unable to move my limbs, or my head. But she's allowing me to talk, perhaps out of boredom—she seems to be alone other than Ling and maybe Alton. Or she's mining me for more information.

"Your presence is less about drama and more about testing the limits of my enemies. With you by my side, killing me will mean killing you. I wonder if they have that kind of resolve."

"I think you'll be unpleasantly surprised," I say.

"It's been a long time since anything surprised me," she says. "It wouldn't be an unwelcome change."

"You sound lonely." The pressure on my body increases. "Just making an observation," I grunt.

"I have lived with the knowledge of what humanity really is, and what your people did to us, for a decade. It weighs heavily."

"What of Alton?" I ask.

"He is a dim light in the endless universe," she says. "Knows as much as he needs to. Were he not already in a position to advance my goals—the arrogant director of the Twilight Directorate—I would have cast him aside."

"And Ling?" I ask.

She laughs. "Ling?"

"She is your companion," I say. "Your friend."

"She is my dog." Her voice loses some of its bravado when she says those words. "I keep her to remind me what your kind does best—serve its masters."

She's lying. I don't call her on it, but I can hear her heartbeat. Know when it speeds up. Can smell her deception, though that is far more difficult. She is deceptive nearly all the time, projecting false confidence, making bold claims. It's as though she's trying to convince herself that what she's saying is true.

Why would she do that? I wonder.

If she is the lone Draun on this world...the mastermind behind my capture... the harbinger of a war to come, why try so hard to impress?

Because she is not alone.

Because she is not in charge.

There is someone else.

"Are they watching us?" I ask. "In this hallway? I assume there are cameras in the rooms, but what about here?"

She glances down at me, squinting. The pressure on me increases. Her mask, which she has not worn since taking it off, hovers up from the sides of her belt and seals itself over her face, hiding her expression. She turns her head down to look at me, and all I can see is a warped vision of my own face.

She's answered my question without saying a word.

We're being watched. Being listened to. All the time.

"Your friends are on their way here," she says, "traveling beneath the waters of the Pacific Ocean, perhaps believing they cannot be tracked. How will they do it, hmm? Will they drop from the sky and hope to gain entry through force? Will they attack from afar, trying to make us scurry out like ants?"

"Couldn't tell you," I say, and that's the truth, but what I saw in the drone video feed before it went dark gives me hope. Not just because they're alive, and together, but because they've found allies on this world.

Powerful allies.

This Draun saw the same thing I did. The felling of a Helion by a human being wearing a Kynolari gauntlet. That alone should be impossible, but he also managed to charge that gauntlet in seconds. I don't know if the Draun understands what that means, but I remember our legends well enough to know that pulling off a trick like that... It hasn't been done in millennia. Few Kynolari believe it was ever possible. But I saw a *human* do it.

A human, who, according to this woman, is a Draun just waiting to be woken up to his full potential. Thing is, I think he's already reached it, and if I'm right about him, whatever Draun might be a part of him is already dead.

"You know," I say, "if you aren't—"

My jaw snaps shut.

I'm unable to speak, muzzled by the Draun.

"Whatever your compatriots have planned," she says. "It will not be enough. This site is one of many."

I stop fighting her control and listen. *Is she telling me something?*

"This battle is already lost. There is no hope for your people. No hope for you. Or this world. It would have been better for you to have never arrived. You'll understand that soon enough."

I struggle and grunt, but my jaws are locked in place.

"Keep an open mind, Gruunlokar, and maybe that tiny brain of yours will be able to comprehend what is to come, and how futile killing me truly is."

She looks down at me. I can feel the pressure of her gaze on my eyes, but I cannot see her.

But I can feel her, scratching at my mind, searching for a way past my regulators.

She shakes her head and lets out a laugh, like she's disgusted. "Trust me."

I've stood on the precipice of a battlefield, where the pull of a trigger could start a battle that would put the lives of loved ones at risk. I've been in that position many times—and never once have I hesitated to pull that trigger first. Risk is part of war.

So, I take one now—

—and allow her access to my mind.

The hallway fades, replaced by a white abyss in which I am still seated, still being wheeled along by her, now maskless.

"I am not your enemy," she says.

I grunt.

"If I were, you'd be dead. What purpose does your life serve? I don't need to hide behind a living shield. I do not fear your allies. I know what I am. What I can do. What I *want* to do. But I also remember who I was before that signal unlocked my true self. A war is being fought within me, between selves."

"We were being watched?" I ask.

"Always."

"By whom?" I ask.

"One of them," she says. "Draun."

"One of them... You mean—"

"A non-human Draun," she says. "Yes. He looks the part. Probably why their genes mixed with humanity's as well as they did. But no part of him is human."

"What is his name?" I ask.

"Lumen Sok," she says.

My stomach knots. "The Visionary."

She nods.

"Impossible," I say. "He's dead. *I* killed him."

I remember the rail-shard, fired from my perch three miles away. The round struck his head, punched through his mask. Dropped him to the ground. Without his guidance, the rest of the battle was a bloody mess but, in comparison to previous confrontations, an easy win.

The Great War's end began with Lumen Sok's death.

"Where is he?" I ask.

"I do not know," she says. "But to reach him, your friends must die."

"How can I trust you?" I ask.

In a flash, the flow of information between our minds becomes a two-way street, full of memories. She was hunted. She sought the signal. Was...a hero. And her power, once unleashed, was vast. Then I see him, Lumen, drawn to Earth, to her power. The scar on the side of his head is revolting but healed. Here, on this forgotten world, he found a sleeping army waiting to be roused. He's been living as one of them, becoming the richest man on this planet, capable of stirring the masses, and influencing society on a grand scale. But nothing will compare to what he has planned. To the awakening.

"How do we stop it?" I ask.

"We don't."

"I don't understand," I say. "Why reveal all of this to me if—"

Her answer comes as a flood of emotion that overwhelms me.

Pain.

Disgust.

Regret.

Hers is a tortured soul, seeking what? Absolution? Redemption?

Those things are not possible for the Draun, and she will not find mercy for the things she has done. Not from me.

"I would expect nothing less," she says, reminding me that she has full access to my thoughts.

"Death is my only path to Lumen Sok," she says. "I am sorry for that, but I hope you understand."

With that, I feel like I've just fallen into an endless pit, plummeting deeper and deeper until all that remains is darkness.

54

"Impressive," I say, looking up at the underside of an anatomically correct Earth horse.

Torel scoffs. "Are Earth men obsessed with genitalia size as well?"

"Not at all," Micah says, while giving me a wink.

I grin and crouch beside him behind the horse.

"We're as exposed as Blucifer's nutsack," Micah says.

"Who is Blucifer?" I ask.

He points up to the horse. "This guy."

"Then I agree," I say. "I did not anticipate leaping into a vast open area. It does not make sense—"

"Unless there was an entrance to a secret underground facility directly beneath the statue?" Torel says, her hand lying flat on what appears to be a solid metal base. "If you two weren't so obsessed with testicles, you might not have missed the seam in the floor beneath your feet."

A small electric charge pulses from Torel's gauntlet, triggering a release mechanism. A hatch lowers and then slides to the side, revealing a ladder that descends into darkness.

"I'm not obsessed with testicles," Micah says, sliding onto the ladder. "Other than my own."

Torel shakes her head and rolls her eyes. "All across the universe, men are the same."

I smile at her, and our gaze lingers for a moment.

Then she climbs in behind Micah, and I follow, shoving the hatch closed above us. Enshrouded in darkness, we descend the ladder, rung by rung, for several minutes, none of us speaking. I do not bother changing visual spectrums. The tunnel around us is so small that I think seeing how tight the confines are might make me claustrophobic.

"Bottom," Micah says.

The tunnel awaiting us is utilitarian and gray, lit by bare lightbulbs.

"For the record," Micah whispers. "There's no one on Earth more obsessed with their nuts than dogs. Probably because they can lick them." He turns to me. "Can you lick your nuts?"

I sigh.

"The time for banter has ended."

"Sure," he says, grinning. He is like a larger, second Chirk. Though I suspect he is trying to mask his concern for Grover. Concern about loved ones can be deadly on the battlefield, as can any distraction. Humor is a common tactic when attempting to reframe one's mind...even when the task at hand is killing.

He transitions to a serious operator as we move down the tunnel, alert, focused, determined. A professional. And much more.

"Door ahead," he whispers.

We approach the door with caution, looking for a security measure to bypass, but there is nothing.

Have we walked into a trap? I wonder.

The door slides open at Micah's approach. We arm our gauntlets and take aim, but the tunnel on the other side is empty.

"Just like the grocery store," Micah says. "Question is, are these doors automatic, or did someone let us in?"

He moves through the doorway. The answer to his question does not matter. Forward is the only path. So, we take it. Two minutes later, we reach a second door...that does not open at our approach. Like the first, there is no clear lock mechanism.

"Let me try," Torel says, lifting her gauntlet to the door.

"Hold on," Micah says. "Even bad guys are polite sometimes." He gives the door a casual knock. He waits a moment, knocks again, and says, "C'mon guys, I mphumphible." The last word is mumbled nonsense.

He waits again.

Something inside the door *thunks*. It slides to the side, revealing a lone man dressed in orange coveralls. "Sorry, but this entry point is closed for—" He looks up. Sees our gauntlets aimed at him. Raises his hands. Drops a metal tool. "Oh. Shit."

"'Oh, shit,' is right. You human?" Micah raps his knuckles on the man's skull. "Feels human."

"Ouch," the man says. "I'm human, man. But what *the fuck* are they?"

He is staring at us with genuine shock. Not a biologic. Not a Draun.

"What are you doing here?" I ask.

His eyes go wide at the sound of my voice. "Talking dogs. Great." He turns to Micah. "Please tell me there is a gas leak and I'm hallucinating."

"Afraid not," Micah says. "Answer the question."

"I'm maintenance. For the airport. I service the outer tunnel systems."

"What are the tunnels for?" Micah asks.

"How should I know?" the man says. "Emergency exit? In case of terrorism, or I don't know, talking freakin' dogs?"

I look beyond the man. The tunnel branches in three directions. "Where do they lead?"

He points to his left. "Airport terminal." He points behind him. "Airport sublevel one. Heat and electrical. Shit like that."

"And down there?" Micah asks, pointing down the last tunnel.

"Hell, if I know," he says. "Another locked door... Guessing that's what you're looking for? I've never been past the door. No one has. We have theories about it. Me and the other guys. Denver airport is known for all kinds of creepy shit. Secret society stuff. Illuminati or Masons or whatever. Hey, if you get past the door, can you tell me what's back there?"

I look the man in the eyes. "We will wake you up upon our return."

"Wake me up?" the man asks.

Torel places a gentle hand on his shoulder. "Don't be concerned. It won't hurt until you wake up."

"Wait, what won't—"

The man convulses from a shock delivered by Torel's gauntlet. He drops to the floor, unconscious.

"Handy," Micah says, and leads the way left, down the tunnel that ends at another locked door. We do not have to travel far before finding it. The tunnel curves to the right and ends at another non-descript metal wall with a door. It does not open when we approach.

Torel places her hand against the door. "I'm not feeling a locking mechanism."

"How does that work?" Micah asks.

"Subtle electromagnetic pulses provide feedback, letting me feel the door's insides. If there is a lock here, it's unlike anything I've ever—" The door sinks in. Slides open.

"I didn't do that," Torel says, and then steps into the newly revealed tunnel.

Unlike the dull, gray, square hallway behind us, the walls are curved, white, and glowing. Bright white interiors are commonplace in the most advanced species in the universe. They help stave off depression during long journeys and make it easier to see something that does not belong. While Kynolari ships are white, they are also quite intricate, with pleasing, sweeping architectural designs. The Draun, in comparison, are minimalists. Everything in its simplest form.

"Starting to feel like they know we're here?" Micah asks.

"Perhaps," I say. "But this feels too subtle, as if—"

"Someone is helping you?" We all recognize the voice.

"Alton," Micah says.

He steps out from behind a corner, farther down the tunnel, hands raised, at our mercy. "She thinks me a fool, you know. Me. I am the director of the most secret black operation within the U.S. Government, and I earned my position long before she showed up. That's why she doesn't know about the microphones hidden in every room and device. From her chair, to the television. I hear everything. And now, I know what she plans to do."

"Turn every human being on Earth into Draun?" Micah asks.

His jaw drops a little. "W...How...Yes. Ultimately. That. But first she intends to kill all of you. As a show of fealty. To him. So *she* can reach him. Kill him herself. She believes to be doing all this on behalf of humanity, but I know the truth. I can hear it oozing from her lips every time she speaks—ambition cloaked in self-righteousness. If she really cared about humanity, she wouldn't have requested that I kill you, nor would she attempt to do so now, herself."

"Her name," Alton says, "is Jenna Flood. A fact I only recently learned, along with this tantalizing tidbit: she was once human. When things got dire for the Draun, they sent a signal to Earth, meant to awaken all of humanity to our true selves. But the signal was brief, perhaps because of an attack by your kind. It was received by just a single person. Jenna Flood. Her change was slow, but she became powerful. The most powerful human on the planet, I'd wager. And yet, she plans to betray us all, by allowing the change and then ascending to the throne. *His* throne."

I feel a weight on my chest. It demands I ask... "Whose throne?"

"Lumen Sok," he says, confirming my worst fear.

The Visionary lives. And he is here on Earth.

"This is far worse than we imagined," Torel says. "If the Visionary is here..."

"Earth is lost," I say to Micah. It is a grim forecast, but he does not argue.

"Where is she?" Torel asks.

"With your unfriendly and grim compatriot," he says. "I believe she is attempting to sway him. To recruit him as she once did me. With false pretenses and wicked lies. She has her talons in his mind."

"Impossible," I say.

"Unless he gave her access. I know the look of a man—or dog—whose mind has been compromised. I see it every time I look in the mirror. But I'm thinking more clearly now. Since your friend's arrival, her attention has been fully occupied."

"He would never betray us," Torel says.

"And I would never help you." He claps his hands against his hips. "And yet, here I am. Please. Time is short. Your friends are en route, and they aren't prepared for what—for who—they will face. You are here for Gruunlokar, yes? I suggest we collect him and leave. Live to fight another day."

"You are trying to save yourself," I say.

"Not sure I'm okay with that," Micah says, extending his claws. "You tried to kill us."

"Y-yes," he says, hands lifted in front of him. "I did. And I won't pretend that I was compelled. I was doing what I believed was right. What I was *taught* was right, trying to gain her favor, just as she is Lumen Sok's. I believed the Kynolari were Earth's enemy, and I was blinded by my own ambition."

"How do you know all of this?" I ask. "If Lumen Sok is behind everything, he will know what is happening here. Everything that is happening here. Including this conversation."

Alton nods. "And I hope you appreciate how much risk I'm putting myself in, telling you all of this."

"He wants amnesty," Torel says with a huff.

"I want to right my wrongs," he says, losing his patience. "Listen. Please. Before Jenna arrived, I had time to make...alterations to the—what do you call them—regulators, on Gruunlokar's head. They did not give me access to his mind...not until he allowed her in. And then, all I could do was listen. Information is my weapon, and I know how to collect it. But now...now you need to do something with it."

"What would you have us do?" I ask.

"Exactly what you came here to do," he says. "Rescue your friend. And leave. With me."

I consider the request and then shake my head. "We do not retreat from the Draun. We do not have mercy on the Draun. The woman you call Jenna may seek to destroy Lumen Sok, but if she intends to replace him, she is no better and must be killed before ascending the throne."

"Okay, okay, I understand all that, but don't you get it? This war cannot be won. Saving Gruunlokar? Killing Jenna? Those will be atomically small victories in the shadow of a world-sized victory."

"Wars are won by thousands of victories," I say, "no matter how small. Over time, they can overpower even the vastest military powers."

Alton nods. "As we've seen countless times on Earth, but...what if you cannot defeat her?"

"If we cannot win here today, we stand no chance against Lumen Sok or his machinations for this world."

Alton sighs. "A fatalistic approach, but better than nothing, I suppose."

"This is the point where you offer to take us to Gruunlokar," Micah says.

"Yes, yes, of course. Follow me." Alton waddles away.

He is far less imposing than I imagined.

"You do know," Micah says, "that if this turns out to be a trap, the first thing I will do is tear out your spine."

"And I believe you capable," Alton says. "I saw what you did in Japan. Best not let your power go to your head as well, eh?"

"Or your head," Micah says.

Alton chuckles and waggles a finger at Micah. "Touché." He waves for us to follow. "Come. Come. It's not far." He looks at his watch. "And your friends will be arriving any moment. If you want them to survive, we best move quickly."

55

CHIRK

"If you need to take a shit, you better start puckering, because there won't be time for a potty break until the Zoignat discharge stops hitting the leap drive."

Jess, my co-pilot who isn't a pilot at all, glances over at me.

"Inference," I say, angling the *Prowler* at a seventy-five-degree angle, skimming the continental slope as we travel from a depth of sixteen thousand feet toward the surface. "You'll figure it out."

"I'm actually concerned about Grover," she says.

"The med-bay is a stable space in the ship's core. The rest of us could be shaken until our brains turned to sludge and Grover wouldn't feel a thing. If he's feeling anything. Besides, Baarfolir's keeping an eye on him. Right now, there is no better place for Grover to be."

She sighs. It's heavy. "When will we know something?"

"MIMIR will fill us in when the procedures are complete. No point in saying anything until then. And there is no point in us worrying about him at the moment. Time to focus up. Forget the wounded. Forget the dogs you might have impregnated."

"What?" she says.

"Like I said, these are things we're forgetting about. Not talking about. Ever."

"Hey, man," Sean says from one of the two gunner stations. The other is occupied by Harth who is already locked in and ready for action. He won't speak unless he's got something important to say. "Far as I'm concerned, you were taking one for the team. You did what needed doing, plain and simple. No one's going to hold it against you, and if I can speak as a bro right now, I think you left her satisfied. At least the one I saw. What was her name? Foxy? Like the Hendrix song. Can't remember the other one, but I'm sure the situation was similar."

"Bacon," I grumble, and I glance up at Jess, who looks aghast. "Her name was Bacon, and she stole my heart long enough to steal my seed."

"*Oh.*" Her faces sours. "God. Let's go back to forgetting your Earth conquests."

"Please do," I say. "Breaching."

Ahead, the water shifts through from nearly black, to bright warbling blue. We slip out of the ocean and into the air without any discernable change in velocity. The *Prowler* generates a cavitation field around her at all times. She can move through any non-solid element like it was open air. The only limitation is when moving from a vacuum—where cavitation is impossible—to an atmosphere.

I level us out just feet above the water, speeding toward the North American coastline, hoping that Micah's information about his country's defense systems is accurate. According to him, all we need to do is hug the water, and the ground, to avoid being detected. Easy enough.

I'm not really worried about the defenses this backward world might throw at us. Things like bullets, missiles, and rockets are easy to defend against, outrun, or outmaneuver. It's the laser weaponry the Draun have positioned around this planet that makes me nervous. Best guess is that there's a land-based source which can be redirected around the world via satellite. We'll need to locate and destroy the source first—if it's in Denver. Then we can wreak havoc on the target zone from above. If we can't, this is going to be the most spastic assault in Kynolari history.

"How the heck are we supposed to hit anything at this speed?" Sean says. "The second I think I see something, it's gone past."

"We're moving at twenty-five thousand miles an hour," I tell him. "Ain't nothing in the universe that can see clearly at that speed. We'll slow down when we reach the target area."

"How long will that take?" Jess asks.

"At twenty-five thousand miles per hour?" I ask. "It's roughly about a thousand miles from the coast to our destination, so...two point four minutes, give or take a few seconds."

I glance at Jess. Her eyes are wide.

"Yeah," I say. "Makes my teats hard, too."

She huffs a laugh and then leans back, surprise building on her face as we race toward what looks like a gray wall.

"Is that the Rocky Mount—hhholy shit!" We reach the mountain range at full speed. Were I actually piloting at the moment, we'd have been vaporized against a mountainside. But MIMIR has already plotted the most efficient course. A blur of snowcapped peaks flow past. Then we clear the continental divide and cruise over forests, rivers, and rough terrain.

Our fledgling crew watches in awe as they tour their country faster than anyone before.

"Almost there," I say, taking control of the *Prowler* and reducing our speed to something a bit more manageable. "We're going to come in all hot and bothered, right? So don't hold back, but also avoid hitting the airport proper. We're trying to get the Draun's full attention, not kill a bunch of humies."

"Humies?" Jess says.

"Better than doggies," I grumble, and then I bank hard to the right as warnings begin to flash in my heads-up display. "Laser fire! They know we're coming! Harth, the laser battery should be kicking off some serious heat. See if you can find it."

"Sean," I say, banking up over a mountain, bringing the airport ahead into view. It's a vast complex similar to the facility in Japan, with the exception of its strange roof. Looks like a bunch of erect Corthonian mammary glands, lit in orange by a fading sun.

"Talon-Actual, Prowler-One," I say. "How copy?"

"Prowler-One, Talon-Actual," Praxion says. "I copy."

"We're taking some heat. Are you milking the Vloraxian Slifmaiden?" I ask, knowing he'll understand the question, while anyone else listening won't have witnessed the majesty of a Vloraxian Slifmaiden...or what its milk tastes like.

This airport has really put teats on my mind.

"Affirmative," he says. "Milking's commenced."

I mute my comms for a moment and lean back. "Harth. Is it just me or is Praxion a little more...relaxed?"

"I have noted the change," he says. "In all of us. He is more...lighthearted."

"Huh," I say, and unmute the comms. "Copy that. Are we orange to start this dance party?"

"Affirmative, Prowler-One. Dance away."

"Commencing dance," I say. "Let me know when you're ready for exfil."

"Will do, Prowler-One. Talon-Actu—." A loud screech cuts into the transmission.

"Shit. Comms have been blocked."

"That sucks," Sean says, "But did you say dance party?"

"It's a metaphor," I say. "Not an invitation to play music! Now, start shooting!"

"Aww," he says, and then opens fire as I swing a broad circle around the airport. The ground below erupts with plumes of dirt, nothing to indicate something substantial has been hit.

I'm not fond of beating the shit out of a subterranean facility while my friends are inside of it. But we're not hitting it as hard as we could. And I'm not sure how long we'll be able to hang around. If not for the *Prowler*'s ability to alter course in any direction without losing speed, we'd be an easy target for the lasers. Right now, I'm barely keeping ahead of—

The ship shakes from an impact. Minimal damage to aft panel B-12. Nothing significant, but that's the point of lasers. A thousand strikes don't take very long, and they tend to add up.

A second strike confirms my fears. Panel B-12.

Which means they're targeting our anti-gravity systems. Going to take a lot more direct hits to achieve that goal, but the moment they do, we'll find out how fast the *Prowler*'s one-hundred-ton weight reaches the ground.

"Harth!"

"Targeting," he says, calm as ever.

A dozen white hot Incinerator rounds arc toward the ground. Each of them exploding with splashes of liquified metal. Several of them strike the airport terminal's roof-teats.

"We're supposed to be avoiding human casualties," Jess says.

"We will not survive unless I am ruthless," he says.

It's not a joke. If anything, he sounds rattled.

"MIMIR, evasive pattern Chirk Seven." With the ship dodging on autopilot, I switch my view screen to Harth's thermal view of the terrain below. I was expecting maybe four batteries. This isn't the Draun homeworld, after all. But there are dozens. The thermal view also lets us see the laser light streaking past us. It's surprising we've only been struck twice.

The ship rumbles.

Three times.

I'm seeing lasers descending from above as well. There are batteries located at other locations, being redirected from above by a satellite. I turn to Jess. "You want to blow something up?"

"Fuck yes," she says, as Sean and Harth continue to barrage targets on the ground, Harth much more effectively.

I point to a headset dangling above her head. "Pull that down. It will connect to your regulators."

She pulls it down over her head. The mask, which self-adjusts to the wearer's head, clicks into place.

"Holy shit," she says, outstretching her arms, confirming that the connection is working. "What the hell?"

"Slow your wag," I say, "you're not actually outside the ship. It just looks like it. And feels like it. You—the real you—are still sitting next to me. But your consciousness is somewhere else."

"Where?" she asks.

"A plasma-disc. Closest thing to it on Earth might be a missile, but this—*you*—have the same flight capabilities as the *Prowler*, and a warhead that could level this airport."

"What the hell am I supposed to do?" she asks.

"Look up," I say, "and fly. To space. Find the satellite redirecting laser fire from other locations and blow it the hell up."

"How do I do that?" she asks.

"The disc is integrated with your mind. Just think it."

"Right," she says, waiving her hand in a broad sweep. "*Imagination is the eye to the soul*—and alien dog missiles."

"Sure, sure," I say. "Whatever the fuck that was, do that."

"Got it," she says, and the disc—one of many—lifts away from the *Prowler*'s hull, launching up through the atmosphere. "Whooo!"

56

MICAH

Here's what I know: We'd be wandering around this labyrinthine facility for hours without Alton guiding us. Here's what I don't know: If Alton is full of shit, killing time, and leading us into an ass rape of an ambush.

He seems genuinely nervous. Is sweating himself into a righteous stink. He presents himself like a cold government operative, but the truth—as it is with so many people—is a far cry.

Torel notices, too. "You seem nervous."

"You'd be too, if you knew what she could do," he says.

"Such as?" Torel asks.

"Oh, I don't know, how about remove your meat from your bones like you're a well-cooked chicken wing?"

"Mm," Torel says. "I've seen it happen."

"Y-you have?"

"They don't die right away," she says. "They lie there on the ground, fighting for each breath, gelatinous, but still able to constrict their musculature. Still able to move. To make gurgling sounds. There's no saving those poor souls. We usually finish the job ourselves."

She and Praxion share a glance and a grin. She's bullshitting him. Testing to see if his fear is genuine.

I can't smell his pheromones, or hear his heartbeat, but they can, and they appear satisfied with the results.

Alton is for real.

"Wait," Praxion says as we pass a nondescript white door. He sniffs around the seam. "Gruunlokar."

"Holding cell," Alton says. "He's not there anymore."

"Where is he?" Torel asks.

"With her. I believe they have formed some kind of...bond." He waddles ahead. "It's not much further."

Every step he takes is almost gentle, like he expects to fall over at any moment. The man is a mess. Very different from the asshole that taunted and tried to kill us. That version of Alton believed himself powerful. Now... Something has happened to him.

"She'll be coordinating the response to your team's attack," he says. "From the dome. Did the Draun have—"

"Yes," Praxion says, and turns to me. "Domes serve as power enhancers for the Draun. They take a toll but magnify a Draun's telekinetic reach. Chirk needs to be warned." He toggles his comms. "Prowler-One, Talon-Actu—"

The comms screech. "You won't be able to reach your friends," Alton says. "Communication frequencies are blocked."

I'm about to complain. Everything about this is starting to feel like an AK-47's muzzle is pressed against my taint, held by an old man with shaky hands. Sooner or later, my nuts are going to get shot off. It's not a good feeling, and it's only getting worse.

"There," he says, pointing to a flat double door embedded in the wall. "The dome."

"How do we get in?" Praxion asks.

"The doors will open for me," Alton says.

Praxion says nothing, but his gauntlet begins to glow with power.

I extend my claws but keep my laser light contained.

Alton slows his pace, creeping up to the doors. He flinches when they slide open. Holds a hand to his chest, breathing heavily. Then he steps inside, and we follow.

The dome is fifty feet tall and just as wide, half of a perfect sphere and covered in a hexagonal pattern of orange lines. It pulsates with warbling warm lights, like seeing a rave from inside a mother's womb. Halfway between the floor and the ceiling is what looks like a woman dressed like part nun, part dominatrix. She's tall, lithe, and mysterious, mostly because her face is hidden behind a smooth, silver, reflective mask with just a thin slit to see through.

This is the Draun.

Formerly a human being.

Awakened by some kind of signal from space, that will soon affect the entire human race.

Beneath her, floating ten feet above the floor, is a Kynolari that appears to be a German Shepherd. Gruunlokar. He looks unharmed, but also helpless, possibly unconscious.

Alton starts slow clapping and turns around to face us. A strange smile stretches across his face. "You made it," he says, but it is not his voice. "I do prefer efficiency."

Praxion lifts his gauntlet and fires a stream of rail-shards. I can't see the rounds moving through the air, but I see the impact they make in the curved wall, off to our left, nowhere near where he aimed.

Torel takes a turn, unleashing a massive electric shock. But it's even less effective, bending out to strike the curved wall, where its harmlessly absorbed.

"What is this?" Praxion grumbles. The deflective technology appears to be new to him.

"Power like you have never faced before," Alton says. His face sags like he's having a stroke. "The Draun you knew were powerful. Conquerors. But they lacked something that humanity has in spades—creativity. Humanity is the next evolution of the Draun."

"That's what Lumen Sok wants you to believe," Praxion says.

"Indeed," Alton says. "But what the old man doesn't realize, is that there is truth to the lie. I am superior, and soon all of humanity will be as well."

I am superior?

"I don't think that's Alton speaking," I say.

"Don't take it personally," Alton says. "I have nothing against your kind. But to reach Lumen Sok...to return the world to humanity's control, I must kill you and gain his trust. And that began with removing Alton."

My brow furrows.

Alton blinks as though awakened from a trance. "Wait, wait, wait!" he screams in a panic.

Then he falls to the floor, a mass of wriggling flesh contained within his clothing like a sausage. His face falls flat, revealing a lump where his brain is located. He breathes, still alive, spraying spittle with each labored breath.

She did it... She removed his bones. Has been speaking through him. Using his body like a puppeteer, guiding us here. While I take a step back in surprise, Torel and Praxion hold their ground, their faces locked to hide all emotion.

Praxion lifts his gauntlet toward Alton and fires a single shard into his brain, destroying it and ending his torture.

"You don't need to kill anyone," I say, stepping past Alton's revolting remains, into the dome. The ground shakes beneath me. A distant impact. The attack from above is underway. I address the floating woman. "You don't need to side with the Draun."

"Humanity *is* The Draun." Her voice echoes around the dome's interior. "*You* are The Draun."

I shake my head. "*I* am Kynolari," I say. "And so are you. We have a choice. You can make a choice!"

"Mine eyes have seen the glory," she says, quoting the Battle Hymn of the Republic, "of the coming of the Draun."

She looks down at me and then turns her body to face me. She glides down. Lands in front of me. Looks me over. Her gaze lingers on my gauntlets for a moment. Then she removes her mask, revealing the face of a beautiful young woman. "Why do you choose them?"

"They're *good*," I say.

"You have no idea who they are," she says. "What they've done to our people. Entire planets wiped out. Babies incinerated. Genocide on a cosmic scale."

"To save the universe from the same fate," I say.

"Well, you *sound* like one of them," she says. "Self-assured. Quick to defend mass slaughter."

The dome shakes from a nearby explosion.

"*Micah*," Praxion says, a warning. I'm playing mental chess with a master. Mentally outclassed. But I'm not trying to reach her mind. I'm trying to reach her heart.

I hold out my hand, and say, "You are as much Kynolari as you are Draun."

She laughs.

"Maybe not in your DNA, but in your mind. In your nature. You can choose a different path. Still."

She glares at me like I've been slowly vomiting as I speak.

"Micah..." Praxion says.

"Please," I say to Jenna. "I don't want to kill you."

"I know," she says. "And that's why you are the wrong person to face Lumen Sok. Only the strongest of us can hope to defeat him and lead our people—our people—into the future."

"Mic-ah..." It's Torel's voice this time but strained. I glance back and find both her and Praxion, pinned against the dome's wall by an invisible force, slowly choking them to death.

57

PRAXION

The Draun called Jenna is powerful. Perhaps the strongest I have ever faced, which lends credence to her claim that human creativity bolsters a Draun's innate abilities. Could be why Lumen Sok does not trust the woman. Killing us might help, but he is no fool. He will be prepared for deception. Draun are compulsively ambitious. He survived several coup attempts, including one I instigated.

I struggle against Jenna's telekinetic grasp, but her stranglehold on my throat remains tight. I can still breathe, but it is a struggle. She wants me to see what happens next.

A quick glance at Torel reveals she has suffered the same fate, pinned against the dome's curved wall, pulsating with color. I've never seen a Draun structure like this, but Jenna seems to be aware of what is inside and outside, controlling the battle above while simultaneously dealing with the three of us.

It is...impressive.

"Mi-cah..." Torel says, her voice strains, but it is loud enough to get our new friend's attention. He turns around and sees us, pinned and struggling to breathe. His demeanor changes. A hardness enters his eyes.

He had been pleading with Jenna, hoping that she might change her ways. Experience tells me that once someone has committed to doing evil, they see it through, even when their feelings about it change. The shame of admitting wrong often overwhelms what a person knows is right. It seems to be a universal truth.

"Last chance," Micah says, extending his claws.

"Last chance..." Jenna repeats, smiling. She glides up off the floor, her mask resealing over her face.

The light roiling around the dome's interior bends around her, pulsating bright red and orange. Is it reacting to her or—

Micah charges up both gauntlets, ready to unleash a double-sized full powered blast. Before he can, a body blocks his path.

Gruunlokar.

What is he doing?

My old friend's face twitches with determination. His movements are rigid.

"Gruunlokar," Micah says. "I'm—"

"I know who you are," Gruunlokar growls. "What you are... Now kill me."

Micah backsteps, unsure what to do.

"Kill him, Micah." Jenna lands behind Gruunlokar. "It is the only way to get to me."

She wants him to kill a Kynolari. Does she believe it will awaken the Draun in him?

Or is she simply torturing him?

Gruunlokar lifts his dormant gauntlet toward Torel. It is an empty threat. Even Micah knows the weapon can only be charged by the user's mind.

When the weapon suddenly shows a charge, I try—and fail—to gasp. The weapon's length increases, forming a rail barrel to propel thin tungsten rods capable of punching through armor—not to mention hundreds of bodies—before coming to a stop.

Gruunlokar growls, resisting, but she has control of him—mind and body.

"Stop!" he shouts, and then to Micah, he says, "Kill...me...now!"

Micah's a soldier. He can do the math. If Gruunlokar dies, Torel will live.

But at what cost? Jenna wants Micah to kill.

If I have learned anything in my life it is that the right choice in any situation is the exact opposite of what a Draun would choose. But does the same idiom apply to Jenna?

I glance over at Torel. Our eyes meet. For a moment, I see and feel regret. Then she gives a nod. We are in agreement.

I fill my lungs with a slow, labored breath, and with everything I have in me, I shout, "Do not kill him!"

Gruunlokar's arm shakes as he adjusts his aim on Torel. "No! God-damnit, stop!"

Jenna is unrelenting. "Any last words?"

Gruunlokar's eyes meet mine. "Prax," he says, using a nickname he has not spoken since we were pups. "Forgive me."

His arm jerks as a sniper rod fires.

Torel's scream of pain is instantaneous—and short lived. I look to her, but her body is concealed in dust—the dome wall behind her shattered.

Gruunlokar's arm redirects to me.

"Praxion!" Micah says, holding his ground, ready to unleash his full power. "I can't do this!"

"You are doing all that you can," Jenna says. "True power—for all humanity—lies dormant in your DNA. You can embrace it and forget your pain, or you can live...and die, in agony with your dogs."

If he does what she wants...if he strikes Gruunlokar down, he will become exactly what she wants him to be—broken. It will undo him. If he's right, that every Earth dog that has shared its life with him has compounded his very soul into that of a Kynolari, what will killing one do?

It is not a risk we can take.

If the Axiom became corrupt, became a Draun, no force in the universe could stand against him.

"Hold!" I manage to shout.

Gruunlokar trembles as his gauntlet points toward me.

It's not your fault, I think, willing him to know.

His eyes dart up, to the dome around us. Then he glares at me. And again, glances up.

Trying to tell me something.

About the dome.

Colors swirl violently, converging above Jenna.

Gruunlokar convulses. Resisting.

The colors above Jenna writhe as though agitated, growing in intensity.

The dome is boosting her power.

I place my hand against the wall behind me. It is smooth. Not like concrete or steel. It's glass.

My throat tightens as Jenna asserts her will upon everyone inside the chamber.

Micah slides back away from her, but digs his claws into the floor, rooting himself, retaining his power, still prepared to unleash it.

Hand against the glass wall, I focus past my need to breathe and find the resonant frequency. Sonizer fully charged, I unleash a full strength burst of sonic fury.

While the regulators protect Kynolari ears from deafening sounds, humans and Draun are susceptible. Jenna's mask protects her, but she cannot stop what happens to the dome. The wall behind me shatters while a clean line streaks up the dome's center, splitting it from one side to the other.

Gruunlokar collapses to the floor.

Jenna flails in pain but doesn't fall.

After sucking in a lung full of air, I shout, "Micah! The crack!"

He spins around, sees me pointing to the shattered glass above me, and takes aim. I dive to the side as he unleashes a full-strength blast of brilliant orange light that decimates the wall. He adjusts his aim upward, carving a deep path through the dome.

"No!" Jenna shouts, surging toward Micah, hooked hands outstretched.

Micah unleashes another full-power blast from his second gauntlet. It's a nanosecond away from erasing Jenna when she lifts her arms to create a telekinetic shield. The orange beam splits and strikes the walls. The force of it shoves her back until she strikes the far wall and drops to her knees.

The dome crumbles. Sunlight flashes through the thick line carved by Micah. The flashing lights painting the surface flicker and dissipate.

Jenna stands, dusts herself off, and then streaks across the floor, hovering just over the ground. She might not have the dome amplifying her powers, but she is still Draun, and still deadly.

Micah sees her coming and rolls to the side. But she doesn't need to hit him to strike him. A telekinetic force knocks him back.

I take aim with my railgun, but she is fast and mobile, closing the distance to Micah before I can take a shot.

He rolls back to his feet, both hands extended.

My eyes widen when I see his gauntlets are fully charged again.

A massive double beam of laser light slams into Jenna head on, enveloping her.

When the light fades, I expect to see nothing but dust. Instead, I find Jenna against the far wall, her outer garments vaporized, but a skintight silver reflective body suit remains, and is apparently capable of repelling laser light.

I aim and fire, peppering the glass where she had stood a moment before.

She launches across the room, this time slamming directly into Micah, using her telekinesis to increase her personal strength. She slams him to the ground, compressing him, holding his shoulders. He grits his teeth in pain.

"There's nothing your friends can do to save you," she says. "And when you are dead, I will peel the skin from their bodies."

"Gross," Micah says. "But..." He tries pushing back. "They're not my friends..." He extends his claws and with a surge of raw determination, reaches up, digs his fingers into her mask and tears it apart. Her enraged face is revealed.

"They're my pack," he says, "Dick-whore."

58

CHIRK

"You sightseeing over there, or are you planning to blow something up? Because shit is getting dicey!" I put us into a barrel roll, as we swing around the airport's outskirts.

"Oh God..." Sean says. While his body is protected from the effects of our rapid course changes, his view from the gunner's seat is a little less adaptive. Inexperienced users can feel nauseous, and on occasion—

The sound of Sean retching fills the air.

—that.

"It happens, man," I say, and then whisper to myself, "to you more than anyone else in the God-damned universe." I raise my voice again. "Shake it off and keep the pressure on."

"Right," he says, grunting, "pressure."

A moment later, his rail cannon starts firing again, shooting the shit out of the terrain surrounding the airport, which might be the roof of a secret base—or just dirt that did nothing to no one and doesn't deserve being aerated by one of the most powerful kinetic weapons in the universe.

"I'm in space," Jess says, sounding awed. She smiles, waving her arms around like she's weightless. While connected to the plasma disc, she's largely detached from the reality of her body. She can hear me, but she can't smell Sean's puke and can't feel the *Prowler*'s movements. There are two reasons the system was designed like this. First, it allows the user absolute control over the disc. Second, it allows the user to complete their mission even if they've been severed in half, or impaled, or are drowning in a crash. I've heard it's the most peaceful way to die. No pain and total freedom until you simply fade away. Jess doesn't need to know any of that, but she does need to snap out of la la land and get down to business.

"Look for glints of light," I tell her. "Or use the infrared to find heat signatures."

"I see a light," she says. "Actually, I see two."

"We have multiple discs," I say, "blow up the first, and then take out the second."

"I'm getting closer," she says.

A volley of Incinerator rounds pummels the ground below. Several punch holes in the secret facility's roof, confirming there is something down there.

"I do not like blindly firing into a bunker containing our people," Harth grumbles.

"*Danger close* is part of the job," I say. "You know that better than most."

Harth was on the ground during an Incinerator strike by another Kynolari vessel. Spent two days beneath the rubble before I sniffed him out. He never complained about it. The mission had been a success.

He grunts, still unhappy, but still launching volleys toward the ground, below which our friends might be fighting for their lives.

A laser blast hits our flank hard. Puts us into a violent spin until I correct it.

"Bllaaarg!" Sean heaves the rest of his stomach's contents onto the floor. "Dude. I'm sorry. Not sure I'm cut out for being a badass operator."

"Floor is non-stick, my man," I say. "Don't sweat it. Keep on firing. Ain't no Kynolari in the Corps that got behind a gunner's seat, in battle, on day one. You're doing fine."

"Huh," Harth says. "That sounded...genuine."

"Shut your trap, big man," I grumble.

"I see it," Jess says. "The satellite. Looks like it's redirecting laser fire from three different locations."

"Don't care about the details," I say. "Blow it the hell up!"

"Closing in," she says. "But so is the other object."

"The other object is closing in?" I ask. "What does it look like?"

"Big shiny ball," she says. "Hard to tell how big it is."

"Destroy it," I say, stomach knotting just from the possibility of what it might be.

"What about the lasers?" she asks.

"We can take it!" I shout. "Destroy the sphere!"

"Sphere?" Harth asks. "Where?"

"In orbit," I say. "Watching."

He leans out of his gunner's station, firing blindly. "She must be mistaken."

"Can't take the chance," I say. "If there's a Visionary Sphere in orbit, it needs to be destroyed."

"On it," she says, biting her tongue in concentration.

"What's a Visionary Sphere?" Sean asks, sounding ill. Despite his discomfort, he's still on mission, firing away, wreaking havoc, causing chaos. He's a good boy, that one.

Cars stream out of the airport. Most are attempting to follow the roadways, but others are driving cross country, fleeing the scene of unfolding madness.

Just as many people are on foot, like Jamangian Fleas abandoning a Goncha's hide as it enters the Flangoi Sea.

"It's a ship," I say. "A personal transport."

"For who?" Sean asks.

"The Visionary," Harth grumbles.

"Except he's supposed to be dead," Chirk says. "Gruunlokar killed him. Put a rail-shard through his head."

"Okay, so someone else has a sphere," Sean says.

"Not possible," I say. "Only the Visionary can—"

"Ahh!" Jess says, her whole body jolts as though struck. "The fuck! That hurt."

"You're fine," I tell her. "The plasma disc was destroyed. It's a shock to the system the first time."

"What do we do?" she asks.

"How good are you at multitasking?"

"Seriously?" she says. "You really don't know much about Earth women, huh?"

"Well, seeing as I shot the first one I met," I say, "I haven't had much of a chance, but your astronomic level of snark answers the question."

"You *shot* her?" Jess says.

"In the leg," I say. "A small hole. I'm connecting you to the remaining eleven plasma discs. Control them as a group, but keep their flight paths erratic, like you're having a seizure. All over the place. If you're lucky, one might get through."

"Okay," she says. "Okay. Eleven at once… Which one will I see through?"

"All of them," I say, and launch her skyward.

"Oh my God," she says, gasping. "Holy shit. Holy shit. It's like kaleidoscope vision, but I can feel them all separately, too."

Sean chuckles, both amused and bedraggled. "Sounds like you're trippin' balls, man."

"Yeah," Jess whispers. "Wow… I'm uh. Okay. Approaching the upper atmosphere."

She's moving faster this time, more comfortable controlling the discs and being detached from her body. But controlling eleven discs simultaneously is no easy task. I've done it myself, but only after years of training.

"Okay," she says. "I see them. Satellite and sphere. Closing in on the sphere."

"More movement," I say, watching the discs' progress. "Remember. Gravity has no hold on you. The laws of physics that bind your body have no effect on you now. Acceleration. Speed. You can do the impossible."

On screen, the discs burst out of their formation, zig zagging through the atmosphere's upper reaches, before entering the vacuum of space. Two of them are instantly destroyed, each causing Jess to gasp, but the rest of them dart in every direction, none of them following a path that makes any kind of sense.

Except one. It's headed in a straight line.

"No way," I say to myself. "No fucking way..."

A moment later, a stationary target explodes. She killed the satellite *while* chasing down a Visionary's sphere.

She's a natural.

I grin. She's a *Kynolari.*

"Fuck you, asshole," Jess whispers, a smile on her face. "I got seven plasma discs with your name on it."

My HUD shows information gathered from the discs. I can see them closing in on the single, round target.

One of them explodes.

Then another.

But they're closing in as fast as Jess can think it, which is surprisingly fast.

And then—the sphere vanishes, moving faster than comprehension, as it darts away, taking whoever was inside along with it.

"No!" Jess shouts. "Where'd it go?"

"Long gone," I grumble. "Could be past your moon by now. Don't beat yourself up. You got the job done. Taking out a Visionary Sphere would have been a longshot for any of us."

A brilliant orange light fills my view, streaking up from below and carving a line up into the sky.

I put the ship into a spin that's so weirdly complicated that it doesn't have a name. But it keeps us from flying straight through the full power gauntlet blast that just carved a straight line in the ground below us.

"Holy shit!" Sean shouts. "Did you see that?"

"I think I know where our people are," Harth says.

A moment later, comms come to life. It's Praxion, whispering. "Prowler-One, Talon-Actual. You have eyes on?"

"Talon-Actual, if you're talking about the big line Micah just carved, yeah, I see it. Nearly was part of it."

"I'm acquiring a target for you in a dome beneath the ground. Hit it with something big."

"Copy that, Talon-Actual. Danger close?"

"Very," he says. "But do not hold back."

"Copy that," I say and turn to Jess. "You catch all that?"

"Already on my way," she says, guiding the remaining plasma discs back toward the ground, on a collision course with our friends.

59

MICAH

"What?" Jenna says, looking like she's been slapped in the face. Despite her confusion, the force emanating from her, pinning me to the ground, never falters. "What did you call me?"

"Uh," I say, wondering if I've just made a colossal mistake. "'Dick-whore.' I don't know. Was doing a favor for a guy."

"'Dick-whore,'" she says, and I swear for the briefest moment, I see a smile.

"C'mon. Jenna. Seriously. You don't need to do any of this. I see you in there. The real you."

Any trace of humor is vaporized. Should have stuck with 'dick-whore.'

"I am *Draun*," she says. "We are *all* Draun."

The pressure on me increases. Breathing becomes harder.

"Only physically," I grunt. "It's just...a percentage of DNA. We...probably share more with bananas."

She shakes her head. "Not when you wake up—and you will. Everyone will."

I stop struggling. "Is...that why you haven't killed me yet?"

"The man who believes himself a dog," Jenna says. "Who can power a Kynolari gauntlet at will. You will make a powerful ally, after you're awake."

Her confidence unnerves me. Could she be right? If this signal wakes up some dormant portion of my brain, am I going to be flooded with memories of the Kynolari that will turn me against them? Will I cease to be me?

"Why...do you need...allies?"

"I might be Draun," she says. "But I am human first. As are you. The Visionary is the last of their kind. A failed leader. He will propel our world to destruction. But I—we—can learn from their mistakes."

"And live in peace with the universe?" I ask.

She grins, and not in a nice way. "Eventually. After they submit."

"That doesn't sound very different from the Draun I've heard about," I say.

She squints at me. "You're buying time."

"So are you," I point out.

Her grin grows crooked. "I wonder whose plan will unfold first. Let's wait and see, shall we?"

I'm expecting a few minutes of awkward silence, but then she counts down.

From three.

"Two..."

"One..."

A buzz fills my body, like there are ants welling up inside of me, spreading out through my limbs.

"The...sig...nal," I grunt, hoping I'm still transmitting over comms. "It's..."

I spasm as the ants reach my mind. A mental dam breaks, unleashing a flood of information. Draun history, ideals, machinations. All of it comes pouring forth, laced with hubris, ambition, hunger, and a disregard for life beyond our control.

Our control.

Draun control.

It overwhelms me, spiraling my soul down into an oblivion from which there is no return. I feel comforted by the weight of it, wrapped in the knowledge that I am better, stronger, smarter.

And I want more.

Until a voice whispers to me.

"No."

A howling wind erases the voice, screaming in my mind, for vengeance, for domination for—

"Micah."

I know that voice.

I've only heard it once before, but I know it.

I'm connected to it.

I *see* through it.

I'm lying on my side. Inside a white room. Robotic arms whir around me. I'm in pain, but...alive.

"Micah here?"

"I'm here, Gro." My insides break. I want to wail in relief. Want to collapse to my knees and retch out my fear.

But I'm not in my body. I'm in his.

"Here, where? Love, Micah."

"Love you too, buddy. Not far away. I'll see you soon."

"Soon," he says. "Hope soon. Love Micah."

The connection between us fades to black. For a moment, I feel nothing. Then I open my eyes.

Jenna's face is inches from mine, her eyes eager. I'm still pinned to the ground, but the pressure isn't intense.

"Now do you see?" she asks. "Do you know?"

I nod. "I know everything I need to."

She smiles. "Tell me."

"Grover is alive," I say.

Her brow furrows. "Grover. The Sesame Street Muppet?"

"The dog," I say. "Woof."

Before she fully realizes I haven't become Draun, I unleash a full strength laser burst directly into the floor with my right hand. We launch up together, spinning. I place my left hand against her torso and unleash another blast of energy. It reflects off her suit, but the force of it flings her away.

We land hard, thirty feet apart.

"Hit her!" I shout.

A crack of thunder rips through the dome. Bolts of lightning wrap around Jenna, crackling just inches from her skin.

Holy shit, I think, watching. *She's holding the lightning back.*

I get to my knees and look at Torel. She looks battered, but she still has fight in her. Her energy is draining, though. "Keep pouring it on!"

Jenna screams, grasps her head, and arches her back. She's been struck by a burst of sonic energy that has no effect on the rest of us. Praxion is doing his thing.

But I'm not sure it will be enough, and unless I can manage a headshot on her unmasked—

No, I think. *I don't want to do that.*

Jenna screams in pain. Then she looks down at a bloody hole in her side. She's been shot by a rod. But from who?

I look to the side in time to see Gruunlokar collapse back to the floor, the sniper extension on his gauntlet still extended. When we hit Jenna, she lost control of him—and the gauntlet attached to his arm.

I climb to my feet and rush over to him. He's conscious, but too weak to move. I feel pretty numb to surprises at this point but am completely caught off guard when his gauntlet retracts and folds itself away—inside of his arm. It's a prosthetic limb.

"Gruunlokar," I say, crouching down. "I'm—"

"The Axiom," he says. "Don't need to know more. Pick me the hell up."

I lie down beside him, head facing Praxion, and haul him atop me.

"Not exactly what I had in mind," he grumbles.

"Hold on," I say, and I feel his claw-tipped hands dig into my shoulders. Then I fire off a laser blast, striking the far wall and launching us across the floor. We slide through some debris, which stings, but is manageable. I kill the laser before we plow into the far wall and slide to a stop just ten feet from Praxion.

He sees us but can't say anything as he struggles to maintain his sonic attack.

His power levels are low. Same with Torel.

I toggle my comms. I don't remember what callsign number Jess is using, so I go informal, trusting no one will actually care.

"Jess, you there?" I ask.

"Here," she says. "There. Feels like everywhere."

"Still on target?" I ask.

"About to slot this coin, yeah," she says. "Please tell me I'm not about to kill you and you called to say goodbye or something."

"Hoping to avoid that," I say. "ETA?"

"Well, since I've never been a plasma-disc before and am not really sure how to gauge—"

"Ten seconds," Chirk says, sounding worried. "Nine..."

I haul Gruunlokar over my shoulder and charge toward Praxion. While he's still firing the Sonizer, I lift him up over my other shoulder and continue on toward Torel.

"Torel!" I shout, closing in.

"Leave me!" she says, struggling to maintain her lightning attack.

"No dog left behind!" I say, and leap at her. I tackle her, crotch-first, knocking her onto her back. Straddling her, I look down, say, "Sorry," and then, "Hold on tight!"

She wraps her arms around my thighs, claws punching through my armor—and my skin. The sting sharpens my focus and helps me to recharge my gauntlets one more time. Then I look up toward the crack in the dome and aim both gauntlets at the floor.

"This feels like a dumb way to die," Gruunlokar says. "But I am glad to be among friends once more."

"Not dying today," I say, as Chirk's voice cuts through the comms again.

"Three... Two..."

As a series of discs shoot down into the dome, I fire both gauntlets, launching us up toward the crack in the ceiling.

Back on the floor, Jenna recovers from Torel's and Praxion's attack in time to see us shooting away and her fate rushing toward her. She shouts, "Nooo!" and is then erased by a series of explosions that vaporize the dome and send a ball of fire into the air. It rises below us, scorching heat nipping at my heels.

Then we soar up above it all...

...and I run out of power. Even if I could recharge the gauntlets, I'm not sure firing them at the ground will slow our fall, or just carve a hole for us to fall through until we're crushed by pressure.

Turns out, that's a problem I don't need to solve.

We land on a large white surface with a collective grunt.

"Everyone alive?" Chirk asks over the comms.

"Singed," Praxion says, sitting up and pulling Gruunlokar up beside him.

"But alive," Gruunlokar says.

"Gruun!" Chirk says. "Man, wait until you hear—"

The *Prowler* shifts to the side as though struck.

"Better get inside," Chirk says. "We are still taking ground-based fire and propulsion is shaky at best. We need a place to settle down and make some repairs."

"My house," I tell Praxion. "With Alton and Jenna dead—"

He nods and relays the mission. "Take us to the original Insertion Zone."

A hatch beside us opens up. Baarfolir's small fuzzy head emerges. "Delighted to see you alive," he says to Gruunlokar, and then to the rest of us, he says, "All of you. And if you want to stay that way, I suggest coming inside." Then he looks at me. "And Micah, there is someone who would like to say hello."

60

Love Micah.

Love Micah.

Love Micah.

See Micah!

Micah hug. Micah kiss.

I lick.

Now I bite!

Now *he* bite!

I jump. And love. And Micah!

Love Micah!

Micah say he love.

"Love Micah," I say.

Everyone happy.

Everyone!!

I lick everyone! I lick Praxion. And Torel. And Jess! Jess is here! Jess, Jess, Jess! "Love Jess!" I say.

Jess cry. And hug.

But then new person! I sniff him butt. He push me away. Me say hello with booty shake on leg. Everyone laughing!

Everyone happy.

I am happy.

"Love Micah," I say.

I in his arms. Out of breath. Him holding. "Love you, too, Grove."

I am happy.

"Home," I say.

"Yeah," he says, face against mine. Smell tears. Happy and sad. "We're going home."

Epilogue

ONE MONTH LATER

The house hasn't been this full since I was a teenager, and my parents were alive to coordinate Thanksgiving with the extended family. While the Kynolari spend their nights in their own quarters aboard the *Prowler*, they spend a lot of daylight hours inside the house.

I still don't know Gruunlokar very well. He, Harth, and Chirk are putting in long hours repairing the *Prowler*, but it sounds like things aren't going well. Damage was more extensive than sensors revealed. According to Chirk, she barely made it back to my house.

The *Prowler* is parked out in the woods, her external skin adapted to blend in with the surroundings, making her invisible from above. But I don't think anyone is looking.

Not with the world in chaos.

Jenna was defeated.

Gruunlokar was rescued.

Grover survived.

But the world...was lost. A signal was broadcast around the globe—the same broadcast heard by Jenna Flood that awoke the Draun within her. The Visionary used an interlinked network of satellites to beam the signal to just about everyone on the planet, moments before we escaped the dome.

I heard the signal. I saw what it contained. The propaganda from a very specific point of view. What it offered. The power. The technology. It held no sway over me, but its impact on the world... While billions rejected the signal for one reason or another, hundreds of millions embraced it, awoke, and began wreaking havoc. Cities have been destroyed. The Draun came together in a patchwork of small armies that eventually congregated in—and overthrew—Japan.

While hordes of Japanese fled the island nation, countless millions more were slaughtered. But not just from the incoming Draun. The factory we discovered was just one of many. As Draun arrived from around the world, finished biologics in all their horrible forms emerged, running amok and killing indiscriminately. Anyone who hadn't changed with the signal was fair game.

Governments failed to respond to the threat, which was both external and internal. When the U.S. President became a Draun and attacked everyone inside the situation room, the country fell apart. There have been some attempts at recovery, but we were a nation divided before some of us became killing machines.

In the past week, things have begun to normalize a bit. The power is back on. Food distribution has started again. But all eyes are on Japan.

The powers that be in Moscow—no one knows who's calling the shots now—launched a nuclear attack on Tokyo, but the missiles never made it to the ground. Some went off course and crashed into the sea. Some detonated against an invisible shield. Others just malfunctioned—which might be the Russians' fault. Point is, the Draun can defend themselves against the worst we can throw at them.

Some are happy to let them keep Japan, as long as they stay there.

But the Kynolari know better.

The Draun are just getting started. The Visionary isn't satisfied with islands, or even with entire worlds. His ambition is galactic. It won't be long until they become aggressive again or make another attempt to wake more Draun.

Torel thinks the presence of so many Lost Tribe on Earth, and their effects on the people around them, might have prevented a total population transformation. If that's true, and Lumen Sok figures it out, dogs might be at the top of his hit list. Remove the Lost Tribe, convert the Earth, take to the stars.

I'm sitting on the couch. Grover is draped over my lap, sound asleep.

He still talks, thanks to the regulator, but he won't be winning any poetry competitions any time soon. It's strange, but the connection between us is even stranger—and stronger now. I can see through his eyes and access his other senses. We can get glimpses inside each other's brains. Feel each other's emotions. I found myself craving moss the other day. It's one of Grover's favorite snacks he's not supposed to eat. It's surreal.

But what isn't these days?

Jess is staying with us now. All but moved in. We're officially a thing. Like really a thing. And it doesn't feel weird, or sudden, just like she'd been missing for a long time, and now she's here.

Sitting right beside me actually, her thigh supporting Grover's head and no doubt getting slathered in drool.

On my other side is Torel. We're watching the news. Looking for signs that the Draun might be on the move. Praxion stands off to the side, his serious gaze on the TV, arms crossed.

Sitting on the coffee table is Baarfolir. With every new report, he shakes his head. "This is disconcerting."

Reports of conflict around the world.

Of governments failing.

Of humans attacking humans.

Power grabs.

Genocide.

Human nature.

"This world is doing Lumen Sok's work for him," Baarfolir says. "He won't attack until there is some kind of organized resistance, and by the time that happens, if it's even possible, it will be far too late."

"You're saying we should attack?" Praxion asks.

Baarfolir shakes his head. "Heavens no. We would all be killed. But...I have a theory that might be worth looking into."

"A theory," Torel says. "About?"

"Anubis," he says.

"Even if he was one of you," Jess says, "he's been gone for a very long time."

"He was an elder of the Lost Tribe," Baarfolir says. "And these statues and ancient stories about him suggest he wasn't merely a legend to your people. He was here." He turns to Praxion. "Could *still* be."

Torel *tsks* and turns to me. "Legend says that Anubis was immortal. It's *possible* he found a way to extend his life, even by thousands of years. The technology is common among the most advanced civilizations. But an extended life is not an immortal one. It has been thirty-seven thousand years."

"And yet," Baarfolir says, spinning around on the table to face us. He's holding one of Dad's old National Geographics in his hand. "I've been going through these historical records." He opens the magazine, revealing a large photo of an ancient Egyptian sculpture.

Torel gasps.

Praxion leans in to see for himself. Grunts his acknowledgement.

Baarfolir smiles. "He was well known on this world just three thousand years ago. And look at how he is standing." The photo depicts Anubis standing on two legs, like a human. "We need to find him," he says. "And if death finally did claim him—then we need to find his final resting place."

"And then?" Praxion asks.

"Nachos!" Sean says, entering the room with two cookie sheets covered in beef and cheese slathered nachos. "And I swear, I didn't add any special spices this time. Except for the tray in the kitchen. That is for me and the little man, capisce? Unless you want to get blazed."

Jess raises her hand.

"I might want to get blazed."

"Same," Torel says, standing with Jess, both of them feeling the weight of Baarfolir's revelation. Praxion sits down beside me, deep in thought. "Could it be possible?"

Not sure who he's asking, but I answer, "At this point, a shot in the dark might be the only shot we get to take. Don't know about you, but if we're going down, I'd rather go down fighting."

Praxion grins and nods. "Ever the warrior."

I look down at Grover, who's been awake since the smell of nachos filled the living room.

"What do you think, Grove?" His tail thumps against Praxion.

"Love nachos." He opens his mouth, smiling, tongue hanging out the side. "Love Micah."

I tousle his ears and kiss his forehead. "Love you too, buddy."

I'm about to get up for the grub when Grover adds, "No love Anbu. Anbu scary."

"Anbu is the common name for Anubis... You *know* Anbu?" Baarfolir asks.

"Grover know." He looks up at me. "All doggu know."

"Where is he?" Baarfolir asks. "Do you know where to find him?"

Grover licks his nose, which he does when his extremely limited vocabulary doesn't do his thoughts justice. Then he says. "In...head." He looks up at me, and the connection between us flares for a moment.

"In his mind," I say. "He's saying we can find Anubis in his mind. In *all* dogs' minds."

"Love nachos," Grover whispers.

"Go ahead," I say.

He leaps off me, before charging into the kitchen chanting, "Nachos, nachos, nachos!"

"Well?" Baarfolir asks, looking at Praxion.

"It's dangerous," Praxion says, and then he turns to me. "How would you feel about visiting Grover's subconscious?"

Three flashes of light announce the return of Harth, Gruunlokar, and Chirk. After relocating and repairing the Leap Nodes buried out in the woods, we can now transport to and from the *Prowler* without walking outside.

"Nachos!" Chirk cheers. "Sean, you absolute badass! I am going to dry hump your leg into oblivion."

"Just call me Bacon, my man!"

Everyone in the living room chuckles. Then I say, "Subconscious of a Golden Retriever. Should be full of tennis balls and happy thoughts. Why not?"

TO BE CONTINUED IN

GOOD BOYS: UNLEASHED

AUTHOR'S NOTE

I'm occasionally surprised by the insanity I get to write. *Good Boys – The Lost Tribe* is a perfect example. It's a ludicrous concept—not for a kids' book mind you, or an animated movie, but for an adult science-fiction novel that can make readers laugh out loud *and* cry? Ludicrous. And I was shocked, after being convinced by my friend Alex Maddern (aka: bigDOLPH), that everyone I pitched it to agreed that it could work. And the more I thought about it, the more it resonated.

I am what's called a 'dog person.' Upon meeting a new dog, I'll get down on the floor, greet them as I would an old friend, accept all the kisses and nibbles, and invariably piss off the owner when their dog starts running in circles, excited because they've just met a human being that speaks their language. I grew up with dogs, and I have had—and lost—my own. They are all dear to me, have shaped my personality, and have always been there for me when life kicked me in the nuts.

As a result, what was meant to be a mostly silly novel became something special. The characters—even though they were dogs—became real and special to me. I feel like I know them. I've met them. And if you're a dog person, too, I think you'll recognize some of your doggo friends in the Kynolari and in Grover.

Speaking of Grover... In reality, Grover is my new Golden Retriever. He was born on the same day, a year later, that my last Golden, Kenobi, died. He's a handful, but he's already a loyal companion and makes every day more fun. And yeah, he is a humping machine.

If you enjoyed reading *Good Boys – The Lost Tribe*, good news! I'm writing a sequel, but we still need Book 1 to be a hit to make that happen. If you want to help spread the news, please post a review on Amazon and Audible. Or post it on your socials. Write your grandma a letter about it. You know she'd love to hear from you. Whatever it takes, let's help the Kynolari save Earth!

If you want to be sure you don't miss the final book(s), all the books to follow, and news about upcoming comic books, movies, TV series, etc., you can visit bewareofmonsters.com and sign up for the newsletter. And, you can join the

TRIBE at facebook.com/groups/JR.Tribe. It's an amazing group of fans and the first place that cool stuff gets announced. Also, we give away free stuff every week!

Thank you for joining me for another wacky adventure. You are an amazing person with impeccable taste. Don't let the people looking at you strangely for laughing, or crying, while reading a book make you think otherwise. Can't wait for you to see what we've got coming next!

—*Jeremy Robinson*

ACKNOWLEDGEMENTS

First and foremost, I must thank Alex Maddern, who, while playing *Call of Duty*, came up with the bonkers concept of talking dogs from space in search of a Lost Tribe. He might be a cat owner, but sometimes he has good ideas, so I put up with him.

Thanks to Kane Gilmour, editor extraordinaire, who helps me turn first drafts into fine-tuned, entertaining word machines. As always, big thanks to our army of proofreaders, Adrian Brooke, Danny Cannon, Julie Carter, Elizabeth Cooper, Dustin Dreyling, Heather Beth Eisenberg, Allison Grant, Cynthia Gregory, Gavin Gregory, Deanna Haddrill, Brian Hemenway, Matt Ingram, Marcy Jaqua, Andre Jenkin, Scott Kehoe, Rebecca Laurent, Janis Levonitis, Rian Martin, Stefanie Maubach, Kyle Mohr, Steven Newell, Jessica Otterstäl, Jeff Sexton, Michelle Stuart, Christine Weatherly, and Courtney Westendorf. You all help conceal the fact that I'm just as bad at typing as I am spelling.

And of course, what would an audiobook be without an amazing performer bringing my characters to life? And for this book—this trilogy—I wanted someone who did amazing character voices. From the moment I first heard Tom's reading of Chirk, I knew he was the right guy. This is my first book with Tom Taylorson, but it won't be my last!

And big thanks to you readers, without whom I wouldn't be able to write stories about talking dogs from space. Talking dogs...from space! And it's not a kids' book! YOU made that possible. Feel good about it. I certainly do.

—Jeremy

ABOUT THE AUTHOR

Jeremy Robinson is the *New York Times* and #1 Audible bestselling author of over seventy novels and novellas, including *Infinite, The Others*, and *The Dark*, as well as the Jack Sigler thriller series, and *Project Nemesis*, the highest selling, original kaiju novel of all time (which is in development for TV with Chad Stahelski, director of John Wick). Robinson is known for mixing elements of science, history, and mythology, which has earned him the #1 spot in Science Fiction and Action-Adventure, and secured him as the top creature feature author. Many of his novels have been adapted into comic books, optioned for film and TV, and translated into fourteen languages. He lives in New Hampshire with his wife and three children.

Visit him at www.bewareofmonsters.com.

Made in United States
North Haven, CT
22 August 2024

56367507R00214